Forged by Fate

THE FORGED TRILIOGY
BOOK TWO

STACY VON HAEGERT

Dragon Crest Publishing

Nashville, TN

Copyright 2023© Stacy Von Haegert

Published in the United States of America
Worldwide Electronic & Digital Rights
Worldwide English Language Print Rights

Forged by Fate
THE FORGED TRILOGY

Book two
Stacy Von Haegert

Cover by Rachel McEwan
Editing by Lara Zielinsky

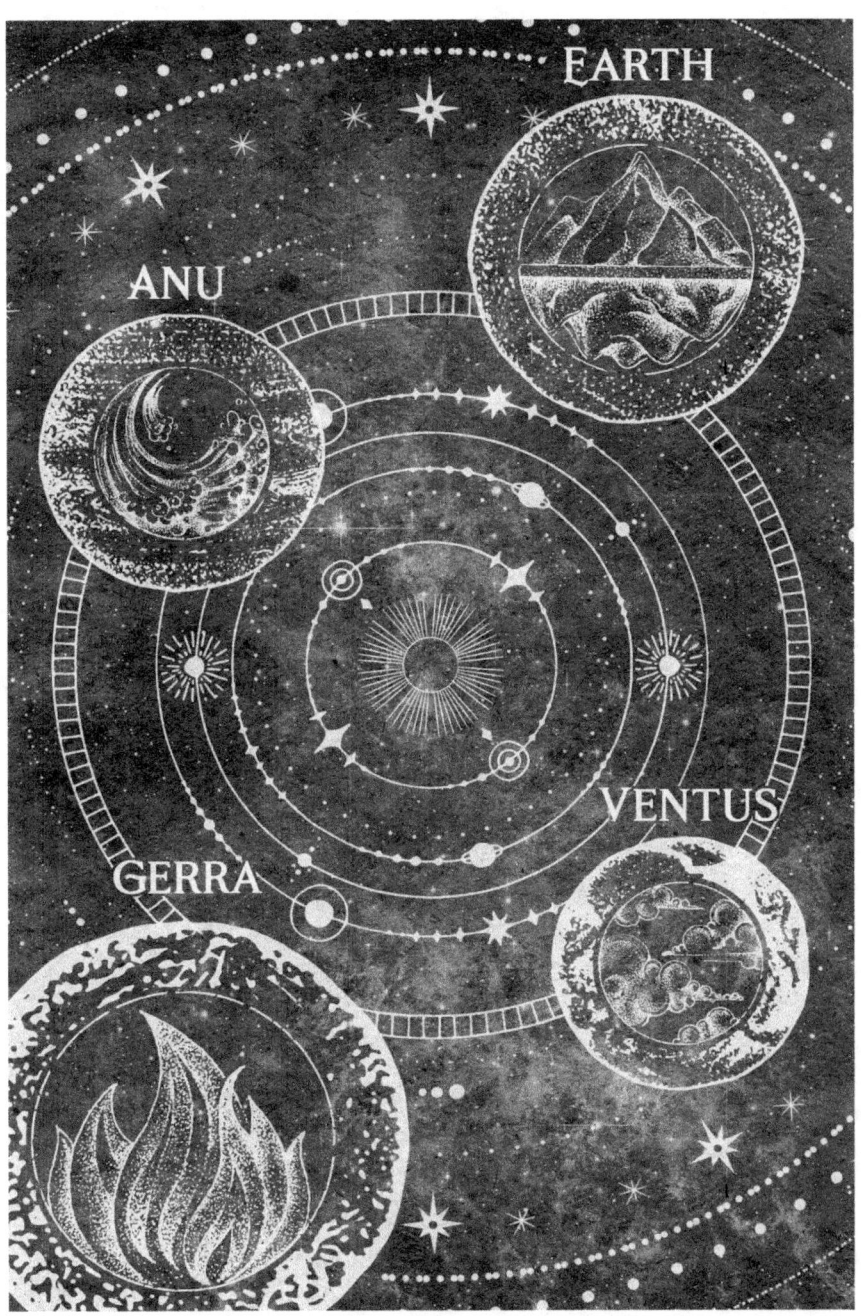

EARTH

ANU

VENTUS

GERRA

Please visit the author's website, stacyvonhaegert.com for sensitive subject matter.

The truth is rarely pure and never simple.

- Oscar Wilde

Chapter One
CASTELLO ALBORNOZ

ITALY

ONE YEAR AFTER THE BATTLE OF GERRA

Stefen,

I write to inform you of the High Council's decision to revoke your admittance into the holy realm of your creation. You have officially been stripped of your lands, your holdings, and your title. You are forbidden by the Gods' Law to sire angelic offspring. Your given name, Von Emmerich, and all claims to the throne have been renounced. In accepting this decree from a court delegate, you have agreed to this ruling. Failure to comply will result in death.

In the gods' name,

Lord Andreas

S tefen folded the letter back into its well-worn creases and looked out into the starless night. Eleven months ago he had received the verdict. A month after his death. Thirty days after his resurrection.

Still...the words on that paper felt as razor-sharp as they had the first time he read them. The pain unsullied. A constant reminder of his failure.

His eyes swept over the expansive fields, stretching like a shadowed patchwork painting across the land, blue and purple and black deepening with each stroke of the night's fine brush.

Three hours from now the grandfather clock by the main entrance would strike midnight. Marking his anniversary. The day the world had shifted on its axis and turned Stefen into the first of his kind. An archangel made vampire. A hybrid with the blood of the dragon running through his veins.

Stefen sucked in a breath and stuffed the missive back into its gold-embossed envelope. "And what have you done with your uniqueness, you stupid fuck?"

Nothing. He sighed.

Other than train daily with Ash and the other fire elementals. Which, he supposed, was something. That's what Kielyn and Ash kept telling him anyway. He was still figuring out who he was. He needed time to come into his full powers. There was no deadline in which to have it all mapped out by. He needed to let nature take its course.

Utter bullshit.

Stefen knew they meant well. Still, it bothered him—not having a defined role, a purpose, an obligation. He'd spent his whole life resenting such things.

But he had known who he was.

Half the time now, he felt like a fumbling teenager. Or worse, an old immortal trying to learn new immortal tricks. He wondered if Alaric lay awake at night laughing at the turn of events. Surely, the High Council of Anu was having it preached to all new souls.

For there was truly no better life lesson than the example he'd set a year ago. *"Spend too much time wishing for a different life and the gods might see fit to give you one."* Just as they'd done with Dante centuries back, casting him out of Anu.

Stefen replaced the decree in his desk drawer, irritated for wallowing in self-pity. He had more to be thankful for than resentful about. He'd been given a second chance. He had friends, a family, and was instrumental in training Ash's new recruits. There was much for him to offer. And plenty more to learn.

He headed for the hall, that last thought top of mind. If he'd gleaned anything during his time at Castello Albornoz, it was that Ash did not like to be kept waiting. While Stefen still derived immense pleasure from annoying his maker...he sensed tonight was not the night.

He took the castle steps at a jog, rounded the door into the parlor, and stepped on a Lego. "Fuc..."

Stefen bit his tongue when Kielyn lifted a brow in warning. "Functioning shoes," she amended for him, adjusting one of the twins in her arm. "They are a requirement in a house with children."

"A requirement I'm not likely to forget again." He walked over, scooping up Eirik on his way.

The cherub-faced baby grabbed hold of Stefen's nose, laughing merrily as he twisted. Of the twins, Eirik was the easiest to amuse. Especially when violence was involved. With a head of auburn curls, a happy heart, and a knack for finding himself in bad situations quickly, he was the most like his mother.

Bastian, by contrast, had midnight-colored locks like his father and a natural skepticism to match. It was unnerving how intensely that child could focus on a person. As if those crystal blue eyes could see right through them.

"My favorite nephews." Stefen blew raspberries on Eirik's round tummy when he let go of his nose, eliciting squeals of delight. "Though I'm not sure what this one just left on my face."

He leaned down for Kielyn to inspect. "Tell me it's clear of color."

Kielyn made a deliberate study of his person, sniffing for added effect, before sitting back and nodding her findings. "Only drool."

"Thank the gods for small favors." Stefen relented his finger to the demanding baby, who proceeded to gum it like a coyote with a meatless bone. "Ouch!" He feigned pain, enticing another round of gleeful laughter out of the red-headed child. "You sure they haven't sprouted fangs?"

"I blame the dragon side for the biting." His best friend smiled. "But no fangs." She cast her eyes back to the raven-haired baby, her voice going soft. "Yet."

Neither Kielyn nor Ash were elites, born vampires. Their children were mortal, just as they had been. It would be a joint decision to turn the twins once they reached eighteen.

Stefen watched his friend coo to the little boy in her lap. It was unfair. That the gods would give all other species such little control over their lives, but saddle one with the ultimate choice.

Kielyn and Ash had already agreed to let the boys make up their own minds when the time came. If one, or both, didn't choose to turn... He couldn't imagine being a parent and knowing your children would not outlive you.

"Good evening," Ash drawled from the doorway.

Kielyn beamed up at him. "There's daddy."

It was still an unreal thing to see the parental smile that curled his maker's lips when he beheld his family. Ironic, really, that life would wait a thousand years to give Ashdon LaGoryen the biggest blessing, and hardest challenge, of his immortal life.

Ash walked over, stopping to tap Eirik on the nose, earning a spit-bubble giggle. The Fire King smiled, and then bent at the waist, taking Bastian from his mate. "Shall we?" He extended his hand to Kielyn.

She allowed him to pull her to her feet, pushing up onto her toes to brush a kiss across his mouth. "You owe them a pony ride later."

"How about I also get up with them tonight?" her mate offered.

"Both of them?" She looked skeptical.

"Of course." Ash led her to the hallway. Stefen brought up the rear. "It's the least I can do for missing our play date."

Stefen didn't bother to hide his eye roll. His maker, leader of the Fire Dynasty, dragon extraordinaire, slayer of Satan; utter sap around twenty-five-pound slobbering coo-bundles. He supposed every mythical hero needed their personal kryptonite.

Two maids rushed over and took the boys.

"Thank you, Darla." Ash smiled before turning to the other and inclining his head. "Penelope."

Stefen side-eyed Kielyn as they continued into the dining room. *Too pleasant.* The look his best friend returned confirmed she knew it, too. Overly agreeable Ash, to those on the perimeter of his world, meant those on the inside were about to get the unedited version.

As anticipated, *it was going to be a long evening.*

Ash had been locked in his office all day, even skipping training. Knowing now that he had also missed time with his sons meant Stefen's chances of making it through this dinner without wanting to pluck his eyes out with his fork was highly unlikely.

They took their places in no particular order, as was the custom. No seat at this table outranked the other. The office was the only room where Ash enforced his rule. The only room where debate ceased once a verdict was made.

A footman came around to each of them, pouring wine. The

chef introduced his menu for the evening next, and servants hurriedly brought the first course. Small plates were placed in front of them, and the warm smell of baked brie and sliced pear over wheat crackers glazed with honey drifted up. Stefen realized he was famished.

The chef nodded once to approve the arrangement and took his leave. The staff exited after him. Stefen fell on the dish, sighing to himself. "Dear gods, can he make this every night?"

Kielyn chuckled, her knife cutting delicately into her appetizer. "You say that about everything he makes."

Stefen wagged a fork at her. "And I mean it each time."

"I'm sure Alaric would have something to say about your new goals of becoming spherical," Ash countered, grinning.

The talk remained light throughout the first course, Stefen briefing them on the day's events in the training yard. All of the Fire-dancing recruits were shaping up nicely. They would reach Ash's goals for testing within a month.

Sparring was a highlight each day for Stefen. Part of why he was ravenous every night. His new body noted fatigue more. Muscles took longer to heal after a taxing day, the sting of an injury clinging to the bones.

Stefen relished it though, these subtle nuances that reminded him he was alive. He had cheated death and been given a second chance. A body that recognized the exertion put into a good workout and appreciated a long soak in a hot bath afterward.

Each day revealed more than the last regarding this new world and his place in it. While Stefen hadn't inherited Ash's ability to control fire, his age and previous training still made him an even match for his maker in the sparring ring. If anything, he was stronger now. Due to Ash's dragon blood. An observation he kept to himself.

He'd unfortunately lost the ability to interrupt the minds of others. With the exception of Ash and Kielyn. Through their shared bond they could communicate mentally any time.

The hardest part had been learning to shut it off. Kie was an unabashed snoop when it came to presents. Stefen had learned the hard way when she had anticipated everything he bought her for Christmas. Ash taught him the next day how to shield against such intrusions. Family or not.

The biggest blessing in his transformation was unquestionably the ability to walk in the sunlight. Something in his angelic DNA made it so he still could. A huge bonus.

Conversation around him turned to the upcoming ball they were throwing. With the couple distracted by Kie's extensive preparation list, Stefen reflected more on all that had changed and what remained the same.

He maintained the ability to shift into his guide animal, a wolf. But his ability to mask his emotions had dulled significantly. That bothered him the most, as it had been a talent he'd perfected since childhood—a means of protection.

He had once teased Ash that he did not want to become an over-protective, brash, brute like his maker. At least, he did not want to reveal it if he was being an unintentional ass. But Ash had dispelled that fear quickly, stating, "Being a vampire didn't make me this way. Falling in love did."

The second offering of food made its way around the table and their plates were removed, and new ones placed before them. "Tomorrow marks a rather important date," Ash said.

"I don't want a cake."

"But, but..." Kielyn pouted across from him. "I made it special."

Stefen cracked a smile and held up his glass. "Well, in that case."

"It also marks another day." Ash sat back in his chair. "The day Dante died. And all hell, literally, broke loose."

"I'm pretty sure you don't want to send Katarra and Zander an anniversary card." Stefen studied his maker—not known for mincing words. "Is there some other significance for tomorrow?"

"This came today." Ash tossed a letter on the table. "From your brother."

Stefen picked it up apprehensively, too many years of royal summons ingrained in his memory. His eyes scanned the words. Alaric needed his help. An angel was still unaccounted for, having never returned after the battle in Gerra a year ago. An archangel, no less, by the name of Anessa.

The connection found its place in his memory. *Anessa*...the beautiful blonde intended for his brother. Stefen had only met her once. It had been an arranged pairing. One Alaric hadn't wanted. Not because he didn't know or accept his duty to take a mate and procure the royal line, but because he didn't think Anessa would do. She was too insubordinate, his brother had claimed. Too reckless to be a queen.

Apparently he'd been right. She had disobeyed him and snuck in among their forces when they infiltrated Gerra. Stefen's mind ran backward in time. Had she been there that day? "Surely, she wouldn't have risked jeopardizing the engagement. By ignoring a royal command."

Ash's droll stare was answer enough regarding what willful females would, or wouldn't, do.

Stefen looked at his brother's signature at the bottom of the letter. "He thinks she snuck over and got herself captured or killed." He reread the last line of the letter again: "*I need your help returning her, dead or alive.*"

Stefen set down the letter. "What's the plan?"

"My presence will be detected immediately if I enter Gerra," Ash said.

"You want me to go."

"I don't want anything. Your brother does."

8

"Why should I care what King Alaric wants?" Stefen ground out, an old familiar agitation scratching at his nerves, pulling at the past like a scab. "He didn't give two shits when they banned me from my home."

Stefen pushed away from the table and stood, chucking his napkin on his plate, sauce soaking through the linen. "He can fuck right off for all I care."

"You're right," Kielyn affirmed, understanding reflecting in her amber eyes. "You owe him nothing. Fuck that feathery bastard!"

Her outburst, combined with Ash's shock, made him smile. It was impossible to hold onto a sour mood with Kie around. She had a knack for knowing just what he needed to hear, and she always had his back. Even when he was dead wrong. She was more like a sibling than Alaric ever had been.

But he still loved his brother, and deep down he knew Alaric's hands were tied when it came to his ban. His brother was born to rule, and he did so justly. It was not fair to begrudge him for not fighting harder. Kings ruled the masses. They couldn't show favoritism.

In all fairness, it was probably time he repay Alaric for his tolerance over the centuries. "When do you want me to go?"

"Tomorrow," Ash stated. "Dante's brats are hosting a celebration in honor of their father. It will be the best time to get in and blend with the festivities."

"*In honor*," he scoffed. "Can I please kill one of them while I'm in that hell hole?"

"No," Ash replied plainly as staff carted in the next course. "Who would you like to take with you?"

"No one." Stefen turned for the door. "This is a debt between me and my brother."

Chapter Two

GERRA

UNDER NORTHDOM CASTLE

The cold water hit like a thousand icy needles. Teakin blinked, the room coming in and out of focus as his vision adjusted to the bright lights. His head was yanked back.

"Awake now?" Zander's face loomed in front of him.

"Fuck you." He spat.

His arms were yanked upward and fastened to iron rings above his head by two guards. His legs were then kicked apart, heavy chains looped through the cuffs attached to his ankles to keep them so.

The king leaned in. "One day, perhaps." With a jerk of his chin, the two guards moved to the door. "However, you'll regret the suggestion if I do."

Teakin lunged but was abruptly stopped by the chains. "Then I welcome it. For that will be the day you die."

Zander stepped back, arms clasped casually behind him. "You

are a mighty specimen, Teakin LaGoryen. I see why my father was obsessed with your brother."

His smile twisted in on itself, growing ugly. "You do you remember him? Your little brother, Ashdon. The one you allowed to be tortured all those years."

Teakin tensed. His memory had been altered by the doctors over the years, but he remembered. Ash, only seven at the time, watching their mother as she was placed in a pool of lava.

Screaming. He remembered his brother's screams. While he stood by doing nothing.

"Ah, I see you do." The king circled. "You failed him. Just as you failed your mother."

Zander stopped in front of him. "There is not much you're good for."

He slid a finger into the loose drawstring of Teakin's pants and gave a sharp tug. The material fell away, catching on his spread thighs just below his buttocks.

"Except," the king's eyes widened with controlled delight, "to serve as entertainment."

Rage igniting his blood, Teakin surged forward again. The shackles clanked and protested against the concrete. Zander wasn't fast enough to hide the flinch this time.

"Your drugs are wearing off, asshole." Teakin bared his teeth. "You can't keep me sedated forever."

And he knew it. Teakin saw the flash of fear. Right before something else lit up the king's vermilion eyes.

"I don't need the ashwood toxin to keep your dragon at bay." Zander pulled a syringe from his pocket and placed it onto a table. "I have her."

Teakin forced down the bile rising in his throat. Of all the memories he had lost. She was not one of them. Zander brought her to see him daily. Usually when the drugs were wearing off. Assuring he would always remember.

A shiver crawled up his spine. *She was to be his new chains...*

The king stepped forward. "Let's play a game. To remind me of your loyalty." His clammy hand reached out and cupped Teakin's cock.

Teakin jerked back, fangs snapping. "Now, now." Zander tsked, stroking the length of him. "The game is that you have to like it. Sell me, if you will. Give this performance your all."

"Never!"

He angled his head. "Would you rather I turn my ministrations on her?"

Teakin's blood turned to ice in his veins, his rage guttering. "No." The word died in the thick humid air.

He would. The fucker was that sick.

Panic seeped into his muscles. He had to control the dragon threatening to emerge. Had to play this game. *For her.*

"Good boy." The king reached up and unshackled his arms. "There are guns aimed at your heart. If you so much as think of harming me, or your fellow actor, you'll be dead. And she will get my wrath." He placed Teakin's arms at his sides, and lifted a finger.

One of the guards at the door took a hesitant step forward. "Take him in hand," Zander ordered.

The guard, a younger elite, stepped in front of Teakin and did as asked.

Teakin hissed, causing the vampire to swallow hard, his eyes shuttering and his grip loosening. "Now, that's not very convincing," the king admonished. "Stroke him."

The guard grabbed him firmly, his callused palm stretching and pulling, rubbing from shaft to tip. Teakin's turned his head to the side, his gaze seeking out a drip oozing out of the rock in the corner of his cell. He focused on that steady leak.

After a few more attempts the guard released his flaccid cock.

Zander sighed. "Perhaps you require more from your supporting actor. On your knees," he commanded.

The elite dropped down in front of him.

"Put your hands on the back of his head, Teakin. Guide him. He's not going to bite." Zander's white teeth gleamed in way that suggested otherwise. "And remember, I need to know you like it."

Teakin felt his dick shriveling. He couldn't do this. He could not make his body do what the bastard was asking.

Something hot stung the back of his eyes. He sealed them shut. *"Would you rather I turn my ministrations on her?"* echoed in his mind. Teakin wouldn't let that happen. His dragon was raging, the physical pull to unleash it unlike any pain he'd experienced.

"That's right," Zander cooed, "control your inner beast. Bend to my will. Prove to me who your real master is."

Reluctantly, Teakin placed his hands on the back of the other male's head, shivering when a hot breath coated the tip of his cock. It would take nothing to snap his neck, then go for the king, releasing the dragon and ending it here.

His fingers tightened on the vampire's skull, just as a pair of multi-colored eyes drifted in from the recesses of his mind.

Her eyes...

He would be damned if Zander laid a hand on her.

Biting back a curse, he thrust the elite's head forward, focusing his own eyes on the wet ceiling. His stomach twisted as he shut out whose mouth was on him—calling to memory another time. A time when he'd found pleasure in a willing participant, behind the stables.

A brief moment he had stolen for himself in this realm. Before the experiments and this cell. Before they'd invoked his dragon.

Before her...

Chapter Three

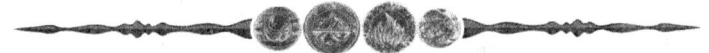

Stefen had been in Gerra for three days, and he was no closer to finding information on his brother's intended than the day he arrived. It was as if he were chasing a ghost story no one had even heard of.

He tossed two silvers down on the bar. "Gin, Hendrick's, and St. Germain."

The barkeep just stared at him.

"Whatever's on tap."

The ruddy-faced vampire turned back to the keg.

Stefen looked around the clay-walled inn, trying not to grimace at the fragrant odors of piss and vomit. No wealthy elite would step foot in this hovel. He needed to really watch his masking here, lest his royal upbringing give him away.

He adjusted the hood of his cloak. Being in Gerra was like stepping back in time. The divide between rich and poor was as prevalent here as it had been during medieval times on Earth. The impoverished were uneducated, working-class peasants. The wealthy were privileged aristocrats thriving on court gossip and politics. The middle tier was the minority, working almost exclusively for those with deep pockets.

The bartender set the drink in front of him, grunted, and hobbled away. Thus far, Stefen had stuck to gathering information from the working-class. That strategy had garnered nothing. He would have to find a way into the middle tier.

The realization had led him here. He'd been told many of the king's guard frequented this establishment after dark, when the whores arrived and rented out the rooms overhead. He took a swig of the dark ale, chewing more than swallowing.

Stefen coughed and the bartender looked in his direction, two bushy eyebrows raised. "A bowl of stew."

The large vampire turned and headed into the kitchen. As he pushed through the swinging doors, a round set of eyes caught Stefen's attention. He took another swallow of the piss water and choked it down.

The barkeep returned a couple minutes later and set the gruel down. The inn's doors burst open and in poured the sounds of drunken merriment. The evening festivities were starting early.

The vampire behind the bar yelled into the kitchen. "Get out here, boy!"

A scrawny lad emerged a second later and the bartender thrust a tray in his hands. "Go get their orders."

The boy approached the motley crew of drunk guards. "He can kiss my lily-white asshole if he wants me to dump one more piss pail from that dungeon," one male slurred.

A second guard chimed in, a bit quieter, "He's the biggest prick I've ever worked for."

Stefen swiveled in his chair enough to see them out of his peripheral.

"And those fucked up experiments..." The male shook his head. "What he did to that beauty."

The first elite, an unusually rotund fanger, with a face full of nose, complained, "Yeah, he should've let us have a go beforehand."

"That's all you," a third guard added. "I'd be afraid she'd cast a spell on my cock if I touched her. Hair that color can only mean one thing: demon witch."

"Since when have you been afraid of a damn demon?" another male quipped. "My cousin has blonde hair. You calling her a witch?"

The second guard retook the narrative. "Her hair wasn't blonde you daft fucks. It was white. There's never been an elite with white hair."

Every nerve ending in Stefen's inner ear perked up. He faced the bar and took a swallow of stale beer. Anessa had snow white hair. The barkeep looked down his way. He nodded for another.

"What about his new baby gi—"

"Shhhh." The guard's words were ended abruptly with a shove. "You'll get us arrested for treason."

"You can't be arrested for treason for talking about a lord already banned from court."

"You can, when the king is involved."

The inn door banged open and more partygoers poured in, their ruckus overtaking the space.

Fuck! What *lord* were they talking about? Stefen had wrongly assumed they were the king and queen's royal guards. He would have to get closer to that table to hear them. The serving boy started back his way.

Right as the child passed, Stefen stuck out his boot and tripped him. The kid crashed to the floor. "Watch yourself, brat," he said with a growl. "You made me drop my coin."

He bent down beside the sprawled-out boy, pretending to rummage on the ground for his loose change. "Meet me out back," Stefen whispered to the young vampire, holding up a coin. "Two, if no one sees you leave."

Stefen stood and dusted off his pants, tossed another silver on the bar, and made for the door. He was taking a huge gamble the kid would keep his mouth shut, but he didn't really see another option. If the white-haired woman was Anessa, he had to locate her.

Once outside, Stefen cut around the side of the building. Within minutes the boy peeked his shaggy head out the back door and he motioned him over.

"I ain't no whore," the lad said, keeping well out of striking range as he approached.

"Good, because I'm not a pervert," Stefen replied. "I need to borrow your ears."

The boy gasped and covered them. "Not literally," Stefen amended. "I need to know what family that table of guards work for."

The boy held out his hand. Stefen placed the two promised coins, and one extra, in his palm. "They're the king's guards," the youth confided.

"Do you know what lord they're talking about?"

"One mentioned Lord Freyberg when they was in the other night."

"Do you know who that is?" Stefen magicked another coin between two fingers.

"Lord Thaddeus Freyberg is the king's uncle." The boy swiped the silver from Stefen's hand.

"Does he live nearby?"

The boy turned his palm over again. Stefen exhaled, but ponied up.

"He lives on the top of Mount Blanc, in Northdom Castle."

He flipped one last coin into the air. "You never saw me." Stefen dematerialized.

Chapter Four

Outside Thaddeus's window the ground fell away, plummeting straight to the forest below. The black rock was peppered with clusters of night-blooming flowers all the way to the valley floor where the lava cut rivers beneath the dirt, snaking under the surface of the land like blooded veins. Beyond that, an inky vapor crawled out of the surrounding mountains, its bony fingers creeping over peaks and slithering between boulders—a creature covering the landscape —the misty death of a thousand sunsets.

A throat behind him cleared.

Thaddeus didn't turn. "Is he done?"

"Not yet," the servant replied. "He wants to know where the wings are."

Thaddeus cast his gaze to the baby asleep in her bassinet, unappreciative of the view he'd been admiring. Unknowing of the horrors lurking just under this mountain. "And what does my grandson want with the wings?"

"He wants to hang them in the prisoner's cell." He could hear the distaste in the male's tone. "A present, if you will."

"I see." Thaddeus continued to study the baby. So beautiful, so innocent...*so dangerous.* "Have Daman take them to him." He rocked the cradle when the swaddled bundle started to stir, her snow-white lashes blinking angrily on her creamy cheeks. "That is all."

Three days. That was all it had taken his grandson to succumb to the same addiction his father had been afflicted with. *The dragon.* Perhaps the time Zander had spent at Northdom Castle propelled it.

Thaddeus looked at his desk where his dagger lay. He should go to the dungeon and end it now. Dragons were not meant to be caged. They did not belong in Gerra.

Zander would die the same way his father had if he wasn't careful. Thaddeus had told him as much. It didn't matter, the king was snared. No amount of logic could argue with whatever power the LaGoryen bloodline wielded. Thaddeus realized the downfall the second his grandson beheld the creature his experiments had awakened. Even in Teakin's weakened state, dosed out of his mind on toxins, Zander had been mesmerized.

He gently picked up the waking baby and took a seat. None of this was going as planned. He wanted to see what could be made from the cross-breeding of an angel and a Fire-dancer-turned-vampire. Nothing more.

The test then, as they tended to do, had grown in scope. What would come from showing the monster his offspring? Would it trigger the foretold dragon sleeping deep within Teakin's royal blood? It had worked on his brother. Ashdon's dragon awoke once his fated bond with the young mortal registered. Thaddeus had rationalized the same emotion could be stirred with the bond of a father to his child.

He was right.

However, *the plan* was to kill Teakin soon after, same as the angel. The dragon had done his job siring the child. The baby Thaddeus now claimed as his own. There was no reason to keep such a liability around.

All that changed the moment Zander laid eyes on what he'd made. The king had hatched a new plan. It was his belief the child would serve as the dragon's shackles. The only thing capable of preventing Teakin from turning on them. So far, it was working.

But for how long?

Thaddeus was a male of science, not whim. Statistics showed fight or flight was a natural response when one was threatened. The problem his grandson refused to see was that dragons did not run. They did not yield.

The king walked the same slippery slope his father had fallen down. It was time to come up with a new plan. Zander could not be trusted to rule. Not while he was under the dragon's spell.

Thankfully, his grandson was needed back at the palace tonight. His presence would certainly be missed if he skirted the closing ceremonies. *A small blessing.* One that would give Thaddeus time to think.

The first thing that needed to happen: disposing of the angel's wings. They didn't need word getting around Northdom Castle was hosting *interesting* guests. If the queen figured out what they'd been hiding, literal hell would break loose. *Not a possibility.* Thaddeus would have the gruesome souvenirs thrown from the mountain and into the lava pits when Zander took his leave.

The sound of scuffling slippers pulled his gaze back up. "Would you like to hold the other one?" the wet-nurse asked from the doorway, his legitimate daughter in her arms.

Thaddeus turned back to the window. "No."

Chapter Five

CASTELLO ALBORNOZ

ITALY

Kielyn flung open the castle doors, Ash right on her heels, the moment Stefen materialized on the first steps.

His maker said nothing from where he stood in the threshold, but his best friend rushed forward when Stefen took the stairs, as if she could heal what he was carrying. The broken remains of his brother's intended.

"She's dead." He passed them both, heading down the long hall off the corridor. "There's no chance anyone could have survived this."

Stefen paused when he entered the study, looking for the best place to lay the wings. Some part of him wanted the next thing that touched them to be worthy. Anessa deserved better.

It had been a stroke of luck he'd even seen them falling from the wide hatch door built into the hilltop castle. They had been intended for the snapping lava pool at the base of the mountain. But Stefen had been faster than the gravity pulling them down.

He'd caught the severed wings right after the door closed, his theft undetected.

His mental walls completely down, Ash read his internal debate with ease. "Put them here." He motioned to the desk, clearing it without lifting a finger.

Kielyn hurriedly unfolded and laid out a soft, thick blanket she used regularly to curl up with. Carefully, he laid the wings down, taking note of the truly horrific destruction for the first time. They hadn't just been removed from her body. *They had been ripped from it!* Muscle and sinew were coated in blood and pieces of broken scapula jutted out in disjointed directions from where they'd been pulled from the sockets and twisted.

"I was too late," Stefen managed, despite the constriction of his throat. "This just happened."

"No." Ash leaned in. "We were months late." He straightened, his blue eyes going arctic cold. "The wings have been preserved. A type of Gerra magic used to halt the decomposition process."

"Why?" Kielyn asked, appalled.

Ash hesitated. "As a way to maintain the life-like effect. So their trophies can be viewed as they were when first killed."

Stefen stared at the mangled wings. He had been a warrior for centuries, slain countless foes, enemies he never knew the names of, and plenty he did. He'd never derived enjoyment from it, never took sadistic pride in it. He certainly couldn't fathom pinning his victims' most coveted body parts on a wall as memorabilia.

The room was suddenly too cramped. There wasn't enough air. Stefen forced his gaze from the grisly scene. "I need to lay down."

"Stefen." Kielyn reached out.

He stepped to the side before she could make contact. "Not now."

There were very few times he shut others out, especially Kie, but this was one of them. He needed to be alone, needed time to process the overwhelming guilt rising up in him—the magnitude of hate that had gone into the angel's destruction.

Stefen marched from the study and took the main stairs two at a time, only slowing when his chamber doors slammed shut behind him. Somehow he made it into the bathroom before retching up the tavern stew.

Once he'd purged all traces of that vile realm from his system, he reached up and yanked down a towel. Bracing one hand on the toilet, Stefen scrubbed the cloth over his face and slowly stood.

Why hadn't Alaric sent word sooner? He might have been able to get her out before those monsters debased her in the most unimaginable of ways. If they were capable of this...*what else had they done?*

He couldn't think about that. If he did, he would go straight back and rip everyone in that castle apart.

Staring into in the mirror, Stefen turned on the faucet. The gods had given him his archangel form and the ability to know right from wrong. But they had also armed him with a sword, knowing he would need it more than his compassion. He might be a Fallen now, but that heritage was etched in his bones. His new vampire body had only heightened his sense of protectiveness and revenge, both coursing like liquid steel through his blood.

Stefen would embrace each of his makers in this atrocity—the gods, and the dragon.

It might take him years but he would strike them down. When he did, it would not be merciful. It would be messy. It would be devastating. He would enjoy every second of it. He would avenge Anessa. He would mete out the justice those bastards deserved.

Steam fogged up the glass, blotting out his reflection.

He would make them pay.

Chapter Six

GERRA

Northdom Castle

The fresh air caressed his skin like a familiar lover—unchained and honest. Though blindfolded, Teakin took a hesitant step onto the soft grass, his lungs filling greedily with the breath he'd been deprived of for a century.

Freedom.

"Do you miss it?" Zander spoke behind him.

"One cannot miss what they do not remember," he lied. The monster at his back might have access to his body, but he would not get his mind. "Still smells like shit."

"Come now, I had the sod brought in from Earth. All the vegetation is from your birth realm. I did all of this for you."

"Is this to be the new stage for torture?"

"Not tonight." Zander slapped a hand on his raw shoulder.

Teakin ground his teeth to keep from wincing. He had been whipped to shreds the day before and given Ashwood that slowed his body's natural healing process. Apparently, his performance with the guard had lacked sincerity. Next time, he would have to look his handler in the eyes for the entirety of the act.

Zander had left shortly after, but not before hanging the angel's wings in his cell. A parting gift. Thankfully, they were gone by the time Teakin regained consciousness. A modification the king raged about upon his return.

"Tonight I have a reward for you."

Teakin's muscles recoiled, rippling under his skin as the blindfold was slipped down around his neck.

"A choice." The king swept his hand around the staged courtyard. "Pick anything in this garden to have, in any way you see fit, for an hour."

He scanned the space. To the left stood two naked females. They pinched each other's nipples and batted their eyelashes.

"You could fuck them however you want. Beat them. Or dismember them." Zander's slithery voice cooed.

Teakin continued to survey the garden. To the right, a table overflowed with various drugs. Drugs that would steal him away from this place and his pain for a short time.

He took a step toward the table, before his sights landed on the open door at the back.

"You could escape," Zander whispered in his ear. "Be free for one glorious hour. I won't even whip you when you are captured and brought back."

Teakin could feel the fucker's twisted smile on his neck, the hot breath against his skin. He cut his eyes to the left. A second table sported every fashion of torture device imaginable.

"I could use those?" He turned back to his captor. "On you?"

The king's smile widened. "For one hour you could do anything you wished to me."

Teakin's fists balled and his blood pumped faster through his veins. He turned slowly in a circle, taking in his options. *One hour...* One hour to bring himself a moment of relief.

But his jailer would be deriving some sort of pleasure from whatever he chose. "I can select whatever I want?"

"Yes."

"Anything in this garden?" He turned back.

The other male studied him closely. "Yes."

"Once I make my choice. Can I take it to any room in the castle?"

Zander tilted his head in contemplation. "Yes."

Teakin walked over to the table of drugs. In the deafening silence of the night, he selected one jar, unscrewed the top, and poured the pills onto the ground. Then he walked to the far side of the garden.

His eyes tracked a shimmering amber light bringing life to the darkness—magic amongst tragedy. Fulgur bugs, Gerra's version of Earth's lightning bugs. All animals and insects in this realm were demons, but Fulgur bugs were harmless.

His hand hovered beneath one, following its dizzy flight path, before folding his palm around it. Gently, he placed it into the jar, and then he repeated the act. Over and over, until the glass was aglow.

After a few minutes he walked back to the table, punctured tiny air holes in the lid with a thin blade, and turned to the king. "Take me to her."

The room was softly lit with candles. The king nodded his dismissal of a wet nurse and she rose quietly and exited the room.

Teakin walked slowly to the crib. "Leave us." He placed the jar on a nightstand.

"This is really what you want to do with your one hour of freedom," Zander stated, more than asked.

"You said an hour."

The king paused, and for a moment Teakin feared he was changing his mind. Then the door closed behind him.

He was alone with her.

Seconds rolled into minutes as he memorized every delicate inch of her perfect skin. After some time, he reached out his hand and brushed the top of her downy head of curls. Little blonde lashes fluttered against rosy cheeks.

She was perfect.

Teakin carefully lifted her into his arms as those crystal orbs opened, one blue and one brown. "Hello, my heart," he whispered.

A tiny yawn, and then a little smile of recognition. "Sorry to wake you."

A chubby hand fought free of the blankets and grasped his finger. "I take that back." He grinned. "I wouldn't change a single thing about intruding on your dreams."

The tiny bundle stirred more, a frown forming on her mouth. Teakin reached for a bottle on the nightstand, before the first cry could pierce the silence of the room. "There, there."

He lifted the milk to her lips. She latched on with a ferociousness that made him smile as he adjusted her into the crook of his left arm. "I have a gift."

With his free hand he reached for the jar of Fulgur bugs.

Teakin watched her intently as he moved the glass into her line of sight. Her focused eyes grew round.

When the jar was within reach, she spat out the bottle and little hands reached for the glass. He turned it around for her inspection. The angelic smile returned to her face, but faded the second he placed the jar back on the table.

He leaned forward to bridge the gap between them and the object of her affection. "Are you ready for the magic?" He twisted the top of the jar.

She protested with wiggles and her fingers opened and closed with tactile want. Teakin chuckled and removed the lid. One by one the Fulgur bugs took flight.

Her eyes widened to the size of saucers, and she rolled her head back to follow them. Their twinkling light danced around the room.

He reached a hand out to one last Fulgur bug leaving the jar. The straggler crawled onto the tip of his finger.

Teakin brought it toward the baby, just as the most amazing sound he'd ever heard filled the room.

Laughter.

He froze, spellbound, as enchantment flooded her eyes.

Teakin brought the bug to her nose and the melodic sound erupted from her throat again.

His heart flipped over.

He would not have traded this moment for anything in the world. His throat closed up and his vision blurred. He would do whatever Zander wanted of him. His purpose in this life was not meant for the monster behind the door.

Teakin's entire soul, his reason for living, was wrapped up in this tiny being in his arms. His heart beat only for the smile of his daughter. His life belonged to this child.

The baby girl he had named *Merick.*

Chapter Seven

CASTELLO ALBORNOZ

ITALY

Alaric stood before him in the library. "What brings you here, brother?" Stefen looked up from his book. "Or, am I not allowed to call you that any longer?"

"You will always be my brother." Alaric's eyes softened a degree. Not so much any other observer would notice, but Stefen did. "I've missed you."

He ignored the sentiment, focusing instead on matters at hand. Questions for which Stefen wanted answers. "Why did you wait a year to check on your intended?" He set the book down. "Seems a rather lengthy lesson."

"It wasn't a lesson. She was presumed dead," Alaric intoned. "Her family mourned her."

So many holes in that excuse. He wanted to poke pins in each one of them. But that was not Alaric's way. He could no more create feelings of guilt or shame in his brother than Stefen could regrow wings.

"Why now? Did you finally develop a conscience?"

"I understand your anger. I will ignore the insult." Alaric took a chair opposite Stefen. "Her mother came to me. She had felt a connection to Anessa, the first since she'd left. She appealed to myself and the elders, citing, if her daughter were dead she would not be able to feel her energy."

Stefen stared at his brother. "You sent me into that godsforsaken realm on a *hunch*?"

"I believed her maternal instincts, yes." Alaric followed his movements when Stefen rose, walked to the sidebar, and poured a drink. "And turns out, they were right."

"Mystery solved." He downed his glass, and slammed it down on the marble. "Why exactly are you here?"

Footsteps down the hall announced his maker's arrival, a second before he rounded the library's arched entryway.

With an elite.

"Sorry to interrupt," Ash said in his usual polished tone, but there was a subtle edge to it, a warning. "We have a visitor."

Before Stefen could take the full measure of the newcomer, Alaric surged to his feet, wings snapping tightly to his back, fangs bared. "What's he doing here?"

Ash kept his body strategically positioned between his brother and the source of his ire. "He's well aware the dangers of walking into this room," he assured, his eyes focused, placating—so very careful. "He has come to discuss the angel."

Alaric, never one to be pacified, snarled. "I will not hear anything this male has to say."

"It has been some time, your Grace." Stefen didn't mistake the glint in the immortal's gray eyes for anything but razor-sharp guile. "Surely, you can afford me a few minutes of your time. After what your brother took from me."

Recognition dawned with the force of a hurling battle axe. *Anessa's captor!*

"You defiled her." The words slipped from Stefen's mouth, low and twisted, like a giant beast yawning awake.

Down their shared mental bond, Ash tensed. But no interference was made when Stefen lunged. His palm connected with the intruder's jugular, shoving him back, and pinning him to the library wall with enough force to shake books off the upper shelves. "I'm going to mount your head in this very room."

"Being made vampire has done nothing to diminish your brother's famed strength," the male rasped, but he made no attempt to break free. Either he knew he was no match, or he had enormous patience. "Your legion must greatly miss him."

Stefen squeezed his windpipe tighter.

"It wasn't...me," the stranger choked out, his skin turning a sickly pallor. "I...knew. Nothing."

His maker's hand landed gently on Stefen's shoulder. "Let's let him talk. Then you may kill him and mount his head wherever you like."

After a few more seconds, once a dull haze started to cloud the Gerra slime's pupils, Stefen released him. "Talk quick, asshole."

He marched back to the bar, his hands needing occupation. If this fucker was going to continue to draw breath for another minute. The interloper coughed, long enough to occupy the length of time it took Stefen to fill his glass.

"First of all." The elite rubbed his neck. "I am a scientist, not a brute. Second, the angel was captured in battle. A war *you* raged against us," he stated pragmatically. "I'm sure you would have taken your own prisoners had we invaded Anu."

Nothing incorrect in that statement. Everyone knew what happened in times of war. Anessa had chosen to engage, despite being forbidden. Still...

Her wings... Stefen's lips pulled away from his gums as his fangs elongated.

35

"All is fair in war," Alaric inserted. "We angels just adhere to a higher standard of morals in the aftermath."

"I only kept her at my estate under orders of the king," the vampire rationalized. "I never laid a hand on her and I never ordered another to."

"The king, *your grandson*," Alaric sneered.

Stefen narrowed his eyes as the elite's identity became clear. *Thaddeus.*

"I am his kin. However, I was banned from court when Dante killed my daughter." He turned to Ash. "So that he could marry your mother. I have been estranged from the throne ever since."

"Then why are you doing his bidding?" Ash asked, unnervingly calm.

Stefen was certain only centuries of training kept his maker from ripping out Thaddeus's throat.

"You are both kings." He glanced between the two. "What would you do if a direct order was not obeyed?" Thaddeus paused. "In Gerra, I promise it would be worse." He looked directly at Ash. "You of all people know how Dante was. Zander is following in his footsteps."

"You're a coward." Stefen's ability to play court politics had never been a bragging point. "What gave you the balls to come here today? And if you say it was to retrieve the wings, you're a dead fanger."

"I had no part in that," he maintained evenly, before addressing Alaric. "I am here to see if retaliation is part of your plan."

"Why the fuck would we be forthcoming with our plans?" Stefen scoffed.

"Because there is more to this story than the demise of the angel." He motioned to a chair. "May I?"

Ash nodded and the elite took a hesitant seat, keeping a close eye on Stefen. Alaric sat across from him, his brother's wings rasping against the back of his chair. Ash selected his seat purposefully—anyone wishing to exit through the only entrance would have to cross his path first.

"As already stated, I am a scientist. I look at things logically." Thaddeus's gaze tracked Stefen prowling the circumference of the gathering. "Logically speaking, you might be interested in knowing she bore a child."

You could have heard a pin drop. All eyes went straight to Thaddeus, various silent challenges were made on who would be allowed to kill him first.

"A baby that is alive and thriving," the elite added quickly, obviously sensing his time left on Earth was ticking down at an astonishing rate. "A beautiful little girl."

Another beat passed before Alaric angled his head, the movement more animal than angel. "Who's the father?"

"For reasons I'm sure you understand, he wishes to be anonymous."

"An elite?" Ash asked, smooth and polished, no hint of the dragon. *Yet...*

Thaddeus nodded. "Yes."

"Then it doesn't matter." Alaric's voice was like a moonless night as he added, "She is no angel."

"What of Anessa's parents?" Stefen snapped. "They have a grandchild trapped in Gerra!"

"A Fallen grandchild is the same as a dead one." Each word out of his brother's mouth was clipped—brutal.

He'd never wanted to clock his sibling more. Ash shot him a warning look, a silent plea to hold his tongue. It was a useless hope on his maker's part.

"But of course, brother." Stefen stopped pacing and leaned over the back of Alaric's chair. "Don't want to upset your *gods*." He was never good at following orders. Why start now. "Anu has standards after all."

37

Ash pinched the bridge of his nose. "What do you want to know, Thaddeus?" he asked, before Alaric could respond. "She gave birth to a child. A child that has no place in Anu. Are you looking for adopters on Earth?"

"Since the child is of no concern. My only remaining question is, do you seek revenge?"

Everyone looked to Alaric leaning back in his chair. "Let me be clear. I loathe you. It is my mission to eventually eradicate your whole species." He let the threat hang between them. "But, war is war. And what is done in war is, as you previously stated, every participant's risk. Anessa knew full well what troubles could befall her, and she broke a direct order in the process. She entered Gerra of her own free will. I can't see waging a war over the actions of one disobedient warrior."

Thaddeus nodded. "Thank you. For offering such practical leadership."

"We're not done here," Stefen said. The next words burst from his mouth before they'd fully formed in his head. "I want the child."

All necks twisted to him.

He continued. "The baby may be of no use to either of these two kings, but its safety is a concern of mine."

"The baby is well cared for and loved by all," the elite assured.

"I don't care to take your word for it." A vein throbbed in his neck. "To believe your kind could cherish a child. Especially after you tortured, raped, and murdered, her mother."

"The child is an experimen—"

"Enough with your bullshit experiments!" Stefen snarled, his fist splaying and closing at his side, wanting for a sword.

He couldn't believe what he was hearing. That his brother and his maker were just sitting here, listening...

Something dark and primal peeled away invisible layers of his self-control. "Am I the only one in this fucking room with a shred of ethics?"

"Stefen," Ash said too softly. "Let him finish." He focused on Thaddeus. "What are you hoping for with this *experiment*?"

The elite's shoulders relaxed a bit. "I want to see what an angel and a vampire mating will produce," he explained simply. "The baby is malleable, uninfluenced by either side. She knows no hate, has no prejudices. I want to see if that will change as she grows. Or, if her ties to the Anu bloodline will shape her differently than her environment."

"So you admit it is not just a scientific observation on crossbreeding." Stefen took a menacing step in the elite's direction. "But rather, an experiment to see how best you might exploit the child's natural merits—bend them to your own purposes."

"These experiments could help us all," Thaddeus insisted. "One day Anu might host an orphaned elite."

Alaric snorted.

It didn't deter Thaddeus. "I will not influence her decisions, only observe her choices. "She will be free of biased opinions in my household. The experiment will be to see how she acclimates outside of it when she is older. What she takes freely from her environment in Gerra. And what she rejects."

"What happens to her when you're finished?" Ash stood, before Stefen could get within striking range of the elite.

"Nothing," Thaddeus said. "She is being presented as a twin to my own child, born just days before. To the outside eye, she is mine. Thus, she will know no different. She will have all the advantages her sister does. She will be taken care of."

"But not loved," Stefen argued. "She needs to be with her own kind!"

"She has no kind," he bluntly pointed out.

For some reason that honesty stabbed at something deep

inside. *A Fallen*. Same as him. As good as dead in his brethren's eyes.

"Let me raise her. Here, on neutral ground," Stefen rationalized, appealing to the other male's scientific brain. Knowing he was the only one in this room on the side of that baby. "Surely, Earth would be less polarizing than Gerra?"

"Ah!" The older immortal's eyes shone. "But the experiment is meant to have polarization. How else will I know how much negative influence society can have on a child that thinks she is one of her peers?" He spread his fingers wide. "Can the light of Anu fend off the darkness of Gerra? Or, will the dark swallow the light?"

"This provision will not go over well with my high council," Alaric finally spoke up.

Stefen cut his gaze to his brother, then to his maker.

Ash only looked at him. *"Let him finish,"* he said down their shared bond.

"It might be enough to serve as the war you wish to avoid," Alaric concluded.

"You just said..." Thaddeus grew noticeably tense. "The child is dead in your eyes."

"She is." Alaric looked at Stefen. "But my brother isn't."

Stefen was sure the world had stopped rotating.

He stood there mute, as Ash took back the conversation. "I think some conditions might go a long way in soothing all sides. The first one being that Stefen, my emissary, will be allowed to check in on the child. To make sure her mental and physical well-being is being seen to. To *our* standards. My second condition; you allow her the choice on her eighteenth birthday. To leave Gerra, or to stay."

Ash walked over to his desk with that casual confidence Stefen was used to—a king, long before a crown had been placed on his head. "That will give you time to see if she might thrive in your realm." He procured a pen and began to write. "It also saves Gerra a war."

"Very well." Thaddeus made one last deliberate glance around the room, before standing and walking to the desk.

"I will grant her free choice on the day she turns eighteen. But your hybrid here," he motioned to Stefen with the pen Ash handed him, "can only check in every five years. Starting on her fifth name day." He amended the treaty. "I can't have our secret pact getting out. The less time you're around, the better. This agreement will be null and void, if the king or queen finds out."

"You have my word," the Fire King agreed.

"Mine as well." Alaric rose to his feet.

All eyes slid to Stefen. This was not the outcome he wanted, but after a lifetime of knowing when to compromise, it was the best he could hope for.

"You have my word." He nodded, turned, and headed out of the room. "See you in five years."

As soon as he was in the hall, Stefen did something he'd never done. He made a promise. A promise to someone he didn't know. A promise to another Fallen.

I will avenge you, Anessa. I will protect your daughter.

Your sacrifice will not be in vain.

41

Chapter Eight

GERRA

FIVE YEARS LATER

Merick watched the cubs from behind the protective glass. They rolled and fought, playing and chewing on each other's ears as their parents looked on. She wondered if the tigers enjoyed watching the offspring of the elite playing on the castle grounds. Did they think Merick and the others were in their own exhibit, set up entirely for the big cats' viewing pleasure?

She sighed and toed the loose dirt beneath her park bench. How she longed to be included. To join in her peers' games. But every year it was the same response; *you're too small, too ugly, and too weak.* Or the worst: *You're too weird.*

She always left the splendor of this place utterly dejected. Each year Merick would do the same thing when she got home. Spend hours looking in a mirror, trying to figure out why they hated her. Even her own sister couldn't stand her, pretending to be pleasant only when their father was present.

Merick had just one friend, Teakin. Recently appointed her

personal guard, he would sit for her tea parties, eat the sweetcakes, and pretend he liked them. He played hide and seek with her, watched while she saw to her studies, and read her bedtime stories at night. Teakin was her best friend.

She turned back to the tigers. The cubs had rolled up to the viewing window and were looking curiously at her. She smiled and scooted off the bench.

They tilted their heads as she slowly approached. "Did you get tired of playing?" One cub gnawed on his sister's tail when she swished it in his face. Merick laughed, and sat down on her knees. "It must be nice having each other."

She lifted a hand to the glass and the little female cub licked at her palm, leaving a wet trail up the observation window. "You must always stand up for each other. It's what family does."

The male cub flopped onto his back, pawing at the air. Merick readjusted also and laid on her belly, putting her nose to the glass. He kneaded his huge paws against the barrier, making her giggle.

They stayed like that for what felt like minutes. Until something snagged the cubs' attention, their ears twitched, and they darted away.

Merick looked up, confused. What had made them suddenly skittish? They'd just become *friends...*

Her heart nearly stopped beating when the mother tiger lunged in her direction, bone white teeth bared. Merick froze, held captive by her own body as the large cat charged, hind legs passing the front, covering the distance faster than she could contemplate escaping.

The large animal collided with the window, the vibration from the impact so resounding it propelled Merick out of her paralysis. She scrambled backward and pushed to her feet with such haste her patent leather shoes became entangled, tripping her.

She landed hard on her bottom and stared—chest heaving, barely able to gulp down enough air—into the glowing red eyes of the beast. Fear and relief. Both emotions clashed for dominance. She wanted to cry, to scream, to run away. But she remained rooted in place.

What would have happened if she had not been protected by the glass? Why did the agitated, pacing mother see her as a threat? How could her honest admiration and curiosity be viewed as dangerous? Someone laughed behind her.

She turned quickly.

"Upsetting the wildlife?" The queen stood over her, the dappled sunlight glinting along the bright thread emblazoned on her emerald-green sleeves as she crossed her arms.

Merick jumped to her feet, giving her best curtsy, despite her shaken nerves. "I...I am sorry, Your Majesty," she said demurely, venturing a look at the female.

Long, perfectly manicured fingers drummed the rich velvet at her elbow. Merick watched their cadence, as if the digits alone would announce her punishment when they finally stilled.

"I did not mean to upset them." Merick took a deep, shuddering breath and cast her eyes back down, dismally aware she was about to cry.

Seconds passed while the queen studied her. Merick kept her sights fixed on the ground, trying not to fidget under the assessment. Her Majesty had never spoken to her before. Now here she was, standing before her, upset that a guest had displeased the beautiful tigers.

Merick's lip wobbled, and one knee knocked against the other under her white muslin dress. She looked up, unable to take the scrutiny any longer.

"Do you know why they hate you?" the queen asked, her gaze too similar to that of the mother tiger.

"The tigers?"

"The brats on my lawn."

Merick gulped and found herself searching out a pebble at her feet. She mentally cautioned against the impulse to kick it. "Because I'm ugly and weird, Your Majesty."

After another long pause, Her majesty said, "No. It's because you're different. That scares them." The female's voice was curiously light. "All creatures are afraid of the unknown."

The queen bent to her level. "Just like the tiger. It did not know you. It only saw you as a threat to its cubs."

Merick nervously bunched her dress in her sweaty palms. "How do I get them to know me...when they refuse?"

The queen smiled, and there was something tender in it, something at odds with the ruler Merick had been raised to fear. "You have to find a way to get their attention. And hold it. Long enough for them to see who you really are."

She stood, a phantom wind playing with her chestnut-colored hair. "But they will still hate you." Her Majesty turned, skirts swooshing around her ankles as she said over her shoulder, "The trick is to make them respect you."

Then she was gone in a susurration of jeweled material and warm dark breeze—that only stirred for her.

Merick sat with the queen's advice. She didn't want anyone to hate her. "Make them see me," she muttered to herself, glancing to the youth on the hillside. *How?*

She turned back to the tiger exhibit. She had always been good with animals. Teakin said it was a gift. All the stray cats around the castle stables she'd lured to the kitchens. It only took patience. After a few days, the feral mongrels would develop trust. Within a few weeks, they'd curl around her ankles.

Her brows furrowed as she studied the giant glass wall that enclosed the habitat. The mother's reaction had to stem from not understanding Merick's intentions. Surely, if the large cat could really see her...it would know she meant no harm.

It was all that stupid wall's fault.

She gathered her five-year-old resolve and marched to where

the precisely trimmed grounds disappeared into the thick deadwood trees. Picking her way down the innkeeper's rudimentary trail, she found a low-hanging branch on the side of the enclosure.

Merick kicked off her shoes and grabbed hold, then carefully shimmied up the tree. When she reached the top of the wall she found another limb stretching out over the den. *If they can just sense my goodness*, she mentally convinced herself as she inched across.

A twig snapped under her hand.

She froze, every sense heightened. Gingerly, Merick tested the limb with a little bounce. She exhaled when the branch held steady.

The noise had gotten the attention of the cubs. Merick continued out further as the inquisitive pair ran beneath the tree canopy, looking up. "I just need to get your parents to see me. Then they will understand."

She stopped, deeming herself far enough out to be spotted. But high enough. Just in case she was wrong.

Confident in her position, and the mother's lack of concern from where she lounged on a large rock, Merick broke off a small branch and dangled it down to the cubs. The two jumped repeatedly for it, toppling each other in their attempts. The male made a new attempt and landed on his sister's head. She growled and rolled him to the dirt.

Merick looked up to get a read on the parents. Her heart nearly quit beating. The tigress's blood-red orbs were locked on her.

The twig fell from her hand when the cat stood, lean muscles stretching as she grew in height. A thrill of panic raced over Merick as realization dawned. The mother was much larger from this angle. The tigress stalked to her cubs.

Her nerve gone, Merick quickly scooted backward toward the safety of the wall. *Just a few more feet...*

Her foot broke off a limb and her leg swung free.

Frantically, she scrambled to right her balance. In doing so, she accidentally pushed down too hard on the support branch. A loud snap was the last thing she heard before her body connected with the hard ground and the air left her lungs.

Merick thought someone yelled, but she could see nothing but the vermilion-colored sky above. And then...*something black.*

She blinked. Black and orange swirls flicked in her right peripheral, like a cracking whip. A second later, they snapped to the left of her vision. Slowly, the shock began to wane and her brain began to focus. The orange and black swished above her again. *A tail!*

Merick rolled to all fours, gasping for breath. The mated pair of tigers circled her.

She heard it again. *A scream.* A child's terror, coming from the other side of the wall.

Both animals flattened their ears as the shouts continued. *Stop! You're scaring them.* Merick wanted to yell, but she couldn't. Noise would only intensify the situation, she just knew it.

Stay calm.

She tried to slow the hammering of her heart. It felt like it would burst from her chest. More shouting.

Merick glimpsed her father running down the hill toward the enclosure. A stranger raced beside him. They would clear the wall with one leap.

No! They would hurt the tigers.

Panic seized her. *They couldn't.* It was her fault. Her stupidity.

Shhh! She closed her eyes, shutting out the chaos. Something —both strange and familiar—rose up somewhere deep inside her. It took over, smothering her fear, snuffing it out. The pounding of her heartbeat slowed.

Merick latched onto that stillness. *Shhh...*she exhaled, slowly raising one hand.

Just see me.

Time hung suspended in the quiet of her newfound courage. The only noise a steadfast confidence and nurturing integrity, speaking without words. *See me.*

She felt it then. A damp heat pressing into her palm. *A nose.*

A sandpaper tongue replaced it. Merick's eyes opened. The female was staring at her. *But this time*...this time the tigress really saw her. A quiet understanding was reflected in those glowing orbs.

Slowly, the large cat turned and walked off beside her mate.

The magical moment was severed by an arrow whistling through the sky. Then another. Like the wave of a heavy arm through a spider's web, it broke the connection between Merick and the majestic animals.

Her screams were hollow in her own ears as both tigers collapsed. She fought, trying to reach them, only to be held back by firm hands. Next she was wrenched up.

A deafening silence rushed in from all directions. The sounds of fear, sadness...*hate*...

Chapter Nine

GERRA

NORTHDOM CASTLE

FIVE YEARS LATER

Thaddeus watched the hybrid peruse his study, hands clasped behind his back. "See anything you like?"

"I like them all."

"Then you'll have to visit the library," he said. "It rivals the one at the royal palace."

This was the second time he'd been in the Fallen's company. Surprisingly, the archangel turned vampire had not threatened his life since their first meeting. Quite the opposite actually. He had been cordial, almost pleasant.

Which was good. Stefen Von Emmerich was not one to cross. Born to the highest nobility in Anu, his strength had only increased when he'd been turned by the blood of a dragon.

"Dante wasn't a scholar?" His guest faced him.

"Only when it came to things that interested him," Thaddeus said. "Which was quite a lot, don't get me wrong. There was a reason he was king."

"Many a monster has been a good ruler." He turned back to the bookshelf.

Stefen was quite the oxymoron. Charming in a natural, easy way, but deadly—as only a warrior who had made himself inaccessible could be. So much strength of character had gone into building the male before him. A priceless work of art, forbidden to touch.

The first of his kind ever recorded. Probably because up until Ashdon LaGoryen, it couldn't be done. Something in the dragon's blood alone could perform the transformation. Thaddeus couldn't stop trying to piece together and dissect the physical and mental differences, where the angel once governed and the vampire now reigned.

It was tremendously easier to observe here, in his own home. He had permitted Stefen to visit them at Northdom castle this year. Partly due to the emissary giving him no choice five years ago, when he broke cover and joined Thaddeus in rescuing Merick from the tigers.

The feat had proved pointless. The child had taken care of the animals all on her own. There had been no need for the guards to kill the beasts. But they had. To this day the girl mourned them.

"It's going to drive you mad." Stefen pulled him from his thoughts. "Working this hard to figure me out."

"What is science if not a dutiful slave." Thaddeus grinned. "Are you ready to see her?"

"Yes."

He led the way, escorting the emissary down the labyrinth of halls. "She has changed a good bit in the last five years."

They reached the doors to the balcony, overlooking the training yard. "Still pure of heart." Thaddeus opened them. "Even if she wishes not to be."

"Why wouldn't she wish to be?" Little curiosity, just a blunt need for explanation, as they walked to the veranda's edge.

"She's different." Thaddeus stopped. "As you probably noted when you were here last. She has a rather ethereal essence about her. Not as intense as other angels. More like you." He continued, despite the look of surprise in the hybrid's sea-green eyes, "Most here are too unaware to really see it. To clearly identify it. But they sense something is *off*. The other children shun her. And the adults are either wary of her, or they're overly curious."

Stefen visibly tensed. "Overly curious?"

"She has an outstanding bodyguard. Most know better." He waved a hand toward the yard. Stefen's eyes tracked the movement. "However, I will need at least four guards in her teenage years I fear."

They watched in silence as Merick loaded her crossbow and took aim, launching the arrow neatly into the intended target. Thaddeus smiled. "I also take comfort in her training."

"Is that the only weapon she knows how to use?"

"She is proficient with all of them," he replied evenly. "Instructed in various hand-to-hand fighting techniques as well. She packs a hard punch for such a slip of a girl."

"Father!" A high-pitched screech pierced their serenity.

Thaddeus exhaled. "Unlike her sister."

He turned to see what Marjory wanted now. "Yes, dear?"

His biological child stomped onto the balcony carrying a new dress, eyes ablaze. "I told her to make it red!" She waved the blue gown about. "Does this look red?"

"By definition of the color, no. It is clearly blue." Thaddeus now wished he had spent more time selecting the uterus that carried this one. She was selfish, mean, and just plain horrible to be around. Her disposition did nothing to help her already plain features. "Marjory, please show my guest you know how to give a proper curtsy."

She looked hell-bent on refusing, until Stefen faced her.

Marjory stumbled into an awkward attempt at what could best be described as a half bow. "Pleased to meet you."

"You as well, Lady Marjory," Stefen replied, smooth and refined.

Thaddeus took the dress when she straightened, saving his guest the misery of continuing the conversation. "Tell the seamstress to make another in red. I will give this one to your sister."

She narrowed her eyes. "Merick got one last month."

"She now has two. You may go."

Her complexion morphed into an angry beet color, before she marched off in a huff. Thaddeus sighed. "You would not believe it but I have raised them exactly the same."

"Father?" A lyrical voice called their attention from the opposite direction.

They turned in unison to see Merick ascending the steps. Aasha, her white Bengal tiger cub, followed in her wake. Stefen cut his gaze to Thaddeus. "Her tiger?"

"She does have a gift with them. We all saw it," he said as Merick walked over. "Daughter, this is Stefen."

The polar opposite to Marjory's disastrous curtsy, Merick dropped into one with practiced ease. "It is a pleasure."

The emissary inclined his regal head. "Likewise."

Thaddeus held out the blue dress. "Your sister does not care for the color. Do you fancy it?"

The child's eyes lit up. "Really? It's beautiful."

"It is yours." He handed her the dress.

"Thank you." She quickly lifted it high, before the playful cub could pounce, which Aasha did. Then looked puzzled as to where the sparkly material had gone. Merick giggled. "May I go hang it up?"

Thaddeus nodded and she turned once more to Stefen. "It was a pleasure to make your acquaintance." Merick smiled again and dashed off, hoisting the dress above her head, the cub trailing after her.

When she was out of earshot, Stefen looked sideways at him. "You really have others convinced you sired them both?"

"Fooling others has never been the problem," Thaddeus replied. "It's convincing them of the truth right before their eyes that's the struggle."

Chapter Ten

GERRA

Five years later

Aasha slinked alongside Merick as they made their way to the base of the cliff. The dewy freshness of the morning lingered in the balmy air. "They say it can't be done, girl."

The tiger nudged her hand with its soft muzzle. Merick absentmindedly stroked the top of the giant cat's head. "Not by anyone that hasn't come of age. Not to the summit."

She tilted her chin, following the rockface, the conversation between Thaddeus and Teakin still sharp in her mind. *"She isn't as strong as Marjory."* Teakin had told her father when they thought no one was around to hear. *"And you know why."*

Her father had agreed, granting Teakin permission to train her alone. She wouldn't be allowed to attend finishing school in three months either. Something she'd been looking forward to since she couldn't remember when.

Merick hadn't asked her mentor, and best friend, why he had such little faith in her. She'd just gone to her room and cried.

Cried until she became mad at herself for crying. For being exactly what Teakin thought of her...*weak.*

Then determination hit. She wasn't giving a hundred percent to her training. Everyone her age had surpassed her physical strength in the past year. Even her damned sister.

Merick had always been on the smaller side compared to other females her age, but there hadn't been a time when she believed she couldn't take them. Now she wasn't so sure. It didn't make sense. She worked hard at everything she put her mind to. Why was her body wimping out now?

No elite ascended to their full potential until the age of eighteen. But everyone else was making great strides. Hearing she would have to wait a year before she, too, could start school was crushing.

To add insult to injury, Marjory's fangs had already started to develop. Merick checked the mirror daily but, nope, not even the hint of hers. What was wrong with her?

The thud of Aasha's large body flopping to the ground to roll in the dirt, drew Merick out of her demise. She smiled as the tigress completely covered herself in the dark clay. "You know Father won't allow you back inside like that." She knelt down and rubbed the Bengal's belly. "Okay, girl, it's now or never. Stay put."

She pulled chalk from her bag, covered her hands in it, kicked off her shoes, and dumped everything beside the large cat. Aasha looked at her curiously. "I can do this." Merick surveyed where to start. "I've always been a good climber," she reminded herself, wedging her fingers into the first hold. "Just one placement at a time."

She hoisted herself up the cliff, her body searching and finding a tempo with the movement. Her confidence grew with her speed, muscles lengthening and contracting. Her one hand loosing its grip before the other found purchase. Momentum was everything. Merick's fingers squeezed into a new crevice, her foot scraping over the rock's sharp surface until it found balance.

Chest heaving, she pushed her back into a fracture on the mountain's face. She filled her lungs greedily with the crisp air as she looked down to where she'd started. Aasha sat at the base looking up at her, the morning fog intertwining around her front legs.

Merick glanced up next. She had made excellent progress, but she had a long way still to go. The hard part was yet to come.

She twisted to find the next hold and a rock broke free under her foot. Loose dirt peppered the breeze when her fingers found their grip. Merick hoisted herself up again. She was close to passing the first crag.

Her left foot lost its placement. In that split second, she pushed off the stone face with all her strength. Her palms connected with the ledge. Her legs hung free as she fought to feel what she couldn't see. She tried to steady her breathing, muscles screaming. Her fingers alone were supporting her weight.

Gritting her teeth, she pulled herself up enough to get her elbow onto the rock. She pushed with all her might, but her arms gave out. She clawed at the ledge, fingers digging up loose rocks. Gravity pulled her backward and the mountain fell away.

Her hands came away with only air. She screamed. Just as something grabbed her wrist and yanked her upward.

Merick's body crumpled like a doll's on the rock's ledge, her elbows barely supporting the effort it took to keep her face off the ground. Her body shook as she tried to keep from hyperventilating.

After what seemed like forever, she dragged a steady stream of air into her stinging lungs, as her eyes followed the dirt to a pair of black leather boots. "What in the Four Realms were you thinking?" the masculine voice asked, full of censure.

Merick's gaze climbed the long legs, past the worn-in jeans

and the T-shirt. Higher, to the broad shoulders and rigid clavicles. Up the tan neck and over the tightly clenched angular jaw. Her visual trek continued until her gaze locked with the most beautiful pair of sea-green eyes.

"You could have been killed." He stared down at her, his tousled chestnut-colored hair whipping around his face.

Killed? His strange accusation pulled her from the appraisal of his person. *Killed?*

It would take more than a fall from a cliff to kill an elite, even one as young as she. Perhaps land her in a coma for the next three years, until she came of age, but not death. Sure, she didn't want to be paralyzed for something so reckless, but come on...*death?*

Merick pushed up onto her knees and looked down. Aasha was pawing the cliff side worriedly. "I'm okay. Stay," she yelled over the edge, bluffing the cat's climbing ability. *Just in case.* It never hurt to let others think you had more weapons than they could count.

"Are you? *Okay?*" the stranger asked. "I think we may need to get your head checked."

Merick looked up, blowing a rogue curl out of her eyes. "Don't you think you're being a touch dramatic?"

His nostrils flared. "Do you actually think, had I not come along, you wouldn't be splattered on the rocks?"

He really did think she'd been in grave danger. Also, suddenly noteworthy—they were having this conversation on a cliff ledge. He hadn't just strolled over here.

Only the strongest elite had the ability to fly, and they were recruited as soldiers to the Crown as soon as they came of age. Surely, she would have seen him during a palace visit.

Merick looked around for another possible way he could have made it up here. Nothing but stone and sky. "Who are you?"

He folded his arms. "You were more obedient five years ago."

Five years ago?

Merick stood slowly. *Those eyes.* She *had* seen them before. The visitor her father introduced her to when she was ten. "Stefen?"

"Yes."

"How did you come to be on this cliff, Stefen? Are you a palace solider?"

"Gods, no!" He scoffed. "I manifested here. When I realized I was about to bear witness to your suicide."

"How do you know my father? Is he your master?" A single brow raise let her know what he thought of that second question. "You're not from here."

"Are you always this nosy?" He looked pointedly at her. "It's not polite to pry."

"I think we have different definitions of the word pry. I'm only trying to discern my immediate danger being on the edge of a cliff with a strange male," Merick said. "Prying would be asking which one of your hands you preferred. In case you try something dubious and my tiger needs to bite it off."

She folded her arms and really looked at him now. He was dangerously resplendent. Tall, well-muscled, with golden skin and a rakish smirk. *And something else...* Something otherworldly about him—elemental—like he'd been forged by the sea.

How had she not noticed this the last time they'd met?

Because you were ten, idiot.

The answer to her own question brought her back to the present. This is what spending too much time with a cat had gotten her. Entire inner dialogues with herself over much too attractive males. She averted her gaze, wiping the dirt off her pants.

"To elaborate on my previous statement, I was headed to your father's when I spotted your tiger. Then I saw you about to plummet to your death." He looked over the cliff's edge. "Don't you have a babysitter?"

Merick narrowed her eyes. "I'm fifteen. I don't need anyone looking after me."

"Yeah, I can tell." He held out his hand. "Let's get you back onto level ground."

She hesitated. "How do I know you won't—"

"I typically don't rescue females just to do them harm," he said. "Take my hand, Merick."

"It's inexcusable," Stefen huffed, pacing the study. "I understand you want her to blend in, but she's not an elite. She's half-angel. We are born immortal, same as you. But there's no telling what her hybrid birth may have altered." He stopped, folded his arms across his muscled chest, and looked at Thaddeus. "Have you run any blood work in that fancy lab of yours?"

"About that." Thaddeus took a draw off a cheroot cigar, rocking back in his chair. "I was ill-informed when your brother asked me if her father was an elite. He wasn't." He expelled the cherry smoke, watching as it curled through the air, creating a mystic white barrier between his desk and his guest. "He was a Fire-dancer, turned vampire."

The vapors parted liked they'd been sliced through with a sword as Stefen's tight face came into focus, his arms braced so hard on the edges of the desk that the wood groaned. "A Fire-dancer?"

"I only recently learned the truth. A recruit in the army. That's all I know." He made to lift the cigar again, but it was swept from his hand and snapped in two.

"All you know..." Stefen started around the desk. "How recently did you learn this? Did you know before she left the house this morning to climb a mountain?" He stopped short of physically swiveling Thaddeus's chair to face him and leaned in, so they were at eye level. "She isn't developing at her peers' pace. Because she is part human!"

"Watch it. You're in my realm," he warned, holding Stefen's stare. "As for Merick's risky behavior, I will talk to her about it."

"Like telling a teenager what to do actually works." He reeled back and marched to the window. "Where the fuck are these bodyguards?"

"It remains singular."

"Why?" he blurted, blinking.

"The male in question is more than capable. He has the strength of three. Besides, I have kept Merick isolated these past five years. There hasn't been a need for more."

"Where was he today? When she was trying to get herself killed," Stefen demanded.

Thaddeus glanced toward the door before speaking. This wasn't the conversation he'd expected to have with the emissary. He hadn't counted on having to come clean about Merick's sire. He certainly hadn't taken into account how overprotective the former angel had become.

Though he should have known after the tiger incident ten years ago. Genuine fear had launched the hybrid down the hill alongside him that day. It hadn't been due to chivalry. There was some connection between the two Fallen. Thaddeus would need to be more mindful of this *kindred* bond over the next three years.

"Detained on official palace business." He chose his words carefully. "I should have insisted she stay inside today."

Stefen, unfortunately, latched on to Thaddeus's apprehension. "Expecting someone?"

Thaddeus stood, walked to the door and closed it. "There are some subjects I would rather not be overheard."

Stefen eyed him as he walked back to his desk. "What sort of business does a resident guard have at the royal palace?"

"Let's just say, the king has particular taste. Merick's guard is favored. On occasions, he is called there..." Thaddeus spread his fingers. "...to entertain."

"Say no more." Stefen's lips curled with disgust and he waved a hand sharply through the air, as if shooing off the conversation's direction.

"I would like you to stay and attend the ball tomorrow. A coming of age party for the girls." Thaddeus changed the subject. "A tradition when a young elite turns fifteen."

"A birthday party?"

"More than that. It gives them a chance to present themselves to their peers and the court," Thaddeus explained. "It's a night most young debutantes look forward to. Many marriage arrangements are made the week following a girl's debut."

"Marriage arrangements?" The words were short, clipped.

"Yes, if two families find a match advantageous."

"Merick is not doing this," Stefen said firmly.

"Don't fret. Sadly, Merick is not one of the highly sought after females."

Stefen looked at him like he had lost his mind. "Does your kind not have eyes?"

"She is lovely, but she is considered different. And *different* isn't a desirable trait in Gerra."

"I find that hard to believe. These are teenagers we're talking about." Stefen shook his head. "But that doesn't matter. You promised us she could choose on her eighteenth birthday. To either stay here or come to Earth," he reminded, mouth tightening in disapproval. "You need to have a good excuse lined up if some simpleton does find her *differentness* appealing."

"Even if a male should want to take her as a mate, he couldn't until she turns eighteen," Thaddeus rationalized. "That's when the female of our kind become fertile."

"Why not wait and have the debuts then?"

"This gives any interested parties time to get to know each other and their possible in-laws."

"Like an old school courtship? Where they're under supervised visits, constantly trying to sneak off, away from watchful eyes to steal a kiss?"

"Not quite so guarded. They are permitted to have sexual relations during that courtship."

Stefen coughed. "What!"

"They can't procreate yet. And everyone is tested to keep healthy."

The other male just stared blankly at him, seemingly working through a mix of emotions and retorts. Thaddeus braced himself for which one would finally surface.

"This is not an option," the Fallen said. "She is half archangel, Thaddeus. They mate for life for a reason. If they fall for someone, they can never love anyone else the same way." He continued, "if she has the heart of her mother's kind; you would be dooming her to a life of unhappiness should she fall in love with someone and they didn't return the feelings."

"And yet, her mother was in an arranged marriage to your brother," Thaddeus pointed out. "Was that not the same sort of fate?"

"That was different. Alaric is a king. Anessa would have been a queen."

Thaddeus tilted his head to one side and lifted a brow.

"I really don't like you," Stefen simmered.

He chuckled. "You have a good soul, Stefen."

"Is that meant as a compliment, or an insult?"

"Usually, a weakness in this realm. However, your energy was strong enough to take on the dragon," Thaddeus said. "I'm not a dreamer, but I know this much: once in a while someone comes along that challenges the norm. A soul is born believing. Not what they are taught to believe, but instead, what they feel—a truth deep inside. An unshackled calling. These are the seekers, the rebels, and the crusaders. The ones whose names will live on well past their death." He stood. "Like Dante. Approve of him or not, he was one of these seekers. He questioned the path laid before him."

"He was a sadist."

"I never said all who dared to dream were pure. He carved a path. Made a name." Thaddeus walked to the door. "Good or bad, Dante created an empire. An empire that will never be forgotten. Not in this immortal lifetime, or the next. And he managed it by challenging what the universe set before him." He smiled, opening the door. "Stay for tomorrow, Stefen."

His guest grumbled a noncommittal response and brushed past him, heading down the hall toward the rooms he'd been assigned upon arrival. "Keep questioning life," Thaddeus added. "Keep seeking."

Chapter Eleven

THE OLD PALACE

"You heard me," Zander said, from the dusty throne in the long abandoned audience hall.

Now crumbling, the ruins were just outside the palace walls, higher up the mountain, looming like an ever-watchful sovereign. At night, the bats danced to a voiceless orchestra around its jutting peaks. By day, the rats darted in and out of crooked towers, blending with the forgotten shadows.

Over the centuries another royal residence had taken its place, but for reasons unknown, Dante never had the original throne room demolished.

Patched unevenly with black ivy crawling over the masonry, wild and uncanny toward the roof's gaping hole. Below, the sun's red glow streamed in. It bathed the ancient stone, overtaken with purple moss and burgundy ferns, in light.

The perfect stage.

The girl at the king's feet had stopped struggling when the

guard shoved her down. She must have gone into a state of shock when the first words left Zander's mouth.

"I said," he repeated them, "fuck her."

"She isn't really my type." Teakin tried to dismiss the order, even as ice pumped like weighted rocks through his veins.

The king's eyes narrowed with hope. "Are you disobeying me?"

He weighed his response. Zander's tone was off, all toying humor gone. He was dead serious. Nothing Teakin could offer would dissuade him.

He tried anyway. "I'm not fully healed." It wasn't a falsehood. He'd been heavily drugged and beaten just last night. "I couldn't take her. Even if I wanted to."

A snicker from one of the guards.

Zander leaned forward. "I said. Fuck. Her!"

The girl shook uncontrollably now. Teakin prayed she would faint. At least if she was unconscious, she would miss some of what was to happen next. "What did she do to upset you?" He stalled.

"Her father pissed me off," Zander said simply, before fixating his eyes on the young beauty cowering at his feet. "You'll like her, she's a virgin."

The girl openly cried now. Bowing her head, she stretched out on the floor and her hands slid to Zander's boots, forehead pressing to the cold stone. *Don't beg.*

"Can I take her to a private room?" Teakin glanced around the room at the four guards lining the perimeter.

Zander stood quickly, yanking up the girl by her hair. Without a word, he dragged her to a table and ripped open her dress. The garment fell to the floor as the girl tried in vain to cover her exposed breasts.

The king walked back to the throne, reclaimed it, and pulled out a folded letter. "This is the invitation to a coming-of-age ball at my grandfather's tonight. There is said to be a girl who is quite the beauty, with hair the color of snow. A rare jewel for sure." He looked up slowly. "As the king, I may have to sample her virtue. Before anyone else can taste such fine honey."

A lump lodged in Teakin's throat, even as he began walking over to the young elite. He had never taken a female against her will. *Except...*

"Just like last time." Zander read his mind.

"You had me drugged last time." Teakin ground his teeth, unable to harness the loathing in his voice. "You created that monster. I cannot recreate it."

The king leaned back, smiling broadly—teeth as white as crow-picked bones. "Which is why I shall enjoy this show even more." He flipped the invitation between his fingers. "If not...I will have to sate my appetite on a certain young debutante later tonight."

Teakin swallowed and extended his arm, brushing his knuckles over the girl's shoulder. She flinched, as if he'd branded her. He turned slightly—appraising his intended victim—angling away from the throne. "Don't beg," he whispered, before spinning her around and bending her over the table.

She sobbed as Teakin nudged her legs apart with his boot. He reached down, his touch a contradiction to his previous actions, fingertips spreading softly over her thigh. He trailed them upward.

"No!" Zander roared, the word barking over the moss covered stones. "This is rape. It's not supposed to be gentle."

The girl started to squirm, fighting to no avail. *Gods forgive me.*

Teakin unzipped his pants and took hold of himself. Stroking from root to tip, he closed his eyes and tried to shut out her tiny pleading mews. He didn't want this, far from it. But he couldn't refuse Zander his perversions. Not without dooming his daughter to the same situation.

69

*But...*he could take away her mind.

He'd been perfecting the skill on the guards and household staff at Northdom Castle, in hopes of being able to use it on himself eventually. All it took was a touch, a passing brush or a gentle nudge, to make the connection. Then he would slip into their subconscious, take over their thoughts and plant his own; what he wanted them to see, to remember, to feel.

Teakin did that now, pressing his palm into the female's spine to stop her writhing, as he forced her thighs wider. Through that shared touch—his hand against her flesh—he entered her mind.

He became a smile from a guard she fancied. Became the sky view she loved at dawn. Became the feather-soft touch of a soothing and familiar hand.

Dividing his thoughts from the ones he was carefully placing, Teakin searched out his own memories. He pictured his first lover, how willing and eager she had been. A slave and warrior-in-training, same as him. She snuck into his bunk each night. With her ample breasts pushing against his chest and her long legs wrapped around him, he had buried himself inside her.

Clinging tightly to the visual, his body responded. He mentally shut out the world around him and positioned himself. When the girl's body didn't protest, Teakin knew she was firmly seated in the spell his mind cast.

Without delay he pushed into her tight heat, his mind one thrust ahead of his body—smothering any pain, transporting her now to a field of tall grass. She was picking berries. The sun was a touch too warm, but she would find shade soon. *Soon.* She would find relief soon.

"Harder!"

He heard Zander in the distance and his body worked to comply, pulling out and slamming back into her slickness. Faster and deeper he thrust, until the room spun and his cock felt like it was going to burst.

"Fill her up," his audience demanded.

He did. His hips bucked upward, pushing the table across the earthen floor, as he emptied himself.

Slow clapping brought his focus back to the present. Out of his hazy peripheral, Teakin saw one of the guards jacking off to his right. The sound of the male's orgasm was like a knife across porcelain. He withdrew from the silent female. The only hint of life left in her was the shallow rise and fall of her ribcage.

"Perfection," Zander praised.

"Are we done here?" He tucked himself back into his pants.

"For today."

Teakin turned from his destruction and walked out. The girl would heal quickly from the physical abuse. He just hoped his mental masking would hold. That she would recall the events of the day as he had painted them for her.

He took the worn, grassy steps at a jog, his mind on another innocent female. He had to find a way to get Merick out of Gerra. The dragon was growing harder and harder to keep caged. He'd gotten away with his hidden ability today. But one slip-up and it could cost her life. Or worse...

He might doom her to his.

Chapter Twelve

T he long hall to the grand ballroom seemed different tonight. The same pictures hung in the same places on the wall. The furniture they passed still sat in the correct spots. Familiar nooks and crannies remained where they always had been.

Music had never drifted from the space they were about to enter. The room they were approaching had never hosted others. Bodies had never swayed in time, the soft sound of their shoes brushing the polished marble.

Now there was chatter where once was none. Hundreds of peers of the realm had collected in her home. All strangers Merick should know. But she didn't.

Somewhere deep inside a little voice breathed, *you are the stranger...you are what is different.*

Merick worried her bottom lip. Just a few more rooms to pass by, sixty-five feet at best. Then all of the royal court would be looking at them, judging them. *Judging her.* Deciding if she was worthy.

She started to wipe her sweaty palms on her dress, but stopped just shy of gripping the blue silk.

"This is it!" Marjory practically bounced on the other side of their father. "My time to shine."

Merick wasn't sure how two people could have such vastly different feelings on the event about to take place. As they approached their father's party coordinator, Merick was sure she was going to pass out. "Your Grace will be announced first, followed by Marjory, and then Merick," the male stated.

"Why does she get to go last?" Marjory protested. "The eldest should get to pick the order. That's me. I was born first."

"It is tradition to announce the house in order of birth rank," the coordinator explained with the patience of a saint. "You are older than your sister, which is why you follow your father."

Marjory stomped her foot loud enough to make an echo in the space. Merick winced, as the noise from the ballroom below dropped a few levels in volume. "I want to go last!" Her sister's voice rose. "The oldest is best. I should be the grand finale."

The poor employee looked to their father. "It's okay," Merick piped up. "I don't mind."

"Then it's settled," Thaddeus said, dismissing the absurd topic.

The servant nodded, turned, and walked to the edge of the banister, overlooking the ballroom. "Attention, attention," he called out. A few seconds passed as the commotion below died down to barely a whisper. "It is my great honor to announce His Grace, Lord Thaddeus Freyberg."

Her father walked fearlessly into the brightly lit ballroom. He looked dignified standing there, his back to them—like a king greeting his subjects. Before Merick could contemplate further, he descended the steps to join the crowd.

The voice of his man of affairs boomed over the din once more. "I present to you, Miss Merick Freyberg."

She froze.

"Go on!" Marjory shoved her. "And don't trip. I don't want any obstacles."

Merick picked up the hem of her dress, righted her balance, and took a deep breath. The shadows from the hall began to peel away, the warmth from the room's light forcing them back. Unsure where to look, she set her gaze on the crystals draping the chandeliers straight ahead. She'd never seen them lit. Until last week the furniture had been covered in sheets, abandoned and off limits.

Her gaze slowly lowered, scanning the paintings hung on the rich burgundy walls. Merick's hands landed on the banister. The smooth stone pulled her focus further down. Then further... Her breath caught when her sights landed on the assembly below.

Every eye in the ballroom was trained on her.

Not a sound could be heard, not even a murmur. Merick forced her legs to move to the edge of the stairs, praying she wouldn't live out her sister's fantasies, toppling head over heels down them.

She took the first step and a lone clap sounded out.

Seconds later, another. Then another. And another.

Her father's man of affairs announced her sister next. But the clapping didn't pause. Instead, more joined in, all eyes on Merick as she continued down the stairs.

She must be so hideously different they couldn't look away. *Unless it was a joke.* Any moment, the smiles would turn to jeers. She was sure of it.

Her foot landed on the last step. If she could just make it through the crowd, she might be able to disappear out the doors on the other side. She could practically feel the heat from Marjory's stare on her back. She didn't dare look back over her shoulder, for fear of bursting into flame.

Merick inhaled deeply and stepped onto the grand ballroom

floor. The crowd reluctantly parted for her, as she started to make her way...*to where?* She didn't see her father. He'd been swallowed up by a sea of elite.

Her heart pumped double time as she glanced around. Everywhere she looked, they stared at her. She tried to look past them, to scout out an exit, but they were all taller than her.

Teakin and her father had been right. She wasn't ready.

The males closed in, pressing in on the tight opening they had allowed her to move through—coyotes around a stray dog. The heat from their bodies started to suffocate her. She gnawed at her lip, throat bobbing.

Father? The faces blurred as she turned in a circle trying to locate him. Her path back to the staircase had sealed shut.

Merick turned again, blindly pushing forward, panic seizing her, when something solid wrapped around her waist, twisting her and pulling her in.

She frantically looked up.

Those brilliant sea-green eyes from atop the mountain the other day stared down at her. "It's okay." He held her securely, cocooning her in his larger frame, blocking out the ballroom. So that all she had to focus on was him. "I have you, Merick."

Her different-colored eyes grew round, but she placed her hand in his. "Let's get you some air," Stefen said, speaking loud enough for those within earshot to hear as he hooked her arm over the crook of his.

He led Merick toward the veranda. The same crowd that had closed in on the young beauty seconds earlier, caging her in, parted like the Red Sea for him. *Assholes.*

The open quiet of the balcony greeted them, chasing away the uncomfortable pressure of the ballroom. The sensation hit him square in the chest...as if it were his own.

It wasn't.

Stefen looked down as she sighed, visibly relieved.

He felt it!

He was feeling her direct emotions. For the first time since the day he was turned, Stefen was experiencing an empathetic connection to another. He turned abruptly to face her. "Can you sense what I'm thinking right now?"

She blinked. "You're..."

Merick closed her eyes, but they shifted with concentration beneath her lids, the skin so delicate the blue of her veins resembled tiny streams. Stefen watched in amazement as the weighted anxiety of the crowded room lessened and her shoulders relaxed.

"Excited! Like I was the day father surprised me with Aasha," she exclaimed, looking up, her eyes alight. "It's as if I'm feeling it with you."

"Because you are." Stefen walked her further away from any prying ears in the ballroom.

"How can that be?" She knitted her brows, tilting her head. "It's gone now. But it was like I was...in your head."

"You were. You no longer feel it because I shut it down," he said. "But what you just experienced was a gift; the ability to read others, to connect to them. Often times when they are needing it most."

"Were you needing me to connect to you?"

"Yes."

Immensely. She'd just unlocked something sacred in him. His angel's ability to feel the world through invisible eyes. A special blessing few were given. He'd resigned himself to never experiencing it again. Turns out, he only needed another with the same unique talent to restore it.

"Why?" She stared at him.

"I'm going to need you to listen to me very carefully and to not get frightened." Stefen took her hands, turning her to face him. "You're not like the others here. You feel that, right?"

He needed to stop. He was breaking his agreement with Thaddeus. But damn it, she did not belong in this realm. Stefen could not sit back and continue to watch this stupid experiment play out. She needed to understand she was special. She had to stop trying to fit into this false world. And the monsters of Gerra needed to stop fantasizing about her in their beds!

He'd seen their reactions. Thaddeus was either a fool, or blatantly lying to him, when he said she was not well received. Every male in that ballroom wanted to claim her.

"I know." Merick slipped her hands free, shaking her head, the candlelight dancing over her soft curls. "You saw the way they stared at me. They know it, too. They're probably all laughing at what a disgrace I am."

Stefen couldn't believe what he was hearing. How could she not sense what he had in that ballroom? Had Thaddeus brainwashed her? Did the brave girl on the cliff really think she was a social pariah? He tipped up her chin with his knuckles.

Her eyes glistened with threatening tears. *By the gods...* She was conditioned to see herself in this light. Because she was different, they'd taught her she was flawed. Anger washed over him as he lowered his hand.

She aggressively swiped at her cheek. "You need not feel bad for me."

"Don't say that. And don't resign yourself to this bullshit!" *Agreement be damned.* "Merick, you may not believe me now, but I need you to understand." He rushed. "You are not from this realm."

A throat cleared behind them and he turned quickly.

Their host stood beside a distinguished looking male. The

younger elite wore a coat of arms on his sleeve, marking him a member of the royal house. "You're right, Stefen," Thaddeus interrupted gracefully. "She looks like something from a fairytale tonight." His smile was tight. "Not of this realm at all."

Merick dropped into a deep curtsy beside him. Stefen followed her lead and reluctantly bowed to the newcomer. "It is a pleasure to reintroduce you, my dear," Lord Freyberg said. "To our crown prince."

"It's been far too long since we've seen you at court." The prince's gaze perused Merick. "Now, I believe it was an effort on your father's part to keep you a secret."

"No secret." Thaddeus's tone was lighthearted, even though his steel-filled eyes cut to Stefen. "Just biding my time. Waiting for the right attention to come her way."

Stefen would kill him. The bastard knew *exactly* how well received she would be tonight. No doubt he'd used her like a lure, hoping to elevate his own position at court.

"With a jewel like this," the younger male said with a smile. "I can understand why." He extended his hand to Merick. "Might I have the honor of the first dance?"

Her eyes quickly darted to her father. Thaddeus inclined his head.

"I would be delighted." She offered her hand, but Stefen could sense her doubt.

He could read every one of her emotions with absolute clarity. She was apprehensive, curious, flattered, but hesitant. Most of all... *She was scared.*

Why shouldn't she be? Stefen had basically just told her she wasn't an elite. Now she had to play the part of one with that nugget of truth.

He was an idiot.

An idiot that needed to teach her how to mask those emotions. In case she encountered another with their unique talent who might expose her. This was exactly what he had feared would happen.

Stefen waited until the prince led her back inside. "You lied to me about how others perceived her." He spun on Thaddeus. "Was it always your intent to use her to improve your standing at court? Or did this just recently occur to your twisted mind?"

"Considering how close I am to having you arrested, I would watch that holier-than-thou tone," Thaddeus said quietly, but not weakly. "We had a deal. Not until she is eighteen will she know of her real birth."

"Oh, I assure you, it's not simply a tone." Stefen took a step forward. "Listen, and listen well, Thaddeus. She does not belong here. As far as I'm concerned, you have already broken our deal. It is clear she's suffered mental abuse under your care. She thinks there is something wrong with her. That she is not worthy of this world," he hissed. "When we both know Gerra is not worthy of her!"

Lord Freyberg met his challenge and stepped up. "I shielded her the best I could. All youth are cruel. Something you may recall from your own upbringing," he ground out. "Tell me, Stefen, how many lovers did you take before the age of fifteen? How many lords and ladies offered themselves to you, the spare?" Thaddeus huffed out a vicious laugh. "Not worthy of the crown, but great for a tumble in the hay."

"Never once did I not know my place. You have led that innocent to slaughter. Allowing her to think she's one of you. Basing her worth on *your* standards. All for some sick experiment."

"I may have taken her on as one, yes," Thaddeus lowered his voice to barely a whisper. "But I do care for her. More than my own child."

"And yet, you're willingly handing her off to one of the fucking Diabolis."

"I had no idea the prince would take a liking to her. Knowing his mother, she has bigger plans for him."

"Great! Then he will just use Merick, and cast her aside." Stefen's tendons stretched under his skin, aching to hit something. "I will not allow it."

"She's not yours to command." The doors to the balcony opened, and a guard stepped out onto the veranda. "Now leave. And do not return here until her eighteenth name day." Thaddeus leaned in. "Or I will bring a war on your maker's lands like none you can imagine."

Without another word, he marched back inside, leaving only the guard.

"I can see myself out." Stefen turned and took the garden steps at a brisk jog, throwing as much energy into his pace as the effort it cost him not to storm back into that ballroom and start a war.

Could he really leave with this knowledge and wait? *For three more years.* Knowing the girl was now being courted, used as a power play by Thaddeus. Possibly for Zander's own son.

He couldn't.

Thaddeus was right though. The bastard had nailed his fears on the head by bringing up his past. The only difference in Lord Freyberg's version of the truth was the implication Stefen had sought out his lovers. It was the other way around. He'd been the coveted prize. The brother to the king. The highest one could go without actually being with Alaric himself.

Stefen took a right out of the manicured gardens and down the twisting mountain path. Their attention had made him feel seen when he was younger. Before he realized they weren't really seeing him. They were using him. In the sickest of ways. He had been a toy. A tool manipulated for personal gain. Preyed upon and exploited by more cunning partners.

He would be damned if Merick lived out a frighteningly

similar experience. Stefen would do anything to keep her from feeling what he had. He just needed a plan.

He continued down the steepest section of the mountain, his feet sliding more than stepping, kicking loose tiny avalanches of dirt and pebble. To this day, his brother didn't know what he'd endured. Alaric would have stopped it.

That was the thing about adolescence, Stefen was reminded, as he leapt off the mountain side and landed with ease on the lush forest floor. Without honesty and guidance, nine times out of ten, the young would make the wrong choices. He strode quickly under the dense canopy of trees, their branches intertwining like cobwebs overhead.

He couldn't let Merick make the same mistakes. He owed it to her mother. Stefen neared the clearing, so consumed in thought he almost didn't register the presence in time.

Almost...

He stilled at the forest edge, inhaling—dragging the intruder's scent across his senses.

The guard from the balcony.

Thaddeus didn't plan on seeing him again in three years. He wasn't planning on him leaving Gerra at all.

The stranger whirled with fluid grace. "Who are you?" Teakin asked, stepping into a patch of light.

The male didn't so much as flinch. Instead, he studied Teakin with the same level of scrutiny, the moonlight gilding his face through the branches. "Who wants to know?"

"The bodyguard of the female you were talking to on the balcony." He took another step forward. "Who are you?"

"Ah, the bodyguard that's never around when his charge is in danger," the insolent stranger replied. Teakin bristled. "Good work you're doing."

"What on earth are you are referring to? I would lay down my life for her."

The immortal canted his head. "Interesting choice of comparisons. Earth." He casually crossed his arms. "I've never heard an elite use such mortal terminology."

"I'm not here to talk about me." Teakin openly took his full measure. *A pretty boy.* The sort the girls would swoon for in his homeland. Judging by the vampires carriage, he knew his physical worth. He was cocky, but in a carefully played fashion, with a gleam in his eyes that marked his intelligence. Something else was there though...*something other.* "You're not from Gerra."

"That makes two of us," the stranger said flippantly. "Now, if you'll excuse me." He started for the clearing. "I have somewhere else to be."

"I heard what you said to her." Teakin stopped him. "About her not being from here."

The immortal turned back slowly. "It was a pickup line." He shrugged. "Just trying to get laid."

Teakin ground his teeth. He was trying to dismiss him with trivial lies. Something had transpired between this one and his daughter. He wasn't letting him leave until he knew what. "I can get the truth from you, one way or another."

The smile the male gave him was nothing short of vulpine. "Are you threatening me?"

"Absolutely," he said baldly. "Tell me why you're here tonight. And what your intentions are with the young lady."

"Why would I waste my time on a guard as inept as yourself?"

Teakin slipped his baldric over his head, then dropped it and the sword to the ground. He was tired of this idle chatter. He wanted answers. His fists would get them.

A jerk of the chin from the stranger. "Go ahead—try me."

He lowered his shoulder and tackled the newcomer.

Their bodies collided, hitting the ground like boulders as they fought for dominance, rolling until Teakin's fist smashed into pretty boy's face. The vampire got in a solid hit. Teakin drew back and punched him square in the nose. Blood sprayed across his knuckles as the stranger pushed him off.

They both hastened to their feet.

He was stronger than expected, but Teakin was sure he could take him. "Who. Are. You?" he demanded as they circled each other.

"Who the fuck are you? That you would fight me over some silly girl?"

"She is not some silly girl!" He charged him again, but this time the other male spun, coming up with a well-placed right hook.

The cracking of bone reverberated through the night as Teakin delivered an upper cut to the jaw. They both reeled backward, chest heaving, the smell of each other's blood and sweat filling the air.

A familiar scent...

It hit him like a physical touch, unlocking a sheath of memories—joyous laughter and devastating loss. Paralyzed by the rush of sensations, the stranger took advantage of Teakin's pause and charged. They went down hard again.

Teakin managed to shove him off. "Why do you smell like him!" he growled, as the male righted himself quickly. "Why do you smell like my brother?"

The other immortal stopped mid-advance. "What?"

"He made you..."

Teakin staggered back in astonishment. *Could it be?* Had they lied about his death?

It wasn't possible. This male was too strong to have been made recently. Could his brother have turned him before the battle?

Before the battle of Gerra that ended Ash's life. His mind scrambled to find answers.

The stranger's aura. The *otherness* he'd sensed. The fight had brought them to the surface. Whereas before, the male had masked them masterfully.

Another beat of silence—in its wake, the anger shifted. "He turned you later." Teakin breathed. "But you were never a mortal." His tone turned thin, brittle. "Is he... Is Ash..."

The hybrid stared, like he was looking at a ghost. "Are you Teakin LaGoryen?"

"I am." His next words drifted into the arid night like a prayer, his heart twisting with hope. "Is he alive?"

A preternatural stillness accompanied the male's answering nod. "Very much so."

Teakin's throat closed up as an onslaught of emotions coursed through him. "They told me he was dead."

"He's spent the last hundred years thinking you were."

A harsh chuckle broke free of Teakin's lungs. "I practically was." He spit blood from his mouth. "Did he send you for her? For Merick."

The hybrid didn't speak. Instead, he seemed to be deciding how best to answer. Or, if he even would. "He did not. She is my concern."

His continued vagueness made Teakin's nails curl back into his palms. "What concern is she of yours?"

The vampire held up his hands. "I have no fight here, but I cannot discuss the young lady. For her own safety. My intentions are in her best interest." He looked him in the eyes. "Will you come back with me? To see your brother?"

Such twisted irony. The universe had just opened a door to freedom. And he still couldn't break these invisible chains.

Teakin looked down at his bruised knuckles. Even as he turned his hands the color was fading, his immortal body healing itself. Yet he was powerless to mend his situation. "I can't."

"Why not?" Shock colored the immortal's voice. "What could possibly keep you..." His words trailed off, only his breath visible in the crisp night air. "The girl?"

Teakin met his gaze. "She's my daughter."

S tefen ran a hand through his messy hair. *Holy shit!* This changed everything.

He refused to return to the Earth Realm without Merick. He couldn't leave Ash's niece in Gerra. Where she may, or may not, be promised to some elite come tomorrow.

Now...now that Teakin was alive...

Stefen looked at him, new complexities and horrors dawning. "Why haven't you taken her and left?"

"I can't." A muscle in his jaw feathered. "During the years Ash believed me dead, I was a prisoner, drugged to the point of insensibility. Only Thaddeus and Dante knew where I was jailed. They kept me there for over a century. When they finally brought me out of that tranquilized stupor, a different sort of experiment started. They pumped me full of chemicals, toxins designed to amplify my rage. To make me exactly what they wanted. A monster."

"When?" Stefen asked, already fearing the answer. "When did they start inducing the rage?"

"When they wanted something of me."

"The child?"

"Yes." Teakin glanced away. "I only remember those months in dismal stages, fragmented images constantly disrupted by the cracks and breaks of my consciousness." He looked back, his golden eyes glazed with pain. "All I want is to forget what little I do remember."

"They knew you wouldn't do their bidding. Would not sire the baby on your own impulses," Stefen hedged, his gut twisting with the knowledge. "That's why they stimulated whatever anger lurked inside you."

Teakin's chest expanded with a deep breath, his dark midnight-color hair, same as his brother's, falling into his eyes. "I had no idea what I was doing. I was out of control. Out of my mind—rabid," he said, his voice rough. "They used me to get the angel with child. Then they sedated me again until she was born."

He was telling the truth. Stefen read his pain like an open book. A manuscript that should have never been written. "What happened when Merick was born?"

"They showed her to me."

"Why?"

"Everything Thaddeus does is an experiment."

"What experiment could possibly be worth putting the child at risk?" He stopped. "Are you..." Stefen didn't need the answer. He could feel it now—something in his very blood making the connection. There, laying just under the surface of Teakin LaGoryen's skin, harnessed like a caged dog, was the same beast his maker harbored. "He wanted to provoke the dragon."

"Our biggest weakness," he confirmed. "Love."

Stefen filled in the rest. "They've been using that emotion to curb the dragon. Keeping you from trying to escape."

The same way Dante had enslaved Ash. By threatening Kielyn. He could only imagine the amount of willpower it took Teakin, knowing his child was the playing piece in this particular game.

Now, the secret was out. Stefen would tell Ash everything. A war, the likes of which Gerra had never seen, would rain down on this realm. "We have to get you two out of here."

"It's not that simple. Zander has a morbid attachment to me." He glanced toward the castle. "Even now, I'm sure he is searching for me." Teakin looked back, moonlight glinting off his sword as he picked up his baldric and slung it over his shoulder. "I can't be gone for more than a couple hours."

"Ash will be here the second I tell him you're alive and being held captive."

"That can't happen. Not yet," Teakin said. "What is the arrangement you have with Thaddeus regarding Merick?"

"He agreed to allow her the choice; to remain in Gerra, or leave on her eighteenth birthday."

"You do realize this realm was built on lies?"

"Yes, well, it's the only thing I've had to work with for the past fifteen years," Stefen intoned. "When Ash learns the truth, he'll come for you both."

"I know my brother and his irrational tendencies. If there is one thing I remember well, it's his lack of patience. But what worked with Dante will not with Thaddeus. He's more level headed. Always one step ahead." Teakin took a step forward, looking him directly in the eyes. "Merick's safety has to be secured first. We need to wait until her eighteenth birthday as you agreed on. In the meantime, I can meet you quarterly on the border with any new updates."

Stefen was not sure how he would convince Ash not to charge in, guns blazing. But he understood the older brother's reasoning. Thaddeus was methodical. An announced attack on Gerra would be too dangerous. "I'll try my best."

"I have to get back. Tell my brother that if he cares for me, he will respect my wishes." Teakin headed into the depths of the forest, but stilled before its rolling fog could completely consume him, and looked back over his shoulder. "Is he happy?"

"Immeasurably." Stefen grinned, images of Kielyn and the boys coming easily to mind. "He has twins. Two boys Merick's age. One as stubborn as his father. The other, more so."

"Two future dragons." Teakin smiled crookedly, and now the

sibling resemblance was uncanny. "Thank you for that." He turned and disappeared into the creeping mist, blending seamlessly with it.

Stefen lingered, his gaze tracking upward past the sprawling span of black forest, over the precipitous mountain, to the castle's flickering lights in the distance.

Maybe three...

Chapter Thirteen

GERRA

THREE YEARS LATER

*Panting, she darted to the right, a low growl releasing as her jaws
snapped shut. White cotton placed a delightful teaser on her tongue.
Adrenaline drummed through her veins. She cut left. The rabbit skidded
to the right, cornered.*
*It doubled back, heart beating wildly in its chest. Thud, thud, thud. She
moved in, fangs dripping with anticipation.*
Lunging, she met only with air. She spun, confused.
*The figure of a man stood at the forest's mouth, rabbit in hand. He
lowered it to the ground and turned away. "It's time to go back."*

Light washed over the imagery—severing the experience
—yanking her from the dream. Merick's eyes fluttered
open. Teakin stood at the threshold of her bedroom, the
fading day accentuating the hard angles of his golden face.

She smiled. "Did I oversleep?"

"Dreams can be dangerous if you stay within them too long. The dream may decide you belong there," her friend said by way of greeting, his brows knitting as he walked across the room. "Was it a wolf again?"

"Yes." She pushed into a sitting position. "This time it was even more realistic. Like I'm really in her skin." Teakin sat on the end of her bed. "Like I *do* belong there."

Merick had only experienced a similar connection once before. Three years ago, with Stefen. Other than Teakin, she hadn't told anyone what he'd said the night of her coming of age ball: *You are not from this realm.*

Those words had unlocked something. A strange gift—a challenge. Something she had the power to change, if only she dared try. So she had.

The day after the ball she made a vow to herself. To start implementing some of those changes. The first one being to get their attention. To be seen for who she really was. To earn their respect. Just as the queen had instructed years ago.

Merick had started her quest by choosing a confidant. Considering her loyal guard was her only friend, Teakin had been deemed that someone. He received daily updates on her pursuits, her failures, and her accomplishments. Nearly everything.

Nearly...

After the ball, her father allowed her to embark on the next phase of her education. Provided she could keep up. *She had.* Training into the wee hours each day to prepare.

She entered finishing school confident, ready for the next challenge. To her shock, the other students seemed ready for her as well. Gone were the snide remarks her peers used to make. If anything, she was sought out, included, even pursued.

Merick turned her face to the window to hide her creeping blush. Kalum, a handsome upperclassman with a quick wit, had been the first to introduce himself. She was sure his popularity played a role in her immediate acceptance, but over time she could confidently say she'd obtained much of the welcome on her own merits.

She was invited to their parties, allowed on their sporting teams, and expected at school functions. Then there were the times she and Kalum were alone—wrapped up in one another, legs and arms tangled, their sweaty bodies pressed together in some hidden alcove.

Merick enjoyed those moments. Almost as much as falling into her dreams. No obligation, no reasons or explanations. Neither of them wanting anything more than that moment.

She'd left those details out of her daily recounting with Teakin...who'd gone utterly quiet at the end of her bed. She turned from the window.

A look of worry was etched on his handsome face. "Is everything okay?" Merick's spine straightened.

"I need to tell you something." He reached out, taking her hands.

"Of course." She drew her legs up underneath her. "Please."

"You know I have always believed in you. I've supported and guided you, but ultimately let you make your own decisions." The graceful line of his mouth tightened. "Tonight I must insist you heed my advice."

"I value your advice above all others." A strange apprehension tiptoed up her spine as she searched his gaze. "What is it, Teakin?"

"The prince intends to ask for your hand in marriage."

The room tilted violently on its axis, her mind scrambling to hold on, to process the statement. The sensation was similar to being pulled from one of her shape-shifting dreams. But dramatically different in that she didn't belong in this one.

Merick blinked. She barely knew Prince Xavier. The only time they'd ever spoken was the night of the ball. Afterward, Marjory received multiple courtship offers. Merick not a single one. Teakin was mistaken. *He had to be.*

"You must have misunderstood," she managed around the lump in her throat. "No proposals came after the ball."

"I wish I were."

She stared at him. "How? Why?" Her disbelief morphed into a challenge. "He made no inquiries. I would have known." Merick shook her head when Teakin didn't immediately reply. She tried again, with logic this time. "Of all the males in the kingdom, why would the prince want me? When no one else did."

"Merick." Her friend angled his head as if he knew a secret she did not. His features softened, a fragile glint lighting those vividly colored eyes, "No inquiries came, because the prince made his intentions known the night of the ball. Only a fool would dare challenge him." The spark faded. "I was hopeful he would lose interest, or find another."

It didn't make sense. *Any of it.* Least of all, the notion Teakin would be unhappy with a match such as the one he now proposed. If he was correct, her father had to be elated. How had Thaddeus managed to keep such a secret? Did Marjory know? *No,* she would have tried to kill Merick in her sleep by now.

To be chosen by the Crown Prince...it was the highest honor anyone could hope for. Why then did she feel a sick dread creeping over her skin? Like a snake had just slithered across her bare foot. "I don't...I can't..."

Teakin didn't move, didn't utter a syllable. He just waited. As he had always done when he wanted her to draw her own conclusions. Ever forthcoming and communicative in his instructions, he never imparted his personal wisdom. *Wisdom could not be taught,* he maintained. Every individual must find it on their own. Through their choices. Through the path they sought to follow.

Merick shot to her feet, wrenching her hands free of his. She could use some damn imparted wisdom now! "Why are you telling me this and not Father?"

She whirled, pacing to her bedroom window before he could answer. The sun was now a hand's width above the horizon, long shadows already smearing the vibrant colors of day. How quickly the light conceded to the night. So fragile—like the silence of the room. One murmur and it too would be gone with the sunset.

"Why would you wish for the prince to change his mind?" A new sort of fear crawled across her mind in that silence, casting a net as far and wide as the invading dark. "Do you find me unworthy of such a position?"

The rush of wind at her back was so forceful it brushed the curls past her face. She forgot sometimes. Forgot how fast he truly was. What depth of power he possessed.

"Merick?" Callused hands landed gently on her shoulders, turning her in place. "It is he who is not worthy of you."

She opened her mouth, but Teakin went on. "You have been sheltered away, unknowing of their depravity. But the Diaboli are a cruel family. You mustn't marry into it." He stared down at her, his golden eyes as unmerciful as the lava churning beneath the mountain. "Promise me you will refuse him."

Merick pulled back. She had heard the stories of their creator, Dante, but she'd never heard anything to denote the other members of the royal family were the same. Her thoughts chased each other around inside her head, only one painting itself clear. What her lifelong friend suggested was treason.

"Teakin, take care," Merick whispered harshly, looking quickly to her open door, then back up at him. "What you speak of is—"

He interrupted her. "Just promise me."

"Do I even have a choice?"

"Not if they have a say in it," he said between gritted teeth. "Which is why we mustn't let it come to that."

Teakin stalked past her to her desk, snatching up a pen.

"When the time comes, I want you to follow these instructions." He scribbled something on her stationery. "Trust me?" He looked up, angst written clearly in his fire-flecked orbs.

Merick glanced to the door again worriedly, but finally she nodded. "With my life."

"Thank you." A faint smile tugged at his lips when she turned back.

She didn't have to feign the one she returned. She loved and trusted the male standing before her more than anyone. Despite the overwhelming urge to cry, to run to her father and beg him to not make her marry the prince, she would abide by Teakin's wishes.

"Your father wants to speak with you tonight. At ten-thirty, in his parlor. He has a meeting before then. If it is running late when you arrive, wait in the hall until it concludes." Teakin walked toward her. "Whatever he has to say, remember... Life delivers blows. Like a hammer striking steel against an anvil. But after the forging, a sword is formed."

He pressed a quick kiss to her forehead—startling her more than any lethal warrior's stealth—and headed for her door. "Never forget your strength, Merick." Teakin glanced over his shoulder. "Nothing can break you if you refuse to allow it."

Then he was gone, leaving only a familiar scent on the breeze. The smell of comfort, of tenderness. And something else Merick couldn't put into a category.

She walked to her desk and looked at the note.

If doubt should prompt flight, follow your dreams into the night.

Chapter Fourteen

" I nfatuation is one thing. But this..." Thaddeus scowled as
Zander tightly racked the pool balls. "This is lunacy. A
crush left unchecked for too long."

"What can I say?" Zander peered up, his vermilion eyes a
garish contrast to the green felt of the billiard table. "He is my son.
He wants what he wants."

The doors opened and Merick's personal guard entered.
Zander leered, blatantly raking him over. "She's packing," Teakin
confirmed, only acknowledging Thaddeus.

"Thank you," Thaddeus dismissed him.

The guard exited the room, as silently as he'd entered. "You
could at least *try* and conceal your perversion." He didn't bother
hiding his disgust. "What would your queen think?"

"Katarra is only interested in grandchildren now. Rotten,
mini-spawn running around the palace. Babies she can groom to
be as evil as herself. And trust me," Zander removed the triangle
and looked at him, "my interests are far more discreet than hers."

"Speaking of discreet," Thaddeus said, as the king walked

around the table. "What do you suppose the queen will do when she learns Merick is not an elite?"

"Have you not crafted a way for her to go, *undetected*?" Zander selected a breaking cue, weighing it in his hands. "You've had eighteen years."

Thaddeus stared blankly at him. "Such as devising the means to produce little elites from her hybrid womb?"

He waved a hand, unconcerned. "We can say she's barren when the time comes. Xavier can then take a mistress and set aside his infatuation."

"Set aside?" A muscle twitched in his jaw. "Like your father did to your mother?"

"A rather grim walk down memory lane, even for you." He made a face, chalking his pool stick. "Why do you care what he does with your clandestine daughter?"

"I don't." Thaddeus schooled his features as the king broke the balls. He needed to stay in control of this conversation. "I do, however, fancy my head on my shoulders. Where it would cease to remain, should I get caught lying to the prince."

"He will be none the wiser." Zander moved around the billiard table, hunting a striped ball. He leaned in, open-bridging his fingers on the table. "He has a hard-on for the girl. Plus," he sunk the five, "his mother is eager for the pairing."

Thaddeus watched his grandson line up, and miss, dropping the three ball. "Why do you think that is?" He moved to the table, choosing his shot.

"My sister is superficial." The king shrugged. "She probably likes the idea of adding her unique genetic makeup to the family tree."

"I would think time a better teacher. To assume anything, as it relates to that sociopath, is an error in judgment." He sunk the seven and Zander's two. "How soon do they wish to proceed with the nuptials?"

"He will announce the engagement tomorrow. With Merick by his side. Then the queen will start the plans. Knowing the prince's eagerness to sink his cock in the girl—one week, tops." Zander took a sip of his brandy. "We can't keep young lust waiting," he added with a slice of a smile. "Of course I have my own selfish reasons for moving that date forward."

Thaddeus pushed down the strong desire to spear his grandson through the chest with his pool cue. "That is?"

"Marrying the hybrid to my son will better endear her real father to me. A reward." The king swirled the contents of his glass. "For his accommodating behavior the past three years."

"You actually believe that don't you?"

He shouldn't be surprised. The fact that he was pissed him off. The only things worse than the unexpected: the ineptitude of sensing it, and failing to plan accordingly. He had given Zander too much credit. Now the king was beating him about the head with Thaddeus's own unpreparedness.

"Why would he not want his child to become a princess? I can think of no greater honor." He gave an assessing look. "It also keeps him loyal to me. For life."

"I can assure you." Thaddeus dropped the one ball. "Teakin would rather fall on his own blade than see Merick married into this family."

Thaddeus had known this day was coming for three years. Known of the prince's desires. Three years to prepare...

He had. He'd let Merick move on in her studies, knowing the *right* families would get word of her proposal and turn their sons' eyes in her direction. The males of Gerra were nothing if not competitive. It hadn't hurt that Merick was the most comely female in the realm. She'd acclimated to her new school and her peers with ease as Thaddeus had hoped.

Same as he'd anticipated, and Zander promised, the prince would grow bored and move on. But the king hadn't made efforts to dissuade Xavier during those years. He'd done the opposite, taking up the cause as his own.

They were all stark raving mad. Thaddeus needed a new plan. Something more than protecting his own hide. Gerra needed competent rulers. Zander was no longer fit. Neither was Katarra. But the queen wanted more from this union. More than another shiny bauble in her trophy case. He needed to figure out what she stood to gain by encouraging the prince's affections for his daughter.

More difficult would be managing Stefen when he came to collect on their deal. Thaddeus took some comfort in one grounding thought. Ashdon and Alaric did not want a war with Gerra. Certainly not one over a mutt.

Something gnawed at him. He mentally shook it off. Emotions had no place in this game. Everyone must play their part. Thaddeus quickly cleaned the table. "Another round? Or are you ready to pay up?"

"What do you want?"

"I want to be named the King's Authority. Acting on the monarch's orders, in their stead, for eternity." He righted himself. "Regardless of which royal sits the throne."

Merick stood paralyzed outside her father's cracked parlor door.

Not her father.

Teakin had left the door cracked when he exited and nodded silently for her to remain in the hall.

Not just her friend...

"Nothing can break you if you refuse to allow it."

Her life... It was little more than a series of carefully crafted, strung together lies. Instead of the violent onslaught of emotions she'd experienced when Teakin told her of the prince's wishes... Merick felt... *detached.*

It was as if every emotion she should be experiencing was just out of reach. Utterly numb. Their harsh summary of her life—and how it didn't matter—was suspended in this moment, hovering precariously in dead space.

Not an elite.

She had as much worth to the two males in that parlor as a marionette doll. Just something to be used. A pawn.

"Why do you care what he does with your clandestine daughter?"

"I don't..."

Someone opened a door further down the hall. She needed to get out of here. While she was in this state of disconnection, her ability to feel diminished, allowing her basic survival skills to operate unimpeded. Life had just landed her a knock to the gut. She intended to wield it as a sword.

Merick ducked around a corner, her heart thumping wildly against her chest as her mind focused on the task at hand— escaping. She picked up her pace, breaking into a run at the next hall. She just needed to get to her room and gather her stuff.

What stuff! They would look for her there first. She slipped inside an empty room and closed the door, pinning her body against it, trying to steady her nerves so she could think. She should stay here. It would take hours for them to search the grounds.

What would they do when they found her? If they realized she'd overheard their plotting? She would be better served going back to her room, pretending she was none the wiser. It would give her time to form a better escape plan.

Then what? They'd cart her off to the palace. Where she knew no one and had no idea how to navigate the expanse of it. As a future bride to the prince she would be under heavy security day and night. If she was taken there, she would never get out.

No, she would not let them transport her to a new location. Merick gathered her courage. This was her chance. The only time no one would suspect her absence. She would be working with mere hours, possibly minutes, before they came to take her away. Teakin had bought her this gift of time. By making it so she heard their plans, he'd given her a chance at freedom.

She hurried to the window and opened it. With only the one driving thought in her head, she leapt out and hit the ground running, straight to the kennels.

L uck was on her side she realized. Sidling along the building, Merick stopped short of the corner. The Master of Beasts was already gone. Likely at the local tavern, where he'd be for most of the night.

She snuck in, going right to Aasha's cage and lifting the lock. The tiger stretched, lazily lifted her large body, and ambled over. Merick placed her hand atop the cat's skull. "We have to go, girl."

The animal sensed her urgency. The sleepy haze in her red eyes vanished in a flash. It was all the prompting the tigress needed.

They bolted toward the rear of the enclosure, then took to the forest, darting around skeleton trees, avoiding their barren branches reaching out like bony fingers to rip and snag. Merick had no idea where to go, but distance was crucial. The realm was vast. If they could cover enough ground it might buy them a day's time.

She paused at the base of a large boulder to contemplate the best direction.

A rustle in the nearby bushes made her jump. Aasha emitted a low vibrating growl, her head dropping below her shoulders, ears flattening as she moved in front of Merick.

"Who's there?" Merick whispered, half to the cat, half to whatever was in the dense underbrush. Aasha lowered into attack position. "Easy girl."

The shadows played tricks on her eyes as the brush shifted, leaves and branches parting under the weight of something large. Merick's pulse quickened, her reflexes preparing for whatever horror was about to emerge from that wood.

The shadows morphed again, a shape taking form as the moonlight caught on a pair of glowing eyes. Clear, intelligent, unflinching eyes.

A wolf stepped onto the path.

Merick leapt back, stumbling over her own feet as Aasha snarled.

The wolf didn't bristle at the larger cat. Instead, it looked past its challenger to Merick.

Just like the mother tigress all those years ago in the palace zoo— a silent understanding reflected in those gold eyes. Like her dreams...

Teakin's written words scribed their message across her mind. *If doubt should prompt flight, follow your dreams into the night.*

Merick slowly moved to Aasha's side. The cat sniffed the air. "He's not here to fight is he, girl?"

The wolf turned and bolted into the darkness.

Aasha took off after him.

Merick had no choice but to follow.

Through the night they fled, over hills and valleys, only the moon above illuminating their path. They ran and ran, until Merick was sure no footfall would soon land behind them. They raced until the landscape changed, her lungs burned, and her legs wanted to give out. They ran until she had no sense of direction, no sense of what lay behind her, or what waited ahead.

Only then did the wolf slow, its gait shifting to an effortless lope over the rocky terrain. Aasha stopped her pursuit and sat back on her haunches.

"What is it?" Merick knelt down beside her companion.

The wolf disappeared behind a copse of trees. "Oh Aasha, we didn't just chase a wild animal," she looked around, "to who knows where?"

A branch snapped and Merick quickly shot back to her feet.

A male figure stepped from the shadows.

Merick took off at a dead sprint.

"Stop!"

Though she thought the voice somewhat familiar, Merick didn't look back, pumping her legs as hard as she could. They'd found her. She neared a ravine, preparing to jump.

He caught up to her, flashing directly in front of her path.

Stefen!

She stopped short, just shy of plowing into him, her eyes searching for an out, her heart slamming into her chest like a battering ram. "Don't touch me!"

He lifted his hands, the universal sign of surrender, even as he positioned himself to physically restrain her if she took off again. "Where's your pet, Merick?"

Realization slammed into her head. She glanced to her left, and then her right. Aasha was not there. "She's okay," he confirmed. "She didn't run when you did."

Merick frantically turned, her worry for the tiger greater than her instincts to not take her eyes off the emissary. Aasha was exactly where she had been seconds ago, sitting in the tall grass, unfazed.

She spun back to face him. "What do you want with me?"

"The same thing I have always wanted. To help you."

"Everyone has betrayed me. How do I know—"

"Your pet has not," he reasoned calmly as Aasha stood and walked to them—as if he had summoned her. "Your real father has not."

"Where is he?" Her voice cracked, those repressed emotions hitting her, one after another in alarming succession.

"He'll join us later." Stefen splayed his long fingers when Aasha reached them. The tigress butted her head into his palm. "For now, I need to get you to your uncle's estate."

Merick tensed, back on the defensive. Teakin had never mentioned any family.

"It's a long story." Stefen seemed to read her thoughts. Then he reached out. "We need to go."

She stared at his hand. She'd been a fool all her life, blindly trusting those around her, caught in a game for which she'd never learned the rules. Could she even trust her own judgment?

What if...what if he too...

Merick looked up into his sea-green eyes, as faceted as gemstones. "I'm scared."

"*I know,*" he said, but she heard his words in her mind not her ears.

The realm drifted away around them, its dimensions and space changing. Color muted as sound and vibration magnified. It was like being taken into someone else's dreams. *His dream.*

Through the beyond, he led her along the twisting web of thoughts and sensations, until she saw through the eyes of another. *An animal...*a wolf padding over the dusty sienna clay, silver paws wet from a recent creek. Then it looked up at Gerra's red moon and howled. The chuff of a big cat answered it. *Aasha!*

She was seeing through the eyes of the wolf they had just followed. Guided there by Stefen's mind.

Merick pulled back, snatching her mind away from his. "How

did you?" She watched as the gold edges of his eyes faded to green.

"I told you on that balcony years ago that you didn't belong here. Neither do I." He took her hand. "I need you to trust in the truths around you. What you *can* believe in. The love you bear your guard. The bond you share with your tiger." Stefen held her stare. "I need you to trust *me*."

Chapter Fifteen

Stefen held tight to Merick as he prepared to make the leap. The air all but chained itself to his limbs, pulling them down, dragging him back, trying to stop him from taking what Gerra thought belonged there.

With one final push, he tore free of its relentless hold.

They entered Earth's atmosphere at a speed too fast to control. He barely had time to wrap his arms around her and rotate, taking the impact when they collided with the ground, tilling up dirt and grass like a meteorite shot from the universe.

Stefen exhaled when the stars stopped racing past overhead. Before he could drag another breath into his lungs, a shadow blotted out the moon and something hot and wet licked his face.

"Of course you landed on your feet." He chuckled as Aasha moved on and the night sky returned.

"Holy fuck!"

The explicative brought Stefen's gaze to the weight atop his chest. Merick's round eyes peeked up through thick lashes and tousled blonde curls. "Are we..." She looked over his head.

Twinkling stars reflected in her multicolored orbs, blinking in and out of focus. "My gods."

Stefen stared, dumbstruck. It wasn't the unexpected words that had rendered him speechless. *It was her aura.* She was luminous.

She'd always been beautiful. But now, her true aura undisturbed, uncorrupted by Gerra's dark influence... Merick was the most stunning creature Stefen had ever laid eyes on. If there had been any questions about what she was, they were no more. The archangel's blood was a virtual beacon.

There was something else. An untapped strength prowled just beneath that moon-kissed glow. A quiet regalness that spoke of another sort of power. Teakin's blood. *The dragon.*

He recognized it now—like the answer to a riddle finally revealed. Pythia's parting words from years ago. "*Three new souls will walk the realms one day, tied to this blood. All will struggle, and all will rise. Three will fly. Two will rule. One will be your greatest test.*"

The Oracle had spoken to Kielyn, Ash and Stefen. But then she had faced only him. "*All of them will need your strength. But one will require your protection.*"

A lump formed in Stefen's throat. He swallowed it down, unable to take his eyes off her. He'd trained Bastian and Eirik for eighteen years. Been their mentor, their uncle, their friend. *Their strength.*

But Merick... Stefen had chosen to look after her. He'd made himself her protector. She was the third foretold soul.

A booming voice yanked him from his revelation. "Are you hurt?"

Footfall crashed through the lavender laden field. Merick shoved off of Stefen and quickly stood. Aasha moved between her and the advancing intruders.

Stefen turned his head to see Ash, Bastian and Eirik coming to a stop. "Answer me, damn it!" Ash barked.

"Everyone is fine," Stefen drawled and pushed to his feet, brushing grass off the backs of his arms. He glanced at Merick. "This is your uncle, Ashdon LaGoryen, King of the Fire Dynasty. And your cousins, Bastian and Eir—"

The wind was nearly knocked out of him by the force with which Kielyn collided with his chest, her arms encircling him in a hug. He embraced her back, looking down to try and see the face of his best friend beneath the head of red hair pressed into his chest. "You're safe," she mumbled, as if saying it out loud confirmed it.

"I distinctly recall promising you I would be." He grinned.

That got her to look up, her pert nose bunching, amber eyes narrowing. "You've never been good at keeping promises."

"Ahem," Eirik cleared his throat. "He was going to introduce me, I believe. Before Mom stole the show. I'm Eirik." He gave a half bow, smiling. "It's nice to meet you, cousin."

Everyone looked at Merick, who wasn't quite quick enough to hide the shock she was clearly experiencing. Stefen gently stepped out of the hug with Kielyn and edged closer to Merick. He wasn't convinced she wouldn't break into a run if anyone else appeared.

"A pleasure," she replied, returning Eirik's smile.

Eirik faltered. They all seemed to. But Kielyn put words to what they were experiencing. "You're absolutely breathtaking, Merick."

Just like that, Stefen was pushed aside as his best friend swooped in. "I'm Kielyn. It's so nice to finally meet you. Stefen has told me much about you over the years. I feel like I know you already. And who is this marvelous beauty?" She dropped down, face to face with Aasha.

The large animal leaned in for head scratches, instantly recognizing the cat lover she'd found in Kie. "This is Aasha," Merick answered, which lead Kielyn into another series of excited questions.

Ash moved to Stefen's side. "Where's Teakin?" he asked, voice lowered to a considerate level Stefen hadn't known was possible.

"I don't know," he said. "He said he would meet us here when he was finished."

"Finished?"

Merick's attention returned swiftly, though her conversation remained with Kielyn. "I didn't ask for an explanation," Stefen replied. "Time was of the essence."

Thankfully, Ash acquiesced to the silent plea to leave it at that. "I'll wait here with the boys. Take the ladies on to the estate."

"I'm not leaving here without him." Merick spoke up, a look of dogged determination on her lovely face.

"Of course you're not." Kielyn rose beside her. "Neither of us are going anywhere until we all do."

Ash cursed under his breath, a sound of long suffering. Eirik slapped him on the shoulder as he strolled past. "Looks like we're camping out here for a while, Father."

Bastian said nothing as he joined his brother, but his eyes stayed fixed on Merick.

Ash just shook his head and extended his arm to Kie. "Come, dear, join me by the river. I'm sure Stefen has more to explain to my niece before my brother arrives."

Kielyn looped her arm over his, accepting, and glanced up at her mate with timeless adoration. Stefen watched the four make their way down the hill to the water's edge before turning to face Merick. "Care to sit with me?"

She walked over and sat on the plush grass, her gaze drifting over the sprawling fields. "There isn't anything like this in Gerra."

He sat down and took in the landscape with her—the twining band of the river below, with ripples like opals, swathes of moonlight silvering the lowlands in dew, and the fresh scent of wild flowers languidly drifting on the breeze.

"Are there lightning bugs here?"

Stefen glanced over curiously. "There are."

"Teakin used to bring me Fulgur bugs. One time he accidentally referred to them as lightning bugs." She stared straight ahead. "He never made accidents, so I delighted in the observation my six-year old brain had uncovered. For a week I teased him, not realizing how uncomfortable it made him, until I did so in front of a group of my father's... My *pretend* father's peers." Merick paused. "It was the first time I ever saw fear in Teakin's eyes. Now I know why."

Stefen stared at her angelic profile, fully aware if she looked over now she would see another first: him speechless. He had no words. They'd flown away like birds. Should he find his tongue, he had no wisdom that could help. None that could absolve himself of the part he'd played in her deception. None that could take away the guilt she now felt.

His hand reached out of its own accord. She didn't flinch when he placed it atop hers in the soft clover. "He'll be here soon. Then he can show you everything he wanted to."

She looked at him. "Are you certain?"

Was he? *No.* But he knew Ash would go in after him if he didn't.

"I have not spent much time around Teakin, but I know one thing for certain. He's almost as stubborn as his brother."

"Almost?"

"Perhaps I'm being too generous." He smirked. "No one is as stubborn as that male down there."

He looked to where Ash was pacing the invisible gateway near the riverbank. Stefen did not want to think about what would occur if Teakin did not emerge in the next few hours. He knew exactly what would happen if Merick's father did not make it out alive.

"Thank you." Her soft voice drew his gaze back to her. "For

everything. Most of all, for hiding your emotions from me." She searched his eyes. "I need your strength right now."

With those simple words he felt something inside him take the final nosedive—off the ledge his emotions had been so precariously riding.

Teakin better drag his ass across that divide soon. He had a long list of promises owed to the beauty sitting beside him. He damn sure wasn't going to let her down again.

Chapter Sixteen

T eakin's feet hit the ground, his legs absorbing the impact as his body contracted into a crouch.

Head bent, eyes locked on one patch of grass, he pressed his fingers into the cool mud. And inhaled.

The past rushed in on that solitary breath, down his throat and into his lungs, seeking out and flooding all that was dark with memories of light—the weeping rain, smoke from a far off chimney, sweet river moss, the downy fur of a cottontail burrowing into its nest.

Then it happened.

For the first time in centuries, his muscles relaxed. *He was home.* He was back on Earth.

Teakin stayed as he was, not willing to move, afraid it would all be a dream, unable to go on if it were. He heard their advance, but he remained still. He'd been too long from this world. Had done too much. Had done too little.

The toe of a high-polished boot came into focus, inches from his sodden fingers. Teakin didn't need to look up to know who stood above him. Still he waited, back arched over one knee, head bent.

The touch on the back of his head was tender—compelling. His vision blurred the outline of those expensive boots.

"Brother." Came a voice he hadn't heard in centuries, but knew as well as his own heartbeat.

Teakin's head lifted until his eyes met with the silver-lined ones of his younger sibling.

He surged to his feet, clasped Ash by the back of the head and dragged him into his embrace. "I've missed you."

"I had no idea," Ash whispered, pain edging his words. "I thought you were..."

"I thought the same of you." Teakin pulled back enough to look him in the eyes. "I'm here now. We are together again. As we always should have been."

Ashdon nodded as Teakin let go and stepped back to fully take his measure. "Besides, little brother," Teakin's lips hitched into a grin, "regret is an awful look on you."

"Still an ass." Ash smiled. "Little has changed."

"A few things have." Teakin looked past him, searching. His heart squeezed in his chest when he saw Merick. "I have more to fight for now." He stepped to the side.

Merick took a tentative step forward, and then she broke into a full run. Tears glistened on her alabaster cheeks when she hit his chest, molding to him as his arms wrapped around her.

"I'm so sorry," he said soothingly. "I couldn't risk telling you. Not until I knew you were safely away."

She held onto him wordlessly. Teakin could feel her heart pounding against his chest. He looked down, needing to know she understood him. "Merick?" He tipped her chin up, enough that he could see her red-rimmed eyes. "Can you forgive me?"

"Forgive you?" New tears pooled in her eyes and her chin wobbled. "You saved me."

His own vision blurred again. "I only wish I hadn't left you alone. To hear their words."

"I had to hear it." She smiled softly. "You gave me a sword in giving me that truth."

He pulled her in, hugging her tightly. An embrace eighteen years too long coming. Not one of a guard to his young charge. A hug between a father and a daughter.

"I have much to explain," Teakin whispered atop her head. "But there's not enough time right now." He stepped back. "I need to get you further away first."

She nodded as Stefen walked over and asked, "Does he know?"

"The alarms sounded when I jumped," Teakin confirmed.

It had been taken into careful consideration. When to make his break. Teakin had waited until he felt Merick cross over. Because he knew Zander would sense his absence the second he folded into the pocket that divided the realms.

Teakin looked at Ash. "Is transportation secure?"

"It is."

The other two males, who had been quietly observing but keenly alert, stepped up beside his brother. Now that they were closer Teakin could see the family resemblance. The dark-haired one was the spitting image of Ash. Olive skinned, blue-eyed, handsome. Dangerous. The larger, auburn-haired lad was just as striking—a LaGoryen trait—but he had an undeniable likability about him. Clearly, a gift from his mother.

"There will be time for more detailed introductions later." Ash jerked his chin to the pair. "But these are your nephews, Bastian and Eirik."

"Fine looking examples of the Ushum bloodline." Teakin nodded. "And it looks like we have added a wee bit of Scottish vitality into the family tree."

"Just wait till you see their mother." Ash grinned. "She should be back any—"

The beauty who flashed before him was nothing short of devastating. Long wavy auburn locks, the most unique amber-colored eyes he'd ever seen, and the same disarming demeanor the one called Eirik possessed. His little brother had done well for himself.

"Lady Kielyn." Teakin inclined his head. "It is an honor."

She smiled. "Ash never mentioned you two looked so similar."

"He told you I was ugly?" Teakin quipped, tossing a smirk at Ash.

"I just omitted the part about the incurable leprosy down—"

"We need to be going," Stefen interrupted.

It had not gone unnoticed that Merick had gravitated to Stefen's side when the introductions began. Right where Teakin had originally found her. *Good*, she needed someone she could trust when he wasn't around.

"A car is at the estate, waiting to take you to the jet," Stefen continued. "The quicker you get to Switzerland the better."

"Where are we going?" Merick asked, skeptically.

"We need to get you and your father further away." Stefen refocused his attention on her. "The Air King, Sidtric, will take you in, until we know it's safe here."

"About that," Kielyn interjected, "there's been a slight change of plans."

"Such as?" The former archangel faced her fully.

"I reached out to Alaric."

"Tell me she's joking?" Stefen looked at his maker.

"We had to ask." Ash's tone was matter of fact, but there was something in his eyes...*an apology*. "It's the safest place for her."

"Why wouldn't we be safe here?" Merick queried.

"It's more complicated than that." Teakin took a step toward her. He could only assume Anu was where they meant for them to travel. If so, they were right. It was the best place for her. Just not for him. "I will not be joining you there. Not yet anyway."

"What are you talking about?" His brother swiveled his head abruptly. "Of course you will."

Ash was no stranger to the Diabolis' twisted fascination with their dragon lineage. This treason would not be overlooked. Zander would come for them.

"That's not what we discussed," Stefen intoned, his words even, despite the fact that he edged closer to Merick.

"We discussed escaping. However, I won't have her running for the rest of her—"

"You will *both* be safe in Anu," Ash rounded on him. "They can't enter—"

"For how long?" Teakin demanded. "How many centuries did Dante look for you? How long did you run? How long did you hide?" He looked his brother in the eyes. He could see what Ash was now gleaning—how deep his scars ran. What manner of destruction had been done, and exactly how much he was willing to sacrifice to keep it from ever reaching Merick. "I won't condemn her to that fate. Please don't ask it of me."

Teakin had stood on that precipice, the ravine that served as the gateway between Gerra and Earth, and considered all their options. The plan he'd set forth with Stefen would serve them well in the short term, but it was no way to live for an immortal. The other option had been not to jump. To remain in Gerra. Zander wouldn't come for Merick if he remained.

There was a third option though. One that would likely see him dead.

He squared up to Ash. "We need this vicious cycle to end. I won't pass down the pain of my past." His gaze once again found his daughter. "I want to leave my child a better legacy." Teakin glanced at his brother's boys, at his beautiful mate, before he looked back at Ash. "None of our family is safe as long as the Diabolis rule Gerra."

"What exactly are you asking?" Stefen inquired.

"For me to fight with him. To end this. Once and for all," Ash answered, his eyes never breaking from Teakin's. "And I will."

"We both will." Kielyn sided up to her mate.

"We *all* will." Eirik clarified proudly.

The quiet one, Bastian, said nothing, but a glimmer lit in those artic-blue orbs.

Teakin looked at Merick. "I will come for you. As soon as this is over. I promise."

She nodded bravely. "I believe you."

He turned to Stefen.

"If someone cuts their palm with a knife and holds out their hand, I'm done with this family," the former archangel drawled.

"Might I ask for one more favor?" Teakin grinned. "No blood required."

"Sure." Stefen rolled his eyes. "I live only to serve your blasted family, it seems."

"Until this is over. Will you continue to watch out for her?"

The warrior didn't hesitate. "With my life."

Teakin nodded and walked back over to his daughter. "Once you're settled in Anu, I need you to start exploring your powers. Being in your mother's realm may help facilitate this. Stefen can help you unlock them." He put his hands on her shoulders when her gaze lowered, the way it always did when she was unsure. "Gerra was a weight on you, pulling your natural talents down. It's time to unleash them."

She looked up, her two different color eyes—as different as Anu and Earth—shimmered with understanding and something else—courage. "I will try."

He smiled down at her. "That's all I can ask." Teakin stepped back and looked at his brother. "Do you have a Fire-dancer that can accompany them? In case she has the gift?"

"I will send my best," Ash assured.

"That would be me," Eirik spoke up.

"Thomas will go."

"I am the best." Eirik stood his ground. "Besides, Merick should be with family. If she has the ability, who best to teach her?"

Ash inhaled deeply through the nose. "Fine," he conceded. "But you're both to fall under Stefen's direct supervision. Understand?"

The younger male smiled broadly. "Of course."

"What are you waiting on then?" Ash said. "Get them to the tarmac. Sidtric will meet you in Switzerland and see that you get safely across from there."

The redheaded beauty put an arm around Merick, but his daughter's eyes didn't break from his until he nodded. "I'll see you soon."

She watched him over her shoulder as she was led away. Stefen hung back. "I'll keep her safe. I can't promise the same of you, if you break your word to her."

With that he was gone, reappearing beside Merick and the others further up the hill. Teakin watched their retreating backs until there was nothing left for his gaze to hold on to. "I don't want you to do this out of regretful obligation."

"I'm not," Ash said. "I am doing it because you're right. And because you're my brother."

"Those Diaboli bastards have been pushing us into submission since we were mere boys." Teakin looked out over the expansive countryside. "In love with what we were born to be. Drawn to its essence like a druggie to a spoon. Propelled by a similar darkness." He breathed in the night. "Dark calling to dark. Within them some primal need to compete for its existence. To harness it for themselves. By forcing us into silence, they in turn become louder. The last voice. The only one standing."

"Well then." His brother stepped up beside him, the warmth of his breath a puff of smoke on the chilled air. "It's time we stopped whispering." Ash smiled, a glint of white teeth flashing. "To challenge one dragon to a contest of roaring is foolish enough. But to challenge two…" He glanced sideways at Teakin. "Is to court extinction."

SOMEWHERE OVER MILAN

The turbulence caused Merick to jump. She wished Aasha was here to comfort her. She hadn't been prepared for having to leave her behind at her uncle's estate. Not that she had been prepared for anything that had happened in the past few hours.

At least her beloved pet was in good hands. Kielyn was a ray of sunlight. Her way with animals was as natural as the beauty and grace that shone from her soul. Merick had believed her wholeheartedly when she promised to spoil the large cat rotten. There was no better place for her to be if they had to be apart.

A voice boomed overhead, startling her. It took her more time than she cared to admit to locate where it was coming from, or what it was asking of her. *Fasten their seatbelts?*

Despite the odd order, she did as she was told. Merick picked up the two belts at her hips and tried fitting them together, the way Stefen had secured them before take-off. She fumbled the first attempt and inwardly cursed.

She'd managed to get them undone, as Eirik had done to his own, once they were in the air. It couldn't be that damned difficult to fasten them back. Before she could try again two large hands stilled hers.

She looked up into Stefen's sea-green eyes. "The smaller one fits inside the larger one."

He leaned in, the heat from his body warming her. His gaze drifted to her lap. The sudden closeness did something strange to the air around her, lighting her skin from the inside out, like the buzz from a second glass of wine. It muddled her senses, leaving her feeling both relaxed and on edge.

He snapped the buckle. "Like this."

She stared at him, snared like some helpless woodland creature caught in a trap. *Look away!* His thick dark lashes lifted slowly. The fool she was, she made no attempt to avoid those piercing eyes when they again looked into hers.

"There aren't any contraptions like this in Gerra," she managed to say. "Thank you."

Stefen only smiled and pulled the belt tighter, his palms spreading out across her hips as he checked it was secure. There was no mistaking the reaction to that. Her core contracted and her pulse stomped out a war dance in her chest. She'd experienced this reaction with Kalum when his fingers would dip beneath her belt line, his breath warm on her throat, words moaned into her ear, anticipation of what was to come.

But she had never experienced anything of the sort from just being near him.

She needed to get a grip. Merick forced her gaze to the left of her seat, taking a sudden interest in the contents of the glass of water on her tray. What in the Four Realms was this male doing to her? She'd always found Stefen positively resplendent, *but now...*

Now she wanted to throw him down and straddle him in the aisle of the plane.

It had to be the elevation. It was clearly messing with her head. Because it most certainly couldn't be the alternative—that she was utterly devastated by the mere proximity to the warrior sworn to protect her. To help train her.

Teakin would kill him.

"You are a mortal," Stefen said, as he sat back in his seat, not bothering to buckle his own belt. "Better to be safe than sorry."

Merick looked to Eirik, to his fastened belt. "You aren't an immortal?"

"Not yet." Her cousin smiled lopsidedly. "I haven't fully committed to the transformation."

"You have a choice?" She was shocked. All elite made a full transformation by the end of their eighteenth year.

"They give you a very one-sided lesson on history in Gerra, huh?" He chuckled.

His eyes glanced to the right and his smile vanished. Merick looked over to Stefen and his raised eyebrow. She refocused on Eirik.

"My mother and father were born human and later turned into vampires," he explained. "Same as my brother and me. It's our choice if we transition or not."

"And Bastian and you are uncertain?"

"I am. Bastian made the transformation last month."

"Won't being human make you more," she glanced at his seatbelt, "vulnerable?"

"No more than I have ever been," he said simply. "But I have a strong gift with fire. So I'm already stronger than the average mortal man."

"About that..." Merick tried to sit forward on the edge of her seat, just to find herself tethered in place by the blasted contraption. She exhaled. "I don't think I like this aspect of Earth."

"You'll get used to it," Stefen said. "You were about to ask about Fire-dancing?"

"Yes. I was educated somewhat on that," she explained. "I

know of the original elemental houses and the gifts that were bestowed on them by the gods. I am aware of Dante's unusual fascination with them too, and how he set about trying to enslave and cultivate them into superior warriors for his army."

"Correct," Stefen answered. "Do you know the significance of each elemental house crest? As it pertains to certain members of each royal house?"

"I know that not every member of a family will possess the gift to manipulate their house's element. And I know the dragon represents fire. I never learned the others."

Merick leaned back into her seat, hating how little she actually did know. If only she'd been more like Marjory, demanding the things she wanted. She should have broken into Thaddeus's library and read every forbidden book housed there.

"They don't permit certain areas of study in Gerra," she said. "I guess now I know why."

"The witch and warlock rules over the Air folk. The werewolf protects the Earth tribes. And the Water clans were said to be protected by the ghormas, or mermen as the human stories refer to them," Stefen explained. "On occasion, it was believed that the spirit of their house crest would pass into a chosen mortal. As it did with your uncle."

"Ash is a dragon?" Merick felt her jaw go slack. "A real dragon?"

"Pretty epic, huh?" Eirik chimed in, grinning ear to ear. "When he's pissed his eyes glow gold."

Stefen cleared his throat. "Let's save the specifics on the family temper for now." He gave her cousin another look of warning before redirecting the conversation, his gaze returning to Merick. "How much did Teakin tell you before I found you in the woods?"

"He only explained the prince wished to marry and tried to prepare me, as best he could, for the conversation that would send me fleeing into those woods later." A niggling of apprehension tickled her nerves. "Why?"

He shook his head and mumbled something that sounded a lot like damning his lot in life. "What do you know of his time in Gerra?"

"Before tonight, nothing. I only knew him as my guard. My friend." She mentally tried to prepare herself for what was about to come. "What do I need to know, Stefen?"

He took his time responding, his only movement that of his thumb rubbing the pads of his fingers where they dangled over the arm of his chair. "Teakin, Ash, and their mother were kidnapped by Dante's army after he sacked their village. They were only boys. Their father was murdered. Dante then took their mother as his forced mate. She later gave birth to Katarra out of that union."

Stefen paused, watching her closely. "Teakin was not a paid guard in Thaddeus's household. He was a slave. And more than that, he was an experiment," he concluded without preamble— like ripping off a Band-Aid.

Merick found the air in the cabin suddenly lacking, her brain only able to put words to one question. "An experiment?"

"Your uncle is not the only living dragon," Stefen said. "Your father is one as well."

"How?" The word slipped over her lips without a thought to propel it. Just a feeling.

How could a dragon be a slave? If her best friend possessed that sort of strength, surely he could have left Gerra long ago. As his brother had clearly done. It didn't make sense. *Nothing made sense.* "Why didn't he escape?"

"He was drugged with ashwood for centuries," Stefen replied. "His inner dragon only awakened when you were born. Before then, he was just a gifted Fire-dancer turned vampire."

"That still doesn't add up." Annoyance quickly was taking the place of bewilderment. "Why didn't he break out then? Once the dragon emerged."

Stefen tilted his head and a faint, almost empathetic smile touched his lips. "He stayed for you."

The reality of that statement sunk like a weighted brick tossed into a still pond. The bruises, the cuts, the despondent look in his eyes when he would return from being gone for days. She'd always asked about them. He's always blamed them on training.

He had lied. Teakin's declaration from an hour ago came racing back. "*I won't pass down the pain of my past.*"

"Was my father tortured?" Her words were barely a whisper.

"Merick..." Stefen sat forward.

"Did he endure these *experiments* because of me?"

He reached for her.

"No!" She made to stand, just to have the fucking belt stop her.

This time she unbuckled it and flung it to the side. "Did he?"

Anger—irrational, scared, and raw—was coming to life somewhere inside her. *Too much.* Her world had been upended in the course of a few hours and those events were now catching up to her in rapid succession. Marriage to a stranger. Her father wasn't her father. Worse, the male she was raised to believe was her father had been using her as a pawn in a political game.

She was not an elite, but rather, the daughter of a slave. *A willing slave!* A dragon—a beast of mythical renown. And her only friend. In a realm pitted against her since birth.

Teakin was her real father. He had put himself through unimaginable torture...for her...

Hold! Her mind tried for control, demanding her emotions listen.

Merick's body had other plans. Her fingers twitched and her vision narrowed to pinpoint accuracy. An invisible weight of armor that should be around her shoulders was instead locking onto her heart, encasing it, preparing to shield it from whatever she was about to unleash. She was not in control.

Something else was.

She focused her simmering wrath on Stefen. "Answer me!"

"He did." Stefen reached out. She jerked away. "That was his choice, Merick. You are not to blame—"

"Who was my mother?" she demanded.

"She died after your birth. She was like me. What I used to be." He moved quickly, his hand landing on her shoulder before she could contemplate deflecting it. "Fuck!"

Stefen recoiled, eyes wide. "You're on fire."

Merick felt it suddenly, as if his contact had registered the sensation. Her skin was burning. She looked at her hands. Wisps of pale smoke were curling over her knuckles.

All tension fled her body. "What do I do?"

The burn intensified. The thin languid vapors became definitive forked flames.

"Stay calm." Eirik lurched to his feet.

"I can't!" Her fingertips glowed like orange glass, the bright light chewing up her nails, leaving black char in their wake as they ate through to the pink flesh below.

"Call it off!" Eirik said, more frantically.

Stefen took both her hands in his. "Look at me."

She did, her gaze locking onto his. "Feel what I feel," he directed.

Tears stung her eyes. "But I'm burning you."

"It doesn't hurt. Just feel what I feel."

Merick focused on the tiny flecks of gold in his irises. Incisive and clear, they glittered amongst the green—like a forest pool shadowed by trees. *"That's it,"* he wordlessly called to her. *"Put the pain on me. I can take it."*

She did, pushing her fear into their shared touch, absorbing his essence. Cool and soothing, healing and courageous, it pulled the angry heat from her. *"You are safe. Trust me."* His thoughts caressed her mind. *"Do you trust me?"*

The pain dissolved, retreating as fast as it had erupted. She nodded, her eyes shutting, succumbing to the calm. She felt her body being gently guided down.

Merick gave over completely to the lulling pull. "Don't leave me."

"Never," he whispered through their shared bond. *"Sleep."*

A breeze kissed her skin and stirred giant palm leaves overhead. The warm sun played peekaboo with the wind. Only a few feet away, water lapped the sand. The swaying seaweed under the waves twined with the current as the ocean rocked it rhythmically over a shell-flecked floor, colorful fish and crustaceans skittering about.

This was where dreams lived. This was where peace reigned. *"Sleep."*

Chapter Seventeen

Thaddeus knew by the tiny 'ping' amongst the crash that the unicorn figurine was no more. Merick had made it for him on her eighth birthday. *Her birthday*. And she'd made him a gift.

Thaddeus smiled where he stood, looking out the window, as the contents of his desk clattered and rolled across the hardwoods. She had fooled them all. His experiment had more courage than he'd given her credit. Merick was altruistic. Even being raised in Gerra, she had never faltered in that.

His mistake had been growing comfortable with the idea that innate goodness equaled blind loyalty. She must have heard them talking. *Heard everything...*

The how and why matter not. He exhaled. She was gone.

"Why are you just standing there?" Zander hissed behind him.

"Are you done rearranging my office?" Thaddeus turned, noting the head of the unicorn rocking to a halt against the baseboard.

"We have to find them." He seethed, eyes blazing, arms spread wide on the empty desk, fingers digging into the wooden edges.

"Why?"

His grandson gawked at him. "Because I am the fucking king and they are mine!"

"Let me ask you this. Why would Teakin risk such a dangerous undertaking? Now."

Zander looked down, head dropping below his shoulder blades. "I obviously allowed him too much freedom." He glanced up, eyes narrowing. "A luxury I won't afford when I get him back."

Thaddeus clasped his hands behind his back. "He's a dragon. He never required your freedom. He could have killed you any time, once you stopped drugging him, and waltzed right out the door."

"He feared me. He wouldn't have disobeyed me."

"He obeyed you only to pacify you. He stayed for her." Thaddeus watched his grandson stewing in his hate, his shortsightedness remarkable. "Think, damn it. What changed? What common denominator shifted, giving him the assurance he could finally save her? Alone."

"You tell me." Zander spat. "If he could have left at any time. Perhaps he decided tonight was the night."

"Tonight?" he mocked. "You think *tonight* would have been easier to steal his daughter than eighteen years ago? When she was a seven-pound infant?"

Zander pushed off the desk. "I will have you killed."

"For what? Calling you naïve?" Thaddeus said through clenched teeth. "For insulting you by stating the facts? That you've become so obsessed you've forgotten how to rule?"

The king sent the desk colliding with the study wall. "Tell me!" He advanced. "Tell me what changed. Why did he choose tonight?"

Thaddeus stared at the king's red face, pupils raging, nostrils flared. "He had support."

"Who?"

"Why, your father's murderer of course."

Several emotions flitted across Zander's face before he rocked back on his heels. "There was no way for him to communicate with his brother. We would have known if Ashdon entered here."

"They had a messenger." Thaddeus stepped around his grandson and walked to the broken desk. "Now, the only question remaining..." He opened a drawer. "Are you willing to go to war over an escaped slave?"

"No." The king strode forward. "But I will take back what is mine. One way or the other."

Thaddeus leaned a hip into the discarded mahogany and folded his arms. Perhaps he'd been wrong. Getting rid of Zander might be easier than imagined. Ashdon LaGoryen would cut him down the second he entered the Earth Realm.

Should his grandson be clever enough to not go himself, he would still be inciting a war. One Thaddeus had no intention of being involved in. "As the King's Authority, I would like to offer a suggestion."

Zander sneered. "I should remove that damn title for your insubordination."

Thaddeus ignored him. "Continue on as if nothing has occurred. Tell the prince and queen that Merick's arrival has been postponed by a few days. Suggest a ball or something to occupy Katarra while I get my spies in place. That will buy me time to locate them."

Zander studied him closely before responding, "Three days." He marched from the room. "Three days to make this right."

Thaddeus rapped his fingers against his biceps as his grandson's tread fell away down the hall.

Three days is all I will need.

Chapter Eighteen

ANU

They had touched down in Switzerland, briefly greeted Sidtric and his entourage, and folded into the pockets separating the realms. Merick never woke.

Castle soldiers lined the cobblestones over the arching bridge, their livery blending with the silent snow. Stoic and resolved they stood guard, like the giant stone lions carved over the portcullis, watching with vacant eyes as their traveling party entered far below.

Once inside the frozen courtyard, Stefen let Sidtric do the talking. He remained silent when they were ushered inside, the warmth from the impressive fireplaces instantly comforting, wrapping their bones—welcoming as a siren on a rocky sea shore.

They ascended the spiraling stairs, their tread on the worn sandstone the only evidence of their arrival. Muted voices drifted by on each level they passed, some brash, some glib, some melodic. Courtiers and clergy, nobility, and dignitaries.

They completed the ninth rotation, the ninth floor of twelve. Still, Stefen said nothing. This was no longer his home. These were no longer his brethren. He was no longer allowed on the twelfth floor.

The angel leading the way stopped and waved an elegant hand, gesturing down the hall. "This level is yours. Take whatever rooms you desire."

Sidtric, ever the definition of kingly elegance, inclined his head in thanks.

Stefen kicked the first door to his right open with the heel of his sodden boot and marched inside, Merick still asleep in his arms.

Muffled apologies were issued behind him, but he ignored them as he gently laid his charge down on the bed. It was no surprise she'd taken so quickly, so thoroughly, to his mental coaxing on the plane. The poor thing was exhausted. She'd been dealt more blows in one day than most immortals could handle in a century.

"I'm sorry," Eirik said from the door after the others moved on.

Stefen covered Merick with a blanket and faced him. "What for?"

"I didn't help the situation on the plane. I panicked when she did." He leaned into the doorframe and shook his head, auburn locks falling over his brow and into his eyes. "I should have been able to walk her back, out of the flames."

"There's an old saying." Stefen moved toward him, snagging a chilled bottle of wine on his way. "Those who can, do; those who can't, teach." He handed his nephew the bottle. "You're an exceptional Fire-dancer. You've never had a pupil though. It's one thing to understand the mechanics of something in your own body and mind. An entirely different thing to show it to another."

"Still..." Eirik looked at Merick, the disappointment in himself still evident. Both he and Bastian had always been overly hard on themselves, Eirik more so. "Is she gonna be okay? When she wakes up."

"Yes. She just needs to rest." Stefen nodded toward the sounds of laughter coming from a few rooms down. "Go join the fun. I know you're eager to explore."

Eirik grinned and shoved off the doorjamb. "Take some of the Air-dancers with you," Stefen added as he headed down the hall. "And don't do anything I would do."

The young LaGoryen pivoted, pointing a finger at him and winked. "That leaves nothing then, uncle."

Eirik was entering a room further down the hall before Stefen could confirm that statement. He closed the door and looked at the bed. Eirik was right; he hadn't been ready for the sudden predicament Merick had found. He would be a great asset for her training when she was in the right frame of mind. Not until then.

Stefen aimlessly walked over. Merick needed guided supervision until she gained her full powers. Likewise, she needed someone she could trust. To talk her off a ledge if she lost control again. Because there was zero doubt she would need some type of assistance in the near future. Removing her from Gerra had unlocked something elemental.

The second they'd landed on Earth he noted it. Each second since then, it had intensified. As if her powers were just waking— the subtle rumble of pebbles underfoot, before a volcano erupts. She needed more than a teacher right now.

She needed a friend.

Before he could reconsider, his hand was reaching out, brushing a rogue curl back from her face. He stood, mesmerized by the tenacity of the ringlet when it recoiled back across her cheek. Fascinated, he pushed the same strand aside once more. Again, it defied him.

Interesting. Such a contradiction to the amicable girl he'd met all those years ago. So eager to please. So seemingly ready to accept her lot.

Or had she been? His mind traveled back to the day he plucked her off the mountainside. She'd been on a personal quest to challenge herself.

The night of the ball, she'd known she was different from the others. It had bothered her, but she didn't seek their validation. Instead, she grew more determined, trained harder, and earned their respect on her own merits. Not because she did what she was told to do.

Had she done that, she would have never fought so hard to attend that finishing school. She could have easily accepted Thaddeus's ruling on the matter and stayed at home, hidden away like the secret doll he had tried to make of her.

It had been her decision to escape. To flee a marriage proposal from a crowned prince. How many well-bred females had Stefen known growing up who would have shunned that union? None came to mind.

Merick did.

Then tonight, when she—quite literally—stood up to him.

Ahhh... There was the curl. How had he missed it before? She'd always been just as willful as that glorious head of thick hair.

He continued to watch her, lost in slumber. Completely unaware of the mental somersaults he was doing over her complexity. Still, why was he just now really seeing this side of her nature?

She stirred, stretching her lithe body under the thin blanket, which caused the material to nestle into the valleys and exploit the hills of her perfect figure, highlighting the room's cool temperature...

For fuck's sake!

The realization was like a mallet to the forehead. He hadn't noticed the nuances of her dueling personality before because he'd been observing her as a child all these years. The finer appreciation of her evolving personality had taken a backseat to his ethical responsibility to look after her well-being. To protect her innocence.

The woman laying in that bed was a far cry from a hapless child. She was strong, determined, and more than capable of making the decisions she needed to better advance her path in life. What she didn't need was some stupid male staring at her sleeping form and pitching a damn tent.

He turned in place, his knuckles welcoming the sharp bite of his teeth. *Fuck, fuck, fuck!* Teakin would gut him if he knew—only a fraction of—where Stefen's mind had just traveled.

The only thing that was a certain; Merick still needed someone who understood her. Someone who could interpret her fears and help guide her natural strengths. There was no cookie-cutter mold for her. No one textbook who would offer the best course on which to study. She needed someone caring for her who could...*relate.*

Relate to being unsure, belonging nowhere definitively, an outsider. He turned back around. *She needed him.*

He reached down and pulled the thicker goose down comforter up from the bottom of the bed. Tucking it neatly around her shoulders, he made sure it covered every inch of her. "Sleep soundly, Merick."

Her hand darted out and grabbed his wrist, stilling him before he could head for the door. He gently rotated his forearm, hoping she would let go and roll over.

She did. She rolled over, pulling his hand with her. He had to follow the movement to not wake her, or snap her wrist. Though he was fairly confident Teakin would opt for breaking it at this point. If it meant not crawling in bed behind his daughter.

"Stay," she mumbled, barely audible, drawing his hand snugly to her chest. Her much too ample chest.

He groaned, but he carefully slipped onto the bed. He did promise to stay with her. Top of his 'to do' list tomorrow was to stop making promises. For he was far too good at keeping them.

*But tonight...*tonight he was exhausted. Tonight her skin felt like silk against his callused hand. Stefen rested his head on the shared pillow, her soft scent enveloping him, coaxing him to join her, to close his eyes.

Just for a few minutes...

This high up, silence had a sound—the wind singing, courting him, paying its respect. It quickened his blood, fed the fire in his soul, called to the magic of legends.
He soared across the land, every nuance from the ground catching his attention. The rustle of the leaves in the trees, the bleating of a stray lamb, an old gypsy snoring against a log.
With the beating of wings, their golden color catching the moonlight, his speed increased. This was what he was born to be. It went back as far as the beginning of time, the link from the past to the present.
Faster and higher he climbed, allowing the anticipation to build, biding his time until dawn would beckon.
The richness of night grew thin, stretching the indigo depth to a bruised purple, dimming the stars. He breathed it in, this fleeting exchange of the moon to the sun, and reversed course.
He dove, racing gravity on a roar—a sound as guttural as his creation, and the aspects of his creation more guttural than he.
Black leather curled back from shining talons as scales morphed into palpable flesh and a foot stepped onto the earth.
He shook off the beast's cloak, his pupils growing round as the morning sun played with the land, bathing it in hues of yellow and pink, highlighting the dew with just a touch.

His lungs filled with the day's warmth as he bid farewell to the
retreating night.
And as the profound darkness crept over the mountains he raised his
arms, allowed his eyes to shut, and fell away...into the crevices of the
dream that called.

"Stefen?" Something soft touched his cheek. "You're dreaming."

He opened his eyes and rolled his head to the side. A pair of multi-colored eyes peered out from thick lashes and white-blonde curls. She looked like something from a fairytale with the untempered morning sun covering her in kisses—winking like stardust atop her skin where she lay.

"You were flying." Merick smiled, pulling her hand back to her chest.

"You were spying on me?" he teased.

"Were you dreaming you were a bird? A hawk?" Her smile grew. "A sparrow?"

Stefen grinned. "A dragon."

Merick's eyes grew round. "How remarkable."

"I've been having that dream a lot lately," he confessed, half to himself.

"I dream I'm a wolf. A white one. Not silver like yours." She paused abruptly, her brows knitting. "How was I able to see the wolf from your dreams last night?"

"You weren't seeing a dream," Stefen said. "You were seeing me. In my animal form."

"How is that possible?" She didn't miss a beat. "Are you a shifter?"

"Sort of." He readjusted in the bed, propping himself up on one elbow. "I am... Rather, *I was* an angel. We can take the form of

139

animals. Our guide animals. Mine is a wolf. I was able to retain that gift after my turning."

"An angel?" Her eyes sparkled with curiosity. "And my uncle turned you?" Merick tilted her head before he could answer. "Is that not a sin?"

"It is. But that's a long story. With more layers than we have time for today." He dodged the question. "I'd much rather hear about this wolf in your dreams."

"It's not nearly as fascinating as being able to actually embody one. But my dreams do feel very real. So much so that sometimes when I wake it's hard to discern which life I'm in."

"Your dreams may be a gift from your mother."

The look on her face turned pensive. "What was she?"

"An archangel. Like myself."

"I'm like you?" She studied him carefully. "Half angel?"

"Yes, though I wouldn't go proclaiming that from the rooftops. Anu will not recognize you as one of them. It's best if we determine what angelic traits you might possess in private for now."

Merick sat up in the bed, sheets falling around her waist, her spine cutting an outline through her t-shirt. Stefen's eyes followed the vertebrae, one by one, up to her long neck. She said nothing for a few minutes. He allowed her the silence. It was a lot to take in.

"What happened to her?" she finally asked.

"She was captured in the battle at Gerra, the one that ended Dante's reign."

"Is that where she met Teakin?" When he didn't immediately answer she looked down at him.

"That's another long—"

"You're only allowed one information escape a day," Merick said. "Tell me. I need to know."

Stefen took a deep breath. "It was a forced meeting."

She stared at him for a long moment before looking away. "I see."

"It's not my place to tell it for him."

"For my father, Teakin?" She looked straight ahead, her ribcage expanding on a deep breath. "I've spent my whole life being lied to and deliberately kept in the dark, Stefen. Now everything about me is changing. At an accelerated rate. I don't think we have the luxury of consideration, or time."

She was right. *Damn it!* Merick came from no ordinary upbringing and she was about to enter a world outside these doors that would judge her harshly for it. *Cookie-cutter rules didn't apply to her.*

"It was an experiment. Your mother and your father. The king wanted to see what their combined powers would create."

The expanse of the room filled the silence between them.

"I'm an experiment then." She let out an uneven breath, turning her profile to him. "Guess they were sorely disappointed. The only trait I inherited was the ability to burn myself."

"Hey." Stefen sat up.

Her gaze drifted to him, just enough for him to detect her fear. "Merick, I beg you, do not dwell on the circumstances of your past. There is nothing in it for you. Besides..." He cupped her chin so that she had to face him fully. "I would rather you focus on the present. Your future."

"It's hard to focus on either, knowing how much hate went into my very existence." She frowned, looking down. "What was her name?"

"Anessa." The word tumbled out of him. "Look at me."

Merick's head lifted slowly.

"She was as beautiful as you. With an ironclad will to match." He stared into those remarkable honey-brown and sky-blue eyes. "She would not want you to relate to her memory with pity in your heart. She was made of truth and light. Think of her as that.

And look for her in the mirror." He brushed a tear from her cheek. "For she lives on through you."

Merick's mouth turned up at the very edges. "I like that." She used the sheet to dab the corners of her eyes. "You have a way of putting things in perspective."

And you, Merick LaGoryen, have a way of making me long to rearrange the galaxies—if it would keep that frown at bay.

"Then I am doing my job," was all he said.

After breakfast Stefen excused himself to deal with some correspondences, leaving Merick and Eirik in the dining room to begin her first anthropology lesson. Rather, her first lesson on the parts of societal history Gerra had chosen to omit.

Merick wasted no time diving right in, grilling her cousin on everything from court politics to what types of animals lived in the different realms. She had always been a good and eager student. Being removed from her place of birth had only intensified that yearning.

A bell chimed from somewhere outside the castle, signaling the passing of an hour, and Eirik decided a tour was in order.

They only made it to the third floor when the tour was cut short. Food—a topic Eirik took very seriously—had come up. Followed quickly by her cousin's shock when Merick explained she knew nothing of the beloved confection he referred to as chocolate.

Her guide left her in a beautiful expansive library to retrieve, what he referred to as "The Nectar of the Gods."

Alone now with just her thoughts, Merick surveyed the impressive room. It had to be over three stories tall, and it smelled of vanilla, freshly snuffed candles, and old leather. The entirety of the space held floor-to-ceiling solid wood bookshelves, each filled with gilt-edged leather-bound books. Sliding ladders provided access to even the hardest to reach manuscript.

Scanning the shelves, Merick took in the different colors of binding-cloth and their smooth textures. She could spend days in here. Reading was her favorite pastime. Something told her she could learn far more about the universe in this one room than she had in the eighteen years she'd spent in Gerra.

She leaned down to better see the inscription on a set of old dictionaries. They dated back fifteen hundred years. She ran a hand over the hand-woven binding. It felt like she was committing some grave sin touching something so valuable.

Her eyes caught sight of another collection of work. Biblical beliefs. All religions. Rows and rows of history. Teachings and theories passed down throughout time. Nothing looked to be barred away in locked rooms, as Thaddeus had done. All this glorious knowledge sat right out in the open; made public for whichever eager minds sought to devour it.

An unbridled excitement ignited inside her. Merick wanted to read every single word written in this room. *This was freedom.* All her life she had been told she should not entertain theories outside of her strict education. She did not deserve to know more than what was allowed. Taught that even pursuing such questions in her mind would make her *different*.

It was all bullshit! Lies created to keep others within limits, enforced boundaries. Gerra, she realized, was a realm based on fear.

Merick turned in a circle, marveling at the new world around her. This was honest. This was where she belonged.

The wind howling against the old stone walls drew her attention to a far window. Something white tapped the panes. *Snow!* Merick had read about the substance, but never in her wildest dreams had she imagined seeing such a thing.

She walked to the crystallized window, her fingers reaching out to touch the cold glass, watching snowflakes sway to the pulse of the glacial winds outside. The leaded glass snipped at the pads of her fingers. She smiled as a cooling sensation spread across her skin.

"I'm going to take a guess..."

Merick pivoted in place at the unfamiliar voice.

A handsome man, refined looking and dark of skin stood by the large leather couch. "You've never seen snow before."

Merick considered him carefully, her formal training at odds with Stefen's warning. Some here would judge her, and find her lacking. "You would be correct."

He smiled warmly, a stark contrast to the world just on the other side of the window. "I'm Sidtric."

"Also known as, Your Grace, King of the Air Folk," Eirik elaborated, as he rounded the doorway with two steaming cups in his hands.

Merick dropped into a deep curtsy. "He's not that fancy," Eirik teased. A thump followed. "Ouch!"

Merick looked up from the floor in time to see Stefen pluck a mug from Eirik's hand. Her cousin rubbed the back of his head. The Air King chuckled, eyes twinkling. "You can just call me Sidtric."

"It is a pleasure to meet you." She smiled.

Stefen came to stand directly in front of her. "Here you go." He handed her the cup he'd stolen from Eirik. "Nothing better than hot chocolate on a cold day in Anu."

"Thank you." Though she wasn't sure thanking someone for bringing you a gift they'd stolen from someone else, after physically assaulting them, was deserving of thanks. She couldn't help but smile all the same. It was refreshing, the familiar bond they shared.

Merick brought the steaming mug to her lips and inhaled the aroma. *God's bones.* Eirik hadn't been kidding. "Smells amazing."

"Try it," Stefen encouraged.

She took a sip. The warm cocoa rolled over her tongue and down her throat. She closed her eyes without thought. "Oh my…"

It was the most amazing thing she'd ever tasted. Was everything in this realm magical? She opened her eyes to find Stefen's gaze glued to her.

"What?" She reached up and dabbed at the corners of her mouth, in case that was the reason for his intense focus.

"Nothing." He averted his eyes.

Sidtric motioned to a couple of worn leather sofas in the middle of the room. "Shall we?"

Merick walked over and took a seat. "Thank you for offering us your home," she said. "I hope to see it one day soon."

"Ash is like family." Sidtric sat directly across from her. "You will always be welcome there." He smiled. "Though perhaps in summer. It's as cold there as it is here right now."

"Much of Earth and Anu has multiple seasons," Eirik explained, taking a place at her left. "They vary depending on geographical location."

Merick had never considered that. She recalled studying it. Only Gerra and Ventus maintained a consistent climate. She added a list of new questions to inquire about in their next lesson.

"I know snow and ice may not be the ideal place to practice Fire-dancing," Sidtric was saying. "But Anu does have impressive indoor training facilities."

"I…" The mere mention of working with fire made her nervous. She involuntarily glanced at Stefen. He gave her an understanding smile.

She looked back at Sidtric. "I can't wait to see them."

"I want to show her around first." Stefen saved her. "Before we start the torture." His lips twitched.

"Perfect," Sidtric said. "I have some new recruits to tend to. Alaric has been most generous in allowing them to train here."

"Hey," Eirik protested, lowering his mug, a frothy white mustache on his upper lip. "I was showing her around."

"I'm taking over. But fear not, I'll save the kitchens for you."

Her cousin tried on a scowl. It didn't work. Merick couldn't help but grin.

"I did see some rather comely new recruits though." Stefen smirked. "Maybe Sidtric can introduce you."

Eirik's attempt at offense changed immediately. Sidtric chuckled as he stood. "Come with me, Eirik." He glanced at Merick. "I look forward to catching up with you more at dinner."

They headed for the library doors, falling into easy conversation, Sidtric clasping a hand on her cousin's shoulder as they rounded the corner. Their voices, so filled with camaraderie you could almost see the shared memories, trailed them down the hall. Like the old friends they were.

Like family.

Again, that feeling. Longing. It washed over her, warm and soothing. The connection they had to one another was a thing of beauty. Same as the one she witnessed last night with Teakin and his brother. It had brought tears to her eyes.

Now...*knowing the story*... These bonds they all shared were more precious than any work of art. It was something to be cherished, to be protected. The most valuable thing in all the realms...

Stefen pushed off the arm of the sofa where he'd been casually sitting and walked over, the movement smooth and unhurried. "They like you."

"How do you know?"

"I know them."

"How long exactly?"

"Since Eirik was born. Sidtric..." He put his hands in his

pockets and eyed the ceiling, making a show of doing the math. "Since before I died."

The look on her face must have done an adequate job of displaying her shock. "You asked earlier why I was turned," he said.

"I'm sorry. I shouldn't have."

"There's nothing to be sorry for. I've just never had to tell the story before." He gave her a crooked grin. "What if I'm horrible at it?"

"I don't get the impression you're inept at very much."

A wicked, taunting smirk curved his lips. "And I am too much a gentleman to disagree with you." He extended his hand.

She took it, more to hide the blush she could feel warming her cheeks than for the assistance. "Where are we going first?" she asked, affecting nonchalance.

He looped her arm over his and led them toward the doors. "Wherever you want Merick. I will show you whatever you want."

From her peripheral she could see a ghost of a smile on his lips.

Stefen took the outside steps at a jog, welcoming the cutting wind into his lungs. Just over the stone railing the world fell away, disappearing into the clouds and drifting snow—as clear as his jumbled mind.

For a split second, he contemplated throwing himself over the edge, just to see if it might bring clarity.

He shoved open the thick wooden door on the fourth level. The winter cold beat him inside, fat snowflakes piling up like soldiers laying siege. They were no match for the heat, melting into tiny puddles before he'd even shaken off the cold. How closely those ice warriors matched his mental state. *Stupid.*

His fucking libido was leading him on a suicide mission. If he wasn't careful he would end up with the same fate as the snow.

Stefen cursed under his breath and headed for the training hall. A good workout would help. At least it would provide some type of release from the tension he'd experienced being in Merick's company for the better part of two hours.

What the fuck was happening to him? Every second he spent with her was like some sort of mental and physical exercise in self-control. Was this some fashion of test? Was it a punishment for being back in Anu as a hybrid? *A Fallen...*

He made straight for the punching bag. Setting an impossible-to-maintain pace he pummeled the dummy. Blow after blow. Not waiting for the weighted return on the downswing, he attacked. Until his heart raced from a different type of adrenaline and sweat beaded his forehead.

Stefen pushed away from the punching bag, grabbed a towel, and wiped it down his face as he walked to the middle of the room. It wasn't helping. He could still smell her. Hear the lilting of her voice as she marveled in the beauty of all he'd shown her on their abbreviated tour.

Such wonder. Such pure joy. She was a kaleidoscope of emotions. And every damn one of them—each brilliant color that marked her soul—had a string attached directly to his heart.

He sat down on floor, pulled his spine up straight, closed his eyes, and tried to locate his center. Meditation might help.

Her image came at him from every corner of his mind. Those soft curls dancing around her face as they stepped onto the eleventh floor terrace. The way her eyes grew round when he explained the each of the paintings that hung in the main hall. How her lips curled, ever so slightly when she really wanted to laugh...

Fuck!

He gave up on finding any sense of calm. Obliterating stuff

was a far better method of escape. He jumped to his feet, stalked back to the sandbag, and delivered four rapid and consecutive kicks before spinning and sticking what would be a fatal blow to the throat.

The bag came swinging back and he lunged to his right, connected again, pivoted and landed an elbow hit to the dummy's face. Someone clapped behind him.

Stefen turned.

Kimberly, an Air-dancer, stood in the doorway, her dark hair pulled neatly to one side and a Cheshire-cat grin painted on her cherry-red lips. "Sweat always looks good on you, Stefen." She looked him over, taking her time. "How long did you plan to keep me waiting?"

Stefen smiled politely and bent to grab his towel. "How have you been?" He dodged the question.

Why? Another anomaly he didn't have an answer for. He'd seen her arrive earlier with the others. He should have been pleased. The flexible beauty was a wonderful stress reliever.

"I'm better now. Finding you in your element, all glistening and primed for battle." The leggy recruit strode smoothly into the room. "I do love watching you train. Be it mixed martial arts..." She passed the punching bag, reaching out to run her fingers suggestively across the dummy's lower abdomen. "Or a sword."

Kimberly stopped in front of him. "Have you had much swordplay recently, Stefen?"

"I wish I could say I was here on a pleasure trip," he started.

"There is always time for pleasure." She licked her fangs. "Why don't you let me remind you?"

"I would—"

She pressed her palm to the front of his pants and cupped his cock. "You would..." When he didn't immediately respond, a pout formed on her mouth. "You're not happy to see me?"

Someone cleared their throat.

Kimberly looked over his shoulder and smiled broadly, releasing him. "If it's not my favorite LaGoryen," she called out.

Stefen turned to see Eirik with a shit-eating grin on his face. There beside him was Merick.

Unexpected embarrassment kicked him in the crotch. He was so caught off guard by the sudden phenomenon he nearly forgot how to speak. That added insult to injury to his perplexed male ego.

Kimberly sauntered over and threw her arms around Eirik, providing some buffer to the uncomfortable situation. He ventured a glance at Merick. Either she hadn't seen, or she was becoming an excellent study at masking.

"This is my cousin," Eirik introduced.

Merick extended her hand.

Kimberly looked at it a beat longer than she needed to before accepting. "Pleased to meet you," she said, with as much sincerity as a snake. "Are you a Fire-dancer too? Like your handsome cousin?"

Merick shook her head. "Not yet."

"Yet?" The singular word was coated in unabashed judgment.

"I'm teaching her," Eirik interjected.

Kimberly, still clinging to his arm like a mink shawl, canted her head. "Better late than never." She shrugged. "My father taught me the art of air at three."

And, we're done here.

"If you will excuse us." Stefen took the three strides it required to be standing beside Merick. "We have training."

"You're training her, too?" Kimberly made no attempt at congeniality this time.

"Merick is half archangel. She will be getting my undivided attention during our stay here." He placed a hand on the small of Merick's back and guided her from the room.

"It's okay, you know," Merick said as the door shut. "I'm used to the assumptions."

"It wasn't okay in your past, and it won't be in your future." Stefen continued to march them down the hall. "Not now."

The conversation clearly over, they walked in silence. And walked...

When they reached a second set of stairs, Merick glanced over at him. His jaw was clenched, spine rigid, his eyes like chips of ice. Stefen navigated them around another turn. *Why?* What had caused this sudden change in his demeanor?

He didn't seem to be in a difficult situation when they entered the training room. Perhaps he was annoyed they'd been interrupted. Some spiteful creature inside her did a cartwheel over the accomplishment.

She immediately shoved that joy aside. It was beneath her. She was here to train. To seek asylum. To do anything, absolutely anything, but feel jealous over that beautiful Air-dancer back there with the male enlisted to train her.

Still... Anger and some strange form of regret dogged her. Whatever emotion it was felt horrible. Almost suffocating. She tried to shake it off but it clung to her like a bad smell.

On the ninth floor, Stefen pushed open a door to a bedroom and walked in. She followed, looking around for any sign of whose room it might be. "I'm going to take a shower." He walked past her. "Then we'll begin."

His room.

"Would it not be best if I waited—"

"No." He picked a book up from atop a chest of drawers and tossed it on the bed. "I won't be long. Start on this."

"I..."

151

The bathroom door shut. Sort of.

As the sound of running water started, the ill-behaved door slowly cracked back open. She quickly averted her eyes. But not before Stefen had discarded his shirt.

Merick looked around the room. A chair was positioned close to the door. But if she took a seat in it, she would have a direct sight-line into the shower.

She didn't realize how fidgety she was becoming until she tripped over a shoe. She supposed bursting from the room, hands flailing above her head, and fleeing down the hall might be a touch overdramatic. Slowly, as if any movement might encourage a draft, Merick sat down.

The bathroom door, clearly conspiring against her best intentions, opened even wider with the sound of the shower door closing. *Damn it!* Her gaze decide now was the perfect time to betray her.

There, through the steam of the glass he stood, head bent, water cascading down his tan back in rivulets—between his shoulder blades, over corded and glistening muscles, making ropes of the strands of wet hair fall around his face. Gods save her... *He was perfect.*

Merick swallowed hard and stood. He would have no idea how far that damn door had crept open. She should shut it.

However, if she walked over to fix it, he might catch her gawking at him. She took a step toward the hall door, her vision at war with her legs' direction. She should leave. He could find her when he was dressed. In her own room. Where she should have been all along.

Yes, leave you fool.

Summoning a strength she didn't know she was capable of, Merick turned to do just that.

And ran smack dab into a wall.

She yipped and leapt backward.

"Merick?" Stefen's voice called out as the sound of the shower cut off.

Speechless, her eyes scanned the wall. Or rather, the large male standing in front of her now. Everything in her being, every instinct she had been born with and every lesson she'd learned, screamed for her to bolt. She took a cautious step back, preparing to do just that.

His fierce hazel eyes tracked the movement. "I wouldn't."

Despite the warning, she took another step away. "Who are you?"

"The better question is who are you?" There was zero curiosity in the question—just one that required the right answer.

Firm hands landed on her shoulders. "It's okay," Stefen said from behind her.

The instant relief at having him near didn't override the need to still voice the concern, "Is it?"

A light chuckle over her shoulder. "This is Alaric Von Emmerich, King of the Anu. But please, don't curtsy to him. He doesn't deserve it." Stefen stepped up beside her, wearing only a towel around his waist. "To what do I owe the pleasure, brother?"

His brother?

He'd failed to mention he was royalty. *A prince, no less.* Just skimmed right over that vital bit of information.

It might explain the glide though. The way he strode across a room, the movement both graceful, and brimming with the perfect amount of unfaltering arrogance. Equal parts danger and charm. Possessing such strength of character, he was dismaying and, at the same time, irrevocably enticing.

Alaric, by contrast, made no attempt at congeniality. He was as straight forward as a falling tree. The two brothers couldn't be more different. "This is the girl?" the king asked, snapping Merick out of her comparison.

"You tell me?" Stefen replied, an invitation more than a question or a retort.

An invitation for what?

The other male continued to stare, his eyes narrowing speculatively. "She's Anessa's."

"What's the first impression?" Stefen pressed.

"I'm standing right here!" Merick's anger flared.

They both ignored her. "She is undeniably angel." The taller blond stepped closer. "It's actually quite strong. Did it get more so when you got here?"

The king finally looked at Stefen, his features softening as he did, his guard dropping just enough... Enough to expose what might be his only weakness. The love he bore his brother.

Those intense hazel eyes now fixed on another, Merick was struck by how beautiful Alaric actually was. One could definitely tell they were siblings. Stefen's features were more refined—as if the gods had made him from poetry. Alaric had a roughness to his beauty—he was conceived from war.

"Seemingly by the second. As are her strengths," Stefen confirmed and glanced over at her. "Apologies for the undignified introduction." He cut his gaze to Alaric, before fully facing her, wet hair dripping onto his much too sculpted chest. "I needed his honest take on your essence."

"Well, I'm not sure what constitutes an *essence take*. As for my strengths, I only learned to hold fire in my hand, without burning myself, an hour ago."

"You did?" Stefen canted his head. "Why didn't you tell me?"

"I haven't exactly been afforded the chance."

"Get dressed," his brother interrupted.

"Not here five minutes and already telling me what to do?" Stefen smirked, unperturbed by the order. "I'll be right back." He nodded to Merick then looked at Alaric. "Don't freak her out with your whole big bad-ass angel king routine."

"Then I guess you should hurry." His brother gave him a flat stare. "My *routine* has a timer on it."

Stefen seemed to take him at his word and headed for the bathroom. Alaric returned to his perusal, looking her up and down, assessing, weighing.

"Is there something else you're looking for?" she inquired, a bit more snarky than she probably should have. "You can smell the angel on me. It's getting stronger by the second. Though we know not what my strengths are." Merick crossed her arms. "Am I missing anything?"

"Yes."

"By all means, please—"

"You should have been my daughter."

She blinked. Once, twice. "Excuse me?"

"Anessa was promised to me," he stated tightly. "Had she not disobeyed my direct orders, entered Gerra, and got herself captured, she would have become my mate. She would have had *my* child."

Not a shred of remorse for her mother in his words, just contempt. It felt like a personal attack. *Because it was.* Stefen's warning again played in her ears. *"Many here will judge you."*

But it wasn't the judgment of herself she was now grappling with. It was the debasement of her mother's memory. It told her everything she needed to know about the angel king's betrothal.

She schooled her face and pushed down the venom-coated words gathering on her tongue. This was not her kingdom. No good would come from going toe to toe with a male that felt he'd been robbed. Somewhere in Gerra, Xavier was likely experiencing a similar irritation right now. His promised mate was gone, too. Left of her own accord.

"Does my presence here offend you?"

He hesitated. She was certain it was not to curb his reply.

"I was promised a royal mate. She was promised a seat at my

side. We barely knew one another." He clasped his hands behind his back. "No, Merick, your presence does not offend. Quite the opposite. You standing here means only one thing to me. My brother is safe. Back where he belongs."

Merick couldn't fault him for that. "We share the same relief then," she said. "My father is safe, too, back where he belongs. There will be no reason for my uncle to send Stefen back to Gerra now."

"Ashdon never sent him," the king said. "I did."

He did?

"To verify that Anessa was indeed, dead," he clarified. "Teakin wasn't even on the radar then."

"I don't understand." Once Stefen confirmed she was gone— why have him return to Gerra and meet with Thaddeus every few years? It didn't make sense. "Because of me?"

"Forgive me for not sugarcoating these next words." *He'd done so with any thus far?* "A half-breed was of no concern to me."

The blunt honesty didn't bother her in the least. She understood court politics. It was the one thing Thaddaeus had taught her well. What wasn't adding up was why Stefen had been in and out over the years. If neither Ashdon nor Alaric had sent him.

"My brother made an agreement with Thaddaeus on your behalf. Ashdon and I backed it. He would be allowed to check in on you every few years. To make sure you were doing okay. In return we would not bring war to Gerra's door for Anessa's death. Part of the agreement was that on your eighteenth birthday your true identity would be revealed, and you would have the choice to remain in Gerra, or to leave. Obviously, none of us foresaw the prince choosing you to be his mate in any of this planning."

Every thought eddied from her head... *But one.*

Stefen had brokered that deal. He'd risked his life on multiple occasions for it.

For a realmless child.

Her knees suddenly felt weak. "Why would he do that?"

Alaric looked at her with such strangeness—like she'd just spoken in a foreign language. "Because he's the best of us all."

Expressions were never forthcoming with Niles, but enough of the apple in his cheeks tightened to let Stefen know he was happy to see him.

It had been almost twenty years. He would hope the lifelong butler of the twelfth floor remembered him. *Fondly.* There had been that disappointing incident with the toads when he was six that could have altered said affection.

He accepted the offered cordial. Niles inclined his head and silently quit the room. Stefen leaned back in his chair and dared a look at the study he'd been actively avoiding since Alaric led them in. He hadn't adequately prepared himself for how stepping onto the twelfth floor would feel. In part because Stefen never expected to be here at all. The fact that he was even permitted back in Anu was astonishing enough. Much less invited to the royal level.

Somehow he'd made it up the grand staircase and down the pristinely maintained hall, lined with familiar paintings, oils so old they brought the past to life—memories chasing him like the voices of their youth, running over the same marble floors.

"You could stay here you know," Alaric hedged, across the mahogany coffee table from him. "Your room—"

"It's best we keep things as they are. I promised to keep a close eyes on Merick and Eirik while we are here."

"Of course."

"Thank you for letting her enter Anu."

His brother watched him, too closely. "Of course."

"Alaric, you've never held back your thoughts." He rotated his wrist, clinking the ice in his glass. "Don't start now."

"She is a lovely."

"Yes."

"Very unique."

"Indeed."

"She's gotten to you."

Stefen raised a brow. "Like a vulture to a carcass?"

"You care for her."

"Well, as you so readily pointed out at dinner earlier, I am a rather sweet fucking sap." Stefen rolled his eyes. "Of course I care what happens to her."

"If you weren't developing feelings, you wouldn't have minded the praise."

"Pertaining to the latter, I've always disliked it when you indicated to others I have a heart." Stefen lifted his glass of Port wine. "Per the feelings accusation, I feel responsible for her well-being, yes. I have been looking in on her since she was a child after all."

Alaric actually snorted. "She is far from a child now."

"So you've noticed?"

Of course he fucking noticed. Any male with eyes would notice.

"You just answered that one yourself." His brother smirked.

"You added a new painting." Stefen looked to the mantle.

Alaric didn't indulge him. "Admit it."

Stefen rolled his head against the back of the chair. "What exactly?"

"You are attracted to her."

"Alaric, I wouldn't have agreed to come up here, if I'd known you wanted to torture me." He sighed. "Merick has a pure soul. She is honest and good. Tell me one male in Anu that wouldn't find those qualities noteworthy?"

"I don't know any that wouldn't." His brother took a sip of his own wine. "But for two vastly different reasons."

Stefen eyed him. "Such as?"

"You know the truth of it." Alaric's eyes grew hard, distant. "There will be those drawn to her natural light. And those that wish to control it, to use it for their own gain. Or worse...to snuff it out. But one thing is certain, they will all seek to benefit from whatever powers she is manifesting."

"No one will be *benefiting* from her." Stefen's fingers tightened around the crystal glass. This conversation was making him increasingly uncomfortable. Leave it to Alaric to call him out on shit he would rather not think about.

Alaric crossed one leg over the other, the tightness fading from his gaze. "She fancies you, too."

"She trusts me," Stefen corrected, looking his brother over for any Victorian clothing he might have missed. "Fancy? Really?"

"Time will prove me right." He sat his glass down on the side table. "On another interesting note. Have you seen the auras around her?"

"I can't see auras as clearly as I used to, but when we entered the Earth Realm, the angel influence was obvious. As was the dragon's. She's finally coming into her own. Now that she's free of that gods awful place."

"She will be quite powerful. If she lives long enough to come into them."

Stefen's focus sharpened on his brother. "What do you mean, if she lives long enough?"

"There has only ever been one other born to a mortal and an angel," Alaric said. "Tobias fell in love with a mortal. She died in childbirth. The child eventually followed her into the grave when he started to make the transformation."

"The boy started to transform into what?" Stefen asked.

"They aren't sure. An animal. His bones broke, and he grew

fangs, but he perished before his human body could complete the transformation."

"His body was forcing a shift? Into his father's guide animal perhaps?"

"I believe so. But it happened over the course of twenty-four hours."

Stefen grew quiet, the blood in his veins going cold. "You think this could happen to Merick."

"Not necessarily. There are differences." Alaric sat forward. "Merick had an angel mother, but not just any angel. Anessa was an archangel. And Merick got her fangs shortly after she turned fifteen, right?"

"She did."

"Tobias's son didn't. He got them only when the transformation started at eighteen." Alaric was watching him like a hawk now. "It's also important to remember that Merick is sired from no regular mortal. She hails from a royal Fire-house. A dragon at that."

"You think bringing her out of Gerra has sped up her transformation?"

"If she's advancing as fast as you claim. She can bend fire now, right? Just in the last twenty-four hours?"

Stefen nodded, mind reeling, sights locked helplessly on the Persian rug under their feet. "She is having dreams about being a wolf." He looked up. "What if her body tries to force her into a shift she can't complete?"

"We will have to wait and see."

"No." Stefen surged to his feet. "We need to reach Ash. Get Teakin here so he can turn her."

"You have to have faith that she is stronger than the only other scenario we have to base her situation on. Again, she is more than half mortal." Alaric continued, as Stefen began to pace. "Besides, to turn her could prove just as dangerous if her angel blood rejects the vampire. There are a lots of variables, Stefen. We need more time to see what she is naturally gravitating toward; angel or dragon."

He stood swiftly and walked over, stopping in front of Stefen. "Listen to me. I have a team studying all options, as we speak. If there is anything that can be found to help her with any transformation, I will find it." Alaric reached out and placed a hand on his shoulder. "I know how much she means to you." A half smile. "Even if you're too stubborn to admit it out loud."

A log shifted in the fire, breaking open and filling the room with a burst of light. "I need to go to her." Stefen didn't bother confirming his brother was right. He *was* stubborn. Merick did mean a lot to him. More than he wanted to admit. "If she is slipping into the wolf when she sleeps, she needs to be monitored."

"My offer still stands. I could have rooms readied up here for Eirik and Merick." Stefen opened his mouth, but Alaric cut him off. "The offer is unending. Should you change your mind."

His brother turned, wings tucked in tightly at his spine as he faced the crackling hearth. "Go. She may need you."

Chapter Nineteen

Merick watched, mesmerized, as Eirik created a thin lasso of fire and whipped it through the air. The angry hiss lashed out at anything and everything, eager to find a connection and spread. It was hauntingly beautiful —a beautiful death.

"It's a delicate balance. You cannot fear it." Eirik opened his palms wide, calling the flame back to him. "But you have to respect it."

"I will never master it as you have," Merick said.

"Ah, but I am not the fire's master." He tossed the flame between his hands. "I'm its servant. I can only play within the confines of what it allows." Eirik snuffed it out. "The second you think to control it, it will try and kill you."

"Why could my father not have been a Water-dancer?" She grinned.

Her cousin chuckled and walked over to where she sat on floor. "Each element has good and bad traits." He extended his arm. "And *you* do not give yourself enough credit. Fire comes naturally to you. That's not the case for everyone."

She took his hand and he pulled her up. "Take Bastian for example. He has been able to control both fire and water since we were little, but water favors him. As it does our mother."

"It's amazing they can control both." Merick dusted off her rear. "But, I'm glad I only have to learn one."

"Don't let my brother hear such flattery." He grinned. "But if you ever really want to piss him off, ask why he hasn't mastered earth and air yet."

Merick had nearly forgotten. Kielyn was the foretold *Chosen One*. Her and Ash's offspring might very well be able to control all four elements eventually. If one, or both, of her cousins possessed such gifts, they might one day rule supreme over all four realms.

Bastian could manipulate fire and water, but not yet air or earth. *Interesting*. Did that mean Eirik could control more than fire? Was there some line-in-the-sand date to accomplish such things?

She was just about to inquire when Eirik's gaze snagged on something over her shoulder. "The blizzard has let up. Want to go out in the snow?"

She swiveled her head. Sure enough, the sun had broken through the clouds. "Can we?"

"Of course! It's part of training after all."

Fifteen minutes later, Merick wondered if she'd even be able to move, as Eirik wrapped a second scarf around her head. "I know I'm new to all this, but shouldn't I be able to see?"

He pushed the wool under her chin. "Stefen will stake my balls to a wall..."

She gave him an arched brow.

"Rather..." His cheeks reddened. "You're not catching a cold on my watch."

She laughed. "I think I get it. Imagery and all."

Eirik's attention went to buttoning his own jacket. Her mind was given time to wander off. To the one thing she definitely shouldn't be thinking about.

Stefen.

After dinner last night, Merick had fallen asleep alone in her room. She'd woken to him resting in a chair beside her bed. Spellbound, she'd watched him. The subtle rise and fall of his chest. The occasional flutter of thick eyelashes against his cheeks, as if his dreams kept him in a state of constant unrest. She wondered what those dreams were showing him in that moment.

Then the rising sun outside her window began its work, bathing him in a gentle glow, filling in details the moonlight had kept secret. Like a sculpture being pulled from the shadows, more of his beauty became clear. The golden color of his skin, the flaxen strands twining through his chestnut hair, the angular cut of his brow, his nose, and jaw. The column of his long neck, the hollow of his throat...

She wanted to touch him there. *Kiss him there.*

Eirik opened the door and the wind whipped into the hallway, nearly stealing her breath and severing the memory. She blinked, her vision fighting to acclimate to the blinding white landscape. "I should have gotten glasses," her cousin said. "Your eyes will adjust in a second."

Certain she could see enough to not fall off the side of the cliff, Merick stepped out into the fresh powder. Trees and bushes lined a path, their branches heavy with ice. Foliage, white with frost, overflowing their flowerbeds.

A world made of ghosts.

Lightheadedness overcame her and she reached a hand out, snagging Eirik's jacket sleeve. "It's like having a buzz," he exclaimed, steadying her, as his voice echoed through the valleys far below. "Something to do with the altitude in Anu."

Merick inhaled deeply. Pine resin and something soft—like sugar cookies cooling on a stove—intertwined in a crisp current of air. A scent like none other.

The smell of magic.

She smiled up at him. "As long as you don't let me roll down the mountain, drunk as a little skunk."

"Not a chance."

Merick followed him further out, the snow crunching underfoot. She marveled in the tracks they left, feeling somehow special. The first to touch this winter day, to be included in its splendor.

She looked to the sky. Snow had started falling anew. Merick stuck out her tongue and caught a few flakes. A thrill went through her, some childlike element tugging on her soul. She removed a glove, bent down, and touched the cottony cold. It was delightful, this snow globe realm made of faceted glass.

She scooped up a handful of it. It was cold and cruel against her skin, but also satisfying. Such a strange sensation. Merick squeezed the snow in her hands before packing more into it. A thrill ran down her spine as she stood.

Without warning, she lobbed the snowball at Eirik. There was surely no better way to start a lasting friendship. It hit him in the back of the head. She squealed.

He whirled in place, a look of genuine shock on his face. It was supplanted quickly with a puckish grin. "Oh, it's on!"

Merick yelped and took off at a run. Albeit a slow run, as the weighted blanket of snow clung to her ankles like tiny shackles. She looked over her shoulder and leapt to the left, just in time to dodge a ball of packed snow.

It exploded against a tree. She squeaked and veered to the

right, getting about twenty more feet ahead before something cold and wet hit her in the back of the head.

Merick laughed and dramatically fell face first to the ground. "I've... been... hit..." She rolled onto her back, reaching toward the sky, summoning her best inner thespian. "Tell them I died a good death." Her arm flopped lifelessly to the side. "A hero's death," she muttered, closing her eyes.

She laid there in wait, listening, fingers curling a ball of fresh power into her hand. Ice crunched nearby and it took every ounce of self-control she possessed not to giggle. *Just a few more feet...*

She could not help her grin when Eirik's shadow blotted out the sun above her. Before she could totally ruin the element of surprise she hurled the snowball.

It made contact with a thud and broke apart, raining cold crystals down on her face. Still she assumed death, half afraid to open her eyes and face the retaliation sure to come.

"In Anu, it's considered treason to pelt a former member of the royal house with a snowball." A familiar voice, one that caused imaginary butterflies to chase each other around in her stomach, drawled.

Merick's eyes flew open. Eirik burst out laughing from where he stood, several feet away.

She stared into star-flecked green eyes. "I never heard you come out." Her swallow wasn't feigned.

A crinkle pulled at the corner of Stefen's mouth, before giving way to a full-on dazzling smile. Merick stared, completely speechless. She'd never seen anything more beautiful.

And the way he was looking at her...*she was the cause of that smile.*

She reached out her arm, proud of herself for the natural segue. Much better than continuing to lay there, entranced—like the world started and ended with that smile.

He looked at her for a heartbeat longer, before taking her hand. "I require an invitation to all future snowball—"

Merick leveraged her weight and yanked him into the snow.

She heard Eirik howling as she scrambled to all fours and pushed to her feet.

She made it one step before something solid encased her waist, and swung her into a snow drift.

"If I freeze to death..." Merick laughed, digging her way toward the light. "You'll have to explain to Teakin it's due to an unregulated snowball war."

The snow cleared, from an effort not her own, and she was tugged from her frozen tomb. "I'll tell him Eirik did it."

"Hey!" her cousin protested.

"He has ears like a bat." Stefen shook his head. "If he ever does turn, all secrets will be known to him."

"Duly noted." Merick dusted off her jacket.

"Are you ready to go inside?" he asked, mischief dancing in his eyes. "Or do you need me to best you again?"

Over his shoulder, others were coming out and actively engaging her cousin, now further down the hill, in a snowball fight. Their laughter filled the quiet winter wonderland. Merick spotted the pretty brunette from the other day among them. *Kimberly.*

She couldn't help but notice the attention the Air-dancer was lavishing on Eirik. Though her sights kept cutting to Stefen. It sat decidedly one way with Merick. Shifty.

She shielded her eyes with one hand and looked up. "I thought the sun was dangerous to vampires in other realms?" She was getting good at this whole 'deflection of unwanted emotions' stuff.

"Only on Earth. And not all vampires. Ash figured out how to manipulate the rays centuries ago, shrouding himself in a protective barrier," he explained. "He's since taught other Fire-dancers the trick."

"Fascinating," she said, catching sight of Kimberly looking their way again. This time the female didn't bother to hide it.

Merick shivered, not entirely from the cold. "Let's get you inside," Stefen suggested.

"Probably wise." As they turned for the castle, a shadow moved across the glittering white snow. A shadow in the shape of wings.

Merick craned her neck back and squinted her eyes. A large falcon drifted effortlessly overhead, its gray wings contrasting with the large white clouds hanging in the cobalt blue sky. The bird shrieked—the wild calling out to the wild—and its head cocked slightly from side to side as it surveyed the ground.

Merick's right arm lifted of its own accord. "She's beautiful."

"Yes, stunning," Stefen agreed, though Merick could feel his gaze on her, not the falcon. "Come now. Let's go inside."

The bird called out again, circling back over the top of them. Merick could no more move her feet than she could take her sights of the expansive wingspan, the tawny feathers blending with the black and gray, the shiny silver of its talons catching the light, blinking like cut glass.

"Merick," his voice was edged with warning. "It will not come to you. It's a wild animal..."

The falcon dove. Straight for them. "Look out!" Stefen lurched for her.

She sidestepped away, her focus entirely on the bird. "She's just curious."

Merick's arm didn't waver as the falcon landed on it. The weight astonishing, the bird's grip firmed around her forearm. "It's okay," she cooed, her heart leaping in her chest. "You only wanted to come say hello, huh?"

"Don't make any sudden movements," she instructed Stefen,

frozen in place in her peripheral. The falcon looked around, keen golden eyes focusing on everything but her. "Isn't she magnificent?" Merick said, exhaling a careful breath.

"Yeah," he said, something like disbelief and unease in his tone. "It's not hurting you, is it?"

"Not at all."

The bird turned its regal head and looked at her once, before pushing off and taking flight. The weight of its presence still on her arm, she watched it climb higher into the sky. Until it was no more than tiny speck on the horizon.

"I think that's a sign," she said.

Stefen stepped up next to her. "Of?"

"I'm headed in the right direction."

Stefen closed the door behind them, shutting out the merriment from the snow-covered mountainside. Turned out even Sidtric's most talented recruits were still kids at heart. He hoped that joy would continue when they met Anu's inner court tonight.

Two young bright-eyed angels, gloves in hand, sailed by as they took the next hall. Merick's eyes tracked them. They were likely the first she'd seen. Other than Alaric.

"You noted their difference," he commented when they were out of earshot. "How?"

The older an angel was, the more discernible they became to other immortals. The 'angel glow' being one of the more obvious differences. But those two that just passed couldn't be older than Merick and Eirik. They should blend easily. A helpful trait for the young.

"They have an energy about them," Merick replied. "Much subtler than you and Alaric."

"Alaric and me?"

She looked sideways at him. "Theirs is far more subtle, but I can still pick out the angel."

He stopped moving. "Are you saying my brother's energy and my own is similar?"

She turned and faced him. "Why would it not be? You're brothers."

"Yes, but I was stripped of the lion's share of angel powers when I was killed and made vampire. I didn't know..." He paused, his gaze traveling to an unfixed point in the flooring.

Could it be? Was she picking up on something that hadn't been altered? Some link to his past angel self he'd long thought gone. She touched him arm. "I can try and show you?"

He looked up.

"As you did with me on the plane," she said. "You took me somewhere quiet and peaceful. Some place your mind created for me." Her gaze traveled to where her hand touched his forearm. "Maybe I could try and let you feel what I feel when I'm around you."

Could she? Could he let her? Did he want to know what she would find if she did?

His inner turmoil must have been transparent for her eyes met his again. "Do you trust me?"

His question to her in the woods.

"I do." His words came out barely a whisper. "Show me."

She closed her eyes.

And just like that...he felt every smile he'd ever given her, saw the flecks of color in his eyes as she saw them, heard the tenor of his voice in a way he could never imagine it sounding. Until the essence of who he was became clear—through her lens.

Deeper still, beneath the barrage of sensations, *the glow*. The ethereal luminosity of the angels. More than that. *The colors of his house.* He'd never seen his own aura before, but she was right; it matched Alaric's in intensity. Marking them as royalty.

Marking them as family.

The vividness shifted, taking on a darker hue. A color so rich the depth seemed limitless. *The dragon.* It pulled from the recesses of the mind, coaxing, stirring some unknown part of him.

He felt the connection slipping. *Not yet.* He needed to know more. He clung to the feelings. This was his past, his future, his fate...

"Stefen."

Not yet.

He saw himself on the mountain ridge in Gerra, pulling her up, felt the adrenaline in her veins, saw the wonder in her eyes. Not from the near fall...*for him...*

It morphed. He felt her hand in his, making the leap. Hitting the ground on Earth. The wonder she beheld when he shielded them from impact. Before her eyes even opened to see the new realm. *Protected.*

"You have to let go."

In the plane. *Attraction, confusion, unbridled connection.*

"Let go!"

He was sleeping, she was watching. Again the desire, but something else...

Destiny.

He was shoved backward, with such force he stumbled a step.

His eyes were open now. Staring into the wide multi-colored ones of Merick's, her breathing coming as hard as his.

"I'm sorry... I didn't know..." he stammered. "I couldn't."

"It's okay." She shook her head, white-blonde curls falling into her face, hands shaking. "I asked you to trust me."

She seemed to notice her body's reaction at the same time he did. Her hands smoothed down the front of down jacket. "I was foolish to try."

"You didn't just try." He couldn't look away from her. As if some part of him was afraid she'd fade from his life like a mirage. "You—"

A door was flung open and two arguing guards marched out of the training facility. Stefen and Merick watched them bicker down the hall. When they rounded the corner Merick spoke first, "I have something I want to show you in the training room."

She looked at him. "Something safer."

"Of course."

Probably best. He could unpack all he'd learned later.

"Will you time me?" Merick jerked her chin toward the obstacle course when they entered the gym. "I'm almost certain I am faster today than I was yesterday."

"Well then, let's test your theory."

Stefen's thoughts circled back to the falcon as they walked over. "When you were five, you fell in the cage at the palace with the tigers." He broached a new, safer, subject. "That must have been a terrifying experience."

"It was. But I was more scared for them. Everyone running down the hill. I knew, in that moment, something bad would come from my curiosity." She looked at him. "No one understood what was happening. They couldn't see the cats were not going to hurt me."

"And you *did* understand?" he asked. "That they wouldn't harm you?"

"Yes."

"How does a five-year-old know such a thing?"

"Instinct I guess." She smiled a secret smile—light years

beyond her age. "How old were you when you learned Anu was a double-edged sword?"

He had not told her of his childhood; all he had endured at the hands of a power-hungry court. Did she know? Had she seen it somehow when they touched?

"Twelve."

"You learned your own kind could not be trusted." Merick faced the agility course, hands behind her back. "As did I."

She moved to the starting line, shucking off her jacket. "Ready to time me?"

The course was designed for immortals, the hardest in the compound. "Eirik let you train on this one yesterday?"

She nodded, lowering into a starting position.

"Why?"

"The mortal courses were too easy." She smirked.

The unexpected show of confidence did something to him— heated his blood, dragging to life every aspect of him that was male.

Stefen shook off his sudden wayward thoughts and focused at the second clock, mounted on the far wall. "Ready. Set. Go!"

She set a pace that would impress a seasoned immortal and cleared the first five hurdles like a deer. Then scaled the tower wall with nary a misstep and disappeared over the other side. His eyes found her again, shimmying up a rope. She swung her body across the widely spaced hanging bars, landing like a cat, before sprinting toward the back loop.

"I suppose there's only one question now," Alaric intoned behind him. "Is her progression due to the dragon influence, or the angel?"

"There's no telling." Stefen kept his sights on Merick. "Dragons are only supposed to emerge when they discover something worth fighting for. Something they love. But she...she is unlike any of us."

"That's not entirely true." His brother stepped up alongside him. "She's a lot like you."

"I was born an immortal, not a human."

"You still died."

Thirty-six seconds. Stefen took his eyes off the clock when her foot hit the finish line.

He looked over at his brother. "A failure of mine you will never forgive."

"I don't fault you brother. In ways, I envy you. You're free of all the political bullshit."

Stefen didn't get the chance to reply as Merick came jogging up. "How did I do?"

"Thirty-six seconds," he said. "Impressive."

She beamed up at him. "Guess what my time was yesterday?"

"What?" Both he and Alaric ask in unison.

"Six minutes and forty-five seconds."

The brothers glanced at each other, neither revealing their shock. "You are advancing quickly, my dear," Alaric praised, the portrait of courtly apperception. "Why don't you head to the showers and meet us back here when you're done."

Merick gave him a mortal military salute—Eirik must have shown her—and headed for the locker room.

"We're fucked," Stefen grumbled when she disappeared inside.

"Which brings me to my reason for coming down here," Alaric said. "I have someone coming to the ball tonight that might be able to shed some light on her unique predicament."

Stefen raised a brow. "Who?"

"No one I want the High Council to know about." He turned for the door. "There's appropriate attire in your rooms. The masquerade starts at seven."

Alaric paused at the door. "Don't be late."

Chapter Twenty

GERRA

Thaddeus had weighed every option. Only to come to the conclusion each one was just as likely to get him beheaded. He slipped in through the servant's entrance.

The objectives were simple. Zander wanted Teakin. The prince wanted Merick. The queen wanted her son to wed Merick as well.

The logistics, however, were complicated. The king was already well on his way to ruining what little respect he had gained over the last nineteen years. Thaddeus had no reason to interrupt him. Zander was no longer a reasonable ally.

Thaddeus did not know enough about Xavier to speculate on his true nature and motives. *A missed opportunity.* Regardless, he could not risk his neck on an untested theory. The prince was also off the table.

That left the queen. Katarra was as unpredictable as they came, but she was magnetic. As with all sociopaths, there was a certain charisma. A sort of singular confidence and utter conviction that made others flock to them. Katarra had it in spades. She was just like her father; deriving more from her enemies than her friends.

Thaddeus moved quietly up the staircase to the royal wing of the palace. His paid guard was waiting, as planned. He nodded and turned down a short hall, stopping in front of the queen's chambers.

According to his informants, Katarra had been entertaining the ambassador of Etteroes, an attractive male with an even more attractive bank account. The ambassador had left her bedchambers at three a.m. each night this week. No doubt to make it back to his mate before she woke and noticed him missing.

For all her inconsistencies, at least the queen took her pleasures on a schedule. Thaddeus hoped tonight would be no different. It was always best to approach the female in question when she was in a decent mood—after sex or killing.

He turned the handle on her door. The sound of running water proved the guard had been right. Thaddeus entered, took a seat, and waited.

The faucet shut off a couple minutes later and the queen emerged. Her cat-shaped eyes immediately landed on him. Unperturbed, she continued towel-drying her hair. "Interesting."

When she didn't expand on the statement, he began, "Forgive the intrusion, Your Grace. I needed to speak to you in private."

Katarra tossed the towel on her bed. "You're not my type, Thaddeus. Too..." She waved a hand up and down. "Dull."

She took a seat at her vanity. "Although, this little visit is rather unexpected." Her gaze watched him in the mirror as she picked up a hairbrush. "You might prove fun in bed."

"I am here on more pressing matters."

Her eyes twinkled. "More pressing than sex?"

Inwardly, he counted to ten. This was standard Katarra. She enjoyed toying with others. Like a cat trying to see how much pain could be inflicted before the mouse's heart gave out.

"Did the king tell you who escaped the other day?"

"I suppose it doesn't matter what lie he told me if you're here to dispel it." She dragged the comb through her glossy tresses. "Who was it? Someone more important than a simple slave, I'm guessing."

"Considerably."

"Don't bore me, Thaddeus. I kill people that do that."

"My daughter left with her personal guard." He watched her reflection in the looking glass. "I hope the prince won't be too disappointed."

She turned slowly in her chair. "You mean, the angel hybrid escaped with her *real* father."

Thaddeus schooled his features. "Zander told you?"

A sly grin. "I've always known she was not yours. She's too perfect." She stood. "There was no way your hag of a mate birthed both of them."

Katarra sauntered over to him. "It was only a simple matter of figuring out who her biological parents were. So I paid attention to those around her. How they interacted with her." She leaned in. "Did you forget that Teakin and I share the same mother?"

He'd underestimated her. *Greatly.* "You play a marvelous game, Your Grace."

"Stop stroking my dick." She straightened. "How are you, and my inept mate, planning to get them back?"

"The king will gladly go to war to reclaim Teakin." If risk could be measured, this one was epic. He steadied the course. "I have asked him for time to think of a better plan."

"A better plan?" She walked back to the bed. "Such as sneaking into my bedchambers in the dead of night?"

"You need to be a part of the discussion. Something my grandson was adamantly against."

Katarra took a seat on the edge of the bed. "You fear he is slipping into the same obsession our father did. You're here looking to switch loyalties." She crossed one leg over the other and leisurely bounced it on her knee. "Let's call it what it is."

This was it. The definitive moment that would either elevate him, or see him dead.

"I do not fear that he is slipping. His obsession will end just as your father's did. I am only here to stop him from disgracing our realm in the process. Teakin cannot be brought back."

She tilted her head. "Because he would kill the king? Your grandson."

"My grandson is dead either way." Thaddeus rose to his feet. "My only concern is for the preservation of Gerra's reputation. We can't afford to keep losing leaders to previous slaves."

"What can you do for me, Thaddeus? That I cannot get others to do."

"You know the answer to that. I underestimated you once, Your Grace. I shan't do it again. I am here to offer my assistance, my allegiance, my mind." He kept his eyes trained on hers. "I'm here to help you kill your brother."

Chapter Twenty-One

ANU

M erick stared at the dress bag like it was a sparring partner. There was to be a ball. It wouldn't be her first. She knew how to dance.

Where then was her sudden apprehension stemming from? She eyed the boxes below the dress. *Why so many?*

Merick took a breath and walked over.

She squatted in front of the armoire and wrapped one arm around her knees, the other reaching out to tip up the edge of a box. *Shoes.* She flicked the lid off and lifted a pair of sparkly heels. They were gorgeous, closed toe and covered with what looked like crushed rose-gold diamonds. She sat them down carefully, afraid they might break.

Merick plopped down on her ass and crossed her legs, eager now to see what was in the other packages. She opened the next box and immediately felt a warmth bloom in her cheeks. *Undergarments!* The likes she never imagined existed.

A black lace corset, backless, except for a narrow band that would strap together at the waist. Why would it button so low? What support did that offer? Merick held up the bra up to her chest. "Good lord!" She struggled to see with her chin pressed to her chest. It wouldn't cover half.

She set it aside and looked at the panties. If you could call them that. They were little more than an expensive looking tissue.

She picked up another box. A box inside a carved wooden box. She lifted the lid. *Makeup!* Merick had never worn makeup in her life. She wouldn't have the first clue how to apply it.

The thought of screwing it up brought her right around to that initial nervous feeling. Why couldn't there have been at least one female at Northdom castle who could have taught her? She nudged away the makeup box with her toe and looked up at the dress bag. She might as well get it over with. It couldn't be more complicated than everything else.

Standing quickly and holding her breath, she unzipped it. Glossy black silk peaked out at her. Merick carefully pulled it from the bag. It was stunning. Thin straps leading to a dangerously low scooped neckline and a fitted bodice. A wide band of satin rose-gold trim at the waist was the only color on the midnight black ball gown. A diaphanous waterfall of dark material cascaded from it, pooling on the floor.

She hung the dress on a hook and stepped back for a better look, her hand running the length of the material, noting a slit in the silk. *Not a simple slit either.* The damn thing ran from the waistline to the hem.

The daring revelation had her apprehensively turning the dress around to look at the back. "Oh my!" Now she knew what the low corset back was for. There was no back to the gown.

Merick took a step back. She could not pull off a look like this. A gown like this required a confidence she didn't know how to manifest. It belonged on a female like Kimberly.

She picked up the only two boxes she hadn't opened yet and sat down on the edge of her bed. Starting with the bigger one, she untied the bow. Her breath caught.

A black half mask swirled with rose-gold and inky-black crystals sewn into the lace, two velvet ties attached to either side. "Gorgeous." Merick placed it back inside its box.

"Last one." She picked up the smallest box. "Not sure how much more I can fit on my body." She removed the lid and gasped.

Her shaking fingers lifted the necklace slowly, exposing link after link, row after row of black diamonds, all falling from and connected to a single choker. It had to be a foot long, she noted, before looking at the dress. It would eclipse the neckline.

Inspecting the intricate piece of jewelry more closely, she realized the strands only hung from one side of the choker. Her gaze darted back to the ball gown. It was not meant to fall in the front. The multiple strands of diamonds would hang down her back.

Merick carefully laid the necklace in the open box and sighed. It was all too grand. She couldn't help but feel like an impostor.

She flung herself back on the bed. Kimberly would surely know what to do with all of this. The image of the Air-dancer with Stefen again came to mind. The familiarity they clearly shared... It made her teeth grind.

"Yeah, fuck that." Merick sat up abruptly, surprising herself with the sudden emotion—a healthy mix of anger and determination. She pulled out the device Stefen had given her and hit one of the three buttons on it. The one that said *Alaric*.

Someone had left her all of this, surely it came with assistance. In Gerra, there were personal stylists hired for formal occasions like tonight. Surely, Anu would have something similar for the masquerade attendees.

The contraption in her hand buzzed twice before the king said, "Hello Merick, is everything okay?"

"Yes. Sort of." She stood up and paced to the window. "The dress and accessories I have for tonight are beyond gorgeous. I cannot wait to thank whomever let me borrow them."

"Not borrowed," he replied, his voice deep and smooth. "They are yours."

"I can't possibly accept. It's too generous. But I would like to thank whomever went to the effort."

He chuckled. "You're welcome."

Her mouth dropped open. "I...It is...Thank you."

"Is that why you rang?"

"Er, not exactly." She walked back to the armoire, secretly challenging the dress to produce an assistant if it was hiding one and save her the next mortifying words out of her mouth. "I was wondering if you might know anyone in the facility that is good with hair." *Good with hair?* She pinched the bridge of her nose. "Someone who might be able to help me with mine. I'm all thumbs, you see. And I want to make sure I get it secured just right."

"Of course." She could hear the grin in his tone. "A stylist is on her way there now."

Great, now she'd insulted him by insinuating he wasn't a proper host.

"Thank you. It's just such a beautiful dress. I didn't want to not do it justice."

"You were well within reason to ask," he said, just as a knock landed on her door. "See you tonight, Merick."

She sat down the device and walked to the door.

A round-faced, middle age woman was waiting on the other side when she opened it. "Well now, aren't you a pretty one. What glorious hair. I'm Ethel." Her eyes scanned the room, landing on the dress bag. "Shall we get to work?"

Merick wanted to hug her. "Yes, pleased to meet you. I'm Merick."

She stepped to the side and the woman passed, towing two large cases. "Let's start with your makeup." Ethel set one case on the table beside the armoire and turned to face Merick. "Have a seat here, dearie."

She motioned to the stool in front of the vanity and shuffled over to the hanging dress. "My, my." Her withered hands inspected the gown. "That's some back. Exquisite design."

She walked back over to Merick. "I have just the plan for your hair now."

"You don't think it's too daring?" Merick ventured. "The dress."

"Not for a masquerade ball," Ethel said, pulling cosmetics out of her bag. "It will be perfect on you. Appears to be cut exactly to size."

"Oh, I have makeup that came with it, too." Merick pointed to the box. "If you think you can use any of it."

Her eyes lit up and she picked up the box. "Let us see what we have then." Ethel opened the top and smiled wide. "Why, someone spared no expense. These colors are perfect for your complexion." She looked at Merick, her eyes crinkling at the edges. "Whoever commissioned this is a very close study of you, my dear."

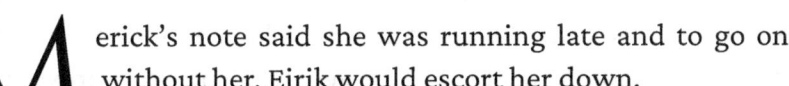

Merick's note said she was running late and to go on without her, Eirik would escort her down.

Stefen adjusted one of his cuff links as he rounded the corner into the formal parlor. Many of the evening's guests were mingling there. He spied Alaric, a head taller than any of the room's other occupants.

Stefen headed in his brother's direction, just to have his progress halted by a glass of champagne. "Here you are," Kimberly purred up at him from behind her demi-mask. "I took the liberty of grabbing two."

"Thank you." Stefen accepted the glass. "You look nice tonight, Kimberly."

She grinned. "You recognized me?"

Of course he recognized her. Her mask barely covered her eyes and she wore next to nothing. Unless she suspected he had become blind or stupid; it was hardly a disguise.

Stefen took a sip of champagne. He'd been spared her advancements yesterday. Could his luck hold out?

Funny though, he didn't remember her being this aggressive in the past. Regardless, nothing enticed him from forced attention. The whole bait-and-troll routine reminded him of his younger years at court, and the games everyone had played.

He forced a smile. "What sort of male would I be if I didn't?"

"I would hope I had made a lasting impression on you." She leaned in, so close her nose brushed his neck—breathing him in. "Perhaps after the dance, I can impress you again."

Her perfume assaulted him. The scent was like repellent now, clinical and insincere. Stefen could almost smell the lab technicians who had created it. Had he once enjoyed this?

Curious gazes started landing on them. Stefen lifted his flute again. The action encouraged her to step back.

What a strange reaction he was having now. He'd fucked her six ways to Sunday the last time he had been in Switzerland. Her perfume hadn't been so *heavy,* and he certainly hadn't discouraged her attention. Quite the opposite. He'd been very attracted to the new recruit then, taking full advantage of her generous hospitality in various rooms of the Air compound.

Stefen checked himself; perhaps he was going blind or becoming stupid. This female was offering her talents up on a silver tray and all he wanted was for her to leave him be. *Quickly.* Before Eirik brought Merick downstairs.

"Brother." Alaric spoke from behind him.

Thank the gods! Stefen turned. "Alaric. I was just coming to find you. Have you been down here..."

His words trailed off when he caught sight of her. There. Merick was coming to a stop at the top of the stairs, the silk panels of her skirt swaying, slipping over the bare skin of her exposed thigh.

The whole room went as quiet as the grave.

Stefen's eyes continued upward, to the belt at her waist, so small he felt sure both his hands could encompass it. On up...*gods' teeth*...her proportions could put an hour glass to shame. Her delicate shoulders, long neck... Those heart-shaped lips.

She tilted up her head, making the crystals on her mask dance in the candlelight when she smiled to her escort. Her hair was pulled up, artfully piled atop her head like a crown. Soft ringlets had been left loose to frame her face. *Those wondrous eyes.* They locked onto him when she looked back at the room.

Something inside him shifted—sundering something vital he'd kept locked. The crowd started to open up, everyone moving to the side. As she moved toward him, he noted a black diamond choker caressed her throat, sparkling like adamant. But she wasn't moving.

He was.

Stefen bridged the distance between them, cutting through the throng of partygoers like an arrow. *That dress...* His vision tunneled in on the outline of her body under the thin silk material. It left nothing to the imagination, yet it hid secrets better than a locked vault.

He felt his head give a slight shake, an attempt to focus. *Yes,* he needed to focus. On anything but her body. His lips were moving before he was sure she could hear him. "You're breathtaking."

A hint of blush rose in her cheeks as she smiled. "You're mighty dapper yourself."

Alaric stepped up beside him. "You look lovely tonight, Merick."

"Thank you." She swept her hands down her dress, appreciatively. "For all of this."

His brother inclined his head, and for some reason Stefen wanted to punch him.

"I wouldn't give him all the credit," a familiar voice said from behind them.

He and Alaric turned.

Marzalla strode up, a pleased smirk on her wine-stained lips. "Alaric has superb taste, but it's not as good as mine."

"I don't know," Stefen teased. "He did always make a fuss over the length of his royal robes."

"Alright, brother," Alaric interjected.

Marzalla laughed and dragged Stefen in for a hug as he said, "I thought you wouldn't be back for another week."

"I had to come back." She released him and wrapped her arms around Eirik, then looked at Merick. "To meet the newest member of the LaGoryen bloodline."

"It's nice to meet you." Merick smiled as Marzalla stepped away from her cousin.

Mar didn't answer at first. Stefen knew what she was doing. *Reading Merick's aura.* "It's truly amazing," she finally said. "For centuries it was just me and your uncle, alone in the world. And now look." Her eyes grew glassy. "He has his whole family back."

The Icelandic beauty pulled Merick into a hug. "And for the record," she whispered loud enough for them all to hear. "I was right. The rose-gold complements you splendidly."

Merick was grinning when Mar let go of her. "I am forever in your debt."

"Have they seen the back yet?" Marzalla asked, glancing from Stefen to Alaric.

Merick shook her head no, a telltale warmth blooming in her cheeks. Stefen prepared himself.

"I have," Eirik admitted, looking slightly uncomfortable.

Mar's grin grew and she twirled a single finger. Merick obliged, turning in place.

Stefen nearly choked. It was completely backless. Except for the long strands of diamonds sweeping her spine. It was an odd feeling being suddenly envious of a gemstone.

"Oh!" Marzalla clapped her hands. "It's stunning."

"A dress fit for a queen," Alaric praised.

This time Stefen had to physically stretch his fingers to keep them from balling into fists. He wasn't a member of the royal court any longer. Surely clocking the king would only get him kicked out of the realm.

Merick looked at Stefen, seeking his approval. The innocent action—that she wanted his validation—was world-ending. It sent a wave of possessiveness through him. *This female...* She was unraveling him at a pace he couldn't keep up with. Wasn't sure he wanted to.

He should say something. Anything. Because that was normal, and normal was most certainly what he should be right now. He should definitely *not* proclaim that dress was entirely too sexy and march her back upstairs to put on sweats. Most assuredly, he should not pluck the eyeballs from the skulls of every male in attendance who was looking at her.

And without a doubt, he should not confess her sheer closeness sent his world spinning, drew his senses as taut as a bowstring, and set every nerve in his body on fire.

Stefen smiled. "It's perfect."

H er feet were starting to hurt but she wasn't about to let that stop her. Merick was having the time of her life. She had hardly stepped a foot off the dance floor all evening as masked male after masked male asked for her hand.

However, she still hadn't received an invitation from the only one in attendance she truly wished would. Stefen had been unusually elusive all night, choosing to stand along the wall. Likely avoiding her.

Which she, a hundred percent, understood. She'd made a fool of herself when she let him into her head this morning—let him see the effect he had on her. She wouldn't fault him at all for putting some space between himself and her school-girl affections.

Nevertheless, she'd tried twice to make it over to him, but she had failed each attempt. Someone new was always right at the edge of the ballroom floor when she was escorted off, requesting the next dance. And perhaps it was just her giving nature, the fact she was having so much fun, or the in-between sips of champagne, but she couldn't refuse them.

Unlike her first ball, tonight she felt free of judgment, able to really experience the evening for what it was, mysterious and thrilling. Merick threw her head back, laughing as her current partner spun her around the floor to a lively quickstep.

They passed another couple and her partner stuck out his tongue. Clearly, a secret competition between him and the other Air-dancer. "Are we winning?" she asked.

"Very much so." He smiled affably. "But it would be hard for me not to with such a skilled partner."

"Well then." Merick grinned, conspiratorially. "Let's make it an indisputable victory."

His eyes twinkled with the challenge and he picked up the

pace. Faster and faster they sped until Merick could no longer make out the faces along the edge of the dance floor. She giggled with glee as he turned her twice in hold. It was the extra push they needed and they sailed past his friend.

They were now on the longest section of floor, no one in front of them. The perfect opportunity for her partner to lead any number of patterns he so choose. He did just that, shifting them into a right box when someone bumped them. Hard.

Their hold broke apart, and Merick went spinning out of control across the floor. She had no choice but to go with the speed, or else she would end up on her butt. She closed her eyes, hoping others got out of the way, preparing for impact if they didn't.

Turning, turning...

Suddenly, she was scooped up, a firm hand on the small of her waist, another securing her right hand in dance hold. Then, with a superb redirection of the centrifugal motion, her new partner steered her back on course. Merick opened her eyes to see who her savior was. But she didn't need to. She knew that scent—storm clouds and the sea.

And she knew his touch, as if it were branded on her very soul.

"Stupid boy." Stefen growled, all the while weaving them gracefully in and out of the crowd of dancers.

"Thank you," she offered breathlessly, as he guided them with easy into a switchback counter-spin that stilled the swirling room. "But it wasn't Brian's fault. Someone ran into us."

"Had *Brian* not been traveling at the speed of light, he would have been able to handle a little nudge." He looked over her head, sights trained on the dance floor.

"I am not sure how it looked from the wall you've been holding up all night, but it didn't feel gentle," she sniped, irrationally irritated at all sorts of implications in his statement.

His gaze cut to hers, but he said nothing, continuing to move her through the dance. Every movement was exquisite, decisive, and thrumming with power. "I wanted to give you space," he finally said, gaze returning to scan the ballroom. "You were having such a good time. You deserve it."

Merick stared at him, the hard set to his jaw, the bob of his throat when she didn't answer. "Give me space? From what?"

"From me."

She didn't understand. He was clearly not himself tonight, but was he embarrassed for her? For having a crush on him and being naïve enough to expose it? Was he avoiding her to save her from making another foolish mistake, like the one in the hall this morning? A million panicked thoughts assailed her. Had she sabotaged their friendship?

Merick pushed aside the deluge of doubt. If any of her fears were valid, she would rather hear them now. "Has something happened?"

"No," he sighed. "Nothing that concerns you."

He spun her in hold and she thought she might die of relief. But that didn't help him. Something was still amiss. "If you're not having a good time, Stefen, it concerns me."

He grumbled, "I would be having a better time if all these idiots would stop drooling over you in that dress."

"My dress?" She blinked. "You said it was perfect."

"It is. Ignore me."

"I can't."

"Why not?"

"Because you're you. You're Stefen." She implored him to look at her again. "Do you really not like the dress?"

He did look at her, those sea-green eyes fierce and clear. "I don't enjoy other's looking at you like they would like to have you as their own."

Merick almost faltered a step. One part of her brain—the rational side—told her this was a practical statement. One her father would approve of. The other side—the stupid side—hoped it was a jealous confession. That perhaps something of what she'd shown him earlier had resonated within him as well.

She went with the former. "Well, fear not. I have no intention of *being* anyone's."

"No one's?" His gaze was direct, holding her eyes as he waited for her answer. "Not one male here has caught your attention?"

Merick swallowed hard. She'd never told a lie in her life. She tested it out in her mind. *No, there is no one here that has caught my attention.*

Vinegar, the words tasted like vinegar. It felt like a betrayal. *Or worse*...the death of something pure and honest. The handsome male holding her in his arms deserved so much more.

"There is one." The tempo of the music slowed and dancers took their final turns on the floor. "Only one."

Stefen moved them in time. "Who is he?"

He lowered her into a dip, his body bowing over hers, taking her completely off her feet and casting her in his shadow. "Who is the only one, Merick?" Her name rolled off his tongue, rough like gravel and thick like honey. "Say his name."

The rhythmic pounding of their hearts was the only sound now. "Stefen."

She lifted her chin and brushed her lips, ever so softly, across his. It was the boldest thing she'd ever done. It was reckless, presumptuous, *insane...*

He kissed her back, tender and soft. A question and an answer. Her entire world went still—retreating footsteps, soft flickering lights, the fading notes of the orchestra—the stars stopped spinning with the whisper of that kiss.

He withdrew, just enough to look her in the eyes, his own bright and full of light. The sounds of the ballroom returned. His mouth parted slightly. "Say it again."

"You." She smiled. "You are the *only* one."

—◦—◦◦—◀◦🌑🌑🌑◦▶—◦◦—◦—

S omething inside him changed the moment her lips touched his.

For a second Stefen couldn't breathe, his hybrid instincts roaring this was the one. This was who held the key.

When he kissed her back, a hunger—a demand—overtook him. So voracious it blinded. A power, staggering and ancient, threaded itself around his bones, pushing into his veins, consuming, chanting; this is your fate.

She is your mate...

He slowly lifted her to her feet. "Your eyes," she said, wonder coloring her tone.

He didn't need a mirror to see what she meant. Stefen was seeing the world around him set to fire. He was viewing Merick painted in gold.

His gaze lifted, landing immediately on his brother, who watched from across the ballroom.

Alaric's arched brow fell with the realization.

Stefen closed his eyes, mentally willing the beast to stand down. Control, he had to find some. *Quickly.*

"Stefen?"

He breathed in, exhaled slowly, and opened his eyes. The colors of the room were as they should be.

"We need to have a conversation with my brother. Posthaste."

Alaric was already walking toward the adjacent parlor doors, slicing a path through the crowd, a shorter guest trailing him.

Merick did not argue as Stefen led her across the floor. The shock on the faces of those they passed was barely concealed behind their masks. He could only hope it was from their public kiss.

Not the golden slitted eyes of the newly awoken dragon.

H is brother did not waste time with introductions when the doors behind them closed. "Does she know what is happening?"

"How would she? I'm still fighting to process it." Stefen looked at the elderly gentleman beside his brother. "Who is he?"

"Apologies," the bent and haggard male said, removing his mask. "I am Trophonius."

It was rare to see an immortal so old in appearance. He had skin like cobwebs, gauntly hung over muscle and bone. His eyes were sunken deep into their sockets, but the pewter irises were clear, shining with a wisdom few could possess.

An oracle.

Stefen looked at Alaric. "I thought you took no stock in them?"

"Let's just say, you convinced me to keep an open mind," Alaric intoned. "Trophonius has been in my secret employment for the past several years. You can trust him."

"Tell me Alaric, how does an oracle serve a king when they are not allowed to impart their secrets?"

His brother had little patience, and if there was one thing Stefen had learned from Pythia, oracles required it. Of course, it was also against angel law to interfere in others' lives. What exactly were two beings, destined to do little more than watch, doing together?

Stefen eyed his brother. "Don't tell me you are looking for a fast way off of the throne?"

"Trophonius does not inform me of anything that will occur, nor do I ask." Alaric clasped his hands behind his back. His, 'my tolerance is running out', stance. Stefen knew it well. "He merely imparts knowledge of the past when I require it."

"A healthy dose of skepticism is natural in you, Your Highness," the oracle addressed Stefen by his stripped title. "A smart way to live. Unfortunately, you also possesses a sentimental heart. The two will forever be at odds with one another."

"Is it my skepticism or my sentimentality that wonders why you are referring to me by my former title?" Stefen put to him.

"Ah, politics. Always reinventing the rules." He put his own question back to Stefen. "Do you really want me to answer that?"

"No."

The oracle inclined his head to Merick, a smile defining the deep ridges of his face. "Another sentimental one. But your intuitiveness is known to none before you. You're like a story that hasn't been written. But the writer dreamed of you at the birth of time."

Relying heavily on his knobbed cane, he took a cautious step toward a chair. "Go on, Your Highness, say what you need to her. We will talk when you are done." The oracle slowly lowered himself into the seat. "Best to not keep a woman waiting."

"I would leave you two alone, but we don't have the time," Alaric stated. "Now that Trophonius is here, we have a vast number of matters to discuss. But first you need to address what happened in that ballroom."

The asshole was right. They didn't have the luxury of time. Or apparently privacy.

Stefen squeezed Merick's hand. "The thing with the eyes..." He faced her. "There's an old folklore—"

"One that's evolving with every second that passes on this story," Alaric said flippantly.

Stefen ground his teeth. "I'll dare you to recall how your provoking ended with Ash some years ago."

"It's okay." Merick looked up at him, ignoring the budding sibling feud. "I can handle it."

"I know you can." Stefen exhaled, thankful for many things.

None more so than keeping him from strangling his brother at present. "You know my turning was not typical, as I was already dead. The only way it was at all possible was due to Ash being what he is. A dragon. That, and a kindred spirit sort of thing."

"Is that the reason for your eyes? Is it also the cause of your dreams?" Merick stared intently, processing. "Are you a dragon, Stefen?"

"Only as of a few minutes ago."

"I don't understand."

"A dragon only emerges with the discovery of true love," Alaric took over before Stefen could structure a reply.

"For the love of the gods, shut up!" Stefen snapped.

Merick's eyes danced back and forth between them. "Stefen?"

"I've always known you were special." Stefen focused on her, his breathing uneven. "But I was unwilling to admit it was more than that." He took both her hands. "I guess part of having the soul of a dragon comes with being unmercifully hardheaded."

"Understatement of the century," his brother quipped.

"It would be a thing of beauty," Stefen said, too exacerbated to threaten death. "To be allowed the basic dignity of professing my desires. *Without* an audience."

"Come, Your Grace." Trophonius tapped his cane on a chair across from his, indicating the king take a seat.

Thankfully, for Alaric's sake, he did.

"Stefen." Merick grinned, a pretty dusty rose color dotting her cheeks. "I just kissed you in the middle of a crowded ballroom. I think I made my desires fairly clear."

He stared at her. "I don't think you understand."

"I felt it, too." Still holding his hands she coaxed him to sit beside her on a sofa. "I have wanted you, in a way I couldn't explain, since we made the leap from Gerra. I know now that my increasing powers were not the only thing heightened."

Her luminous eyes grew misty, searching his. "Kissing you

tonight might have awoke some mythical creature in you, but my heart was already invested." She smiled. "There is only one for me, Stefen. You."

He had so much he wanted to say. So much he wanted to do. The dragon in him was screaming to kill the other two room's occupants and be done with it. To lay her down and claim every inch of her as his own.

He swallowed hard, pushing the primal side down, relying on every ounce of courtly behavior bred into his bones demanding he pull his shit together.

Stefen leaned in and kissed her forehead, then he brought his lips to her ear. "That's the last chaste kiss I ever intend to give you."

"Fabulous," Alaric concluded, the word coated in glorious boredom. "Now, moving on to her predicament."

"What predicament?" Merick asked

Stefen cast a frozen glare in his brother's direction. "Regarding your transformation." He refocused his attention on Merick. "Since we are not sure what aspects your body might gravitate to during it, we have to prepare for any possible complications."

"Such as?"

"Perhaps I can explain?" Trophonius politely spoke up.

Stefen nodded his consent. The older male went over the issues, detailing the same limited history Alaric had relayed earlier. Through it all, Merick sat utterly still beside him. He rubbed the inside of her wrist with his thumb when Trophonius moved on to the possible outcomes if the transitions didn't go smoothly.

"It will be easier if the angel side takes over," the oracle stated. "There are theories."

There it was, the annoying aspect of oracles; knowing the damn future, but honor bound from telling it. "What theories?"

"The eclipse," Trophonius replied. "If she can encourage her body to shift during it, the angel part of her will embrace the transition."

Merick scooted to the edge of her seat. "When is the next eclipse?"

"Friday," Alaric said.

"What happens if she can't?" Stefen asked.

"She must." His brother kept his gaze on him. "You need to prepare her. For if, or when, her body tries to shift."

"That's not a plan." Stefen stood abruptly, looking pointedly at the oracle, the dragon raking claws down the inside of his chest. "Tell me what happens, damn it!"

Trophonius's eyes grew round in their sockets right before Alaric moved in front of him.

Stefen cocked his head, his vision narrowing.

A gentle touch and her fingers curled around his. "It's okay." She stood. "Look at me, Stefen."

He did, and an instant calm enveloped him, pulling away the anger—like the moon slipping beneath the sea. "You can teach me," Merick said. "You will show me everything I need to know to complete the transition."

"What if I can't?" His voice broke on the words.

"You can." Her half-smile wrecked him. "This is our fate being forged. We don't need anyone else to tell us how it's going to unfold."

Chapter Twenty-Two

TUSCANY

TWO HOURS LATER

H is body sliced through the water, muscles stretching long as they propelled him under the glassy surface. The silence, the weightlessness of another world, the utter stillness of being submerged had always called to him. Soothing, here in the depths of calm water—after a lifetime of fighting each breaking wave.

Teakin's head broke the pool's surface at the far end, the past beating inside him like a second heart.

Breathing in deeply, he inhaled the mixed aromas of the conservatory's lush flora and fauna. His brother's distinct voice, weaving down the cobblestone walkway toward him, was issuing someone an order.

Teakin placed his hands on the edge of the swimming pool and hoisted himself out. "I'm not sure why you don't take advantage of this space more." He grabbed a towel and started drying off. "I'd make it my bedroom."

"You'll have to fight Kie for it." Ash walked over and pulled out a chair. "And I'll go ahead and warn you; redheads don't fight fair. As for me," he took a seat, "this whole *king* business is rather time consuming."

"Have I mentioned how relieved I am it ended up being you that has to wear that crown." Teakin wrapped the towel around his waist and took a seat opposite his brother. "You always were the more orderly one."

"Yeah, well, don't think that your return from the dead won't be discussed at the next Council meeting." Ash smirked. "They may decide, now that the heir is alive, they don't need the spare."

"Perhaps we won't tell them."

They had only been reunited a few days, but he'd already seen just how valuable Ash was to this realm. His brother was made for ruling. He was smart, cunning, and respected by all. Teakin couldn't be more proud.

He looked over at the water. "I admire you. But I don't envy your obligations."

"That makes two of us." Ash chuckled, the sound bouncing around the vast atrium, before drifting away on a current of air. "I spoke to Stefen."

Teakin's gaze swung to him. "How is Merick?"

"She's good. Advancing quickly." He smiled. "Quite the budding Fire-dancer apparently."

"Really?"

His brother nodded. "Just took getting her out of Gerra."

A sudden, but familiar remorse crept in. Teakin had missed her first steps, her first word, countless birthdays. So much time stolen. His jaw clenched.

"I can't imagine." Ash voiced all that Teakin hadn't said.

"Soon enough, brother. Soon enough." He changed the conversation to the most important matter at hand, "What did Stefen say about the transformation speed?"

It had taken a near act of the gods to keep him from heading straight to Anu when Ash informed him yesterday of the potential dangers involving Merick's shift. But his brother assured him she was in the most capable hands. There was nothing he could do in time anyway. After Teakin had got over blaming himself, he turned that angst into training with Ash's recruits, later apologizing for sending most to the camp medic.

"Alaric, a total pain in the ass that you'll learn to like eventually..." Ash shrugged. "Maybe... Has called in someone with better insight. If Merick can will her body to start shifting into her guide animal on the next eclipse, her angel side should take over and make the process easier."

Teakin sat up in his chair. "She can do it. When's the next eclipse?"

"Next Friday." Ash steepled his fingers, tapping two.

Most would interpret the action as simple contemplation. Teakin knew better. "You used to do a similar thing with your hands when father would make you wait in the hall outside his study, while he pondered your punishment for whatever horrendous act you'd committed." He smiled. "What is it? What's got that big brain churning?"

"Somethings never change." Ash grinned wistfully but ceased the tapping. "We are no longer the only two living dragons."

"What do you mean?" Teakin had seen Bastian only an hour ago. "Has something happened with Eirik?"

"It's Stefen," Ash said.

"How?"

"I imprinted many of my own traits on him when he was turned. We had no idea at that time what those traits would be.

Over the years, the only real difference seemed to be that he got stronger. Nothing to denote any fire gifts." He paused, as if going over past indicators. "I never imagined it might be possible for him to evoke the dragon."

"He has your DNA?"

"No, testing shows he took only molecules that applied to my abilities, not ancestral ties," Ash explained. "His base makeup is still angel."

"Did he say what prompted it?" Teakin asked.

"He did." Ash looked him dead in the eyes. "Your daughter."

Teakin nearly choked on his own saliva. "Excuse me?"

"I had a similar reaction." Ash watched him carefully, like one might a coiled rattlesnake. "Stefen is not the *falling in love* type. I can't imagine the trail of broken hearts he is going to leave behind him."

Teakin shoved out of his chair, sending it skidding backward on the stones.

"That might have come out wrong."

"Your prodigy is a whore?" He fumed. "A whore that seduced my daughter?"

"Not a whore per se." Ash spread his hands, as if the obvious laid between them. "You have seen him, right? They literally fall in his lap."

"You're not making it better," Teakin warned.

"Here is what I do know," his brother said. "Stefen is a good guy. Ten times the male I was before finding my mate. Ten times as charming too." Ash stood. "However, if Merick woke his inner dragon—it's real. You know what that love is like."

Teakin sighed, running a hand through his wet hair. "I only know it as it pertains to a child."

"Then you're just going to have to trust me, big brother. Be it paternal love, or that for a mate, it is real."

"Does Merick return his feelings?" He held out hope.

Regardless of how *swell* a fellow Stefen was, Teakin was not ready to give up his baby girl so soon. Especially after just getting her back.

"Are you sure you can handle the truth?" Ash stuck his hands in his pants pockets and rocked back on his heels.

"Simply slice off my head and be done with it."

Ash grinned, enjoying the torment entirely too much. "She feels the same for him."

Teakin reclaimed his chair by throwing his body into it, feeling physically ill. He had known this day would come. Merick was as beautiful on the inside as the outside. It was only a matter of time before some male wanted to make her his.

If he was being honest with himself, it could be worse. She could have been trapped in a loveless marriage, bonded to a family of monsters. Teakin exhaled, his gaze tracking a puddle on the stones trying to find its way into the moss and mortar.

"If you're done losing your mind." Ash interrupted his downward spiral. "We need to discuss the logistics on entering Gerra. Timing will be critical. There's to be a festival in honor of the prince's engagement. It would be the ideal time to strike, unless Zander thinks you're bent on retaliation. If he does, he'll be prepared."

Teakin's head snapped up. "Xavier has chosen another bride?"

"That's the narrative their going with," Ash said baldly. "Unless it's a trap, of course. To make us think all is quiet on the western front."

"It's impossible to know what that lunatic is playing at." Teakin scoffed. "His delusion with himself is an unprecedented wonder. One he fights hard to maintain."

"Not unprecedented. His father shared the same delusions. Any fruit off that tree will eventually fester and rot."

"I'm surprised he hasn't already tried to find us," Teakin said, taking a breath. "His obsession with torturing me went too deep. Too dark."

"They need a pawn to enforce their power over us."

"He won't let it go." He looked up at his brother. "He'll try to regain control."

"That's why we're going to kill him," Ash stated, a glint in his eyes. "We're going to kill all of them."

Chapter Twenty-Three

ANU

*The soft scents of the carefully manicured garden were swept away,
replaced by the organic aroma of the ripe forest. The wolf padded
through the wooden gate that barred and bridged two worlds. The safe
with the feral.*
One step—soft white fur pulled back from pink flesh.
Two steps—two legs took the place of four.
Three steps—ten human toes sunk into the soft moss.
*Four steps—she looked back at the white picket fence with its fragile
pristine yard...*
And chose the depths of the wild.

Merick woke when the mattress shifted under the weight of another.

Her senses opened up like a flower to the sun as his essence wrapped around her. In that moment, she couldn't even recall what unhappy felt like. A funny giddiness, edged with elation, and a healthy dose of desire was all she knew now.

But, as much as she wanted to roll over and bombard him with questions and kisses and tell him about her dream—how she felt certain it was a sign she could make her transition—he needed to sleep. Instead, she laid there quiet, listening for the sound of his breathing to change, for the subtle shifting of his muscles to slow.

It took only seconds for slumber to claim him. She envied him that. Perhaps she should have Alaric lecture her for hours each night. Merick was fairly certain exhaustion would come easy after playing court to that king.

She smiled, nearly laughing, wondering what the two brothers and the oracle had discussed after the ball. Whatever it was, it had been of enough importance to rob her of her first evening alone with her future mate. Stefen had apologized profusely after escorting her back to her chambers, promising a normal, quiet life, once the threat of her looming transformation was behind them.

Falling asleep had been nearly impossible after that. Strange fears kept plaguing her. What if she woke up in Gerra, all of this having been a dream?

It wasn't a dream. He was right here beside her. She was safe.

Merick rolled to her side and watched him, the slight part of his lips, the gentle rise and fall of his chest. She wanted to be that close to him, to be the air he breathed in, be the breath his lungs expanded with. There was something astonishingly intimate about sleeping with a male, not just bedding one. The fact Stefen could let down his guard around her, trust her as she did him—it spoke more about their connection than sex ever could.

Though she very much wanted to test that theory. *A lot.* She was no stranger to sexual euphoria. Merick also knew better than to even contemplate how many females had enjoyed Stefen's body.

But this...shared sleep...it was limited to just him. This male who was to be her mate. The one she'd love until she was nothing more than dust blowing whimsically over open land.

She exhaled, sliding her gaze over the planes of his torso, from his broad shoulders to the chiseled cording that created a V on his lower abdomen. All muscle and bone. Such strength contained in one beautiful depiction of masculinity. It was hard to fathom such a tender heart beat beneath.

Her thoughts pulled her back to the narrowing of his waist, and the way the ridges of his hipbones dipped beneath the thin cotton of his pajama bottoms. Some inherently female part of her tightened to the point of pain.

Two loosely knotted ties were all that separated what lay beneath the material and her desperate eyes. *Shameless.* Her curious fingers reached out, her brain screaming at them to heel.

Slowly, she ran one finger along the waistband of those damned pants. His stomach muscles tightened and she lifted her hand, fingers hovering above his tan skin. Holding her breath, she waited. Gradually, the tension eased from his body. Then her traitorous desires betrayed her again, the need to feel him too great.

This time she traced the stitching from the waistband down, down, further down the mounded edge... The material rose, filling out those seams and stitches until there was no denying what lay just under the cotton—no longer asleep.

Merick's breath caught in her throat. She could no more control her hedonistic impulses than she could stop the snow from falling outside. *Sleep was overrated anyway.* She ran her index finger over the rigid line of his impressive shaft. It jerked at the contact.

Her gaze darted to Stefen's face. Emerald green eyes were locked on hers, glazed and foreign. He said nothing—no amusement, no excitement—nothing but a predatory intensity focused on her every movement.

With exaggerated caution, Merick untied the string at the waistband of his pants. He continued to watch her as she pulled the material over his hips, exposing the proud, thick, length of him. Her mouth went dry.

The ache between her legs increased as she tentatively reached out and touched him. Satin stretched over steel. Her fingers wrapped the girth of him.

Her gaze found his again. His eyes were bright, his ferocity a living thing, simmering in the air between them like steam rolling off lava. They tracked her every breath.

She stroked the length of him and he hissed. It sounded like torture. *Or a warning.*

For a split second, Merick wondered if she had made a mistake. She was playing with fire. *Would he be so willing to help her escape this time...*

She lowered her head, her gaze pinning him to the pillow as she licked the broad width of him. He fisted the sheets, white-knuckled. Merick became aware of every nerve in her body when she took him fully in mouth. Her vision lowered and she moved on him, one hand taking hold of him at the base, the other splaying out over the rippling muscles of his abdomen. She wanted all of him, wanted to become full of him. She wanted to make him burn the way she was burning, until they were nothing but heated wax, molding to one another.

A knock fell on the door.

"Stefen, get up." Alaric's voice was muffled, but too clear to ignore. "We need to talk."

Merick slowly lifted her head. Stefen's eyes were closed, a look of pain etched on his handsome face as he silently mouthed out something in Latin. *Was he counting?*

"Nine. Ten." He wordlessly said, eyes opening. "Give me five minutes."

"Two." Alaric countered from the other side of the wooden door.

Stefen grabbed Merick's wrist and pulled her up his chest, kissing her thoroughly in a clash of tongues and teeth—a dance, unbounded and feral—a claiming.

A growl rippled from him as he broke the kiss. "He won't leave until I exit this room."

"As little thought as I would give to that right now," Merick grinned, "I would like to have your undivided attention our first time."

"Only the first?" He arched a brow. "What the little exhibitionist."

She pushed off him and rolled to the side. "What can I say, you're bringing out a rather primal side of me."

"Good." Stefen smirked and threw his legs over the side of the bed, rising in one graceful movement. He tied his pants at the waist, still gazing at her intently. His next words were a lethal caress as he said, "Feel free to wake me up like this every day."

"This better be the most important thing you've ever needed to tell me." Stefen snarled, taking the lead and marching down the hall.

"Did I interrupt something?"

"You know what, Alaric." Stefen pivoted, continuing his pace backward. "Thank you."

His brother had the decency to look shocked. "Thank me?"

"I was heading down a path I'm not yet ready to travel. So, thank you." Stefen turned back around. "For assuring the family tree doesn't produce fruit anytime soon."

Alaric's tread on the polished marble faltered behind him. "Who are you?"

"A changed male, brother."

Alaric jogged the two steps it took to reach his side. "You're taking this seriously."

"Of course I am." Despite the affront on his moral code, he could understand the quandary. He had no moral code.

Until last night.

If it were possible to ignore the dragon, he couldn't deny his own heart. Even before Merick had gone and provoked the damn beast, Stefen had known. Known she was the one. The one he had been searching for over the centuries, restlessly biding his time, waiting... *for her.*

She deserved so much more than anything he'd given anyone before her. Not because she was some innocent, with delicate sensibilities and limited experience. She was daring, wild, impulsive—unchained. But she was likewise, wholly feminine, refined, warm and steadfast. A paradox.

A treasure.

No, he would set the pace and take this slow. Even if it killed him. Which right now... His balls were making the case that it might.

"I dare say, I'm impressed," Alaric said.

"Don't be. My newfound ethics were almost undermined by a five foot nothing, wisp of a female back there," Stefen intoned. "Care to place a bet on how long my best intentions shall endure?"

"You're not mated yet. There is always time to slake your thirst."

Stefen cut his gaze to his brother, selecting his words like throwing knives. He held them, bit back the retort, as a strange realization replaced his anger. It wasn't a deliberate provocation on Alaric's part. His careless suggestion came only from practical indifference.

His brother had never known love and as a king, he likely

never would. He could not afford to dabble in emotions. Alaric had only one partner in this life—the crown.

For the first time ever, the gravity of that changed the lens through which Stefen viewed his brother. Alaric was a pillar of strength, the definition of courage, as unmovable as the stone lions that guarded the castle gates, and... Stefen pitied him.

They took a right into a study. Sidtric was waiting, relaxed in a green velvet chair, legs crossed, the portrait of courtly equanimity —despite the black fighting leathers he wore and the tattoos whirling over the sides of his shaved head. He smiled, pearly white teeth accentuated against his dark skin. "I knew she'd be the one to tame you."

"I'm not sure why you didn't feel the need to share that revelation sooner."

The warrior turned king chuckled. "Telling a man what is right in front of his eyes does not make him see."

"I'll remember to be as helpful a guide if you ever find yourself blind." Stefen narrowed his eyes on his longtime friend.

"We heard back from Ash." Alaric closed the doors behind them, getting straight to the point. "They plan on attacking on Wednesday, during a festival."

Stefen feared this was what he was being dragged here to discuss. It also explained why Ash would have gone straight to Alaric and Sidtric, over trying to reach him down their shared bond. His maker wasn't looking for an opinion or a debate. He was looking for support.

"What are we to do?"

"Nothing," Sidtric answered. "We wait for word the deed is done."

"Then what?" Stefen walked to the sofa. "Just watch and see who jumps on the throne next?"

"That's been decided," Alaric stated.

"Who?" Stefen voiced the question, despite the niggling feeling he was not going to like the answer.

"Thaddeus."

"Fuck no!" Stefen spat. "Thaddeus is a vindictive, cruel, calculated monster."

Alaric scoffed. "He already sounds better than the current occupants."

"Gerra will be in a state of emergency after this goes down." Sidtric leaned forward in his chair. "Every overreaching royal in that godsforsaken realm will be in competition for the throne. Thaddeus, as big an asshole as he is, is well-respected enough among his peers to be accepted." He spread his hands. "And the easiest of the monsters to control."

"For how long?" Stefen looked from his friend to his brother. "How long do you think he'll play the puppet? Because I know that male better than any of you. He's too damn smart to not already be thinking five steps in advance."

"We only need him in the interim," Alaric said. "Once everything has calmed down in Gerra, we can be rid of him too."

Stefen ran a hand through his hair. "What happens if they don't succeed?" he challenged. "What happens if they get killed?"

His brother didn't hesitate. "We annihilate the whole fucking realm."

Going back to sleep after Stefen left was as attainable as calling a cat and having it listen. Thoughts of his tanned, toned body and that hooded sultry stare... Merick thought she might go blind if she didn't find a distraction.

She pulled her hair back in a ponytail, threw on a pair of track shorts and a tank top, and headed for the training facility. She wanted to get there before the other recruits and take out some of her pent-up tension on a punching bag. She started to jog. She needed to sweat. Merick took a hard right and nearly collided with Kimberly.

A giggling Kimberly. Exiting Eirik's bedroom.

The slender brunette smiled beatifically. "If it isn't your cousin."

Eirik appeared in the doorway behind her, a dusty rose creeping up his throat. "Er, Merick. What are you doing up at this time?"

"Getting a head start on training." Merick continued on, shuffling past Kimberly.

"I'll meet you there in just a few," Eirik said over the Air-dancer's head.

Merick gave a quick wave as way of acknowledgment. She did not want to think about what they had been doing together at this early hour. "Oh, Merick?" Kimberly called out gaily.

It would be rude to ignore her. Merick turned back.

"A few of us are going to a party further up the mountain tonight. Want to go?"

"I shouldn't. I have too much training."

"Oh come on, cuz," Eirik chimed in. "We all need a little fun."

Don't you know it. However, Merick was pretty sure anything involving Kimberly would not end well. Why she would even invite her was perplexing. Perhaps she wanted in her good graces, now that she'd set her sights on Eirik.

"I'll think about it," she lied, and continued her trek down the hall.

Thirty minutes into Merick's work out, Eirik sauntered in. "You left the ball early last night."

"I think I might have overdone my training yesterday." Another white lie.

She was becoming quite good at them apparently. A habit she needed to break. Something about withholding the truth had always made her uncomfortable. Like covering dirt over a secret that would eventually be excavated.

She gave him a wry smile. "Sooo, Kimberly?"

"Is not a topic I want to talk about with you." He gave her a pointed look. "Let's work on the technique we started exploring yesterday." His own way of changing the subject.

"Fair enough." Merick lifted her hands and held them about two inches apart, fingers spread wide, and closed her eyes.

"Eyes open," he reminded. "You need—"

"To see the trail," she finished for him, opening her eyes.

Focusing on nothing but the thin air between her palms she called back the memories of her past exercises. Summoning them from both, fear and awe. That's what fire was to her, elation and terror. Merick never wanted one without the other.

Concentrating, she planted the seed—a tiny ember glowing between her palms.

Whispered the desire—a hint of smoke curling around her knuckles.

Painted the flame's recollection, the swirls and light—they danced in the space between her hands, traveled through her, moved with her...for her.

"That's it," Eirik praised. "Contain it. Don't let it slip."

She obeyed, her gift listening in turn. He continued his tutorial; when to increase the intensity and when to ease up; how to feed it and how to disarm it.

Merick was exhausted, sweat dotting her forehead, by the

time the last spark fizzled to ash, drifting away when the training room's ventilation system kicked on. Eirik took pity on her and called it a day, promising to touch base with her later about the invitation to join them.

She went back to her room, took a hot shower, and curled up on the bed with a book she'd snagged from the library. When she woke the sun was setting.

Merick looked over at the clock and sat straight up. She had slept for six hours!

She reached for the tabella Stefen had given her to reach him. A note appeared on it. *"Sleep as much as you can. Your body needs it. I will meet you after dinner. I have some things to take care of. Stefen"*

What things?

The tabella vibrated, startling her. *"Come out with us later. Eirik."*

Merick felt herself smile. Despite knowing she shouldn't go, it did feel good to have others wanting to include her. *"Maybe next time. Thanks for the invite,"* she mentally sent.

Her stomach let out a sound that was utterly terrifying. She hadn't eaten today. *How could that be?* She supposed accidentally invoking a dragon from a sexy archangel turned vampire and vowing to be said dragon's mate...might make a girl forget to eat breakfast. Food was definitely in order.

The dining room was empty when she entered. Of course it was. She was an hour late.

She was just about to head to the kitchens when a sweet looking maid appeared. "Are you Merick?"

"Yes. Sorry I'm late. Can I grab a quick snack?"

"Nonsense." She shuffled over. "I was told you may arrive

later." The female smiled and pulled out a chair. "I have a dish waiting for you."

"Oh?" Merick took a seat.

"Yes, Sir Stefen instructed us before he left."

He left! Merick tried to hide her shock. "Did he say when he would be back?"

"I'm afraid not, dear. He left with King Alaric," she said, before trotting off to the kitchen.

Something felt...*off.* She took out her tabella to send Stefen a note asking where he was, but stopped. She was overthinking this. Simply concerned because she'd been caught off guard. Merick pushed down the restless feeling. He had said he would meet her after dinner. She set down the tabella.

Thirty-five minutes later, Merick's plates had been cleared, her stomach was full, and she was still waiting. Maybe he had meant after, after, dinner? The tabella pinged, shooting an adrenaline spike through her, and nearly causing her to drop the device.

She quickly displayed the message. *"Heading out in ten. Sure you don't want to come? Eirik."*

Merick sighed and replied, *"No, but thank you for the offer."*

She set the tabella on the white linen table cloth. Five more minutes ticked by. Still, no word came from Stefen.

Merick picked back up the device. *"Have you left yet?"*

Her cousin's response was instant. *"Nope. Change your mind?"*

"What should I wear?"

A couple seconds passed. *"Are you in your room?"*

She pushed her chair back from the table. *"I'm heading there now."*

"Kimberly is dropping off a dress."

Merick stared at the tabella, debating the best response as she took the stairs. *"I have something. Can you give me ten minutes to get ready?"*

"She's already heading your way. See you on the main level in ten."

Merick pocketed the device and stepped onto the ninth floor just as dark locks sailed around a corner at the other end of the long hallway. Sure enough, something was hanging on her door. *Something small.*

As she got closer, the article of clothing didn't get any bigger. Merick reached her chamber and lifted what she was to wear tonight. Two strips of sequined material. A tiny black skirt and a low cut V-neck blouse with sheer sleeves.

She hurried inside before she could start formulating an excuse. Her cousin was right, she *did* deserve to have fun. After the last week, she'd certainly earned it. What was she going to do here? Besides worry about where in the Four Realms Stefen was. Merick continued her pep talk as she changed, held her breath, and turned to the mirror.

Holy mothers above!

The skirt, if indeed it could be classified as such, barely covered her ass. And the shirt... Merick looked down. She could see her navel! Or, rather, she would be able to, if her breasts weren't blocking the view. The corseted top was so snug it displayed them like a serving tray.

Oh, no, no, no. Merick reached for her discarded jeans. Her tabella buzzed. *"Hurry up, slowpoke."*

She inwardly cursed. There wasn't enough time to rethink this. She tossed the denim and made for the vanity, dabbing some gloss on her lips, before grabbing the heels from last night.

"On my way," she replied, slipping on the shoes and making for the hall.

Rounding the circular staircase at the fifth floor, she sent another message, this one to Stefen. *"Heading out with Eirik. Be back later."*

Merick continued to traverse the twisting stairs. Somewhere

around the second floor she felt it—a thrill. The same giddy feeling she used to get when heading out to a party after school.

Finally... a memory from Gerra that didn't make her instantly sad. Maybe tonight would be the first step in reshaping the way she viewed her past. Perhaps she had just needed a little shove to see it. *Or a little black dress.*

Chapter Twenty-Four

kay, she might have grossly underestimated what constituted a *party* in Anu.

Merick wasn't sure why she had assumed they would be going to some old barn or hidden cave, sneaking in pilfered bottles of booze and hiding out like teenagers. It occurred to her, as they descended the rock steps etched into the side of the mountain that was her only point of reference. Memories from an old life in Gerra, which now felt like remnants of a distant dream.

This was her new life. She was about to enter an establishment, the first one of its kind she'd sought admittance into, as her true self. Carefree and able to make her own rules. Be her own person. Here she could ditch the false pretenses of her past and introduce herself as she truly was; a Fire-dancer.

Merick only wished her skin shared the same enthusiasm. She pulled the fur jacket closer around her chin. "I promise it's warmer down there." Eirik nodded toward the conservatory built into the side of the mountain, comprised of steel and floor to ceiling windows, some thirty feet below.

Supernaturals of all variety were gathered in groups on the snowy ledge, warmed by fires lining the perimeter, the flames swaying to the heavy bass resonating from the club. Merick could see through the glass roof that just as many were inside. Some were dancing, others mingling. In the center, an energetic bartender flipped flaming bottles behind his back, while a cook roasted spiced apples on a spit, drizzling them with cream.

"The wind cuts from the north." He pointed. "The club's protected on three sides."

He was right. As soon as they made their way another fifteen steps down, the howling wind let up and Merick could again feel her nose. "Once you start dancing, you'll discard that coat in no time," Kimberly said over her shoulder as she eased through the first crop of partygoers lounging along the edge.

The Air-dancer plucked a smoke out of someone's hand, took a drag, and handed it back before sashaying on. Merick stayed glued to Eirik's heels. As usual, she was one of the smaller individuals here and her vision quickly became obscured when they pushed deeper into the fold.

"I'll grab drinks," her cousin said over the thumping music.

Kimberly motioned to three large cages suspended off the side of the mountain. Inside the cages, supernaturals gyrated and grinded to the approving catcalls of those on the dance floor. "I'll be in there." She winked. "Care to join me, Merick?"

"Er, maybe later."

Kimberly shot them a smirk and disappeared into the crowd. Merick followed Eirik to the bar, the path clearing for him. He acknowledged many as they passed. Seemed her cousin was quite popular. She wasn't surprised, he was impossible to not like. But here tonight, with his windswept curls, jacket collar flipped high on his neck and a playboy smile at the ready, he truly looked the part of a king's son. Striking, powerful, a bit rakish, but easy to be around.

Eirik gave Merick the only seat available at the bar and leaned across, hailing the bartender. The male came right over with a ready smile. "Hello, LaGoryen, the usual?"

"You know it." Eirik looked to her. "What will it be, cuz?"

"A vodka. On the rocks, please."

Her cousin grinned approvingly. "Nice."

"Expecting something fru-fru out of me?"

"I'm learning not to underestimate anything from you." His eyes drifted up.

Merick followed his visual trajectory. Kimberly had gotten into one of the iron cages and was giving a performance that had half the males on the dance floor foaming at the mouth. Judging by her cousin's slack jaw, he shared their sentiment.

Drinks landed on the bar top behind them. Merick grabbed one and lifted it up. Eirik tapped his glass against hers and tossed it back.

The alcohol burned going down, like a spiritual awakening or a saging. She held up her empty glass. Within seconds, another was in her hand.

Merick finished it off just as Kimberly slithered back over, dabbing a napkin to her shimmering chest. "That was needed."

"And very much appreciated." Eirik nodded, taking a sip of his drink. "You should take Merick with you next time," he mouthed around an ice cube. "I bet every male in here would fall over."

Kimberly slid her gaze to Merick. "Would that turn you on?" She walked her fingers up his chest. "Me and your cousin getting freaky?"

Merick fought the urge to vomit, her need to stay close to Eirik suddenly flung from the mountain. "I think I'll try it solo." She set her glass down and started for the ominous-looking cages, mustering the liquid courage coursing through her with each step.

By the time she reached the angel manning them, she felt pretty damn confident. She loved to dance. Always had. In private.

She smiled up at the large shirtless male, his fawn-colored wings tucked in to his muscled back, as he lowered one of the cages back to the floor. "I would like to go up."

The iron scraped against the rock when the cage landed, the sound as jarring as the way he craned his head and looked her over. The male straightened to his full height, dwarfing her in shadow. "Interesting," he said, lips curling over sharp fangs.

Before Merick could adequately pick a response, he leaned in and inhaled deeply. "What's a decadent little hybrid doing in a place like this?"

She stepped back. "Excuse you!"

The angel looked over her head, scanning the crowd. "Where's your protector?" His gaze returned to her, smile widening. "It's not safe for spring flowers to be out in the snow."

Something inside her—likely the vodka—railed at his blatancy. *Fuck you, asshat!*

Merick met his insolent stare, letting him read the disgust solidifying in her with absolute clarity. "Not everything is as it seems."

A murmur of smoke curled over her fingers. Like claws. His eyes tracked it. "I guess not." He tugged on a rope and lowered the middle cage, swinging the door wide and extending his hand. "By all means, tiny Fire-dancer."

Merick stepped inside. The door was shut behind her and locked. A quick jolt of the cage sent her reaching out to steady herself on the bars. The angel laughed.

"Asshole," she muttered.

Shucking off the fur coat, she dropped it at her feet as the cage swung up and off the mountainside. His eyes changed from taunting amusement to something much darker. It only served to make her more resolute, feeding a defiance she hadn't realized she had been hiding.

Let him look. Greedy males had been looking her whole life.

Xavier's face came to mind, how he'd thought to cage her, too. The other males at her coming of age party, audaciously raking her up and down. The aristocrats that used to visit Thaddeus, undressing her with their roving eyes.

Merick had been an object to all of them long before she even realized it. Back when she'd worn the restrictive garments and hidden her body under layers and layers of material...to appear less appealing...*to them...*

Yeah, *fuck that!* She might be inherently modest on a good night, but that wasn't tonight. Tonight, *she'd* chosen the cage. Tonight, she wasn't hiding.

The cold nipped at her, but she didn't mind. Instead, she focused on the music, the brilliant twining of stars above her, and the silky feeling of moonlight against her skin.

A few heckles rose up, threatening to rob her of the experience, trying to make it about them. She closed her eyes. *No,* this dance was for her and the snow-laden mountain. For the winter night.

Slowly, she moved to the beat, swaying her hips in time with the melody sweeping over the top of the song. She focused on the haunting lyrics, lifting her hands, fingers gracefully dancing in time above her head. The tempo changed and she followed it seamlessly, rocking her whole body to the earthy underbelly of the dominant, driving, bass line.

She could hear cheers from below. For the first time she could ever recall, the attention did not resonate as negative in her ears. The noise became part of the song and she became its visual extension. Lost to the sensual ebb and flow of the music, she completely blocked out the world. It was just her and the wind.

Until the wind shifted. A shuddering over the mountain. A

subtle change in the environment below—a shadow snaking through the dancers—searching...

The speakers blasted out the music around her, but something had changed. Something was coming for her. Merick's eyes snapped open.

She didn't need to search out the interruption. It had already found her.

Watching from a barstool, the casualness of his pose contradicted the intensity of those stormy sea-green eyes. His penetrating stare didn't stray from her face, her body, or the hitch of her breath. As immovable as the frozen mountain, his gaze was as piercing as the frost bitten wind.

Her mate...

No words were needed between Stefen and the male operating the cages when their gazes met and he started across the room. The angel quickly fixed his attention on bringing her down. The fucking show was over!

To her credit, Merick had already slipped on her coat by the time the gate swung open. Stefen took her by the hand, much to the disapproving looks of the surrounding crowd, and headed for the exit. "Let her shake it." One drunken male made the stupid mistake of stepping into Stefen's path. "My cock wants the image for later."

A fist to the face was his answer. Merick gasped as the angel hit the floor. No one else said a damn word.

Eirik came running up from wherever in God's creation he'd been. "What happened?" He fell in line behind them. "I just went to the pisser..."

He shut up when Stefen's gaze swung sharply in his direction. "Get your shit and meet me at the castle."

Stefen didn't wait on him. He continued through the doors with Merick in tow, past more outside gawkers, to the stairs. He was so singleminded and focused, he almost didn't stop in time when Kimberly stepped in front of him. "Leaving so soon? We just got here." She pouted. "LaGoryen still owes me a dance."

"I suggest you go find him then." Stefen moved to walk around her.

She blocked him. "I was hoping to get you in one of those cages."

Stefen brushed past her. "I don't do cages."

He continued up the rock stairway, pulling Merick behind him. It wasn't until he was at the top he realized he wasn't helping her up the steep incline, but instead he was dragging her. He stopped and turned.

Sure enough Merick had her heels dug into the snow and dirt in an effort to slow him down. "What is the matter?" She huffed, white ringlets whipping around her face, cheeks flushed from the cold and, no doubt, the exertion to keep up. "I was just dancing."

"*Just* dancing?"

"Yes, dancing. Like everyone else."

He scoffed. "Oh, that was not like anyone else."

Her brows shot up. "I have no idea what you are inferring. Everyone goes to clubs. Everyone dances."

Stefen tugged her closer, his temper slipping its leash. "You and Eirik are not like everyone else in that club!" Not releasing her, he turned back toward the castle. "He should have known better than to take you there."

"He's my cousin. He would not have taken me anywhere that would put me in danger."

"Not intentionally," he grumbled. "But he's thinking with his cock, not his head."

"I can take care of myself."

"Can you now?" Stefen whirled around, teeth grinding hard

enough to make his bones ache. "Because all I saw up in that cage was prey."

He could have sworn hurt flashed in her eyes. "I'm not prey!" She bared her teeth. "My powers are developing faster than half the beings in that bar have advanced in decades."

"Listen to me." He stepped up to her, the wind gusting around them. "That power stalking through your veins, purring against your bones..." He gripped her chin—gently enough to not hurt, but firm enough to make her look at him. "It purrs for them too. Like a damn beacon calling them in."

Stefen let go. "Until your ability to decipher others' intentions matches your budding powers, you won't be on an even playing field with them. For, as you so aptly pointed out, they've got centuries on you."

"How do you know what their intentions were? Are you a mind reader?" Uncompromising will shined in her eyes. "Perhaps you're wrong."

"I don't need to be a mind reader. I am male." He let his gaze travel to her much too short skirt. "I could have that lifted before you could blink. Have my hands sliding up your thighs, fingers dividing your panties before you could catch a breath." He leaned in. "How would you stop me?"

Her eyes widened, even as she produced a silver flame in one hand.

Stefen grabbed her wrist, faster than her eyes could track and caused the flame to falter.

She lifted her free hand. Before she could enact another little fire display, Stefen had that one clenched, too. He wrenched both hands behind her back.

"That's a stupid test," she protested. "I'm not really trying."

"Why not?"

"Because I know you wouldn't hurt me."

"I wouldn't?"

She swallowed hard when he walked her backward. "And I have no intention of trying to hurt you?"

"You don't?" Stefen pressed her against a nearby tree, bent his head to her neck and breathed, "Even if I did this?" He kissed the sensitive flesh below her ear.

She shuddered and her pulse thumped quick and warm against his lips. "I wouldn't—"

His fangs elongated. "Wouldn't what?" He trailed them down the slender column of her neck. "Hurt me?"

"No," her whisper was barely audible.

"That's good." Stefen pinned her to the rough bark with his body, wedging one knee between her legs, parting them with his thigh. Her little black skirt hiked higher and higher, until he could feel her heat through the material of his pants. His words were feather-light when he spoke them to her lips. "Because I'm not really trying."

He released her and stepped back.

She stared at him, her breathing uneven, as the snow again did start to fall. "That's not fair."

"About as fair as me having to watch a club full of deviants eye-fucking my future mate. All hoping to get her against a tree and claim her as theirs."

"I would never—"

"You wouldn't have a choice."

She looked at him like he's physically hit her. "How can I be your mate if you think me so lacking? So inept? So...*frail*?"

Her words were daggers, each one hitting its mark. "I don't think of you as any of those things," he said. "I think of you as—"

"Prey." She pushed off the tree, her voice honed as sharp as a blade. "You told me already. Everyone here sees me as prey. *You* look at me like I'm prey."

"I look at you like what you are." Stefen stood there, the frost-kissed mountainside plummeting on either side around them, the howling wind carrying off his next words. "The most important thing in the Four Realms to me."

⸻

M erick stared at the dresser in her bedroom, a million emotions at war with one another inside her head, none of which would concede to the battle.

The problem was he'd made good points. Her confidence *was* exceeding her grasp. Whatever powers were getting stronger within her were also blinding her with accolades she hadn't yet won. She'd been in a state of constant growth since breaking free of Gerra, but she knew she hadn't really been tested. Not against another.

On the other hand, she knew who she was. She felt it more and more each day. Like a braided light was attached to her soul, pulling her toward her true path. Only, she had no evidence to support the feeling. Just blind faith in herself.

And that was what hurt the most. That Stefen didn't see it. Or worse...he might see it, but simply did not agree.

Merick pulled out a drawer and took out a t-shirt and sweatpants. She wished Teakin were here. She could use his sage advice. She could use a friend.

She wiggled out of the minuscule club dress and pulled on the cotton lounge wear. Slipping on a pair of sneakers, she picked up her borrowed clothes and headed for the door. A mundane task would take her mind off the events of the evening. Returning the clothes that had gotten her in hot water—to the female that wanted to bang her future mate—seemed a mundane enough place to start.

First she would wash them. Because it was the right thing to do, and because she didn't want Kimberly scenting out Stefen on them. Merick smirked and turned the blouse inside out, looking for the laundering directions. Though, it might serve her right. To know how he'd turned Merick's legs to gelatin on the top of that mountain.

She closed her bedroom door behind her. What was Kimberly's deal anyway? The Air-dancer was hooking up with Eirik now, but she'd practically stuck her tongue in Stefen's ear when they were leaving the club. *Who does that sort of shit?*

"Desperate bitches."

Merick jumped and whirled.

Marzalla stood in a doorway down the hall, framed by candle sconces, her unbound hair gleaming and rippling like liquid gold around her ivory shoulders.

"Did I say that out loud?" Merick grimaced.

"You might as well have." The beauty grinned.

Merick tried to rein in her shock. "You can read my mind?"

"Only what you don't conceal."

"I had no idea anyone was around." A nagging inner voice—sounding a lot like Stefen's—chastised her. *Young and careless.* She arched a brow. "Did you hear that?"

"No." Marzalla smiled. "You've blocked me. But, now I'm dying to know who the harlot is." She pushed off the wall, her pale blue dress swirling around her legs as she sauntered over. "Elemental or angel?"

Merick felt herself grin. "Elemental."

"Ah." The leggy Air-dancer clucked her tongue to the roof of her mouth. "Kimberly."

"You're good."

"She's just that bad." Marzalla chuckled. "However, rotten females do make for great gossip. I left a couple bottles of Alaric's best pinot noir in there." She nodded to the library's open door down the hall. "Care to vent?"

"I think I can get on board with the way you think."

"Great!" Marzalla looped her arm through Merick's. "We can also talk about infuriating dragon males."

Merick cut her eyes to her as they walked to the library. "Stefen told you he turned?"

"He didn't have to," she said. "My only wager was how long it would take." The look of confusion on Merick's face must have been encouragement enough to expand on said wager. "I knew the second I saw you that you were meant for our handsome angel vamp." She steered them into the ninth floor library. "But with these headstrong males you just have to wait until they actually accept it for themselves."

Marzalla untangled her arm from Merick's and walked to the sidebar. "Now, to Stefen's credit..." She poured two glasses of wine. "He's much quicker to see reason than Ash."

"He sees reason?" Merick plopped into an oversized chair with a guttural snort. "He just decked a male in a club for watching me dance." *Hard to imagine it could get less reasonable than that.*

Marzalla walked over and handed her a glass. "You dropped your guard again." She smirked.

"Shit."

"It's easy to forget to shield when we're worked up," she explained. "And clearly, he's got you worked up."

"*Clearly*. There's certainly been a lot of new revelations in the past couple of days." Merick took a sip of wine. "Now that you know, I could use some female counsel." She sat forward, bracing her elbows on her knees. "Is this sort of irrational, territorial behavior typical of dragons?"

Marzalla took a seat across from her. "Honey, storms are less capricious than they are. Landslides more restrained." She grinned and wagged a brow. "But that's what makes them so damn hot."

"I suppose I have a lot to learn then. Like what triggers the mythical beast." Merick did away with the sipping and took a swig. "Apparently dancing. And certain articles of clothing."

The pretty Air-dancer laughed heartily. "I did wonder how long it was going to take him to run a sword through every male at the ball last night after he saw you in that gown." She eyed the black sequined material sitting beside Merick. "I can only imagine how that costume went over."

"I guess I should order potato sacks by the hundreds."

"I'm sure he could even find fault with those."

They both laughed. It felt good. Merick didn't realize how much she'd been craving the company of another female. This easy banter, the levity, the honesty. It was everything she never knew she'd been missing—like opening a new world. A world that hadn't existed until now. Right here, in this library, over a bottle of wine, a friendship was born.

Marzalla relaxed into the tufted sofa and draped an arm over the back, the other elegantly dangling her wine glass over her crossed knees. "Has he talked about this place?" She tipped her head up, scanning the expanse of shelves.

"He likes to dodge those questions. The ones pertaining to his past."

"Keep asking them." Marzalla's gaze landed back on her.

"I'm not going to like the answer when he finally does confide in me, am I?"

"No, most of it you will not." Her new friend gave her a sad smile. "But you can't have his future without his past."

Merick stared into her glass, getting lost in the kaleidoscope of burgundy hues. "It's hard to imagine him any way but how he is now; powerful, confident, caring." She looked up. "Impervious."

"There's a special kind of strength that comes from enduring darkness." It was Marzalla's turn to get lost in her own wine glass. "And still manage to choose the right path afterward. To remain kind. To remember how to trust, and to love."

Merick had the distinct feeling Stefen wasn't the only one that had overcome such hardships.

Marzalla's blue eyes lifted and she smiled, vanquishing any trace of melancholy. "But, let us talk of less complicated matters." She gave Merick a pointed look. "Like concealing those thoughts of yours."

"Please!" Merick nodded, thankful for the help, the timing, and the friendship. "Make me an impenetrable vault."

Chapter Twenty-Five

Teakin watched Aasha roll in the grass of her newly constructed enclosure. Ash had it made the night they arrived, insisting she couldn't roam freely across the Tuscan countryside. Teakin quickly realized the wisdom in this after the tigress nearly took the head off his brother's kennel master.

Thankfully the poor man had been okay, but the incident only further confirmed what he feared. Aasha couldn't stay here. She was a product of Gerra, a demon. Her wild instincts could no more be controlled than her glowing red eyes.

His heart twisted at the thought of telling Merick her pet would have to eventually find a new home. Perhaps Ventus. The fae had a wider range of animals, and more tolerant inhabitants. Some place where apex predators were more readily expected and accepted.

Teakin's eyes sought out Aasha's large round ones. The cat

rolled to her back for a belly rub. Sighing, he knelt down, running his fingers through her soft fur. "It's not fair, is it girl?"

Aasha looped her giant paw over his forearm, pulling it toward her and licking him with her sandpaper tongue. "Don't go getting any ideas," he warned. "I'm the one that's going to make sure..."

Somewhere nearby, a door was flung open. Hurried footsteps followed.

He jumped to his feet.

Orders were being issued and, one by one, lights flickered on inside the nearby training facility. Teakin quickly exited the enclosure and locked the gate. When he turned around, his brother was already marching in his direction. "They're here."

"How many?" No names were needed.

"More than we have," Ash said. "They're lined up on the border. Waiting."

"For an audience with the Fire King. I think I can guess their terms."

"They better be prepared to fight then." Ash turned.

Teakin grabbed his arm. "Remember what Father used to say? Judge a man by his enemies."

Ash finished it, eyes aglow with the stars above. "They tell of his character and his potential."

"No matter what happens here tonight, brother." Teakin nodded tightly. "It's not over till we win."

They materialized on the moonlit field, three hundred Fire-dancers at their back. On the opposite side stood twice as many elite, Zander—looking wild-eyed and crazy—at the front of their line.

"Teakin, my pet," Gerra's king called out, "we need to talk."

Ash visibly bristled beside him. "He's lost his mind."

Teakin scanned the army. "I don't see Thaddeus."

"Katarra's not here either. He is acting on his own."

"Let's get this over with." He started walking toward the center of the field, Ash right beside him.

Zander approached from the south, accompanied by two soldiers. "Where is your queen?" Ash asked.

"Where's yours?" Zander cocked his head, grinning odiously. "I do wish I had gotten a chance to fuck her. Perhaps when I ransack your lands, I'll do just that. Before I gut her."

A stillness crept into his brother's features, a far better warning than Ash's next words. "Is that the reason you're here?"

"I have come for something better." The king looked at Teakin. "It's time for you to return home."

"You have come to do battle then." He surveyed the line of elite behind Zander. "Care to tell us how you want your body sent home?" His gaze returned to meet the Gerra king. "In pieces, or ashes?"

"Oh," Zander tutted. "How I've missed that smart mouth of yours."

Teakin stepped forward. Ash halted him with a palm to the chest and addressed Zander. "Shall we begin then?"

"Why, that doesn't seem fair at all." Zander looked theatrically past them, at their inferior numbers. "I have a better idea. Just hand over your traitorous brother and let us be on our way."

"You were there when I ripped the head off your father," Ash said boredly. "Do you really want to witness what two dragons would do to your little group?"

"I keep forgetting." Zander snapped his fingers, a gleam lighting in his eyes. "There's one other minor detail. Should I die here tonight," he looked directly at Teakin again, "your son will too."

Lies, Teakin reminded himself, Gerra was built on lies. He knew to expect the unexpected when dealing with Zander. The monster's depravity knew no bounds. *But still...*a shred of possibility tore at that logic. "You've completely lost your mind."

"You do remember her, don't you?" Zander's cruel smile was a slash of white. "Funny that both your brats are products of rape," he crooned. "I wonder if all that hate will affect them someday. To be born from such brutality."

"You're lying," Teakin managed, over the bob of his throat.

Zander had always given his victims a pill after he'd made Teakin bed them. The king was adamant about it, his fear of another living dragon too great. This was just another trick.

"You tell me?" Zander leisurely lifted a hand.

Teakin's heart beat a rhythmic tattoo against his chest wall as the line of soldiers parted and a child, no older than three, was led forward. His expert vision tunneled in on the boy's face—the stubborn set to his jaw despite being in the middle of an army in a foreign realm, the dark-olive complexion, the gold eyes...

The dread that gripped him was staggering. Teakin did not need to look at his brother to know Ash saw it, too. The Fire King's aloofness was gone, replaced by a barely restrained beast.

Zander seemed to understand the danger for he gave a curt nod. Just like that, the child was gone, swallowed up by the front line. "I think it's safer if he stays with his mother," the king said. "While we work out our—"

With a palm to the throat, Teakin took him completely off his feet and slammed him to the ground. Hands were instantly on him, pulling, hitting, and trying to pry him off. It was futile. The dragon felt no pain. Teakin struck again and again, until all he saw was red. Until it dripped from his fists and his brow, coloring the world in blood.

Still, the maniac laughed, raw and wet, edged with hysteria. "If I die..." Zander rasped between blows. "So does he."

Teakin hit him one last time, crushing his eye socket.

He surged to his feet and yelled into the night. Entwined in that scream, woven into the fabric of hatred and pain—a thread of acceptance. An unwavering resolve.

Zander coughed and rolled to his side, spitting out blood. "A father's love." He chuckled, a slimy gurgling sound. "No better shackle."

Teakin hauled back and kicked him in the ribs. "Shut the fuck up!"

Ash put a steadying hand on his shoulder, coaxing him back from the lingering edge. *"I defer to you."*

Teakin shook his head, the past, the present, and the future conspiring and colliding all at once. They'd been so close. *So fucking close.*

Ash stepped in front of him and grabbed him by the back of the head, forcing his attention, boring into his mind. *"It's not over till we win..."*

Chapter Twenty-Six

T he sun was just starting to sneak across the hardwoods when Stefen slipped into bed beside Merick.

He'd spent all night theorizing and pouring over literature with Alaric after Marzalla messaged him, confirming her and his future mate's whereabouts. No stone would be left unturned until they felt confident Merick could make the transformation when the time came.

At some point, Eirik had stuck in his head. Despite Alaric's encouragement to send him back to the Earth Realm, Stefen had instead laid out a few more ground rules. Thankfully, Eirik understood. Too much was on the line with his father and uncle seeking revenge on the Diabolis. Both he and Merick needed to keep a low profile.

Many hours later, when Marzalla's thoughts became fragmented down the tabella, Alaric sent a guard to casually stroll the ninth floor. Stefen had been adamant; he didn't want Merick to feel spied upon. Especially after how he'd behaved at the club. But he needed to make sure she was safe when she did eventually fall asleep.

Once his fiancée and Mar made their way back to their designated rooms the guard took up a closer post outside Merick's chamber.

After combing through two more ancient texts and a half bottle of brandy, Stefen retired to the ninth floor, still wondering why he'd reacted as powerfully as he had upon seeing her dancing in that damned cage.

The fucking dragon. It had to be. He had never been possessive or jealous.

Though, if he was being fair with his past self, he had never cared for anyone as he cared for Merick. And he was right! She shouldn't have been out there with those supernaturals. Every reason he'd given her was based on logic.

Still. He couldn't help but feel there was a lesson in this for him, too. He was going to have to come to terms with these new emotions. His future mate was not a female to take orders, and he did not want to be the sort of male to issue them.

Everything would settle down once she made the transition. She would come into her full powers, and he could stop worrying so much. Everything would be set to right. *It had to be...*

She stirred beside him, pulling his attention back to the present.

He watched the advancing morning light wash over her golden skin. *Gods, she was captivating.* The most beautiful thing he'd ever seen.

His fingers reached out to caress her shoulder. She smiled in her sleep. The reaction instantly made his cock hard. She was so responsive to him, so eager and honest.

Reluctantly, Stefen withdrew his hand and tugged his shirt over his head. He had to get some sleep. If he kept touching her that simply would not happen.

And despite Alaric's urging to '*go ahead and fuck her,*' Stefen wanted to wait. He needed her to get through the training and transformation. He also wanted their first time together to be void of outside stress.

He cursed under his breath and adjusted his pants. If he could hold out that long.

Laying back down, Stefen closed his eyes. He simply needed to call on every ounce of patience he could muster. *Fucking patience.*

A pained whimper made him sit straight up in bed.

Merick gripped the sheets, knuckles white, mouth twisted in anguish.

"Merick?" He touched her cheek. She was burning up.

Her lips parted on another muffled groan. "Merick!" He shook her and pushed to his knees, just as her spine arched and she cried out.

He grabbed her face. "Wake up."

Her arms flailed, hands reaching for purchase, ripping at her throat when they found it.

Stefen yanked them down to her sides but her body bucked in protest, twisting the sheets and exposing large dark veins. The labyrinth of blue and black crawled over her skin, rolling under the transparency of her much too pale complexion. "Wake up!" he yelled, shaking her harder.

Panic gripped him when something in those veins started to take shape and move, undulating, snaking over her muscles like a serpent. *"Alaric."* Stefen screamed out in his head as he straddled Merick, pinning her to the bed.

She was trying to turn. Her head thrashed from side to side violently. He put his hands on either side, trying to steady it.

The bedroom door burst open, nearly shattering from the hinges. "What's happening?" Alaric's large frame filled the doorway.

"She's turning."

"Wake her up," he ordered.

"I can't," Stefen said.

Her eyes flew open, and then rolled back in her head.

"Pull her out of the dream." Alaric stormed over and made to push Stefen to the side.

He shoved him off as a thought occurred to him. *That wasn't the way to her.* He couldn't forcefully remove her. "I have to join her."

Stefen placed his palm over her heart. It raced so hard he feared it might explode from her chest. Cupping the back of her neck with his other hand, he supported her head. "Be quiet," he hissed at Alaric.

Closing his eyes, he tried to shut out the world around them and focused all his energy on finding his connection with Merick. It was like trying to see through a tornado. Colors raced around her, angry and confused. Stefen pushed through the tangled mess.

*There...*deep within the swirling chaos—a spark of gold. *Her true aura.* He locked onto it, his mind traveling over and around the gnarled root system, pushing the other hues aside as he made his way toward that thread of gold. *"Come to me, darling."*

The dense, suffocating colors separated, one by one, parting for him. Stefen reached out with all his energy. *"I'm here. I have you."*

The golden light grew. He dug deeper. *"Trust me."*

Her body went pliant in his hands and the dark spider web of colors fragmented into tiny motes of dust. "You did it!" Alaric broke the mental connection.

Stefen opened his eyes.

Merick's blonde eyelashes fluttered softly against her cheek. Then she gasped, a gulping, desperate sound that told a story all its own.

Stefen cradled her head and lifted it gently as relief washed over him. "Shhh. You're safe."

Her panicked, darting gaze found its focus—on him. Slowly, her pulse regulated, the adrenaline subsiding. She pulled deeper, controlled breaths into her lungs. The fear in her eyes waned, as she absorbed his words.

She trembled, the shock setting in. Stefen pulled her to his chest. "It's okay." Something wet landed on his cheek.

Merick's head snapped up, going straight to the lone tear, as if she'd heard it fall. "Stefen..." She stared at him in wonder. "You're crying?"

A breathy chuckle escaped him. "You go through all that, and your first words are to poke fun at me?"

She gave him a wan smile. "Only a male would consider that a taunt."

"You scared me to death." He swallowed.

Alaric cleared his throat. "You scared us both."

"I'm sorry," Merick rasped, not taking her gaze from Stefen. "You saved me."

"You did not make it easy."

She wrapped her arms tighter around him, as if he was the only solid thing in the world, and buried her head in his chest. "I love you."

Stefen held her, speechless. All he'd said to her last night flooded back. He had been such an ass. It was not her fault she did not yet know who and what she could trust. It was his fault for being gone all day. Had he been there, Eirik would have never taken her to that stupid club.

Alaric slipped quietly from the room.

The action pulled Stefen out of his self-admonishment on a fleeting thought; it was only slightly disturbing to see his brother behaving with care—as though he might have emotions, or at the very least, recognized them in others.

A few more seconds passed in silence, and the gravity of what had occurred started to sink in on a different level. The fear he'd felt. It was like none he had known before. Stefen would have given anything to alleviate her torture. He would have traded places with her if he could. He would have died for her.

Because he loved her.

He hadn't told her. Not in words. Hell, he'd barely done so in actions.

Stefen rested his chin atop her head and exhaled slowly. "I think I've loved you since before I drew breath in this life." He let his heart speak. "I loved you in another. When we were both stars."

Chapter Twenty-Seven

"I loved you in another..."
The trees, the animals, the seasons—they all share a beginning and an
end. Even the stars eventually die, and those among the living know
nothing of it.
But the stars remember.
They are born again, out of their due place. Forever searching for
something permanent, a space to belong. Some deeply rooted sense of
home singing to them, calling them back to the lands of their ancestors.
To a location where their dreams and their memories walked together.
To a fifth realm. Where there is no new beginning...no end.

Merick woke to the sound of someone stoking a fire. She must have fallen asleep. *Again.* What the hell? Was she trying to hibernate?

She sat up as another log was placed in the library's hearth. The book she'd been reading still rested in her lap. But a blanket had been placed over her.

Stefen. They'd come here after breakfast for him to get some correspondence done. Merick had selected a historical romance to fill the time; she obviously had dozed off.

She looked to the window and gasped. It was black outside. She'd been asleep all day.

"Sorry to wake you." A servant turned from the fire and smiled. "I was trying to be as quiet as possible."

"It's quite alright. I needed to get up. What time is it?"

"A quarter till six," the young woman replied. "Are you hungry? I can bring your dinner in here."

Merick shook her head. "No, thank you. I will join the others in the dining hall."

"Everyone is in a meeting right now."

"A meeting?" She rubbed her eyes. "Everyone?"

"The High Council called for it," the girl explained. "The Air recruits have already taken their dinner and are in a late training session."

Merick stood, folding the blanket. "I should join them."

"I'm afraid that's not possible. I was instructed to attend to you on this floor."

"Attend to me?" She tilted her head, instantly suspicious. "On this floor?" Merick glanced to the library door. The hallways were empty. Not a hint of movement came from anywhere except the crackling fireplace.

She looked back at the servant. "Am I grounded?"

"No. It's just that..." The girl blushed, eyes searching out the rug, clearly uncomfortable being questioned. "I was told to watch over you. On this floor."

"Watch me for what, exactly?"

"Nightmares. It was the only time your mentor wished to be interrupted during their meeting," she amended. "If you fell victim to one."

Merick felt herself getting more annoyed by the second. So, Stefen was now her mentor, and she was to be supervised. Like a child. Still didn't explain the ninth floor part of this poor woman's job. "I would like to take a stroll. Outside."

The servant took a step toward the door. "That is not allowed either."

"Why?"

"No one is permitted to leave, or enter, the castle during the meeting."

The last of Merick's patience snapped. "What's going on?"

"That's all I know. I swear. You are to remain on this floor." She wrung her hands together. "Would you like some tea?"

"I will get my own food." Merick stomped to the door.

Just to have it slam in her face.

She spun back around, indignation replaced with resolute anger. "And here I thought you were just a servant."

The female straightened her spine, completely discarding the babysitter façade she'd clearly been working. "Thank you."

"Thank you?"

"Yes."

"I obviously need to work on my delivery." She studied the other woman more closely.

It was like looking at an entirely different person. Or rather, it was as if Merick were seeing the room's only other occupant for the first time. *How could that be?* The female standing before her looked nothing like the servant, yet, she couldn't even recall what exactly the servant had looked like.

It would be hard to forget the supernatural standing before her now, though. She had a flawless umber complexion, glossy ebony hair, and honey-brown eyes the size of lotus leaves. Three striking features she had not noticed before.

Merick continued to take her measure. She was lithe of build with long delicate bones, almost fragile in appearance. What she lacked in physical intimidation, she more than made up for in the set of her shoulders and the look in her eyes.

249

The stranger folded her arms, waiting, enjoying the assessment, challenging Merick to get it right this time. This was no meek young servant, tasked with keeping an eye on her. The female before her was confident, intelligent, much older, and more experienced than originally perceived.

Merick reached out with her mind, trying to find a connection she might be missing. She wasn't an angel or an elite. Not human either. Something more melodic, her footprint on the realms lighter. Not water, earth, or fire... *Air.*

Her gaze darted back to the other female's face, past the high cheekbones and kohl-lined eyes, to the points of her ears—daring to poke through her thick hair.

Fae!

"All done?" One side of the stranger's mouth lifted in a half smirk.

"I'm not sure." Merick took a healthy step back, unapologetic for her obvious hesitancy. "Who are you?"

"My name is Palomi, and as you have just ascertained, I am from Ventus." A glint lit in her eyes. "Two things you pegged completely wrong upon first observation."

"Why have I not seen you before?"

"Perhaps I did not wish to be seen." She shrugged. "Perhaps you simply failed to notice."

"Perhaps I have never been good with trickery." Merick narrowed her eyes.

"There's a fundamental connection between seeing and being. If you only see what is presented to you, you'll miss what is being hidden." The female clasped her hands behind her back. "In this case though; I didn't trick you. I only embodied what you expected me to be."

"That's ridiculous. I never expected to wake to a servant stoking a fire."

"You didn't expect anything," she said. "Which is part of the problem. The second part of the problem, when you did encounter me, you chose the path of least resistance. A maid, in a castle such as this, would make sense. Your brain filled in that role for me. I did not choose it. I simply adapted to it."

Merick stared at her. "Why?"

"I'm told you could use some help regarding these issues. Not being so..." She paused, as if the point could make itself. "Trusting."

Merick snorted. She would kill Stefen later. It was bad enough he found her lacking in her ability to read people correctly, but now he was out telling everyone her faults. Like this stranger, *Palomi*.

Why should she believe her anyway? She wasn't exactly thrilled by her particular skill set. It felt deceitful. And why was she sequestered to this floor? Why not the other recruits? What was the sudden High Council meeting about? Something told her Palomi would not be forthcoming with any answers.

Merick took a seat with a huff that would have made Marjory proud. "So, you're to be my new instructor?"

"For the day," the fae replied simply.

"Fine." She sat back and crossed her legs. "Show me how to be skeptical and untrustworthy."

"To see things as they truly are," Palomi corrected with a sly grin.

Merick rolled her eyes. "Tomato, to mah toe."

Stefen's advancing tread rang out, bouncing off the corridor walls with each step. It was a little past midnight now. The High Council meeting had lasted well over eight hours. *Too long.* It always took them too long to decide to do the right thing.

He took a deep breath and stopped in front of the library

doors. Now for the real test. Could he deliver the news? Better yet, could he handle the reaction to it?

Stefen only made it around the corner before she was standing in front of him. "What's going on?" Merick demanded.

He glanced to Palomi. "Would you mind leaving us?"

She nodded and walked over. "She's a quick study." The fae warrior smiled at Merick. "We can practice more tomorrow."

"Thank you," Merick replied. "And sorry, again."

Stefen knew there was likely an interesting story to that apology. One he couldn't wait to hear. Mostly because it would mean he was well past this next moment in time.

They stood in silence until the door clicked shut behind Palomi. "It's cliché, but you need to sit," he said.

Merick did as suggested without question, taking the closest seat. Stefen sat down beside her. "Let me start by saying we're working on a plan."

She worried her bottom lip. "Are we falling under attack?"

"Not yet."

"Is it the Diabolis?"

"The only one we're sure of is Zander. He has your father." Her eyes grew wide, fear bounding across them. "We will get him back," he rushed to assure her.

Merick jerked to her feet. "How did this happen?"

"I'm not going to sugarcoat any of this." Stefen stood, looking for consent. When she nodded, he said, "You have a brother. A child Teakin had no knowledge of until Zander confronted him last night."

Merick's gaze drifted from his, as if searching for answers in the thin air. "Where? Where did he confront him?"

"On the border of Ash's estate."

She continued to stare into space. "He willingly went back with him."

He swallowed against the lump forming of his throat. "It was the only way to keep the boy alive."

She turned slowly and walked to a window. Stefen waited. Waited for her to decide what she wanted to do with this knowledge. If she wanted to cry, he would be here. If she wanted to scream, he would be here. If she wanted to run, he would be here.

When she finally did turn from the window, something Stefen hadn't anticipated reflected in those multi-colored eyes—understanding. "I would expect nothing less from him."

Merick crossed her arms and walked over to the bookshelf. "As much as I want to hate Thaddeus for all that he did, I can't," she said. "Because of all that he allowed." She reached out and ran a finger over the spines of the books. "He could have kept Teakin from me, but he gave him a role that would keep him close."

She selected a book, studying the cover, a wistful smile curving her mouth. "Alice in Wonderland. This was one of the first stories Teakin read to me." Merick opened the well-worn version and flipped the pages, before pausing, seemingly finding the one she was looking for. "Alice asked, how long is forever?" she read. "White Rabbit replied, sometimes, just one second."

Her smile grew. "Teakin said it didn't mattered how long a soul lived as long as it loved well. That forever was a clock unset if you knew the meaning of true love."

"Your father is a wise man."

Merick looked over at him. "When do we go get them?"

"We're waiting to hear back from Thaddeus. He has been working with Ash. Though it looks like Zander overthrew their plans. So we are reassessing the strategy."

Stefen walked to her side. "But there is no 'we' when it comes to getting them out of Gerra, Merick."

"That's my father in there." Her focus grew lethal. "You can't expect me to not be involved."

"Of course I can," he said firmly. "You have yet to come into your full powers."

The look in her eyes grew down right mutinous. "When the time comes to take action," he continued. "You will stay here with your cousins, keeping your bloodline protected."

"Bastian is here?"

"Just arrived."

"He and Eirik are not going?"

"Their duty to the realms is to stay safe."

"In case the king should fall," she concluded.

"Yes."

"I'm not a prophesied ruler. I should be allowed to go," she protested. "My powers are getting stronger by the day. Marzalla taught me how to hide my thoughts and Palomi—"

"You are a LaGoryen," Stefen cut her off. "You and your cousins are the last of a bloodline that predates the coming of Christ. You are royalty. Which means you also have a duty to the Crown. And as my future mate," he added. "You have an obligation to respect my wishes."

"What about my wishes?" She stood her ground.

"Ask of me anything but for you to go to Gerra and you shall have it."

Noise from the hall made them both turn their heads toward the door.

The twins walked in. "I need a drink," Eirik proclaimed, heading for a side bar.

Bastian's intense gaze didn't miss a thing, taking in the distance between Stefen and Merick, the tensions still hanging between them. "Alaric wants you, uncle, back in the meeting room."

"Of course, he does." Stefen rolled his eyes and looked at Merick. "We will finish this discussion later." He asked down their bond, *"Are you going to be okay?"*

254

She nodded, then replied, *"We sure as shit will."*

Stefen inwardly sighed and walked to the door, eyeing both boys as he passed. "Look after her."

E irik handed his brother a glass and walked over to Merick, offering her one as well. "It's going to be okay." He smiled down, sympathetically. "My father will get him out."

Bastian let out a short, mirthless laugh. "He shouldn't need to." His steely gaze met Merick's.

"Cool it, Bash," Eirik warned.

"Why?" The word cut through the room like lightning on a stormy night. "Our father is putting his life on the line for someone that wouldn't return the favor."

Merick felt like he had physically slapped her. Which she supposed was the intention.

Another person she had read wrong.

She thought Bastian simply aloof that night in Italy, but it went further than that. A depth of hate she had never discerned. He resented Teakin.

By the way he was coming at her, he resented her too.

"That's enough," Eirik said.

"It's true." Bastian's eyes raked over her with a sort of insolent appreciation. "You are here to learn, right?" Before she could answer, he continued, "Here's a little lesson in history. Our father fought to save our grandmother when Dante tried to burn her alive. Your father merely watched."

Eirik advanced toward his brother. "Stop!"

"No. She needs to hear it." His icy gaze didn't break from Merick's. "Our father never gave in. He fought the monsters that killed his mother. Your father submitted and stayed. Their willing slave. He would still be their slave, if not for Stefen," Bastian said, his voice dripping with loathing, lush with disdain. "Now he is their slave again."

It wasn't true. Teakin would have never sat back and let the Diabolis have their way. He would have fought them. As he fought for her. Week after week, year after year he endured, he stayed... for her.

"Did he though?" A razor sharp claw scraped down her mind.

Merick's eyes snapped up, realizing too late she had let down her guard. Let Bastian hear her thoughts.

A slice of a smile as he wordlessly added, *"Or did he just need an excuse to stay?"*

The back of her knees connected with a chair and her drink sloshed over the rim of her glass. The cold liquor jostled her out of her head. She needed to get out of here.

"Shut up, Bastian." Eirik stood in front of his twin now, red creeping up his neck. "She's our family."

Bastian met his brother's challenge, stepping toe to toe with him. "You're one to speak of family," he sneered. "Where will you be when the war begins? Here? Safe and protected behind these walls in your mortal skin. Trying to get your dick in our cousin while the rest of us do the fighting?"

Eirik punched him.

Bastian stumbled backward, catching himself on a side table, his drink shattering on the floor. Merick lunged to intervene, but Eirik held up a stiff, halting arm. "Stay back!"

Bastian's face filled with cool amusement as he straightened, the blood from his lip disappearing on his skin, reminding Merick he had already turned. "Go ahead, hit me again brother. I bet it feels good, knowing I won't hit you back."

"You have forgotten yourself," Eirik said, not backing down.

"No, I'm the only one that hasn't lost my mind over a piece of ass."

Bastian shoved past Eirik and strode to the bar. He filled a fresh glass, downed it, and turned back, looking directly at Merick. "You may be family by blood." He angled his head, eyes taking on a fervid gleam. "But neither you, nor your father, have earned the name LaGoryen."

Merick stood speechless. The doors opened and Kimberly waltzed in.

The Air-dancer quickly took in the uncomfortable scene around her. "What do we have here?" She looked at each of them. "One big happy family reunion."

Bastian turned back to the bar, bracing both hands on its top. Eirik threw himself into a chair. The weight of the room was tangible with heated emotion. But they would say no more on the subject. Not in the company of strangers.

Merick was not sure how she felt about the sudden realization —that she was one of them now. A family that, despite their issues, didn't share them with others.

She lifted her glass. Though it shook against her lips, she managed a sip. The scotch burned the back of her throat but it couldn't snuff out the hate-filled words or the hurtful accusation.

She needed to be alone. The itch to run was firing on all cylinders. She wanted to race until her legs gave out, climb until her muscles screamed, begging her to still. To hit something until Bastian's biting words no longer nipped at her.

Merick headed for the door when Kimberly crawled onto Eirik's lap and slipped her hand through the opening of his shirt, her eyes scanning the backside of Bastian at the bar. The shiftiness only made Merick flee faster.

She slipped out the open door, her legs launching her into a dead run the second she was out of earshot.

An hour later, Merick slowed to a jog on the gym track. After climbing the indoor rock wall seven times, racing the agility course twice, then sprinting until she thought her legs would snap in two, her physical goals of pushing herself to the point of exhaustion were achieved.

It helped with the mental ones, too. Thirty minutes in, she had stopped thinking about Bastian's venom-spewed opinions of her and Teakin. Instead, she considered what she might do to prove him wrong. This soreness in her body was temporary. The sting from her cousin's accusations was temporary.

Whatever Teakin was going through in Gerra right now; that was permanent.

She might not be able to get him out on her own, but she would be damned if she let that entitled shit Bastian belittle his good name. Her father deserved their respect. Merick would do everything in her power to make sure he got it.

Breathing hard, she stopped and bent at the waist, watching as sweat dripped onto the track floor. *Everything would be okay. Ash would get him out. He had to.*

Merick forced herself upright and headed for the showers. Hopefully, Stefen would be back by the time she was done. There was no better stress relief than what she wanted to do with that male. She wanted him to break her apart, obliterate every doubt in her head, steal her away to that beach in his mind, and ravage her until she knew nothing of this world.

Her nerves almost hummed with anticipation by the time she started down the hall to the showers. She turned the corner, a smile on her lips, and froze.

In the dim light, just inside the adjacent locker room entrance, was the naked backside of a man. Broad shoulders, tapered waist, dimpled ass cheeks flexing in at the hips from repeated thrust...

Merick commanded her eyes to look away. They willfully disobeyed. Not as his large tan thighs, braced apart, rocked forward, and up, forcing whoever was in front of him up onto their tiptoes. It was all she could see of his partner, apart from splayed fingers against the wall, bright red nails clawing at the stone.

He rammed into her from behind, over and over, hard and unrelenting, like punishment. His head was dropped between his shoulders, lowered to his partner's neck as she gasped and whimpered. Merick's mouth went dry and her pulse fluttered unexpectedly.

She needed to leave. *Now!*

As slowly as was possible, she made to take a step backward. Before she could avert her gaze, the man's head lifted, exposing his partner's profile. *Kimberly!*

Only, *that wasn't Eirik.*

Merick took another step away. Her foot caught on something and her balance listed dangerously to one side. Her hand flew out, smacking against the wall and catching her weight before she could hit the deck.

The male's head pivoted, disheveled dark hair falling over piercing sapphire eyes as he looked over his shoulder and grinned. "What's that?" Kimberly squeaked, still caged in front of his larger body.

"Nothing," Bastian growled, fangs dripping red as he stared Merick down. "Nothing." He thrust into Kimberly so hard she cried out. "At all."

Chapter Twenty-Eight

Merick was sprawled out in the middle of the bed under the covers. Stefen was getting used to such a small thing needing so much space.

She did make a serene picture in the center of the silk and goose down. *The little bed hog that she was.*

Stefen had to smile as he pulled his shirt over his head and kicked off his boots. He only had minutes before needing to leave, but he could thinking of nothing better to do with those fleeting minutes than hold her.

She scooted back instinctively, seeking out his heat, when he crawled in behind her.

His cock turned to granite the second she wiggled her bottom against him. "Merick?" he whispered.

That shapely ass rotated again and he realized—to his utter undoing—she was not wearing undergarments. The only thing separating them was his pants.

She arched her back, pressing firmly against his aching, swollen member.

He bit through his bottom lip with a fang.

"I know you're awake." Stefen exhaled through his teeth, "Vixen."

She mumbled, "Prove it."

He reached around and cupped her rounded breast. "Like this?" He rolled her nipple between his thumb and forefinger.

Her breath hitched.

"Stefen..." She moaned when he kissed the shell of her ear.

"Humm?"

Merick shifted in his arms to face him. "I know you want to wait. For our first time together to be...ideal. Romantic." She pushed his hair back from his face. "But right now." Her mouth tilted up, her breath hot against his lips as she whispered, "I need you to just fuck me."

It was all Stefen needed to hear to snap the thinly stretched string of control holding him in check. He rolled her beneath him, their mouths colliding. Her hands were in his hair, across his back, fingers digging into his scalp, exploring every inch of him. A primal desperation unleashed.

It was like falling out of the sky. Tumbling uncontrollably, momentum building, the ground getting closer with each breath —the high worth the crash.

His body pressed into hers, his forearm by her head, holding the bulk of his weight off her chest, some part of him screaming to be gentle.

Stefen broke the kiss, lowering his lips to her collarbone, then lower, stopping at each breast to thoroughly lavish them. They were perfect, round and firm, soft as silk against his lips. She inhaled sharply when he sucked one pert nipple into his mouth.

He moved his attention to the sensitive flesh of her navel. Her hands on the top of his head encouraged his worshipping as he worked his way down.

He pushed her legs apart with his knees, his hands fanning out across her abdomen as he nipped the inside of her thigh. She wiggled under his touch when his fingers found the heat they sought.

Stefen made no apologies as he rocked back and took in the sight of her, his fingers glistening as he slowly worked her. "You are beautiful."

He spread her wider and lowered himself, kissing her dewy curls. She smelled amazing. Like lilacs, aspen wind, and feminine bliss. She tasted even better. His tongue made tiny circles as his fingers continued to probe, doing exactly what his cock ached to do.

Merick arched her back off the bed in response. He pressed the palm of his free hand to her stomach to keep her still. She gasped and ran her hands through his hair, fisting it when his tongue took over for his fingers.

He wanted more. He lifted her hips off the bed to grant his mouth better access.

"I want you," she rasped, pulling on his shoulders. "All of you."

Stefen had his pants off and tossed across the room in a flash. He rose up over her, poised at her entrance, his cock thick with need as he nudged into her heat. Just the tip.

She was on fire.

Her legs quivered as he slowly lowered his weight back onto his forearms, bracketing her head with his arms. Holding painfully still, Stefen's eyes locked on hers and he pushed, inch by inch, by torturous inch.

The speed alone was enough to kill him. He could hardly breath, hardly think at all. His eyes searched hers, needing some unspoken permission to fully claim her.

She tilted her chin, her breath mingling with his as she whispered against his lips. "Please."

It was all the invitation he required. Arms braced on either side of her, caging her in, he buried himself to the hilt.

He almost lost vision when her body clamped down around his shaft. She gasped and clung to his shoulders. With more willpower than Stefen thought possible, he lowered his head and kissed the hollow of her throat.

Slowly, he withdrew, marveling at how her body shuddered from the loss. He looked down at her. Her breasts were suffused with rosy color from the friction of his chest, her nipples as round as pebbles. Mouth slightly ajar and eyes half-closed, she was magnificent.

"Look at me," Stefen urged.

She did, her gaze meeting his as he sank into her. Her hands ran the length of his back and gripped both his ass cheeks tightly, her nails biting into his flesh.

Still he withdrew slowly, rocking his hips forward, filling her thoroughly with each new stroke. Her body joined the dance. And when she moved...the sun, the stars and the moon collided.

He felt her everywhere; where their bodies fused together, her mouth crushed against his, her thighs squeezed his waist. He moaned. Deeper and faster with each new thrust, until the pace took over, demanding he take all.

"Stefen." Merick buried her face in his chest, her legs shaking as he continued to pump into her.

He yielded completely to the primal roar of his body, moving with a hunger he'd never experienced. He consumed all of her, thrusting harder and faster until her body clenched around him, her muscles convulsed, and she took him over the top.

His kiss found her mouth. With one hand, he reached behind her head, cupping it. His breathing clashed and moved with hers, until a final thrust sent him spiraling over the edge.

He pulled out as he came, panting as aftershock after aftershock racked his body. She held him tightly, her own body riding the wave of his release, her mouth on his collarbone, his throat, his jaw and his lips. Stefen dropped his head down beside hers and closed his eyes, his heartbeat ragged.

When the room finally stopped spinning, he pressed his forehead to Merick's. "I think I might have just died."

"That...was..." She rasped out in short little breaths. "I can't uncurl my toes."

Stefen rolled to the side, taking her with him. "Then my job is done." He smiled. "For now."

She nipped his chin. "How many minutes do you need?"

"Minutes?" He scoffed.

Merick pressed against him, her soft frame melding seamlessly to his length. He took a labored breath, feeling every inch of her perfect body—her thighs, stomach, nipples—hardening anew against his chest.

His cock answered the call, eagerly pushing into the cleft between her legs. She grinned wickedly.

"Unfortunately," he said, and her smile began to fade. "You're going to have to take my word for it."

"What does he need you for now?"

"It's not Alaric this time." Stefen kissed the pout on her mouth. "But I won't be gone long." He gently disentangled her and sat up.

"When will you be back?" Merick propped herself up on an elbow.

"As soon as I can." He hated being close-lipped with her, but the less she knew the better.

Stefen pushed to his feet, locating his discarded pants and pulling them on. "Can you forgive me for rushing off?" He reached for his shirt. "I did want our first time to be, *memorable.*" A pang of guilt washed over him. "Certainly not ending in me having to rush out the door right after."

She moved to her knees. "Come here."

He obliged, leaning in. Merick cupped his face, kissing him

softly on the lips, his cheekbones, and jaw, before whispering, "There is nothing to forgive."

She sat back. "As far as memorable..." The crumpled white sheets bunched around her, framing her body like a winter rose. A smirk on her berry-red lips, she said, "Ask my toes how they've recovered when you get back."

Chapter Twenty-Nine

GERRA

It swept over his mind like a susurrating wind through dead trees. Pain, anger, hurt and loss. He would bleed it all. The sharp, sting of reality was the lancing price of admittance. The only way to face what was to come next.

Teakin watched his blood fill the syringe. It danced with the poison, both striving for dominance. It only took seconds for the drug to win, stealing passage when the pressure was released.

It entered the vein on a hushed moan and time hung suspended. Then it raced, gathering strength, raging with a cavalry's intent, obliterating all that he knew. All that he was. Like a lover, it wrapped its long legs around his waist, ran its fingers through the roots of his hair, and whispered in his ear...*I am here.*

Teakin's head rolled back. The monster could have his body, but his mind would be gone from this world. A needle crashed on a hard surface. It made no more than a murmur. His eyes fluttered closed.

Let it take me. Let it steal what is left. Let it end.

The present and past swirled around one another—one last

memory. Faster and faster, they whirled until there was nothing but silence. Nothing at all.

Something inside him had other plans. A pain, like none he'd ever felt, gouged at his slumber, a faint noise ringing out like a tiny bell. The intrusive sound grew in volume, louder and louder, as a scream worked its way out of his bones.

Then the weight of a hammer landed in the middle of his chest. *The dragon waking.* Teakin's eyes snapped open.

He was in the same room, a richly decorated bed chamber. The place of his torture. He did a mental check of his body. Other than the stabbing sensation in his chest, and some superficial wounds leaking from his head, he hadn't been violated. *Yet.*

Teakin's gaze drifted to the syringe laying between the cracks on the floor. He made to move for it. He couldn't. His mind fought to push away the haze as he tried to locate the damn ringing bell, still getting louder.

Something hit the side of his head, wrenching his face to the left.

The slap served two purposes. To drag him to clarity. And piss off the dragon. "You think you can escape me?" Zander yelled, his body coming into focus, looming over Teakin. "Who gave you this?" He was holding the syringe now.

Teakin sucked on his teeth, trying to draw enough saliva back to his mouth to answer. "I thought you wanted me compliant."

"Subservient," Zander spat, hurling the syringe at the wall. "Not fucking dead."

"Not into that sort of thing?"

Teakin's head snapped violently to the side again. This time the delivered blow had come from a closed fist. The taste of copper filled his mouth. He spat it out. "I must have struck a nerve."

"Tie him over that." Zander pointed to the railing at the end of the bed.

"No foreplay?" Teakin hissed, as someone hauled him to his feet.

"Just be thankful you won't have an audience."

His shirt was ripped up the middle of his back and he was pushed face forward, over the end of the bed. Fighting would do no good. This was the deal he had made. To keep Zander from decapitating the boy upon entering Gerra, as he had done his mother. Teakin's arms were yanked wide and tied out to the posts.

Zander leaned down, his breath hot against his ear. "Tell me who gave you the drug and this will go much *smoother*."

"Why does it matter? I'm awake now."

The king snarled. "Leave us!"

He took a deep breath when Zander moved behind him, the dragon raging just under his skin. It would take an act of the gods to keep the beast at bay for this. But he had to. For their sake.

Teakin braced himself for what was to happen next. He heard a zipper. Felt rough hands at the belt of his pants. Then...

A razor thin whooshing sound sliced through the air.

Something heavy fell on his back.

Teakin jerked his head from side to side, but his arms were bound too tight to get any kind of visual.

The weight slid slowly off his back, then dropped with a thud to the floor.

Someone, faster than his eyes could track, cut the ropes at his wrist. Teakin leapt up, whirling in place.

Zander lay at his feet, looking up with vacant eyes, an arrow through his skull.

Teakin stared at him. "How—"

"A little bird told me where to find you."

"Did that little bird happen to tell you where my son is being kept?"

"Only that you will be reunited with him." Stefen looked to the prone body of the king. "Once you finish the bastard off."

"Killing him won't assure my son's safety." Teakin jerked Zander up and slung him over his shoulder. "Making him a prisoner might."

"The deal I struck was his life for yours. I don't know what they will do if you don't fulfill your end of the bargain."

"They'll get their fulfillment when I get my son." Teakin marched toward the door. "Not before." He stopped in front of Stefen. "Thank you."

"Don't thank me until we make it across."

They stole into a servant's stairway. Less than a minute later, they were through the palace gates and crossing the rocky terrain, covering the ground with lightning speed. They reached the border and made the jump without even glimpsing another elite. It was almost too easy.

As soon as their feet landed on Earth's soil, Stefen mentally reached out to Ash. He would ask for forgiveness later. He never was one to follow directions.

His maker shot from thin air like a spear of darkness. "Of all the stupid shit you've pulled..." His words faded when his sights landed on Teakin, their archenemy strung over his shoulder like a slain deer.

Stefen shrugged. "You knew the risk when you turned me."

Kielyn manifested beside her mate, her lips twisting upward. "That should probably be the Fire Dynasty's motto at this point."

Ash looked back pointedly at Stefen. "He still shouldn't have broken with my orders."

"I wouldn't necessarily call it *breaking with them*," he retorted. "More like, speeding them up a bit."

Zander twitched. Teakin dropped him to the ground, wrath twisting his features. Yanking the arrow out of his skull, he plunged it back through Zander's eye socket.

The amount of aggression in the action spoke more to Teakin's brief stint in Gerra than any words. Ash's mouth tightened as he stared down at his brother—rage, not worry flickered in his eyes. "He didn't?"

Teakin shook his head as he stood. A beat of silent understanding passed before Ash inquired, "Where's the boy?"

"Thaddeus wouldn't tell me," Stefen answered. "He only told me where to find Teakin. Claiming he would bring him as soon as Zander was dead."

"Which clearly he isn't." Kielyn wrinkled her nose, looking from the king's limp body to Teakin. "I'm guessing you had doubts about him holding up his end of the bargain?"

"The Diabolis are nothing if not dishonest. You can trust them on that," Teakin said, meeting her eyes. "They can have the son of a bitch when I get my child."

"They will no doubt agree to the trade, but then what?" Kielyn looked at each of them. "We'll be inciting a war if we kill him. I don't care how bad the queen wants her brother dead, she cannot let obvious disrespect go unpunished. She'll owe it to her kingdom to exact revenge. Are we prepared for that?"

Ash motioned to Zander. "Let's get him in the dungeon." He looked at Stefen. "Alert Alaric. And get Eirik and Bastian out of Anu."

He didn't have to expand on the order. The twins had designated strongholds assigned to each of them. In the event of a war. Two secure locations that would provide security. In case something happened to their parents.

Stefen grabbed Zander and heaved him over his shoulder. Ash stepped up. "You know I would send Merick with one of them, if she wasn't so close to turning." Though the words were delivered with practical wisdom, the look in his maker's eyes begged understanding.

Stefen nodded and Ash turned to his brother. "We will join them in Anu after we can get things in order here."

"I'll consult Alaric's oracle," Stefen said. "There might be some benefit to the coming eclipse. If we can hold them off until then."

"Any help would be welcome," his maker agreed. "Since it looks like I'm about to have an elite army on my doorstep."

Stefen and Kielyn started for the castle. "I'm sorry, brother." The anguish in Teakin's voice was palpable. "I can leave as soon as I end him. Hopefully they'll follow me, realizing you had no part in this."

Stefen glanced back in time to see Ash's pupils flare. "The fuck you will!" he snapped. "You are my family. What they have done to you, they have done to me." He grabbed Teakin by the back of the neck. "We will kill them all."

Kielyn reached out and took Stefen's hand in hers as they continued to walk away. "We will stand together," she said softly. "As a family."

Chapter Thirty

ANU

M erick headed into the training room sore but completely energized. She spotted Eirik descending a rope and smiled.

Her joy faded when he dropped the remaining ten feet and landed beside Kimberly. The Air-dancer giggled and curled her arm around his waist.

"That wasn't the only thing you were curled around last night," Merick mumbled.

"Aww, you're jealous?" a snide masculine voice said.

She whipped around, coming face to face with Bastian.

While a small part of her could rationalize away his issues with her and Teakin, since they pertained to his own father being involved and the risk arising from it, none of them had anything to do with Eirik. That had just been cruel. Strictly for the sake of being cruel.

"More like sickened." Merick glared up at him. "Do you always go after your brother's sloppy seconds?" She could barely believe her own words—the bite to them. But before she could contemplate further, more came tumbling out. "I would guess that your inferior dick complex must be to blame, but sadly, I'm no shrink. And to think," she folded her arms, "Just yesterday you were touting such a *noble* bloodline."

He only smirked. "So much to learn."

"Whatever." She started for the climbing wall.

He gripped her elbow in a movement too fast to detect. "It's my day to train you."

Her eyes narrowed to where he touched her. "Pretty sure I've never heard your name spoken as anyone skilled enough to do so."

A blatant lie. Merick knew all too well how talented Bastian was. She'd heard more than a few angels and elementals alike praise his abilities. *Regardless...* She was team Eirik. The evil twin wouldn't be getting an accolades from her today.

"Let's ask, shall we." He released her arm, looking over the top of her head as he called out. "Eirik, who did Stefen want working with our dear cousin today?"

"You," Eirik shouted back. "Why?"

Bastian smiled slowly. "Just wanted to be certain I heard him correctly." He cast his gaze back down and lowered his voice. "I was so thoroughly spent when he asked me last night."

"I need to talk to Eirik first." Merick turned around. She'd see how his answer changed when she told him what she'd witnessed last night.

Three strides in, Merick definitely expected Bastian to try and stop her. He didn't. By her fifth step, she realized he wouldn't. She glanced over her shoulder. Only to find the raven-haired twin patiently waiting.

What the actual fuck? Did he really not care if she ratted him out to his brother?

She lost her nerve. Merick knew firsthand the only thing worse than having jokes made about you behind your back, was having them made to your face. She would not humiliate Eirik in front of these traitors. She would tell him later, in private.

Merick spun on her heels and marched back, past Bastian, toward the obstacle course. "Fuck you!"

Bastian chuckled. "I'm sure you'd enjoy that."

Thirty minutes later Merick was sure of one thing; Bastian was trying to kill her.

"Run it again." He flew by her. "You're the slowest mortal ever."

Merick fought back a curse and pushed harder, trying to keep up with him. She landed on the other side of the last wall, her breathing doing its own part to end her. "Please tell me you're better at Fire-dancing," he said.

"Since you're the teacher, you tell me." She shot a fireball at his head.

He dodged it. "Ready for sparring, are you?" A blue flame lit in the palm of his upturned hand.

"Just testing your reflexes," she intoned bitterly. "You seemed a little slow on that last lap."

"Are you always this witty?"

"You must bring out my inner bitch."

"Well, let's see how mouthy your inner bitch is when you're in combat." Bastian threw the blaze at her feet.

Merick leapt back, but the fire had already formed a ring around her and the obstacle course wall. She quickly climbed up, flames snapping at her feet. "What are you doing? You can't use the elements in this room. You'll burn it down."

"Something you should have considered before you threw the first punch." He stood, arms crossed, watching as the embers latched onto, then climbed the wooden wall. "What are you going to do now?"

Merick looked around, panic beginning to set in. She could jump over it. If she'd thought of that ten seconds earlier. She had only dabbled in fire of her own making. Only witnessed fire Eirik called to him.

Neither of those examples could compare to the hungry, wrathful fire Bastian had just created. This fire was born of darker magic, kindled with rage and menace. The flames were spreading out, teasing at what the structure harbored, the wood giving itself freely to that intimacy.

The blaze gained momentum, its heat singeing the hem of her sweat pants and melting the plastic tips of her shoestrings. Coughing, she looked up, the fumes burning her eyes. *A rope.* If she could reach it, she could climb high enough to swing across. But if she missed...

She looked back at Bastian through the rising inferno, and something inside her shifted. An awakening. A shimmering ripple of clarity. So bright it chased away the constriction of fear in that instant. She couldn't outrun this. She would have to subdue it. She would have to bend it to her will.

Bastian's words collected like an avenging army in the back of her mind. *Weak. Unworthy. Not one of us.* Merick drew them forward, feeding them to the mounting power drumming to life deep inside her.

Her vision narrowed as it had on the plane. A similar anger festered now. Her cousin had his mind made up about her and her father. This was his trial by fire. He was testing her. Seeing what she was made of.

The pain of her childhood—outcast, judged unfairly, never given a chance—assembled and simmered.

No more!

She was born of fire, same as he was. She had as much a right to claim the LaGoryen name as he did. The words from the queen of Gerra played again in her head. *"They have to see you to understand you."*

Marzalla and Palomi had taught her how to avoid being a target. By interpreting intentions and concealing who she was. A valuable defensive.

However, other times you had to show *exactly* who you were.

Merick didn't recognize the growl that rumbled low in her throat. She might not be one of the realm's 'Chosen,' but she had the blood of the dragon in her veins. *And it was pissed.*

But not at the blaze.

She cast her gaze to the inferno raging beneath her. It wasn't the element's fault. It had been willed to life. Drawn here by a vengeful host. Merick stared into the fire. *So Angry.*

'Perhaps you are just like me,' she said to the firestorm. *'Born to a life you didn't choose. A life others fear, they run from, or try to control.'*

One by one, she mentally latched onto the invading flames, pushing them gently back. Heat swirled, licking at her flesh, but she could no longer feel its burn.

The same enchanting call pulled her to the fire. She let its song drift around her, but she didn't let it in. Fire was a wicked lover, Eirik had warned. Once you became lost to its hypnotic sonnet, it would consume you.

Merick funneled her thoughts into one singular goal. *Understanding.* Just as she'd done with countless creatures over the years, she let the fire see her. Let it feel every intention. Let it understand she meant not to run. She would not fear it. Half of her was molded from it.

She lifted her hands and forced the element to heel.

It did. The room cooled and the flames fell away, almost as quickly as they had risen. As they descended, crackling and hissing, she saw again her cousin's face.

He, too, saw her clearly.

Merick smiled at him. Shockingly, it was not an effort or an act. She smiled because she knew fear now—had shaken its hand, looked it in the eyes. It possessed fangs. It was beautiful.

She had smiled at the fire.

The flames knew her now, too. It saw her white hair and two different color eyes, and called her an angel. It also felt the heart of the dragon beating inside her.

The fire smiled back at her.

Order out of chaos. That was what he needed.

In another time, not so distantly removed, Stefen would have reveled in the hustle. Everyone buzzing about, energy high with the adrenaline of an expected war. Grand masters would be darting here and there, securing intelligent property in case of a siege. The High Council would be arguing, war chieftains strategized, soldiers received their marching orders, and Alaric, the king...would remain unnervingly calm, sitting amongst the chaos, waiting for it to die down.

Stefen would have been absent during most of this, likely off fucking some chit in a hidden alcove, while pandemonium ensued around him. When his presence, or lack thereof, was eventually noted, they would come for him. At which time he would sit back and delight in his brother's torment.

He was such a shit.

Looking back on it now with a totally different mindset, Alaric had been calm out of necessity. Staying behind his pack, letting each individual preform their designated roles without hindrance. Lower ranking members would then follow the agreed upon edicts of their superiors, never realizing the true direction came from the leader at the back.

Controlling chaos meant being able to trust the process, to

trust the *wolves* placed strategically in a well-maintained court. Control was patience. A good leader knew when to assert his role and when to trust the process. Alaric had learned this at a young age, while his little brother was out doing whatever he wanted. Life had not prepared Stefen to rule. It barely had taught him to obey.

Actually, he mentally corrected, it *hadn't* taught him to obey. If it had, he wouldn't have gone off script and snuck into Gerra, slipped into Thaddeus's household, learned where Teakin was being held and freed him.

No, life—this one or the last—had not altered his personality in the least.

Until now.

Now he was the one sitting still in a room filled with activity. Sidtric was on a virtual meeting with Kizer and Dax. Marzalla was going over new details with three Air generals. High Council members were doing what they did best, argue. A few scholars had already left the room in search of 'secret documentation'. All that was needed to complete this bit of nostalgia was Alaric—busting in to scold Stefen for causing this.

As if on cue, his brother walked through the door. He'd brought his oracle. Stefen waited for the chastising to commence.

Alaric took a seat across from him, Trophonius hung back, observing from the doorway. Stefen unclasped his hands and spread them. "I'm waiting."

"I see that."

Great, he was being gifted 'cryptic Alaric'. "Alright then." Stefen started to stand. "Now that you're here. I'll be back—"

"You were never a still child," Alaric cut him off. "An even twitchier teenager. And a downright obstreperous warrior."

Scrutinizing Alaric, his favorite. "Do go on." He relaxed back into the seat. "I bet you have considered this lecture all the way from the twelfth floor."

"Actually, it just occurred to me."

"All my shortcomings *just* came to you?" Stefen eyed him suspiciously. "Like you don't have them permanently etched in chronological order by annoyance?"

"Not your shortcomings." Alaric waved his hand up and down, referencing Stefen as a whole. "This..."

"As much fun as charades is with you," Stefen said. "We are a little pressed for time."

"Why are you so calm?"

He looked around the room. "Everyone is busy getting things in order. I'm simply not adding to their stress."

"Yet the complexity of your emotions is drastically different from your days in my court." Alaric raised a brow. "You used to live for the drama. Bathed in it really. You wanted to be the first to battle and the last to pass out from drink afterward."

His brother studied him closely. *Too closely.* "You were one of my best and most bloodthirsty fighters. It was the only thing you seemed to enjoy." He shrugged. "Apart from debauchery."

"Well, that was before I was killed, re-born, and cast out of your court."

"Nay, it was before you fell in love."

The truth out of his brother's mouth was both a beautiful and terrible thing. It painted a clear picture of everything. As liberating as that might be, it rightly pissed him off in the same breath.

Stefen was patiently watching everyone else scramble about, but he wasn't enjoying this. He was not looking forward to what might come next. He was preparing. The sort of preparation unknown to the selfish.

He was afraid. Afraid for those he loved—Merick, Kielyn, Ash, the twins, Alaric. Terrified of his role in bringing this to their doorsteps. And while he did not regret, not one bit, rescuing

Teakin. He could only hope whatever happened next ended in their favor. He wasn't sure if he could live with himself if it didn't.

"It's in times of great conflict, or love, that leaders are forged." Alaric pushed his chair back from the table. "Your time has finally come."

"My time for what?"

"To lead."

Stefen snorted. "You just got done listing off each of my personality traits that completely contradict this theory." He shook his head, incredulously. "Have you taken a crack to the skull?"

"Look around, Stefen." Alaric leaned down, his voice pitched low, "You're the only calm one in here."

"Being calm hardly correlates to being suitable for advising others."

"No, there is more to it than that. Factors such as, you are the only one of the Earth kings raised in a royal court. Ash was taken from his when he was only seven summers. Dax, and Sidtric were generals' sons, and Kizer is too young."

"What exactly are you saying?"

"The realms need leaders, not just kings, from all corners that are willing to pull from, and share, their experiences. No one who keeps their talents to themselves during times of great strife will be remembered when the history books document the days that mattered."

"I wasn't born to lead, Alaric."

"Neither was Ash. And look how efficient he has become. He was born with the capacity, and has learned the will, to rally his people around him with a strength of character that inspires confidence in each of his subjects. Now you have much of his inherent power, coupled with what you retained from your angel lineage. That makes you one of the deadliest warriors alive. Also, the only one with inside knowledge to the type of court politics Gerra and Anu were built on."

"Your point?"

"Leaders aren't born. They are made. As with your maker, the universe has been honing and polishing you for a similar role for centuries." He glanced around the room. "They could all use your insight." Alaric looked back at him. "It's time they wrote your name in that history book."

———————◆◆◆◆◆———————

M erick made her way down the dimly lit passageway beside Eirik and Palomi. The wailing sirens from above drifted after them as they descended further into the underbelly of the mountain. She ventured a glance over her shoulder. Others were still filing in from the hidden doorway, their shadows filling the tight space, cutting off any remnants of natural light from the castle's kitchen.

"Everything will be okay," Eirik assured, though she wasn't sure if it was for her benefit or his.

Merick focused her sights straight ahead. The passageway was just wide enough for the three of them to walk side by side without brushing shoulders. She rubbed her arms as the temperature continued to drop. "What do you think it is?"

"Probably just a test," Palomi reasoned. "In all the years I've been here, there has never been a breach in security."

"The last war was before I was born. And now that Teakin's back in Gerra there shouldn't be a reason... " Eirik paused. "I mean..." He looked over at Merick. "Sorry. That was insensitive."

"It's okay," she said. "It's a rational deduction."

"Rational? My brother?" A voice, Merick was becoming annoyingly familiar with, quipped from behind them. "Unfortunately he's woefully lacking on his intel." Bastian pushed between them, his customary cruel smile in place. "Teakin escaped."

"What?" Merick gasped.

"I caught Stefen leaving the High Council meeting." Bastian strolled ahead. "He said not to tell you."

"I knew he'd escape." Eirik grinned with pride. "He's a LaGoryen."

"Is Teakin with him?" Merick asked.

Bastian didn't bother looking back. "Nope."

"Does this new development have anything to do with the sirens?" Palomi rejoined the conversation.

"Don't know," Bastian replied. "He was ushered away by King Alaric before I could ask. He only said to find you three and stay close."

"Fuck!" Eirik's sentiment matched Merick's. "That can't be good."

"Best to not draw conclusions," Palomi reasoned. The tunnel opened up into a massive cavern that mimicked an amphitheater. "Let's hear what they have to say first."

The entirety of the space had been carved from the mountain; from the black spiky-edged walls with speckles of glassy gold, the chiseled out coliseum seating, to the stalactites hanging high above, glistering wet—like stars being born.

Merick wordlessly followed the others down the worn center steps. She had always loved mountains. They'd served as her escape many times over the years. Anytime her life had gotten too difficult or too lonely, she'd sought out their powerful solace. There, above the reach of life's expectations, among the wild expanse of nature, she found silence in the midst of eternal noise.

Albeit, her experience was one from atop. Never had she been beneath the rock. This mountain was different from any in Gerra. More ancient, like a gap between two worlds. She could feel it. This mountain had seen untold sunrises, standing reverent since the beginning, under the thunder's praise. It predated the winged creatures who ruled over it.

A force for nature to break itself on from the outside. On the inside...this space, this cave, felt like a temple. A terrestrial manifestation of the gods. It filled every pore and cell, welcoming her home.

Bastian's broad shoulders moved out of her way and she saw for the first time the center of the giant semicircular arena. Its own form of worship. A throne.

The stage, same as the polished stone where Merick took a seat, rose out of the onyx bedrock. The towering gold throne stood out in the middle like the sun emerging from a solar eclipse. Five smaller replicas were positioned on either side of the gold one, each upholstered in a signature color; frost-kissed silver, royal-blue, emerald-green, crimson-red, and one of snow-white with light blue trim. Lining the edge of the stage, three steps down from the raised dais, stood twelve ornately carved wooden chairs, each bearing a unique crest.

"I've always preferred an empty throne to one with an ass in it," Bastian said out of the side of his mouth, somehow making the hard rock he was sitting on look comfortable.

An image of him seated on a throne flashed in her mind. He would wear it well. Was born for it.

"Careful, your Highness," Palomi warned. "Many a heart would break to see a noose around that handsome neck."

"The gold is obviously Alaric's." Eirik pointed to the others. "Four of those belong to the Earth kings; blue for water, red for fire, green for earth, and silver for air. No one ever said elemental dancers were creative." He chuckled when his sights landed on the white velvet-covered throne. "That one I have never seen before."

"The fae king?" Merick hedged.

Bastian snorted. "Which one?"

"It's a complicated situation." Palomi's gaze slid to the dark haired twin. "A conversation best left in Ventus." She refocused on Merick. "I don't have a clue who the white one is for."

"Must be some honorary bullshit," Bastian said.

Palomi grinned sardonically. "Perhaps it's yours."

Bastian yielded no tinge of emotion as he unfurled his hands. "White's not my color."

More supernaturals, elemental and angel alike, filled the space around them, similar inquires and speculations whispered amongst themselves. Though everyone grew silent when twelve High Council members filed onto the podium and took their seats before the dais. Then, one by one, the elemental kings came out.

Her uncle took the crimson throne and Sidtric the silver. A male with long golden hair, who could be described as nothing short of beautiful, claimed the blue. A fourth male lumbered more than walked onto the raised stage and plopped down in the emerald-covered throne. Huge, he had flaming red hair, hard features, and eyes that probably could kill by just looking at you.

Finally Alaric emerged, walking to stand in front of the golden throne. Merick could not help but be impressed. All five kings were a sight to behold. Each exceedingly handsome, all commanding in their own way.

"This is not a drill," Alaric addressed the crowd. "We have good reason to expect a provocation from Gerra soon."

Nervous murmurs drifted around the cavernous room, their concern bouncing off of the agate walls like echoes in a hollow canyon.

"Anu will join Earth in uniting under one banner if they wish to escalate matters," the Angel King continued. "For ill intent against one of us is an affront on all of us."

"Looks like your daddy really threw his name around," Bastian snarled low beside her. "If any of my friends die fighting his battle—"

"Stop!" Eirik cut his gaze to his brother.

The Water King was speaking now, but Merick couldn't focus on his words. Her mind was racing forward in time with too many scenarios. Would they really go to war? Was her father the reason? Where was he? Where was Stefen?

A soothing caress feathered over her frenzied thoughts, *"Everything's going to be fine. Teakin's here now. I'm going to strangle your cousin."*

Merick looked around the giant room. She didn't see Stefen anywhere, but his words were a balm to her frayed nerves. She smiled down their bond. *"He really is a prick."*

"For too long the realms have been divided, each species sticking to their own," Alaric's voice interrupted her from saying more. "All that changed with the birth of our Chosen One. But there are still many without a direct tie to any particular realm. Some that are born hybrids and some that were made such by circumstances beyond their control."

Merick's blood quickened in her veins. Like Stefen. Like her...

Alaric continued. "It's time those individuals have a house. A supernatural faction welcomed openly on both Anu and Earth soil. It is my honor to introduce you to house Rigel, named after one of the brightest stars in the galaxy. A beacon to any seeking a home."

A white banner lowered behind the six thrones—a light blue crest bearing an image of a windblown tree. Its roots spread wide at the bottom of the tapestry then crawled up its ornately embossed sides.

"The Joshua tree," Eirik whispered. Merick looked quizzically at him and he expanded the statement. "Biblically, it was said to be named after Joshua. A sign to weary travelers that they were headed in the right direction. Dendrologically, the tree is a symbol for thriving amidst adversity."

"Culturally." Bastian leaned forward with a Cheshire cat grin. "A cool band named an album after it."

"But what is a great house without a great leader?" Alaric's rich baritone voice filled the space again. "I present to you..."

A light from above illuminated the back of the dais, driving out the shadows that had concealed a form Merick knew all too well.

"King, Stefen Von Emmerich."

———————◆◆◆◆◆◆———————

"What in God's armor did you just do?" Stefen stormed after Alaric down the tunnel.

Unrestrained tongue-wagging could still be heard from the throne room. He needed to get to Merick and explain. All of this bullshit. But first, he needed to understand it himself. "Have you lost your mind?"

"Don't act so surprised." Alaric opened a door and held it. "I said you would make an excellent ruler an hour ago."

"No, you said I should use my training to help the others. Which is not even remotely close to *'here's your new king'*. And you damn well know it." He made a beeline to the room's side bar. "Besides, you can't just proclaim a damn king." Stefen filled a glass. "They have to be selected by the popular vote."

"You were."

"You are not the majority, Alaric. No matter how much you think it."

Alaric leaned his weight into the back of a leather couch. "All four elemental kings voted you in."

"I stand corrected. You've *all* lost your minds."

"I honestly thought you would approve. Having been cast out

of your own home. And then witnessing Merick's struggles to fit into a realm she didn't belong to."

"Do not bring her into this!" Stefen snapped.

"Why not?" he challenged. "It's the truth. Same as Ashdon. Once he escaped Gerra, he had nowhere to go. No legion he belonged—"

"Exactly as he wanted it."

"Had Bane, as twisted as his real motives were, not reestablished the ruling elemental houses on Earth, your maker would have never met Kielyn. Never sired those two boys. His purpose would have benefited no one. Simply another lone vampire with the ability to manipulate fire."

Stefen stared at his brother. "There's the real answer to why you're doing this. It's not about inclusion. It's about strategy." He scoffed. "You don't give a rat's ass about *'lost souls'* finding their true home. You only care about building stronger alliances. Growing your numbers."

Alaric watched him, a deadpan expression on his face. "Can they not both achieve the same results?"

"Do the others share those same agendas?"

"Stefen, they're kings."

"Unbelievable." He slammed back the drink. "Well, find another one to rule *Rigel*. I will not be your puppet." Stefen poured a second glass. "Did you, even once, consider my opinion on this?"

Alaric folded arms. "I considered your personal feelings as much as anyone did mine when I was named king."

"This is not the same." Stefen glared at him. "But it doesn't matter, I'm no longer under your rule. You can't make decisions for me anymore."

Alaric pushed off the couch. "You would deny me?"

"Yes."

"Would you deny Ashdon? Would you deny Merick?"

"Don't." He tipped back the glass. "This is about you. Still trying to control my life."

"Oh, but it's very much about them. Your maker needs your support. Not just as another sword in his army, not as his emissary. He needs every asset I listed off in that chamber room earlier. Assets only *you* can provide."

His brother started toward him, willful determination residing in those hazel eyes. "His wife, your best friend, sacrificed everything she'd ever known to further this cause."

"They were mates."

Even to Stefen's ears the excuse sounded feeble. Some part of Kielyn had to have felt the mating bond early on. Still, without any guarantee of what she was walking into, she had volunteered up her body and life for the betterment of supernaturals everywhere. Without hesitation.

Alaric persisted like a hound wearing down a fox. "Your future mate needs this, too. To feel safe bringing up your children. In a world that won't scorn them for being different." He stopped, directly in front of Stefen. "Does she not deserves that?"

"Do not dare tell me what she deserves." Stefen growled. "And don't think for one more second to saddle me with some made-up crown."

"Fine." Alaric stepped back, his eyes growing hard. "Play the selfish Stefen card if you like. It's what you're best at. Disappointing others." He turned and marched swiftly for the door.

"Fuck you!" Stefen lashed out. "You have no idea what all I endured living under your damned rule."

"And what was that?" Alaric stopped in his tracks, turning ever so slowly. "Dodging anything remotely similar to your duty?"

"Oh, I did more than my share at keeping up your perfect appearance." He could feel his fists clenching, his spine growing rigid, the alcohol loosening his tongue. "You were their crowned king. The highest and closest to the gods. Everyone loved you. But you know what's stronger than love?" He downed the last of the scotch. "Lust."

"However, you were not obtainable to slake their perversions on." Stefen set the empty glass on the bar top. It made a hollow sound. "Guess who was?"

The words hung in the air, the silence stretching long between them. "Stefen..."

"At first it was just praise. Praise for a stupid boy starved for attention." He went on, despite the bile rising in the back of his throat. "But I think we both know that nothing in this court is done without careful consideration of political gain. Praise turned to touch, and touch turned to... Well-laid snares. Once I started making mistakes, getting sloppy, their pursuits changed."

Stefen faced the bar top. He'd never spoken these words to Alaric. Only Kie, Ash, and Mar knew this part of his past. Knew how it had shaped him. What it had cost him.

"They now had something to hold over my head. Something they could use against me. Against you and our family name. I had a choice to make; play by their rules, as varied and ever-changing as they were, and keep my indiscretions a secret. Or embody the persona they had manufactured to use against me." He paused, still unable to face Alaric. "The court whore."

Stefen stared at the amber liquid in the crystal decanter. "So you see," he said finally. "I do know a thing or two about appearances. I kept up an award-winning one for most of my life."

"I had no idea...I..." Alaric faltered behind him. "I assumed..."

"Good." Stefen let out a breathy chuckle. "I worked very hard to maintain that deception." He faced his brother, fully expecting to see the disgust in his eyes.

Alaric's gaze reflected anything but. "They groomed you for a role you never wanted. Then they used it against you." His voice all but galvanized. "Names!" He marched to a desk. "I want names."

"Brother."

"They'll die for this." He began digging for a pen in one of the drawers.

"Alaric?"

"Damn it, Stefen! Tell me who they were." He looked up, something etched on his face Stefen had never seen before— anguish, hate, *guilt*...

"I've already made my peace with it. I have forgiven them."

"Forgiven?" Alaric asked in a brittle, accusatory tone.

A small smile. "A few might have met with an unfortunate end outside of Anu."

His brother was across the room, hand on the back of Stefen's head, dragging him in for an embrace. "I should have known. I should have stopped it."

"Please don't do this. Don't take this on." Stefen pulled back. "This weight is not yours. That time is behind me. Life must be lived going forward, ahead of past wrongs."

Alaric looked him in the eyes. "Can you forgive me? For being blind. Insensitive."

"I already have." He grinned. "Nineteen years ago, to be exact."

"So recently?" The corners of his brother's mouth turned up. "It's good to know you only hold grudges for a handful of centuries. That'll give me a good timeline when I piss you off in future council meetings."

They both laughed, then fell into silent reflection. "Do you really think I have what it takes?" Stefen finally asked.

"Without a shadow of a doubt."

"I don't think I'm ready to be a king," he admitted.

"It's because of that..." Alaric stepped back, his smile widening. "I know you are."

Chapter Thirty-One

GERRA

Thaddeus drummed his fingers on the arm of his chair. It had been six hours since Zander had been taken and still no word from his captors, publicly or privately. But that wasn't his biggest problem. He had lost the upper hand with the queen.

The little witch broke their agreed-upon strategy the second the alarms sounded. Instead of curbing the palace chaos; she chose to incite it. Delivering a fiery speech about revenge, intolerance, and promised mayhem. Half the surrounding village was wielding pitchforks and vowing to get justice for their captured king before she stepped off the damn rostrum.

He tried to get an audience with her after she was whisked away to her chambers, but he was turned away. *'The queen needs her rest.'* A blatant lie. The queen needed to plot. All of which reminded Thaddeus why he'd been hesitant to involve her in the first place; she was as unpredictable as a tornado with the attention span of a lightning bolt. One did not simply *deal* with Katarra. They survived her.

The only thing he considered a blessing was no one had been

ordered to stay at court after the declaration of war. Although most did, all eager to hear what their orders would be, Thaddeus had wasted no time heading straight back to Northdom castle.

Stefen's arrival had been a setback. Be that as it may, he'd sworn his allegiance to Ashdon. So Thaddeus did as the angel hybrid asked when he showed up in his palace chambers. However, it robbed Thaddeus of the show he had been counting on. A bloodbath to put the last LaGoryen fiasco to shame.

Which is what would have happened if the Fire King had come for his brother. Exactly what Thaddeus was banking on to convince all of Gerra the Diaboli reign was weak and in need of revision. A new regime only *he* could provide.

Now, there would be war. Stefen and Teakin had assured that by taking Zander. Gerra would demand what Katarra had promised in her speech. A battle the queen seemed eager to deliver.

It was time to pivot *again*. Overthrowing a throne was a complicated science. It was a damn good thing he excelled at research. Making mistakes, calculating changes, anticipating failure—it all made for success. He only needed one of these narrow margins to line up correctly. As long as Zander and Katarra both ended up dead, all would be as it should.

A commotion outside the study made him swivel his chair away from the window.

"Open up!" someone ordered, just before his doors burst open.

The prince marched in and scanned the room, flanked by two royal guards. "You've been busy, great grandfather."

"Your Highness." Thaddeus rose, inclining his head. "What a pleasant surprise."

"Is it?"

"But, of course." Thaddeus chose his next words carefully. "Does the queen need me?"

"Not even past the pleasantries and already you're insulting me?" The prince glowered. "Tell me, Thaddeus, do I look like a messenger boy?"

"Forgive me, Your Highness, no. I am just surprised is all."

"Let's not start this meeting off with lies. I'm done with those." With the flick of his wrist, one of the guards closed the doors behind them. "Who has the king?"

The king. The clinical title wasn't lost on Thaddeus. "Assuming I know, I would like to put a question to you first. Do you want your father returned?" He decided to go with the direct route. "Dead or alive?"

Xavier chuckled, but the mirth did not reflect on his face. He clasped his hands behind his back and walked up to Thaddeus. He was taller, bigger than his father, with striking green eyes and tawny hair. The boy had grown into quite the man— distinguished and handsome, with a commanding presence.

As Thaddeus continued to take the measure of his great grandson, he realized something even more unique about the crowned prince. *He looked nothing like Zander.*

Twin flames lit behind Xavier's emerald irises. "You already know the answer."

"You don't care," Thaddeus said. "He's not your father."

ANU

The throne room became a buzz of activity the second the last High Council member quit the room. Bastian, Eirik, and Palomi wasted no time fanning out in different directions. Likely for three vastly different reasons.

Merick remained in her seat, listening to the excited whispers of a group of young Air-dancers behind her. "I heard the dragon emerged in him. That's why he was chosen. Dragons make excellent rulers."

"If you stay on their good side."

"I think it's romantic," a female said. "That a creature of such power can only be awakened by love."

A male scoffed. "Or good pussy."

That earned him a slap. "If that was the case, King Alaric's brother would've been turned a million times over."

Giggling erupted, and then a long sigh. "That male is sexy as fuck."

"I heard he was still boinking Kimberly."

"Didn't he make out with that stunning little hybrid at the ball?"

Merick cringed, pulling her hoodie over her head.

"Her, and half the castle." Sounds of agreement. "Kings don't have to be faithful. Regardless if their dragon has been *sprung to life*."

More laughter. "He will always have his cock. If I were him I would set up a harem."

Another female's voice. "Not all males are pigs."

"If you're talking about the male with the golden cock," a familiar feminine voice joined the conversation. "He will most definitely never settle down." A pause. "I have it on good authority."

A lowered whisper. "Are you the one that awakened his dragon?"

"Who knows." Kimberly chuckled. "I was too busy making other parts of him rise."

Merick had known she didn't like the Air-dancer the day she met her. Now, that verdict was signed, sealed, and delivered. She hated the bitch.

"This blows." Eirik reclaimed the seat beside her. "I wanted to go to the club tonight."

Ah, the mandatory curfew the High Council had issued. "They did say you could be out until ten," Merick offered.

"Nothing fun happens before ten."

"You won't be going out at all." Palomi delivered the sentence as she walked over. "Your father wants to see you." She looked at Merick. "You too."

Eirik huffed out a long sigh.

Merick stood and offered him a hand. "Come on."

He lazily accepted and let her haul, more than assist, him to his feet. Palomi lifted her arm and waved someone over. Merick did a quick scan of the room, avoiding the Air-dancers behind them, and located Bastian, lounging near the dais, a gaggle of approving females around him. His intense blue eyes noted Palomi's signal briefly before refocusing on his spellbound fans.

"This way." The midnight-haired fae led them down the stadium steps, past the dais where Bastian joined them, and through the same doors the High Council had used earlier.

The three cousins fell in step behind Palomi and trode down a short hall. Again, Merick reached out mentally, as she had done when Stefen left the stage. *After being proclaimed King of Rigel.* She received the same reply; nothing. He had locked her out.

Palomi stopped in front of a door and knocked twice. Alaric's voice answered. "Enter."

The door opened to reveal Stefen, Alaric, Ash, and Kielyn within the chamber. Each of their faces somber. Merick's heart flipped over in her chest when those sea-green eyes locked on hers.

Then he was moving, heading straight for her, his long legs eating up the distance between them. His large hand went to the back of her neck, cupping it gently and pulling her into his arms.

Stefen wrapped her up tightly, his scent enveloping her. She breathed it deep into her lungs, feeling his relief and his exhaustion as he exhaled. She wanted to cover him in kisses. But now was not the time. This was their own council meeting. As a family.

Merick looked around. *Except...*

"He'll be here shortly." Stefen squeezed her reassuringly.

"Is that where you went this morning?" she dared ask into the folds of his mind. *"You went back for Teakin?"*

He nodded down their bond and she buried her head in his chest. *"Thank you."*

Ash began. "Long story short, Teakin went back to Gerra with Zander when the fiend revealed my brother had a son, a boy he then threatened to kill if we didn't comply. Stefen went in and got Teakin out. They took Zander in the process, to assure a trade for the boy. Fast forward to now—I've just received word from Gerra. Katarra has agreed to the trade."

"That's excellent news," Merick exclaimed, stepping out of Stefen's embrace.

"Unfortunately it won't end there," Kielyn continued. "Gerra wants revenge for stealing their king. They've already started issuing their conditions." She paused, shadows moving across her amber-hued eyes. "They are demanding a sacrifice."

"Who?" Bastian asked, terrifyingly calm.

Ash looked from him to Eirik. "One of you."

Merick turned to ice. This wasn't a trade. It was a declaration of war. An internal touch skimmed her mental shields, Stefen reminding her not to panic, silently assuring her all would be okay.

"We have agreed to this. To get them into Anu." Alaric took over. "My oracle has informed us of a rather unique phenomenon that will occur during this particular eclipse. Something so rare it was last documented in 15,743 BCE. For a brief moment, when the sun is obscured for all four realms, the borders bridging them close up."

"An eclipse of this magnitude triggers a locking mechanism on the universe, so to speak," Stefen explained. "It temporarily prohibits travel between the realms by sealing shut the pockets."

"Our plan is to lure them here with the promise of sacrificing one of the twins in the name of keeping the peace," Alaric said. "Once the eclipse starts, they will be trapped. Unable to flee, and unable to bring in any more troops. This will give us time to do as much damage as we can before the eclipse passes and the pockets again become passable."

"With luck," Stefen added, "we won't need more time."

"Once we cut off the head of the snake," Teakin said from the door, "its body should slither back to Gerra to lick its wounds."

Merick loosed a shuddering breath and was across the room before anyone could respond. She flung herself into Teakin's arms, tears falling like rain, all her fears unburdened by the warmth of his hug. "I thought I lost you," she sobbed into his chest.

Teakin cocooned her in his arms and kissed the top of her head. "It will take more than Gerra to keep me from you."

"We have less than twenty-four hours to get ready then," Bastian summarized straightforwardly.

"Correction. *We*"—Ash motioned to Teakin, Stefen, Kielyn and Alaric—"Have less than twenty-four hours. You and your brother are going to the safeholds."

"Like hell we are!" Eirik bristled. "I will not let others fight for me, while I hide like a child."

"You are still mortal," Kielyn stated flatly. "It's not up for debate."

"Turn me now."

299

"I've made the transition," Bastian interjected. "I'm strong enough. I will fight."

"Neither of you are experienced enough," Teakin replied, with a warrior's frankness.

Bastian narrowed his eyes. "You don't know anything about us."

"Teakin is correct," Ash said. "The most valuable thing you can do is live." He nodded to the door. "Go collect your things. I want you off within the hour."

Barely contained anger rolled off both twins, but they turned and marched out of the room, slamming the door behind them.

Ash heaved a jagged breath and rubbed his temples. "Palomi, can you see that they get an escort to the border?" She inclined her head and slipped quietly out after them. He turned to Teakin. "We need to strategize. And Merick needs to prepare for what is to come next."

Her father released her into the outstretched arms of Stefen, looked him directly in the eyes as he spoke softly—more gently than she'd ever heard. "You have my blessing."

The second the bedroom door locked behind them, he had his body pressed against hers, walking her backward as he yanked her hoodie over her head. "We have much to discuss."

As if by magic, he had her pants and panties pulled down. She stepped out of them as Stefen continued to move her further into the room. He growled, "But first, I'm going to worship you."

Her hands greedily pawed at his button-down shirt, finally yanking hard and sending buttons flying across the floor. "Good. I am in need of some devout faith right about now."

The back of her bare thighs connected with her writing desk

and he took full advantage, shredding the lace of her bra with one finger down the center. Merick pushed the rest of his shirt over his shoulders and her breath caught at the beauty of him.

"Then let me clear an altar." With a swipe of his arm, the contents of the table went flying. He laid her back on it, following her down as he kissed her hard. A kiss with such desperation, such unbridled need, it felt like a collision of stars.

Stefen broke the kiss, grinning down at her as she protested. Then, faster than she could fully process, he hooked his hands under her thighs, gripped them tightly and yanked her to the edge of the desk, placing her legs over his shoulders as he knelt before her.

Slowly he kissed the inside of her thighs, making his way up until his tongue circled her twice. She nearly cried out, her nails digging into the wood of the desk—like it could hold her onto the edge of the realm—when his wet heat slipped inside her. He growled his approval, feasting with ravenous vigor and skill that should be criminal until she broke into a million pieces around him.

Only when her legs were shaking like a leaf did he rise up and stand over her, a pleased smile on his handsome face. "Say you're mine."

Merick stared up at him. "I am yours."

His hands clamped around her waist and hoisted her up off the table. One hand repositioned, cupping her ass. He carried her to the bed, kissing her slower this time, the taste of her still on his lips. "And you are mine," she whispered against his mouth.

Merick heard the unbuckling of his belt, his other hand her only support. She wrapped her arms around his neck and lifted her legs higher around his back. She hooked the waist of his jeans with her feet, then helped push them over his muscled thighs. They hit the floor and Stefen kicked them to the side.

Returning his hand to the small of her back, he hoisted her up and turned in place, each movement as fluent as a dance. Slowly, he sat on the feather mattress, lowering her with as much precision as someone holding a bomb. Her knees pressed into downy covers, but his firm hands around her waist kept her weight suspended above him.

Merick bent her head, her hair falling around his face like a curtain, her lips parting his as he eased her down. Her entire world constricted to the feel of his arousal against her. His hands fanned out across her hips, giving her full control. She would set the pace.

Inch by torturous inch, she lowered herself onto him, her body working to accommodate his size, her gaze rooted on his. His whole body shuddered, ripples racing up his chest, when she thought she could take no more of him. His hands still on her hips, he gently rocked up, proving her wrong when he filled her completely.

She gasped, the sensation almost too much. He was everywhere—under her, around her, inside her. One of his hands moved to her breast, cupping it, testing its weight, before rolling the nipple between two fingers. Fireworks exploded across her skin, sending a current of need lancing straight to her core—like flint against tinder.

His smoldering, hooded eyes watched her intently as she began to move on him, rocking forward and back, finding her rhythm, reveling in every inch of him. Faster and harder, she worked him, hips rotating, grinding down on him, her body clenching and unclenching, chasing the building sensation, the rushing desire within her.

"Merick," he rasped. "Say it."

"Mine..." She panted. "You're mine."

She came undone, slipping over the edge as his growl reverberated through her. His body bucked, taking over, as she collapsed on top of him. His hands grabbed her hips, moving her up and down on his shaft, pounding into her, swelling evermore with each thrust.

Stefen roared as he came, burying himself in to the hilt. Molten heat filled her. Merick's body continued to shake and pulse as she clung to him, her cheek pressed firmly to his chest, her heartbeat so wild she could hear it in every corner of her body. It matched the cadence of his, as if their hearts beat as one.

She could barely think beyond that steady drumming. Minutes passed as they laid there, tangled together, listening to their breathing even out. Merick held him tightly, relishing the feel of her skin on his, the fullness still lingering inside her.

A feather-light touch down her spine made her lift her head. Stefen was looking at her with something like wonder in his eyes. As if he were seeing her for the first time.

"I was afraid," he breathed. "Afraid that if I started to feel, started to explore my feelings for you...they would be taken from me. Like so many things in my life have been." His hand moved up and his fingers shook as he brushed them against her mouth. "I wasn't sure I could bear it if you left, too."

The quiet sorrow in those words, the weight of his confession... "I'm not going anywhere," she reassured. "However, I am realizing something altogether new to me."

He looked quizzically at her, a hint of a grin on his mouth. "Please don't tell me it has anything to do with my performance just now."

"The *performance* was the best I've ever had." Merick smiled. "My realization is that I'm a very jealous partner."

"A little jealousy is healthy in a relationship, I think. But what, or who, could possibly make you jealous?"

"Your past."

He arched a brow. "Well, I can assure you, nothing of it will ever change the way I feel about you."

"I believe you. But I want to know all of it. Every aspect of your life, past and present."

"I suppose that's fair. I know all of yours. It's only right that you know mine." He sighed. "Just know this; my truth, and our future home, lives out there"—Stefen turned his head, his gaze going to the window—"in gathering storm clouds. Formidable from a distance, but far safer than the past I've buried here."

"Stefen, I will not share you with the ghost of this place. All I want is to bury them with you." Merick laid her head back on his chest. "I want to know every part of your story. I want to hate who you hate, respect what you hold dear, fight the battles you wage, and the ones waged against you. Beside you through all of it. As your mate."

She looked up. "And know this, Stefen Von Emmerich. I will love you through every bit of it. Through the anguish and injustice of your past, to the trials, tribulations, and joy of your future." Merick searched his eyes, so completely focused on hers. "I will go with you into those storm clouds. As formidable as they might be. Because I love you."

He sucked in a shuddering breath, silver lining his eyes. "Then let us start at the beginning."

Chapter Thirty-Two

Merick woke to a flurry of activity outside her room. They had stayed up most of the night, Stefen telling her everything. As heartbreaking as it was, she now felt closer to him than she could have ever imagined. She knew he felt the same when he kissed her goodbye and slipped out of the room just before the sunrise.

Palomi was waiting outside her door when she opened it. Together they went to the dining hall. Bastian and Eirik had left during the night. The giant castle felt empty without them. Merick wondered if it was due to the blood ties.

Regardless, despite all the nasty shit Bastian had said and done to her, she would still fight for him if he were in danger. *"A dragon's greatest strength, and their punishing weakness, is love."* The words came drifting back to her as she took a seat beside Palomi. Merick wondered if Bastian would do the same for her.

Recruits, soldiers, angels, and elementals darted past the dining hall, clad head to toe in fitted fighting leathers. Strapped to each of them were wide belts, some hung at their waist, while others crisscrossed their chest. Even without their wings, the angel warriors were the easiest to pick out. They were outfitted the same; impressive metal armor, silver breastplates and helmets bearing Alaric's crest. They reminded Merick of a time long ago—though she wasn't sure how she knew that.

The elementals were far less uniformed, attired in a wide array of materials. Some wore chainmail, others wore next to nothing. Many had painted themselves in camouflaging white and gray, meant to blend into the snowy landscape. While others had chosen head to toe leather. It all depended on their unique skill sets, Palomi explained.

Marzalla appeared in the dining room, dressed in all white, fur rimming her boots, her gloved cuffs, and her jacket's collar. It was a complete contradiction to the lethal looking bow and arrow strapped across her back. She snagged an apple and walked over to them.

Merick didn't miss the way Palomi's gaze tracked her, the way she subtly averted her large honey-brown eyes, letting her thick tresses fall forward to conceal the appreciation reflected there. "Are you ready?" Mar asked, taking a seat.

"Yes," Merick lied. She was to remain here, with only Palomi to see her through the first stage of her transformation. The angels remaining in the castle would take over after that. It all made perfect sense, but selfishly, she wanted Stefen here with her. Under Mar's lifted brow, Merick dropped the show and sighed, "I honestly have no idea."

"Good," the Air-dancer chuckled. "Confidence is learned, not gifted."

Marzalla took a bite of the bright red apple. The contrast of her pale skin and white attire against the ruby-colored fruit made a pretty picture. She sucked an escaping drop of juice off her lip. The simple action changed everything.

It wasn't a clear nectar that dotted the Air-dancer's lips—*it was blood.*

Merick nearly stopped breathing as the room morphed into a muddy and war-torn battlefield. In the middle was Marzalla, fallen. Her eyes glassy, one hand clutching a spear, embedded deep in her chest. The tiny dot of red at the corner of her mouth became a steady stream. It rolled down her chin and dripped to the ground, mingling with the blood of others.

Merick tried to speak, tried to scream, but it was as if she were being muzzled, yanked back by an invisible force to the farthest perimeter of the grisly scene. On the edge of the battlefield now, she looked at the whole of the picture. Bodies covered the valley. In the middle, flying high and proud—the familiar flag of Gerra.

Merick stumbled backward. Strong hands caught her around the waist. "Shhh, it's okay. Listen to my voice. Follow it out."

She clung to his command like a lifeline, staying with his voice, closing her eyes, and pushing away the image. Just like that, it was gone, covered up with fresh snow.

She opened her eyes. Stefen held her in his lap on the floor. Marzalla and Palomi stood above them. Merick tried to shake off the lingering images, but they were too clear, too tethered in reality.

"You can't go. I...I saw you..." she stuttered, canting her head up to Marzalla. "I saw you. You were dying."

"A premonition?" Palomi asked. "Can you make them?"

"I have never felt anything like it before." Merick looked from Marzalla to the others. "You can't go. None of you can."

"Steady your breathing," Stefen instructed. "What exactly did you see?"

"I saw Marzalla dying on a field covered in elemental and angel bodies. Above them flew the flag of Gerra. I was there." Merick's panic returned. She twisted in Stefen's lap, searching his eyes. "Something is wrong with today. You cannot go."

"The young lady has the gift of Sight," a haggard voice drawled behind them. "The ability to see the most plausible outcome," Alaric's oracle said from the doorway. "There are too many moving variables though. It's not possible to know which outcome will come to fruition."

"This Sight gift, or whatever it is, just painted a picture in my mind too real to not be taken seriously." Merick pushed out of Stefen's arms and stood. "If I am channeling the most plausible outcome, then this must be called off. For it is most likely that you will all die today." She was shaking now. "You cannot engage in this madness!"

"Merick." Stefen rose beside her. "Yes, your visions are a possibility. But it's only one possible scenario. Out of thousands." He turned her to face him. "It is not definitive enough to risk all we have put in place. We have the numbers. The eclipse on our side."

"He just said it was most plausible outcome. You can't—"

"Listen!" The sternness of the single command silenced the whole room. "No one ever freed themselves from the shackles of oppression without taking risk. Even if the odds were against them."

Merick stared at him in disbelief. *He knew it too.* Yet he'd kept it from her. After everything they had shared last night. His promise to not hide things from her. He had withheld the most critical information of all...that he might not be coming back.

"You feel it, too." When he didn't respond, she asked, "And you're going to fight regardless?"

Stefen reached for her, but she drew back. "Merick, we have no other choice."

"Wars have been won with lesser odds," Palomi chimed in, though there was now a subtle unease to her normally level tone. "We have a good strategy and well-trained soldiers. It's normal to have doubts the day—"

"Why keep this from me?" Merick tuned out everyone in the

room. They didn't understand. *He did.* "So that I might wake from my transformation to...nothing?"

She felt it then, the gentle tapping on her mind—Stefen trying to speak to her, to calm her. Privately. *No!* She sealed shut the connection. If he was willing to leave her in the dark, he could damn sure have a taste of what it felt like.

"Wouldn't it be kinder to prepare me for what I might wake up to? Or was it just easier for you to send me naïvely into my confinement, thinking everything would be fine when I woke?"

Marzalla touched her arm. "You have enough to be concerned with today. Your energy needs to be focused on what you have to do to make your transformation. Worrying about a war you can do nothing to change will only work against you."

"I will decide where my energy is best served!" Merick snapped.

"You're right," Stefen agreed. "You deserve full transparency. But tell me..." He stepped toward her, his gaze both honest and determined. "What good does knowing the elevated risk serve? It's all a risk. Be it a premonition, or just war. Fate will have the final say today."

The weight of his words sunk into the pit of her stomach like a rock. There was no way to make the others see. No way to make them feel what she had just experienced with that vision. They were working off experience. She had only her senses.

Stefen had both, but he was willfully choosing to ignore his gut instinct. Be it from some devout sense of loyalty or sheer determination to alter the outcome, she wasn't sure. But Merick was certain of one thing; no one in this room would listen to her. Either they didn't believe her. Or they thought she was still too new to their world to really understand how it worked.

She knew something else, too. She still didn't belong. Not entirely. Not yet.

Outside the window spread a clear blue sky. Gusts of wind

blew between the castle towers, brushing freshly fallen snow off the slate shingles. The morning sun struck ice on a distant tree, making it sparkle so brightly she thought, for just a second, it might be the cause for the sting in her eyes.

"You're correct." Merick averted her gaze before anyone could see her tears. "Knowing the risks does not serve me at all."

She turned and walked from the room.

Chapter Thirty-Three

The snow drifted around them, dusting their armor, same as it did for the army across the expansive white field. The snow knew no loyalty. The snow took no sides.

Katarra was easy to spot in her crimson robes and long flowing hair. Thaddeus stood tall beside her. Their army behind them was a dark mass rippling as far as the eye could see. It spread up and over the mountain ridge.

Stefen stood beside Ash and Kielyn, atop a broad knoll overlooking the battlefield. Not far behind, Dax and Kizer, gave the order to halt. Their soldiers obeyed, shifting into a wide flanking formation.

Sidtric landed effortlessly from the sky on a summoned wind and crossed the flat-top knoll. "We underestimated their numbers."

Ash's eyes scanned the opposing army of elite. "Do you see the boy?"

"Not yet," the Air-King replied, stone-faced.

"We need to show them that Zander is alive first," Kie said.

"Do it slowly." Alaric marched up, flaring and then settling his wings, testing them. "The eclipse is thirty minutes from beginning."

Ash nodded, attention still fixed on the waiting army, smoke coiling at his fingers. "Bring him."

The sounds of shifting bodies and the crunching packed snow behind them confirmed their prisoner's progress. Stefen tried once more to send a message to Merick. It fizzled in the dry air, unable to get past the protective wards surrounding the castle. At least he'd had time to send her one before leaving, right after Ash had summoned him here. Letting her know he was being called away sooner than expected. That he loved her. That he was sorry for not sharing his concerns with her about today. And, finally, he would see her as soon as he could.

Because he *would* see her soon. Those concerns were typical before a battle. It would be more unnerving not to have them. Though he hated having to raise his voice to make her see reason, he had needed to dispel her overactive imagination. Even if a fraction of her premonitions were to come true, it still served no good purpose. Merick needed to stay focused on her task today; transitioning. All of this would be for naught, if she didn't survive. He would rather be slain in battle than to live without her.

The bound and badly beaten body of Zander was dragged across the knoll and dropped at their feet. "Ready, brother?" Teakin asked.

"You really think you can get out of this without blood being spilt today?" Zander glared up at them.

Neither LaGoryen said a thing in response, they just grabbed him under his arms and hoisted the bastard to his feet. Ash turned his head and gave Kielyn a quick kiss. The love reflecting in his eyes conveyed more to her than any words.

Stefen watched with the others as the brothers dragged Zander like a plow through the snow, down the hill, and across the barren field. On the opposite side of the battlefield, Katarra and Thaddeus escorted a small child. The three started their way.

This was how it was done, same as in days of old. The kings, or king's generals, of either army would meet in the center of a battlefield to discuss any last minute proposals. These discussions would determine what would happen next. Either terms would be met and both armies would turn around and go home, or they would fight until a clear victory was claimed. It would then be up to the winner to decide what was done with any survivors.

But today wasn't about proposals. Both sides had already laid out their terms. Gerra wanted a sacrifice. Anu and Earth wanted to be done with the Diabolis for good. The terms were set. The lines drawn. The plan in motion.

The only thing going against them was time. Gerra had arrived too early. Ash and Teakin would have to stall if they stood any hope of stopping any more elite from crossing into the realm.

Which they would. Today would play out exactly as planned.

Again, as Stefen watched Ash and Teakin meet Katarra and Thaddeus in the center of that vast field, a niggling sensation formed in the pit of his stomach, begging the question *what if it didn't?*

Merick let the curtains fall closed and turned from the window. They were gone. Aside from the remaining staff and Palomi, the giant castle was a ghost town.

She had not been able to watch them leave since her room was on the west side. Not that it would have mattered. By the time Palomi told her, Stefen and the rest were already over the mountain.

This was not how she had wanted to send Stefen off to battle, sulking in her room like a stubborn child. Gods, was there anything she could get right? What if they were not victorious? What if she lost him on that mountainside?

Merick walked over to the bed and curled up in the middle of it. Tears blurred her vision as she wrapped her arms around her knees and hugged them to her chest. What if they won the day, but she was not strong enough to make the transformation?

A knock at her door signaled Palomi was back. "It's open." Merick wiped her cheek and sat up. At least she could appear to have her shit together.

The thick head of distinct auburn curls that peaked around the corner was not that of the female fae. "You sure you're decent?" Eirik asked, one hand covering his eyes, a lopsided grin on his handsome face.

Merick on her feet and across the room in less than a millisecond. "Eirik!" She threw herself into his arms. "What are you doing here?" She shoved him away just as quickly. "You're supposed to be in hiding."

He held up his hands, the universal sign of surrender. "Don't ground me, Mom."

"I'm serious. You can't be here."

"You think I would let my cousin go through something like this alone?" He grew serious. A figure moved in the hallway. "Besides..." Eirik kicked the door fully open. "This idiot insisted."

Bastian scowled from behind his brother. "I only insisted we be here for Father."

"Whatever." The lighthearted twin blew him off and walked past Merick into the center of her room. "What should we do first? Paint our nails or gossip while we wait?"

Merick laughed. "I do have a makeup case around here somewhere."

She watched him plop down on the end of her bed. Bastian moved into the room but hung back, leaning against the wall.

"But in all seriousness." She walked over and took a seat on a chaise lounge. "You two are really taking a chance by coming here. I think the Diabolis may be the least of your worries when your mother finds out."

Merick wasn't joking either. Ash might be revered as the 'Dark King' but his mate was a force to be reckoned with in her own right.

"We will weather that storm when the time comes," Eirik said, though the tone of his voice lacked confidence. "What's important now is that we are here to help you through this."

She ventured a glance at Bastian. "Are you going to try and join the fighting?"

"I will, after I deal with this," the dark-haired twin stated.

So he hadn't come back solely for his father. Was it true? Did dragons put not only love, but blood, too, above all others? Merick had to know. "Is there some unwritten blood tie rule that you're bound to or something?"

"Yes."

"No." Eirik rolled his eyes at his brother. "There is no blood tie, or dragon code of ethics. But there is a familial bond. Not one strong enough to compel or anything. Nothing like the mating bond."

"For example," Bastian added. "It will be nothing at all for my father to kill Katarra today. Regardless of her being his half-sister."

"That's different," Eirik said. "The queen is the spawn of Dante. She is neither a Fire-dancer nor a dragon."

"She's still blood," Merick pointed out.

"What blood she has of ours is so thin," Bastian groused, "it might as well be water."

Merick's mind traveled back across the years to the day outside the tiger enclosure. Most would consider the advice the queen had given her bad. It landed her in a maneater's den after all. And perhaps it was bad advice. Mayhap the queen was as evil as everyone claimed.

Yet, the lesson Merick had learned that day greatly outweighed the risk. She had pulled from it numerous times over the years. Most recently with the very male now boasting his father would kill the infamous queen of Gerra. He, too, had challenged Merick to do something she didn't think herself capable. Did that make Bastian and Katarra the same? She wondered. Did society paint them both as dangerous and untrustworthy? Or did they pass around the oils and canvases themselves.

"I met her once." Both brothers looked at Merick, as if they had forgotten where she was raised. "She was not unkind in that moment. Might have even been helpful."

Bastian scoffed. "She was probably setting you up for something. The queen does nothing unless it directly serves her."

"I heard she looks like our grandmother," Eirik mused.

Merick wasn't sure what their grandmother looked like. It was rumored Dante had all traces of her existence removed from Gerra after her death. "The queen is quite comely. Regal, feminine, intriguing, and curiously approachable. An interesting paradox, considering all the horror stories detailing her personality."

She walked to the window. "I always imagined she would make an excellent cat." For what had to be the tenth time in the last hour, she drew back the curtains. "If she were feline, I suppose her perceived disposition would vary greatly based on who was judging her. The farmer, or the mice."

"Interesting theory," Palomi said from the bedroom door. Merick turned. "I would advise you to remember that cats also enjoy hunting for sheer sport. Hardly a trustworthy animal." She glanced from one brother to the other. "There is going to be literal hell to pay for this, you know?"

Bastian gave a curt nod. Eirik simply shrugged. "Our cousin

needs us." He tossed Merick a grin. "Even if she fancies the misunderstood—gods, demons, and cats."

As expected, Zander was the first one to talk. Or curse rather. Thaddeus could remember a time when his grandson would have remained levelheaded enough to stay silent. Apparently not even being taken hostage, beaten nearly to death and tossed to the ground at his sister's feet like a half-eaten turkey leg, could humble him enough to keep his tongue still.

"Kill them at once!" Zander barked. Everyone ignored him.

"Brothers." Katarra smiled, resting her hand on the little boy's shoulder in front of her. "What a lovely day for a family reunion." She looked past them and waved to the other kings staged around the open glen. "But where are my nephews?"

Thaddeus had to hand it to her, she had no fear. Probably because she lived in a parallel world to the one where the rest of them resided. A world without consequences or empathy. Katarra only cared about the here and now. Because of that, she was the most free of them all, unchecked by anyone or anything. She was also the most dangerous.

"Let's cut to the chase," Ashdon said. "We all know you can't kill Zander in front of your warriors."

"What the fuck does he mean?" Zander sputtered, trying to get his feet underneath him.

Teakin shoved the heel of his boot into the king's back, crushing him back down. Ashdon continued. "We also recognize that you cannot simply turn around and go home, ignoring the insult of us taking the impertinent shit."

"Which was sort of the point of the sacrifice." She crossed her arms, looking bored.

"Sorry to disappoint," Ashdon replied, the graceful line of his mouth tightening.

"Very well," the queen sighed, flipping her wrist. "A battle to the death it shall be."

Teakin's lips pulled back from his teeth. "You really are a cold bitch."

Katarra beamed. "It's been a whole three hours since anyone complimented me. For that, I'll allow you to get to the front line, with the boy, before we begin."

Teakin's fists balled at his sides, but it was his brother who spoke. "I have your word?" The Fire King watched her closely. "On the honor of our mother."

Katarra lowered to the child's level and spoke softly, almost tenderly to him. "Go to your father, little one." She gave the three-year-old a gentle nudge.

"Guards!" Zander bellowed in vain. "Attack!"

Teakin scooped up his son, then kicked the King of Gerra toward Katarra. The queen straightened. "Let the fun begin."

"If I may," Thaddeus said, "propose a slightly alternate ending."

All eyes fixed on him.

"What are you doing, Thaddeus?" Katarra wore a saccharine grin, but there was an edge to it.

"Merely playing the game."

Zander pushed to his knees with a gravelly chuckle. "I knew you'd have something up your sleeve, grandfather." He held out his bound wrist. "Cut me free so I can kill my sister. Then have my army lay waste to these fools."

"Oh, Your Majesty." Thaddeus tutted. "I'm afraid it is you who is the fool. In everyone's game." He looked down at his grandson. "You will die here today."

"Thaddeus..." Ashdon cautioned.

"Gentlemen." He regarded the LaGoryen brothers. "Thank you

for putting your trust in me, but it seems another player has made an offer. One even better than ruling Gerra myself."

Katarra whirled on him. "You dared to conspire against me?"

Both males visibly tensed, their fighting leathers growing more taunt across their chest and shoulders—like coiling pit vipers—anticipating, calculating their strike. *Dear gods,* they were perfection. He wouldn't stand a chance against them in battle. None of them would.

It was no wonder the Diabolis had been obsessed with them since the dawn of time. *Darkness calling to darkness.* Only an idiot would stand against them.

Or a male with another hand still left to deal.

"As you know, I am a man of science," he started. "I work with numbers. I study and I observe. Acting only when I know the outcome is as I predicted." Thaddeus unfurled a hand in the queen's direction. "I'm not charismatic and opportunistic like you. Others don't notice me, and they certainly don't fear me." He looked at Ashdon. "I don't have your power and instincts." His attention moved to Teakin. "Nor do I possess your bravery or loyalty."

"I have no weaknesses." Thaddeus's gaze landed on Zander. "I am the perfect ally. Which is why you've all sought me out." He looked back up with a smile. "Correction... Why I sought each of you out."

"Untie me, Katarra." Zander snarled. "We can destroy them together." His grandson continued to go unnoticed on the ground. Toy dogs had more sway.

"Who? Whose side are you on then?" The queen chaffed, looking around in exaggeration, though the tone in her next words belied the casual levity, "Who the fuck is left?"

Ashdon spoke, his voice like shadows given form, "What is the ending you propose, Thaddeus?"

"Quite simple really," he answered. "You let me leave here. Alive. With my daughter."

Teakin took a menacing step forward. "Your only child is in Gerra."

"My biological child is in Gerra, yes. But we both know Merick is the only one that matters. Why do you think I raised her as my own, kept her locked away from others for so long? Because I knew how special she was. Knew she would be my endgame. You did not honestly think I would approve of her and the hybrid, did you?"

Teakin's nostrils flared, smoke rising from around his neck, rolling over the leather baldric at his back, stroking the deadly blades it held dear. Smoke born in a lightless dungeon, a drug-induced prison meant to break him. Instead the warrior had learned its heartbeat, mastered its modulation.

"You see." Thaddeus looked to the sky, the light around them fading. "I have an oracle too. She's confided Merick has more to offer. Certainly more than becoming the mate to a fallen angel."

"Here's your endgame." The older LaGoryen growled, his eyes glacial. "You're going to walk back to that row of soldiers and die alongside them. By my hands."

Thaddeus knew the only thing keeping Teakin from eviscerating him on the spot was the child in his arms. Apparently Ashdon knew it, too, for he stepped forward. "Brother, take my nephew back to the frontlines," he said calmly, smooth and cold.

Thaddeus's palms began to sweat, but he had come too far to back down now. "I already factored in you refusing my offer." He steadied his voice. "Which is why I brought a backup plan."

"Enough with the tiresome riddles." Katarra had a blade to his carotid artery before he could blink. "Answer my question."

Thaddeus had expected that too. Counted on it.

"Who could offer you more than any of us?" she hissed in his ear.

"Why, my dear." He craned his neck to meet her eyes, as the first drop of blood bled into the white of his starched shirt collar. "Your son's real father."

The queen's face paled. The first fear he had ever seen in her. Proof he had aligned correctly. The brothers had offered him a kingship. But it would only be a matter of time before they sought to dethrone him. No LaGoryen would ever trust an elite. Rightfully so.

He swung his gaze toward Ashdon, just as a deafening roar sent sound waves crashing down around them, shaking the ground beneath their feet.

"Surely, Stefen's recent evolution taught you not to discount the improbable." Thaddeus smiled thinly. "You're not the only living dragons."

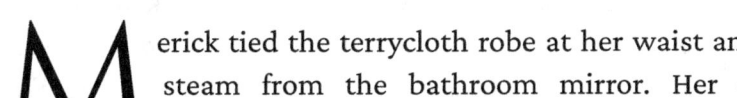

Merick tied the terrycloth robe at her waist and wiped steam from the bathroom mirror. Her different colored eyes stared back, her most unusual feature— nature's mark. One blue, one brown. They both begged questions of her now. Questions she couldn't answer. There were no words in existence yet to frame them. No description for what she was.

The steam reclaimed the glass. She didn't bother disturbing it. Mirrors had never provided her clarity. Only her dreams did that. Thankfully, those dreams were becoming stronger. Her mother's lineage calling to her. She was fairly certain she would be able to make the shift.

When Merick first had stepped into the steaming shower, she'd been resolved in her decision. She could channel the wolf. It was the most logical guide animal to try and invoke. She knew its form best.

But during that fifteen minutes of contemplative reflection, the water beating down on her head, wings kept appearing to her. Reflecting in the marble tile. The shape of the soap suds pooling around her feet morphed as the drain pulled them down. A sparrow perched on a window ledge outside her shower stared at her with wide eyes.

Either the universe was convinced she was a bit slow on the uptake, or it had a wicked sense of humor. She was choosing to believe it was a good sign. As soon as she landed on that decision, the exact species of bird came to mind. A dove.

Dove was the endearing pet name Teakin had called her as a child. She recalled it fondly. After every bedtime story, he would kiss her forehead and say, "Good night, little dove." Merick could think of no better spirit to invoke.

She felt herself smile. *Another sign.* Both her parents would be with her now.

A soft knock fell on her door. "It's time," Palomi said.

Merick pushed away from the counter and walked into the bedroom. Someone had lit candles and pulled down the thin muslin hung around her four-poster bed. "Every woman likes candles, right?" Eirik grinned sheepishly.

She smiled. "They are nice."

Palomi drew back the curtains on one side of the bed. "Bastian suggested you might be more comfortable with some privacy."

Merick looked at her darker-haired cousin. He had his fingers laced behind his head, leaning back in a chair, half concealed in shadow. She was shocked he'd considered it. The possibility of returning to her human form naked, with all of them in the room, was something she hadn't given much thought. Now that she was... The fact that Bastian had thought of it... It touched her. More than she could adequately express.

"Thank you," she said.

Perhaps it was the sincerity in her voice, but he gave a faint nod.

"We'll remain right here the whole time," Palomi assured, urging her toward the bed.

She climbed in. "I know you will be."

The curtains closed behind her and she laid down. The room grew darker by the second. The eclipse was beginning. Merick closed her eyes and sought out the image she desired. *The dove.*

I magining the sky above, a weightlessness began to take over. She was rising over the branches covered in fresh snow. Climbing higher into the downy clouds as a warmth enveloped her.

A soft yellow glow lit a path. Merick followed it, her skin tingling, as the ambient noise of the bedroom melted away.

A melody drifted on a current of air—the sounds of nature. Suddenly, her whole body felt cradled, suspended by invisible hands. She focused her energy on the vision in her mind's eye, the dove.

Her arms extended and her legs curled inward. Tiny sensations by the thousands tickled her flesh as, one by one, white feathers replaced skin. It was happening. She was becoming the bird. Touch by touch, the invisible embrace let go. Until only one was guiding her.

A flap of virgin wings. Then the hold was gone. The wind caught under her body and she soared, higher and higher, toward the call. The tranquil melody lured her, a seamless, unified beckoning.

Except...

Something was off.

Merick tuned her ears to it. There... Somewhere in the perfect lullaby—a note off key. Faint, but persistent. It pierced the other infallible notes with a knife.

"Ignore it," a voice urged from above.

She couldn't. There, again. The strange interruption. This time louder, edged with fright.

Pushing the brilliance aside and fighting backward through the layers and cords, she sought the part that was wrong. Again, she heard it. This time it was clear. Coming from below.

Without a thought, she changed direction and looked back. Her room lay there in miniature, three figures circling one another. A fourth lay bleeding on the floor.

Merick's heart hammered in her chest as she forced her vision to see clearer, pushing aside the drug-like pull to climb higher. Palomi lay clutching her chest, her cousins moving around an intruder. She gasped.

Xavier!

The prince held a sword dripping with crimson as he stared down the twins.

"No!"

Suddenly, hands were on her again. She fought them, pushing and shoving to be freed. From somewhere, she heard the voice again. Warning her to stay away.

But that was her family. And they were in danger.

With all her might, she struggled until the music morphed into a screech and the wind bit her face, ripping at her hair with angry talons and peppering her skin with a stinging reality.

She fell free.

Frantically extending her wings, she tried to slow her descent, but her feathers flew away, pulled off like dandelion petals in the wind.

Then it happened. Something inside her—foreign and primal, enticed without song—began to fight.

The only sound was shifting wings and absolution. Merick's vision grew acute and her spine arched backward. Time slowed and curled, halting her in midair. Her muscles constricted, and her limbs expanded as the last white feather was pulled from the bone.

In its place...

A shiny ivory scale.

Flames rippled across the sky, painting over the sun and moon. Their violent swirls and whirls devoured the light and the dark, radiating a heat felt atop the snow covered knoll. Then the beast emerged from within the inferno, carving a path through its own vibrant destruction, its scales and wings the color of burnt sunset, blending with its fiery kiss.

The realm took a collected breath. Just one. That was all anyone was afforded. Footing dug solidly into the earth as stances hardened. Resolve collected en masse like hounds at the leash.

Stefen felt his own body transforming. He did not need to lay eyes on Ash or Teakin to know their dragons were already answering the call. He could sense them—a language all their own—reaching out to each other, summoning the clan.

His vision morphed, peripheral narrowing, as fangs lengthened to the point his jaw hinged open. Beside him, Kielyn brushed the back of his arm with hers, a silent affirmation.

He glanced over and she gave him a faint grin. "Don't go getting killed this time."

Before he could answer, darkness reclaimed its right, wrapping them in night. But the eclipse had not come soon enough. On the far side of the battlefield, the mountainside became a sea of black as elite poured over the ridge. Above them, its giant wings clipping the tallest peak, a second dragon crested the horizon. Blood red and twice the size of the first.

Teakin appeared in front of Stefen, his eyes aglow, the flesh around his cheekbones growing taunt as his tendons stretched beneath his skin. He thrust his son into Stefen's arms. "They mean to take Merick." His voice was honed sharper than any blade. "Protect them."

He shot into the air, wings unfurling as gold scales replaced skin. Angels and elementals alike braced themselves as a hurricane-force wind hammered the ground. Kicking up snow, the dragon flapped once, twice, then was gone.

Ash joined him in the sky, his black and red alongside his brother's black and gold. Battle cries rang out as steel was dragged from metal and arrows whispered against bows. Both sides charged when fire blew from Ash's lungs, the sound like thunder breaking across the knee of the realm.

Stefen shielded the toddler as best he could and hurriedly pushed toward the safety of the back line. He could not dematerialize with the child. He would have to travel by foot and hope no one got to the castle before him.

The ground beneath his feet rumbled, and the boy started to cry. Stefen looked to the right and saw its source. Dax and his Earth-dancers were working the land, pushing and pulling it with their energy.

A subtle shifting of pebbles and stones on the cliff-face suddenly gave way to a thunderous crack, which echoed around the valley. Chunks of granite broke loose and the side of the mountain crumbled, tumbling and gathering strength, like a building wave toward the elite's rearguard.

The howling wind made Stefen look to the left. Trees were being uprooted by the Air Folk and hurled through the sky. Icy hail was thrown down like blades by the Water-dancers. The Fire Dynasty wielded lassos of flame, their angry hissing pops searing through muscle and bone.

Kielyn stood atop the knoll, between the water and fire elementals, conducting the offensive like a maestro. Watching her was always like watching a dancer, graceful and decisive. *But today...* Today she looked like a phoenix rising out of the flames, the ocean bowing to her—devout at its priestess's feet.

When Stefen finally made it to the ridge, he looked back in time to see Alaric land in the middle, unleashing himself, his archangels sundering the Gerra front line.

It was a battle like none Stefen had ever seen. Magic filled the air and fire lit up the clouds. His dragon fought him, eager to join in the carnage. The rush of combat flared, potent in his veins.

Stefen pushed it down. He had no idea what had been said in that center clearing. And he didn't require an explanation. The wrath and worry in Teakin's eyes was enough to keep him moving in the opposite direction with this child.

He slipped over the mountain ridge with the sounds of war chasing him, encouraging him, ringing in his ear like a battle chant. Get to the castle...*get to Merick...*

Eviscerate anyone or anything that dared come near her.

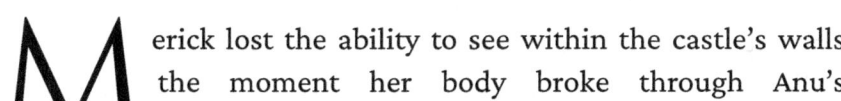

Merick lost the ability to see within the castle's walls the moment her body broke through Anu's atmospheric barrier on her descent.

Trees and rock rushed past as she fought to get control of her new body's movements. One of her wings clipped a branch and sent her thrashing into the side of the cliff. Instinctively, she folded inward and rolled down the jagged surface, plowing through the snow and earth.

She found purchase, claws digging into the granite and scraping large gashes in the side of the mountain. Finally, she started to slow, gaining her bearings. "Fine," she spoke breathily to the beast within her. "We'll do it your way."

Merick stopped trying to control it and, instead, propelled herself off the cliff. Surprisingly—having also thrown her rational mind over the edge—she caught a current of wind and, with a few awkward flaps, took flight.

This time, she soared. Sounds, smells, and sights raced by her, but they were not her own. They were the dragons. Merick surrendered everything to the beast. Letting it take control, to do as it wanted.

And what it wanted was blood...

She landed hard on the roof of the castle, tiles cracking under her massive claws and ricocheting away. Alarms sounded. Without a thought of her own, she was moving again, scaling down the stone walls, until she was outside the ninth floor.

A commotion could be heard from within. The muffled words sounded foreign. Merick strained to make them out, moving to her bedroom window. Her acute vision locked onto the movement inside, though the images themselves were fuzzy. Figures circled one another. She couldn't discern who was who. Her mortal memory, the structure used to identify, was skewed by the more predatory lens of the dragon.

Frustration mounted within her new form and attempts to navigate around it only served to feed the beast. Merick felt its agitation— a crazed animal clawing at its cage. Then, faster than she could process, primal instincts usurped higher reasoning, and the window pane exploded.

Glass shards rained down on the ledge and onto the floor, and the warmth of the room flooded out through the newly exposed opening into the thin winter air. The bedchamber's occupants stopped moving.

Smell... She could smell them.

The beast opened its jaws and sucked in their scents—their blood, DNA, fear—all of it. It was a visual map to each individual. The fog-like haze of her senses lifted and once again, she saw clearly.

Eirik Bastian, and...the prince of Gerra. Her eyes tracked

Palomi, bleeding out on the floor. The tangy scent of some fetid chemical oozed from her chest.

"Ah, my bride." Xavier chuckled darkly. "I was hoping you possessed the dragon. Now I know our offspring will rule the world."

Bastian lunged for him. But the prince proved quicker. With a twist, Xavier ran his sword through her cousin's chest.

'**N**o!'

In her head, it was a scream. But externally that scream manifested into a deafening roar. It shook the very foundations of the castle, sending pictures crashing to the ground and cracking furniture.

Her field of vision shrank, narrowing in on one object. All human emotion blurred simultaneously with her muddled peripheral. Merick couldn't breathe fast enough, couldn't think above the shouting in her head.

The dragon was taking over.

She lunged when Xavier leapt behind Eirik. A silver blade flashed at his neck. The prince's words were lost on her now. She was no longer in control.

Merick fought inside her own imprisonment. She needed to see, had to be able to discern friend from foe. How else would the dragon know who to kill? If she didn't regain some modicum of control, she might destroy her own blood.

She recalled what Stefen had taught her. Latch onto an energy and either pull it to her or push it away. Merick focused on the heart first. Tracked the pumping of her blood, the drumming in her veins. She centered her weight and isolated her thoughts to one. *Connection.*

She felt it—herself within the dragon. And linked her mortal understanding to its rage, its needs, and its passion. Slowing her heart rate, she visualized the tranquility of an isolated cave, gently coaxing and subduing its wrath through her thoughts. Just enough to see clearly from its eyes.

Her pupils widened and Xavier's speech was again recognizable. He seemed to sense it, too. A slow smile spread across his face. "There you are, love."

Eirik jabbed him in the ribs. The prince only laughed and yanked her cousin's head back further, crimson gleaming now around the edge of the blade. "I never understood why your uncle didn't force them both to turn on the day they came of age. An astonishingly bad oversight on his part." Xavier glanced down at Bastian. "Not that he was much stronger."

His gaze returned to her. "Here's what is going to happen, Merick. You are going to force your dragon to heel, and return to your human form. I will give you to the count of ten." A casual shrug. "Or he dies."

Merick felt the beast fighting against her hold. She wanted to let it out, so desperately it physically hurt to keep it restrained. But she couldn't risk hurting Eirik. She had no guarantee Xavier wouldn't kill him after she transitioned, but at least she maintained an advantage if he tried. She could call it back at any time, awaken the monster inside her—remind this prick what hell looked like when it wore the skin of a gentle mortal.

The prince began to count. Merick closed her eyes. With each number, she fought off the form she had taken, forcing it out of her mind, willing it to be still. "Ten..."

She heard the final number as she collapsed to the floor.

Eirik hit the ground a few feet away. "Fear not." Xavier stepped around her cousin's lifeless body as if he were a soiled area rug. "It's just a tranquilizer."

Merick's arms buckled when she tried to rise. "How could you?" She looked from Palomi to Bastian. "You had no right!"

Xavier grabbed her robe off the bed. "I had every right." He walked over and stood above her. "Get up."

"They did nothing to you," she accused, tears stinging her eyes.

He reached down and yanked her to her feet. "They were in my way."

"I would have done whatever you wanted." She jerked out of his hold, unsteady on her human legs. "Without you needing to harm them."

"I know you would have." The prince stepped back enough to look at her, his gaze like a brand running the length of her body. "Just as you will cherish and obey me?" A question and a challenge. "As your future king." He watched her closely. "And your mate."

"That's the reason for this senseless bloodshed?" She shook her head. "Surely there are plenty of females to choose from in Gerra."

"Ah, but there are no dragons." He grinned and picked up his discarded sword, circling the others methodically.

Merick had a vague feeling the world was sinking, pulling her under with it like quicksand. Her mind frantically scrambled and grasped for options. There were none. None that could be called to favor without risking all the lives in this room.

"I'll go with you," she said, treading so very carefully. "But it will be a union in appearance only."

He paused, his eyes narrowing on her. "I heard rumors of your infidelity. I had hoped that was all they were."

She drew from the training most applicable—*perception*. She had been raised in Gerra. No matter what the prince had learned of her since, he would expect her upbringing to at least reflect her birth home. If that realm was known for anything, it was loosely defined morals.

Invoking every nuance of teaching Palomi had given her,

Merick slipped on the mask of perception and angled her head at him. "Have you not lain with others since asking for my hand?"

"I think you know I'm not referring to the simple act of sex." Xavier studied her. "Has your heart been unfaithful to me?"

"No." She looked him directly in the eyes. "I love no one."

The silence in the room could have lasted one second, or sixty. "Then I think it's only fair you prove it," he finally said.

"How?" Merick asked, her heart rate picking up dangerously.

The prince looked slowly to the bed. "It reeks of him." He looked back at her, not a shred of emotion on his face. "Prove your loyalty to me by leaving him with the scent of our coupling."

Merick swallowed hard. The tether on her calm façade and the dragon prowling under her skin pulled to the point of nearly snapping. *Keep it down. Remain calm.* Her friends still needed her.

She tried for reason. "They will be coming for me soon."

"No they won't." He started for her. "*They're* in the middle of a war."

Merick found it increasingly hard to think. The handsome prince who had treated her with such care and attention years ago, now looked at her like he would love nothing more than for her ruse to be exposed. He had her exactly where he wanted her, trapped between her lie and his desires. If she succeeded in this, he would win. If she failed...he would likely still take her back to Gerra. Only he wouldn't be gentle in doing so.

"Get on the bed, Merick." He prowled toward her.

Her eyes darted to Bastian bleeding profusely on the floor, his body showing no signs of healing. She had no way to know if the blade had pierced his heart. All she knew was she had to get Xavier away from her cousins before he could finish them off.

"I wanted to be your mate," she rushed. "Take me back to Gerra and let me prove it to you there."

"Interesting that you ran away then."

"I was scared."

"Why?"

"I heard rumors of your father's taste for the perverse, and I was warned you might suffer the same afflictions." Not entirely a far stretch of the truth.

"Tell me." He stopped in front of her. "How long did it take the hybrid-mutt to get in your pants?"

"It was just sex."

"I hear your words." Xavier reached out and tipped her chin up with his index finger. "Yet, you're still not on the bed to prove it." He began walking her backward toward it. "Though in full disclosure, before I show you what real fucking is, I feel compelled to share with you why I believe you. When you say it meant nothing."

The back of her knees hit the mattress. "Angel boy already confessed as much to Thaddeus. It was all part of the plan actually." He pushed her down. "Your birth father and your uncle paid him handsomely to seduce you. To make you feel like you belonged here."

"Clever really." The prince looked around the room. "First, they convinced you I hail from a family of demons, selling you on the idea Anu is composed of saints." He laughed, but the sound was tinged with darkness. "Then they made him a paper crown, when I possess a real one."

Despite the sting of the accusations, and the barrage of questions, Merick kept her focus. "I fell for the first mistruth when I fled Gerra, it's true. They failed to convince me of the latter." Merick swallowed, but she didn't balk. "I never felt like I belonged here."

After a moment, she looked up at him. "Can we go home?"

He grinned, but it didn't quite reach his eyes. "After I make him pay."

Her heart all but stopped beating. "What do you mean?"

"Stefen Von Emmerich is a prideful male." Xavier unbuckled

his belt. "Even though you mean nothing to him, it will still piss him off that I claimed you in his bed. Plus, we don't have much time left."

"You're right." Merick started to stand. "There are guards coming to check on my transformation."

The prince blocked her path. "To get you with child."

"What!"

"The eclipse." His smile widened. "Not only does it allow passage between the realms, it makes supernaturals that are able to shift ten times more likely to conceive. I'm going to fuck you, fill you with my seed, and turn you." He shoved her onto her back. "Stefen will lose his mind."

"He doesn't care." Merick crawled backward.

Xavier grabbed her by the ankle, pulling her back to the edge. "I beg to differ."

The dragon was raging now, slashing at her willpower, snapping at what little dampener she held over its power. She could set it free. As easy as flicking a switch. Its darkness flowed through her like a black fog encroaching over the land.

"Ruined sheets." She spat. "That is all you will give my mate!"

The split second of recognition in his eyes was the only warning she got. He backhanded her so hard her teeth went through her lip. "Your mate!"

Merick saw stars and tasted the blood in her mouth, as her head was wrenched to the side. "You stupid little slut." He was on top of her now, straddling her midsection, his hand around her throat, pinning her to the bed. "You *do* love him."

Everything was happening too fast. She couldn't think. Only fight to get even a wisp of air down her throat, into her lungs. Her heels and the backs of her legs slid over the cool sheets as she kicked and thrashed, feebly trying to get any sort of leverage.

"We'll see whose mate you are when I'm done with you." The loathing in his eyes shimmered there as he wedged his knees between her legs, forcing them apart. "You're mine. You belong to me!"

The voice that came from her lungs was at once the light and the dark. And every inch of her body bowed to it. "I belong to Stefen Von Emmerich. King of Rigel."

His fist drew back, but the smashing sound that followed was not that of her bones breaking. It was the door flying off its hinges.

T he last thing Stefen saw with his normal eyes was Eirik, Palomi, and Bastian lifeless on the floor, and Merick pinned under the body of the prince. She was naked and bleeding.

Then the room went red.

The male on the bed leapt to his feet. Stefen's dragon laughed coldly, his body already shifting.

"You are not the only male dragon in this room," the prince bolstered. "You can't have what belongs to me."

Stefen's acute senses did a mental scan over the bodies on the floor. Eirik was only knocked out. Bastian was in a bad way, but he was not dead. *Yet.* The entry wound of whatever had stabbed him just grazed the edge of his heart. He would need blood quickly if he were to pull through. Palomi was the worst. From the strong smell emitting from the wound, Stefen knew the blade that had run her through had been dipped in some type of poison. He had minutes, at best, to render aid.

The fact only made it harder to hold back the inevitable. He was damn eager to give the dragon his due. As soon as he got Merick out of that bastard's reach.

Stefen's vision tunneled on him. "A real dragon wouldn't need poison to fight his battles."

Xavier made a wild grab for Merick, but she jumped to the side. Stefen lunged.

He collided with the prince with such force, he drove him back over the bed, through the solid wood headboard, and into the wall. The crack of his head against the stone reverberated through Stefen's bones. The prince groaned and Stefen sent him sprawling to the mattress, taking it to the floor with a splintering crack.

He grabbed the piece of shit by the throat and dragged him out of the pile of linens, dust, and drifting feathers. "What? Finding it hard to talk with me crushing your windpipe?" Stefen did just that, the cartilage around the trachea scrunching like a straw. "Let's hear you make your threats now, asshole."

Xavier wheezed and pawed at Stefen's hand as he tried to suck down air. Stefen released him and stepped back, the dragon chomping at the bit to deliver the next blow.

"Stop!" a feminine voice ordered.

Stefen turned to the window to find Katarra. Holding a knife to Merick's throat. "She won't recover the same," the queen warned. "Let him live, and we will leave."

"I can heal her before his blood seeps between the cracks of the hardwoods."

"You'll still have to make a choice." She looked at the bodies on the floor. "Them. Or her. Even you can't save all three in time."

"This has to end." His voice was not his own. The dragon was taking over. "Today."

"It will end. Just not today." She sounded uncharacteristically rational, not a trace of macabre humor. "Not without us both losing too much." Katarra stepped forward, pushing Merick with her. "I don't want to kill her."

Something was off. Stefen forced the beast, hissing in his veins, to quiet. The queen was a master of deceit but... She let him in—through some connection he hadn't known was possible.

Allowed him to see what she harbored deep inside. Laid herself bare for him. Every agenda, every truth.

Something else was hidden deep within her heart. Something no one else was privy to. A blood bond. She cared for Merick, her niece.

"I'm still a monster," Katarra clarified. "I'm not trying to convince you otherwise. But I promise to let her go, if you release my son."

Stefen ran a hand through his hair and exhaled. *Fuck!*

He hauled back and kicked Xavier in the ribs, sending him careening into a dresser. *She was right.* Stefen wouldn't be able to save them all in time. Not if he had to fight her first. The little sociopath had literally tied his hands.

He looked from her son, curled up on the floor coughing, to her. He had no other choice at this point than to take her at her word. "If I ever cross paths with him again..." Stefen stalked over to the prince.

"You can kill him," Katarra finished.

"No." He hoisted her son up by the back of his jacket collar. "I'm going to bring him to my mate and let her do it." He tossed Xavier out the window like a rag doll.

The queen lowered the knife and Merick rushed to him.

He reached out, gently framing her face with both hands as he searched every inch of it, taking calculated measure of the damage done by Xavier. Stefen was certain his blood could be heard popping and hissing where it boiled in his veins, and he had to force his legs to not propel him out the window. And finish off what he'd started.

Stefen pulled Merick to him, needing the feel of her to know she was okay. Also for the strength he required to stay firmly planted in this room. He kissed the bruise on the left side of her cheek and then the angry split of her lip, before looking back up.

Katarra took a step back. A shadow moved behind her. Before

Stefen could grasp what was happening, a blade tore through the leather breastplate of her armor.

The queen's eyes registered the surprise, widening slightly, before she looked down to the sword point jutting from her left breast. One delicate hand lifted to the steel, as if she needed the blood on her fingers to fully accept it. Slowly, her gaze lifted, fixating on Merick.

"Remember," she whispered, a drop of crimson dotting the edge of her ruby-red lips. "They have to see you." Her eyes twinkled vividly, one last spark of life—a soul's farewell. "Then they will respect you."

Katarra fell forward, her body sliding off the blade.

"And sometimes..." The shadow of her killer stepped into the light. "They need not see you at all." Bastian swayed where he stood, sword still in hand.

He stumbled forward and Stefen caught him as the blade clambered to the floor. "Get a Gilcolm," Stefen ordered. "As many as you can find."

Merick wasted no time wondering if she would know what one looked like and headed out the door. She didn't have to look far. At the end of the long hall stood about ten servants, all nervously looking her way. "We need Gilcolms," she shouted.

A rather determined looking redhead pushed to the front. "Hurry!" Merick waved the girl forward. Another pale young man stepped up. "You too."

Merick ducked back into the room and rushed to Eirik's side. Dropping to her knees she checked his pulse. It was faint, but he had one. "A Gerra sedative will have him out for a while," Stefen said, moving from Bastian to Palomi.

Merick jumped up, grabbing a pillow and blankets off the demolished bed. The redheaded servant burst into the room, her eyes growing round as she took in the sight. "Him." Stefen motioned to Bastian.

The Gilcolm hurried over to her cousin. Merick returned to Eirik. Carefully lifting his head, she repositioned him. The male attendant rounded the corner, his breathing jagged.

Stefen jerked his chin to the female, now offering her wrist to Bastian. "Take over when she's done."

The male servant did as told and Merick looked back over at Stefen as he bit his own wrist. He turned his arm, positioning it over Palomi's mouth. Merick held her breath. *Drink.*

Palomi did. Slowly at first. Then in large hungry gulps. After a couple minutes Stefen pulled away his wrist and looked at Merick. "Get the head cook. She's part fae, and a healer. She'll know of anything that can be used to get the poison completely out of her system."

Merick quickly rose and made for the hall. The gawking crowd was still clustered at the end of the hall. "Is one of you the cook?"

An older portly woman raised her hand. "You're needed," Merick said and stepped back into the room.

Stefen was on his feet. Merick looked to Palomi. Color was returning to her lovely face, but she remained on the floor, still too weak to stand. "I have no idea what the fucker used," Stefen cursed.

Merick's eyes darted to Bastian, who was now standing, using his thumb to wipe blood from his lower lip. He looked no worse than if he'd just woken from a late night out. "I must find Father."

"Like bloody hell." Stefen looked ready to physically restrain him. "You're staying here and looking after your brother and

Merick." His tone offered zero quarter. "If I so much as sniff you near the battle, I'll finish you myself."

"Fine." Her cousin had the good sense to comply. "But if you're not back—"

"No!" Stefen snapped. "You will stay here. Period. For as long as it takes. Regardless of who returns and who doesn't." He pointed to Palomi when the cook entered. "I gave her my blood, but poison was used. It's inhibiting a full recovery."

The woman rushed to the pretty fae's side, seemingly unfazed by the ransacked room and the slain body of Katarra. "I'm going with you." Merick stood.

Stefen just stared at her, like the look would be answer enough.

"Uncle," Bastian started.

"Each of you is taking centuries off my immortal life." Stefen scrubbed a hand down his face.

"You might need her," Bastian replied simply, shocking Merick to her core.

"What I need..." Stefen focused on her dark-haired cousin. "Is for her to try and make the transformation." He turned to Merick. "There's still a chance. The eclipse is only—"

"Stefen." Merick cut him off. She could explain everything in detail after they made sure Ash and her father were okay. "I already made my transformation." She walked to the window, willing the beast back to her side. "I chose the dragon."

The prickling sensation under her skin returned like a loyal familiar. Her dragon was ready, eager and thirsty. This time she would not hold it back. Merick climbed onto the open ledge and looked back over her shoulder. "Who do you think blew out this window?"

She didn't wait to hear his answer before she dove out the opening.

Teakin circled, preparing to collide again with the red dragon. Ash had disappeared over the horizon with the orange one. He could hear the fighting on the ground, the clang of steel on steel, bone on bone. Occasionally, pops of electric light lit up the clouds from below as elementals worked their craft.

A nasty gash on his left side made itself known as he redirected his flight pattern. The wind gathered under his wingspan. He collected its energy, generating lift, hovering long enough to lock the red firmly in his sights.

His opponent charged, flames licking the sky. Teakin drew back, ready to launch.

Suddenly, he was struck from above.

Razor-sharp spurs penetrated his scaly armor, gouging into his muscle, and he was driven down. Twisting against the pain, he rolled, tearing loose of the orange dragon's talons. But their combined momentum was too great to break free. Locked in a tangle of snapping jaws and slashing claws, they plummeted toward the ground.

Out of his peripheral, he saw Ash emerge, taking a hard hit from the red. For a moment, his body fell freely through the clouds.

Teakin thrust up with all his strength and kicked off his attacker. His wings unfurled with a cracking snap and caught the air. Unfortunately his aggressor was just as successful not far below.

He flew toward his brother, as the red dragon death-spiraled through the sky, bearing down on Ash. A desperate sound, fathomless and misshapen, rumbled up from deep inside, reverberating Teakin's giant maw. The taste of fire singed the roof of his mouth. He zeroed in on the red beast.

His target disappeared suddenly into a cover of unexpected smoke. Teakin cut straight through it, eyes watering from the heat, the smoking cinders fusing to his scales. Around him, he heard a guttural roar and thrashing wings. He was blind to anything amidst the thick smog-like blanket. Something clipped him on its heavy descent, but he couldn't make out which dragon it was.

A sliver of an opening presented itself as the smoke thinned. Through it, Teakin made out two forms, though he still couldn't discern their colors. He increased his speed, his vision clearing with each beat of his mighty wings. A third speck was coming into sight. The blood pumped harder in his veins.

A gold streak flew past, just as Teakin broke free of the smog. It dove hard and hammered into the red, sending it barreling through the sky. *Stefen!*

Ahead of him, he could now make out two more dragons. Ash's black was locked in battle with the orange. The abundance of glistening red on his brother's underbelly was more than the shine of his crimson breastplate. He was in trouble.

Teakin bared his teeth and gave chase. Faster and faster he sped. The two dragons broke apart, blood splaying from their talons like rain. Ash wavered, his adamant-colored wings dipping too much with the wind. The orange corrected quicker and reared back his long neck, its throat a radiant forge.

Ash was in its direct path...

Fire exploded across the sky, just as a flash of white collided with his brother, knocking him free of the blast.

Ash and the intruder tumbled out of the inferno's path in the nick of time. Teakin tracked their decent. The white pushed off and swooped away with the nimbleness of its smaller size.

His brother now free of the orange's rage, the attacker set its sights on the newcomer. Teakin inhaled, trying to get a scent on the white. A fear like none he had ever known seized him.

Merick!

Heart pounding and rage coursing through him, Teakin charged. She was fast, and leading the orange beast on a challenging course, but she would be no match if the larger male got a hold of her. She cut to the right, then back to the left, but he was gaining momentum. Quickly, she changed leads again, preparing to dive. *Lose him in the clouds.*

The male anticipated it and snared her.

A scream pierced the sky. Teakin wasn't sure if it was hers or his. He felt the pain in it—as if it were his own, as if they shared the joint sound—that of glass shattering.

Out of nowhere, the gold dragon reappeared, sideswiping the orange and causing him to readjust his flight pattern. In doing so, his hold on Merick must have loosened for she broke free. The orange roared at the loss and shook his huge head, right as Ash emerged below Teakin.

No communication was needed between them. As a unit they moved, indomitable, merciless in a way that had no words. Only a feeling. A savage, unconditional compulsion reserved for those threatening their own.

Flickers of recognition reflected in the glassy orbs of the orange dragon as they—a legion of blood-kin—descended upon him. He shrieked twice, the call resonating abroad, before blowing out a curtain of fire.

They pulled up short of being burned by it. The temporary barrier bid their opponent enough time to flee. The flames died out as the shadow of the red joined its brethren in their escape over the mountain ridge.

Teakin's dragon ached to pursue. But the father's heart inside him was stronger. Love had freed it, untwisted the thorns and chains of a hundred years. Though his flesh remembered the wounds that once bled, the scars forever marring his body and mind, his heart had been unlocked.

Now that it was open, it would be impossible to ever close again.

He looked over at his brother flying off his left wing, gold eyes scanning the ground, searching, his worry almost tangible.

"Go to her," Teakin sent down their bond. *"I'll meet you at the castle."*

Ash's black craned his regal head in a silent response and peeled off, diving under a layer of thin clouds. Teakin looked down, surveying the battlefield for the first time since taking to the sky. His large body cast a long shadow over the army below. The fighting was over. Bodies and blood covered the muddy field. The elite were retreating.

Victory was theirs.

With the sounds of cheers ringing out from below, he took one final loop around the perimeter. Ash had already morphed into his human form and was locked in a tight embrace with his fiery-haired mate. Teakin turned his large body in the direction of the castle. In the direction of *his* most cherished. Later he would find out what became of Zander, Katarra, and Thaddeus.

After he made damn sure his son and baby girl were okay.

The second Merick's feet touched the cold stone of the south facing balcony she looked over. And as those sea-green eyes of his met hers, she realized something else...

She opened her mouth, but only a broken, small sound cracked out of her.

She started to move.

Her legs gave out and her knees hit the floor.

Stefen was right there, sliding on his own knees to get to her. His hands on her face, he frantically kissed every bruise, every nick, as if he were memorizing them. Finally, he slowed, his lips trembling against her skin.

Merick pulled back, concerned. "What's wrong..." Her voice came out weak and raw.

A lone tear escaped down his cheek, tinged pink from the cold. She brushed it away, wanting nothing more than to alleviate the pain reflected in his gaze. She tried to speak again, but he put a finger to her lips and shook his head, his chestnut hair falling around his face.

"Give it a second. I'm fine. *I just...*" he said down the bond— that braided bit of light that linked them, *"I thought I was going to lose you."*

Merick's throat closed at the heartbreak in those words. *"The universe is going to have to try harder than that. There are no songs, no poems,"* she kissed him softly, *"no words to describe how hard it would be to steal me from you."* She pulled back enough to look him in the eyes, and managed to say out loud, "I've loved you for too long to lose you that fast."

He stared at her, eyes bright, full of color and light...

Almost as brilliant as the gold of his wings.

Massive, membranous wings, arching high over his shoulders, two claw-like tips at each peak. The color of molten gold flecked with hints of iridescence—like fireflies danced within them. They were the same smooth, leathery texture of his dragon's wings. Only now they were structured as ornately as any angel she had seen. But not a feather in sight.

A stunning combination of what he used to be. *And who he was now.*

He was speaking, but she'd missed the words. "Stefen?"

His mouth stopped moving and he grinned. That sideways tug of his lips that always did her in. "You want me to skip to the good part and get to the ravishing?"

"I guess that depends."

He angled his head, delighted curiosity dancing in his eyes. "On what?"

"Can you ravish me with those out?" Merick looked past his shoulders, to the wings.

The look on his face faded in alarming degrees as he seemed to realize all at once. His head snapped to the left, then the right. Then he was on his feet, those magnificent wings so long down his back they touched the ground.

Stefen lifted them out of the snow, as if muscle memory forbid letting them drag. He looked at her slowly, silver lining his eyes anew. "I have them...I have them back..." he breathed.

The stumbling words, the earnestness in his eyes...

Merick knew in that moment, if ever anything was to break her; it was this male. He was the light and the dark, the restless night and the breaking sun. He was her other half. He made her whole.

She stood, drinking him in, honored to be the one standing with him when he was bestowed this gift. This was his past. Everything he had sacrificed. But this was also his future. Everything he deserved. All woven together by the threads of eternity. The threads of fate.

And beautiful golden wings.

Chapter Thirty-Four

Six months later

Castillo En Las Estrellas, Costa Rica

The best perk that came with being king of a hybrid army was getting to pick its headquarters. It had only taken Stefen the time it took to throw a dart, nailing it perfectly, on Alaric's map of Earth. He had always felt a deep connection to water, and ever since his first visit to the part of Earth known as the Caribbean, he'd understood why.

It had been the image he mentally sent Merick her first day in the Earth Realm. Later she had confided how soothing she found it, adding she wanted to visit the actual source. But why visit, when they could call it home?

Kielyn and Ash had wasted no time helping them secure the perfect location in Costa Rica. Although, Kie did most the work. Ash only peered over her choices and either nodded, or scowled, based on how well his mate's romantic ideals corresponded with his more practical compound requirements.

In the end, they narrowed it down to two. The first was by far the most ideal for having a training facility quickly up and running. But "ideal" took a backseat to wonderment when Merick stepped out of the helicopter and onto the old castle's grounds. Perched high on a mountaintop, surrounded by rainforest and overlooking the Caribbean, the second location was love at first sight for his mate.

The sounds of the early morning crew getting to work on the west wing roof competed with the boisterous monkeys in the trees. It reminded him exactly how much they still had left to do. Thirty hybrids already called Castillo En Las Estrellas, the castle in the stars, home. Thirty more would be joining house Rigel by the end of the month.

Stefen looked down at the outdoor training courtyard. Some of the sun-tolerant recruits already were sweating under the heat of the Central American sun. From his spot on the balcony, he could also see the indoor gym. A UV-protectant window allowed the others to practice safely inside and provided him the perfect bird's-eye view of both spaces.

Marzalla, presently handing a male trainee his ass with the nunchakus in the gym, caught him watching and waved. Then she took the guy's legs out from under him.

Stefen smiled. Six months ago, they weren't sure if the stunning blonde Air-dancer would pull through. Merick's vision before the battle had been correct. Marzalla had faced off with one of Gerra's best warriors. It nearly cost her her life.

Thankfully, Alaric had gotten there in time to deflect the second blow. But the first one had nicked her heart. It took Alaric's best field surgeon, and Sidtric and Dax hiking a full day to locate a special root grown high on a mountainside, to repair the damage.

He focused on another blessedly spared that day. Palomi, never far from her flaxen-haired companion, was in the courtyard teaching a fae Water-dancer to use a type of magic only her fairy side could conjure. She nodded up as Stefen passed overhead and resumed her session, after a quick glance toward Mar of course.

"You're being too easy on them," Alaric said from behind him. "And where's your shirt?"

Stefen turned and spread his arms wide, coffee splashing out of his mug and onto the tile. Enzo, the parrot on his shoulder, squawked at the disturbance. "How else can I maintain this tan?"

"Really..." His brother gave him his token droll stare.

"Hey." He shrugged. "You made me a king. You never said I had to act like one. Besides." Stefen looked over the other side of the balcony to where Merick was just emerging from a forest trail with Teakin and Aasha. "My mate likes it."

Alaric joined him in gazing over the lush landscape. "Is she ready for him to leave?"

Stefen watched the two below. No, his beautiful, strong mate would never be eager to part from her father. They were as close as a child and a parent could get.

"She understands the role he must play," he said.

They all had new roles to play now. Zander had been killed in battle, trying to flee like the coward he was. Thaddeus somehow had managed to escape, and a price had been placed on his head. A price that would keep him in hiding for years to come. Xavier had fled as well, but it would only be a matter of time before he returned to reclaim his throne. Pride was too strong in that bloodline.

On the heels of the battle and with no clearly defined ruler, Gerra's elite had been willing to make concessions. An agreement had been struck between Alaric, the Earth kings, and the surviving generals. Until Gerra elected a new ruler who Anu and Earth agreed was suitable, Teakin would serve as regent over Gerra.

Unfortunately, for Merick's father that meant overseeing the very realm that had once enslaved him. An ironic twist of fate.

At least his son, Sterling, would be safe. Kielyn had been adamant, to the point of near violence. The child would stay with her and Ash while Teakin was away. It was a good plan. Teakin would visit every chance he could and hopefully, the gods willing, Gerra would decide on a new successor sooner than later.

A pair of colorful macaws took flight from a nearby guanacaste tree and crossed in front of Teakin and Merick. Both father and daughter tracked their path. Nearby, Aasha rolled in the green grass, batting at a butterfly.

Stefen faced Alaric. "Excuse me, brother." He handed him Enzo, despite the look of abject protest on his face. "I have a morning date with my true love."

"I'm not babysitting your damn bird..."

His words fell away as Stefen jumped over the edge of the balcony with a smirk. He landed neatly beside Merick, arms clasped behind his back.

"I see my time is up." Teakin grinned.

"She beats me up if I don't adhere to a strict schedule." Stefen dodged an elbow to the ribs from his mate. "See!"

Teakin chuckled and leaned in to place a kiss on Merick's forehead. "Good girl."

"See you after lunch?" Merick asked.

"Absolutely." He turned for the main entrance. "Come on, Aasha."

Stefen looked at her. "Are you ready, darling?"

She kissed him and nodded, her smile widening. Stefen summoned his wings and scooped her up. Then he shot into the sky to the sounds of delighted giggles. He would never get tired of that sound. Nor would he ever bore of their routines.

Each day, before either started their daily training or correspondence, they explored the jungle. Each night they took to the sky, two dragons soaring into the Caribbean sunset. Their life together had become everything he could have ever wanted. Had he allowed himself to even dream it before...*before her?*

"Do you have my poem?" he asked down their bond.

"Eager, are you?" She hugged him tighter as the wind whipped her hair around her face.

"I'm always eager for you." He nipped her ear.

"Then who am I to deny such want?"

Stefen started his descent, carefully avoiding branches as he weaved into and under the dense rainforest canopy. He touched down by their favorite place on the property. Beside a crystal clear waterfall and plunge pool.

Kicking off his sandals, he lowered her to the plush moss. Another of his favorite things were the love letters his mate wrote and sent to him daily. Some funny, some reflective, and others made it down right uncomfortable to concentrate. In the best possible way.

Hence his first rule; all notes were to be mentally or physically passed when he was not in a Council meeting or the training yard. Appearing the proper king meant not walking around with a raging hard on.

Merick toed off her shoes, walked to the water's edge, and stepped out of her thin dress. Stefen became aware of the exact number of steps, of breaths, it would take to reach her. "Dear gods, help me." He placed his hands in his pockets to keep from reaching for her.

She stepped into the cool pool. Goosebumps feathered her skin and her rosy nipples pebbled. "Into the wilds of your dreams —I want to explore with you," she began.

"As the night spins on silent wheels, say you'll take me too." She walked backward, hands pushing gentle ripples across the glassy surface. "Up among the stars—infinity heedless of hours. Or on the ground, in a field searching for a four-leaf clover." She smiled. "Eternity, a single flower."

Stefen stared at her as she dropped into the water up to her chin, that smile traveling to her eyes. "I..." He had no words.

None were adequate for the praise she deserved. None could articulate the emotion coursing through him. The love he felt for this gorgeous creature in front of him. This female so pure of heart.

How could he ever be worthy of her? She had known adversity, struggle and loss, ridicule and judgment. But she'd never let it dim her spirit. Instead she used it, appreciated it, and learned its lessons. Merick had never succumbed to it. Never allowed it to rob her of her sensitivity and compassion. Be it with other supernaturals, or with the simplest of the gods' creatures.

She made the voiceless heard. Saw fragments of light in the darkest of night. Those wings, her ethereal white wings, had been earned with the weight of the universe on her shoulders. And she had managed it all with the grace of a queen.

"I want you always with me in my dreams." A tear slid down his cheek, swift and warm, as he let her in. Let her feel what was in his heart. Showed her how she looked through his eyes. *"You are my four-leaf clover."*

"Stefen..." Her chin wobbled as she stood, the shimmering water and the glinting sunlight writing its own poetry over her skin. The forest stilled around her, as if it too were in awe. Even the waterfall seemed to quiet out of respect. Merick held out her hand.

His wings vanished and he untied the string to his loose-fitted pants. When the linen fell to his feet, her expression changed. Stefen walked out of the puddle of fabric and into the crisp clear water.

"Eternity is a long time." Her gaze traveled over every inch of him.

He moved through the water, single-mindedly. "I think you're wrong."

She bit her bottom lip and dropped back into the water, playfully pushing away as he neared. Not fast enough. Stefen caught her around the waist and pulled her to him. "It's not enough time."

Merick wrapped her legs around him and kissed him slow and long. When she pulled back, that smile had faded. "What is it?" he asked, concerned.

"You never asked me about my transformation the day of the battle."

He was confused. They had talked at length on more than one occasion about her experience. *Unless...*

"Do you mean what woke your dragon?" he ventured, surprising himself with how frightening that question was, voiced out loud.

Her gaze drifted down. "Yes."

"You told me it was the fear you had felt for Bastian, Eirik, and Palomi?"

"It was," she whispered. The words were barely audible above the splashing falls behind them.

"I don't understand."

She looked up. "You never asked why it didn't surface before then." Her eyes searched his. "Why it wasn't you that woke it. As I did for you."

"Oh, darling." He rushed to assure her. "It doesn't matter what triggered the dragon. It means nothing to me that—"

"It means everything!"

Stefen stared at her, words suddenly foreign, and as hard to reach as the moon.

"You didn't awaken my dragon because I already knew. Same as I knew Marzalla would get hurt in battle. The way I've always felt things," she said. "Some part of me recognized the day we made the jump from Gerra, you were meant to be mine." Merick smiled softly, those luminous multi-colored eyes glistening with

353

unshed tears. "You didn't have to awaken my dragon. Because it already recognized you as its mate."

Stefen exhaled a breath he hadn't been aware he was holding. He didn't have her gift for sight, but he had felt it then too—*the bond*. From about the same moment in time. In that field in Italy. He had known then she was going to mean more to him than he could have ever imagined. His mind had stupidly found other excuses for the connection. But his heart...his heart recognized their souls were linked.

"It's never felt like I was getting to know you," he confessed. "Only as though I was remembering who you are."

She reached up, her fingers feather-light across his cheek, as he continued, "Every interaction, each touch and word." He turned into her open palm and kissed its center, his gaze never breaking with hers. "Was me finding my place." A tear rolled down her cheek and he kissed it too. "Finding my home."

Stefen drew back enough for them to share a breath. "Within your soul."

That's when he saw it...

Merick's unique aura and his. A swirling band of white and gold wrapped around each other. Between them, faint and soft, as if painted by the wind itself—two family crests. The insignia Stefen had been born into, and the one he'd been made from. The House of the Dragon.

They both stared at the bond. *The fated bond...*

At the same time their gazes lifted, locking on each other.

"How?" Merick breathed.

"Your admittance? Mine?" He shook his head. "It doesn't matter."

Stefen kissed her. Kissed her for confessions under a waterfall, for friendship, destiny, and love letters. He kissed her for being his muse, his salvation, and his mate.

Together forever, *forged by fate...*

Chapter Thirty-Five

A stink bug landed on Brock's broadsword. The mountain of a fae stared at it, like one might consider an unpleasant and indiscernible odor. Clearly unable to process whatever thoughts were running around his meaty head further, Brock lifted his fat thumb and drilled it into the insect in a twisting motion.

His nostrils flared when a pop was heard. "Stinks."

They continued on in silence, Brock scratching—with surprising enthusiasm—at the drying bug guts. Twenty minutes later they came to a fork in the road. Brock looked up from his persistent scraping. Just as a ratty-haired boy darted out from a thatched roof hovel, and froze.

Brock looked down at the lad with the same obtuse consideration he had shown the bug. Archer shot the kid a raised brow, a look that would have sent any city urchin scrambling.

Apparently street smarts didn't make their way this far north. The lad's gaze stayed fixated on Brock's shiny metal armor.

A lesser fae female ducked out from under the low hanging roof. Her eyes widened and she called the boy to her.

"Where's your mate?" Brock grunted.

She pushed the lad behind her. "Inside."

Brock's bulbous lips twitched and he heaved a leg over his saddle. Hitting the dry ground like a barrel of ale, the behemoth-sized knight marched toward her. Archer exhaled, mentally cursing his rotten luck.

As a prisoner, a disguise Archer was quite proud of, he had easy admittance into the dungeons of Windsong Palace. From there he could gain the information the crown wanted. Then, he would present those details and be welcomed back to his rightful position, Commander of the King's Knight.

The only life he knew. The life he had earned. The life he had bled for.

Before he had displeased the King's Regent, his mother.

Archer was yanked back to the present when the woman shrieked. She was attempting to run as his traveling companion gained momentum striding toward her. The boy struck out with a stick to try and trip Brock. He failed, and was backhanded to the ground.

Archer looked down at his tied hands. He had loosened the binds hours ago when his captor was taking a piss. He glanced back up in time to see Brock snatch a handful of the female's hair and drag her inside the hut.

It had been a good plan.

Archer sighed and threw his legs over his own horse, dropping to the ground. *Simpleton Brock and his bug-popping brain.* Why couldn't he have lured a classier knight into arresting him? He passed the boy, who scrambled away, his courage skittering off with the dust. He would need a new way into the palace now.

"Oh Brock, you stupid sack of shit." Archer kicked in the swinging door.

To his surprise, Brock lay face down on the dirt floor, gurgling on his own blood, his throat slit cleanly. Archer's gaze lifted to see who was responsible for the large fae's demise. It wasn't the female who had just run. The lesser fae wasn't in the hovel at all.

Standing above him, leisurely wiping clean a kitchen knife and backlit by the room's only window, was a stunning creature. Petite, so much so that she couldn't have stood higher than the center emblem on Brock's breast plate, she had thick brunette hair and eyes the color of gold.

Decidedly *not* fae.

Then what? She'd just dispatched a knighted male three times her size. And she had either disposed of the lesser fae female, in the length of time it had taken Archer to get in there. *Or become her...*

He cast out his senses, trying to discern exactly what she was.

She chuckled, the sound melodic. "Take your time."

He reeled back in his efforts. Whatever she was, her masking was too advanced to penetrate. Archer stepped around Brock's prone body, righted a toppled chair, and took a seat. "Consider me intrigued."

She finished cleaning the blade and set it on a makeshift counter behind her. "Exactly how I prefer my allies."

"Allies?" Archer cocked his head. "With a lowly prisoner?"

"Come now, commander. Your disguise may have worked on this one." She wrinkled her nose at the dead male on the floor. "But you can't hide who you are; the generational power thrumming through your veins, nor the hunger to conquer that rages wild beside it." She lifted her gaze, a twinkle in those strange large eyes. "No more than I can hide who I am."

"And that is?"

"The one that's going to help you get your title back."

357

"The king will grant me that when I get the information he desires."

"Will he?" She looked him over as she walked forward and took the room's only other chair. "Your nephew is only ten. We both know who makes the decisions now that his father is dead."

There was no point arguing. What she summarized was fact. The king had died less than a month ago, and already Archer's mother was ruling the kingdom with an iron fist.

His sister, the queen widow, had never been interested in anything beyond her gardens. Her son could barely hold a sword. Archer's mother had swooped in and seized control with a letter, written in the late king's own hand before he took his last breath, naming her regent until the boy came of age.

Her first order of business; securing the crown and all ties to it. By blood.

That started with Archer apparently. He must agree to take a mate by the next full moon. An easy proposition for any other High-fae. Just not for Archer. He couldn't be the commander if he took a bride. The Kings Knight were forbidden to marry.

An issue his mother didn't share. She needed power. No amount of servitude from a mere commander would give her that. She wanted him trussed up at their ancestral holding, given a dukedom, and siring a legion of House Voltaire's.

But his mother wasn't his biggest problem. It was the king's new advisor, Lord Ulrich. The male had come to court the day after the late king's death, and made himself a fixture by the regent's side, in her ear. Archer was convinced it had been Ulrich's idea to strip him of his title and ban him from court for not complying with his dear mother.

"Who are you?" he asked.

"That depends on who you ask." She grinned, a dangerous, beautiful grin. "Give me three names, and I'll tell you how each knows me."

As much as Archer enjoyed a challenge, he was losing his patience. But something told him now was not the time to stop playing alone.

He spread his fingers. "How would my mother know you?"

"As the daughter of a king."

Interesting. He mulled over who to choose next. Someone with immeasurable insight and reach.

Archer studied her closely. "How would the gods know you?"

She crossed her legs, leaning back in her chair, a pleased look on her face. "They call me Sekhmet."

"After the Egyptian deity?"

His mind replayed its history lessons. Depicted as a lion-headed warrior goddess, Sekhmet, also known as the Red Lady and the Eye of Ra, was considered both a creative and destructive force. The story of her bloodthirsty rampage at the behest of Ra, was considered by many to one of the oldest vampire tales.

He searched her genetic makeup again, allowing his magic to travel a different route this time, a power very few High-fae possessed. The ability to see bloodlines.

Archer's gaze drifted over her until it found the best source, the artery at her neck. He closed his eyes, listening to the steady thumping there. When he could picture the color of the blood, he then followed it in—a map opened up inside his head. Like a chemist's charts, he saw names, forks on the invisible paper of her history, end lines. Back, farther and farther through time, on and on...

A chair squeaked and his eyes flew open.

"You're as good as they said." A slow clap. "Ready to ask the last question? So you can be on your way to King Calian's." She folded her hands neatly in her lap. "Find out which LaGoryen will be marrying into your enemy's house."

"For it will be a LaGoryen that wins," she continued. "And

what an awful mess for you if it's the wrong one. The right one could eliminate your whole court."

Archer watched her closely, choosing his last question carefully. "What name does Gerra know you by?"

"With your help." The stranger leaned forward. "They will again call me, Your Majesty." She smiled, a flash of pearly white fangs against her blood-red lips. "But you can call me Katarra."

Preview of Forged in Blood - Book 3
THE TEMPLE

VENTUS

TWENTY YEARS AFTER THE BATTLE IN ANU

Reclining back against the hillside, Bastian folded his hands behind his head and inhaled the eternal aroma of autumn–bitter and honeysweet–intertwined with the briny tang of sea. A crisp breeze drifted over his bare skin, kissing away the heat from the noonday sun. He closed his eyes.

"How much longer?" a wispy voice whined beside him.

"As long as it takes," he replied.

An exhausted huff. "That could be *forever*..." Silence. "This is so boring."

Bastian grinned. "It is only boring because you are eight."

"What does age have to do with the untimely arrival of a ship?"

Bastian cracked an eyelid, needing visual proof it was, indeed, a little girl sitting to his right. Not some wise old crone, too long-lived for this world.

Bright citrine-colored eyes glared at him. As if he had personally caused the ship's delay.

"Patience is a virtue, Oakley." He closed his eyes again.

"Hog poo! You sound like Master Warelow." Another tortured sigh. "Why allow me to follow you from the training yard, if this is all you planned to do?"

"I do not recall *allowing* you to do anything," he chuckled. "Don't you have piano lessons? Or something else befitting a young lady?"

"I'm not a lady!" She toed her velvet slipper into his ribs. "And piano lessons are for Hanna."

More disgruntled grumbling, and then the tiny vibration of her flopping onto her back. "Tell me a story about the old days."

Bastian rolled his head to look at her.

"Please," she added sweetly, thick lashes batting against cinnamon-colored skin, her auburn ringlets fanning out around her like a halo in the rich, verdant golden grass.

"The old days in Ventus?" he clarified. "Before I arrived here?"

Her eyes filled with excitement as she flipped onto her stomach and propped her head in her palms. "Were there really horses that could fly?"

"Pegasuses." He smiled at her innocent wonder. "But not like the ones in the books Anne reads to you."

"Oh, no." Her little face grew serious, as her brows creased. "Scary, big beasts with glowing eyes and razor-sharp teeth."

"More suited for warriors than little ladies." Bastian tapped her nose, but continued before she could protest. "A good thing the latter is not present. I fear such tales would be too frightening."

Oakley beamed. "Only those possessing pure magic could ride them?"

"So it is said. Same for the wyverns."

She studied him carefully, the way she often did, as if she were deciphering some great puzzle. "Do you have pure magic, Bastian?"

"Not in the way the fae define it. I can control the elements, harness the energy, direct it for my own use, but I cannot become it."

"Have you ever met anyone that can?"

"No, I have not."

She grew pensive as those brilliant-colored eyes slid to the sea beyond. "Anne says they're all extinct. The pegasuses, and the last of the pure magic lines. Neither has been seen since the fall of Arrowren."

Bastian looked toward the ocean. The sun, high in the sky, bathed the water in diamonds of light. The white caps sparkled and broke on the reef where gulls swooped in between the crashing waves. He could very well understand the child's fascination with the history of her birth realm. Likewise, he found it interesting, if also sad.

Fifty years ago, the Great Siege had played out, propelled, as with all conflict, by fear and greed. Brother turned on brother, city gates were barricaded, alliances were forged in dark rooms, and division took root and spread across the realm.

In the end, it proved to be about more than the sacking of one castle–the fall of one family.

It had been an extermination. A carefully crafted one. The annihilation of an entire bloodline: the Astameres. And with them, a magic deemed too unpredictable and dangerous.

Pure magic.

Though, it was whispered around campfires and taprooms in the dead of night when voices weren't prone to carry that a few practitioners had survived. And with them, a nameless child; the heir to the Arrowren throne.

After the siege, Ventus had been divided into two kingdoms. A caste system was put in place and magic was sanctioned. Anyone possessing it must register with either Windsong or Hornhall by the age of ten. What fraction of magic one possessed determined where they would be placed next.

Most ended up in the royal armies, others in covens. A select few were chosen as champions for the king's inner circle. It was a great honor to be counted among the High-fae, a life far superior to lesser fae. In reality, it meant a life of servitude. A life not of one's choosing.

An archaic way of thinking. Even Gerra allowed its' own the right to choose their path. Provided they were willing to claw their way to it. Ventus was the only realm in history to travel backward through time, tightening its control over its people, alienating itself from the other realms. Permitting only two ruling houses to dictate all.

Yet, there was such beauty here, such hope. As if half the population had forgotten what sacrifices it took to keep them protected. What limitations shackled this realm's potential. What rights they gave up.

Bastian was not of that mindset. He couldn't look at the staggering splendor of this land and not see the corruption used to maintain its prosperity. He could not ride past the pregnant mother in the village and keep from wondering if she lay awake at night praying her child was not blessed. He certainly couldn't find comfort in the invisible cloak that dulled his own powers whenever he set foot outside of the Temple grounds.

Such had been the price of admittance. One of two conditions the fae demanded of him and his kin. To willingly subdue their natural gifts, and to abstain from drinking from another living being while in the realm.

Synthesized blood was the means of nourishment for Ventus's vampire guest. The taste was one step up from drinking warm piss. But it was a sacrifice worth making to advance his craft.

Which was the entire reason Bastian was even here. To hone

his powers and study under a coven of wizards renowned for their wind-magic, the final element in his training. Once he mastered air he could go home, rejoice in modern day technology, and wait...

Wait for the hand of fate to decide who would lead all four realms. Who would wear the crown.

"If I had a pegasus, I'd meet that ship out at sea." Oakley stood, pulling him from his thoughts. She shielded her eyes with both hands, her delicate pointed ears peeking out through windswept curls. "A ship!" She hopped in place. "Teakin's ship!"

Leaves crunched behind them with someone approaching and Oakley turned, eyes gleaming with excitement. "He's here, Sterling. Let's go."

A chuckle was all Sterling was afforded before Oakley grabbed him by the hand and dragged Bastian's cousin toward the beach. Sterling smiled over his shoulder, and then disappeared over the cliff's edge with Oakley.

Bastian sat up as the ship dropped anchor. Sterling and Oakley appeared in miniature minutes later on the beach. Teakin waved from the bow of the boat.

Uncoiling to his feet, Bastian felt two emotions warring with each other–joy and apprehension.

He was happy to see Teakin. The male who had trained him, fought beside him, and had his back for the better part of the last twenty years. But, as with everything in his life, this reunion would come at a price. He could just feel it.

The only question now; would he be willing to pay it?

About Stacy Von Haegert

Stacy Von Haegert is the International Bestselling Author and Top 100 Amazon Bestselling Author of two genres: Historical Romance (the White Rose trilogy, and Lords), and Dark-Fantasy Romance (the Forged series)

Stacy currently lives in historic downtown Franklin TN with her hubby, son, calico cat, and Belgian Tervuren, where she writes by day and teaches ballroom dance in the evenings. She is obsessed with old houses, good literature, and boogie boarding.

You can find all her work at: www.stacyvonhaegert.com

Don't forget to stalk me on social media!

Want more from this author?

Check out her historical romance trilogy, the White Rose.

"Fans of Bridgerton and Outlander will love this richly textured and adventurous New Adult Historical Romance by International Bestselling Author Stacy Von Haegert!"

Start with book one: **Under his protection**.

https://books2read.com/u/m0ENky

Most debutantes meet their intendeds at polite societal gatherings, not over a duel in Hyde Park.

However, Greyland Kingston is not your typical young lady, and her family is far from conventional. The gossip fans start to flutter when Greyland, her two older brothers, and distinguished father, make their debut. Who is this family? How do they know The Queen? Why does the patriarch look like the ghost of the long-ago Plantagenet King, Edward the IV?

Alexander Hamilton, the bons ton notoriously dangerous "Dark Lord" and new Duke of Ravenswood, is about to learn how unique the family is, when he becomes unwittingly entangled with the Kingston's from New Orleans—one family member in particular. With her spirited personality and innocent aversion to all things proper, Greyland Kingston completely throws him off his well-established game.

When trouble ensues in the form of jealous women, ambitious men, and a vengeful Irish clan, Alexander quickly finds having Greyland for his own will come at a steep price...

And he must risk everything to keep her protected.

Want steals and deals from this author?

Sign up for her monthly newsletter at:

https://stacyvonhaegert.com/newsletter-signup/

You can find all Stacy's work at

https://stacyvonhaegert.com

You can stalk her on social media to:

https://linktr.ee/stacyvonhaegertlinktr.ee